Vicky Newham grew up in West Sussex and taught Psychology in East London for many years, before moving to Whitstable in Kent. She studied for an MA in Creative Writing at Kingston University, where she graduated with distinction. She is currently working on the next instalment in the DI Rahman series.

Out of the Ashes

Vicky Newham

ONE PLACE. MANY STORIES

HQ
An imprint of HarperCollins*Publishers* Ltd
1 London Bridge Street
London SE1 9GF

This edition 2019

1
First published in Great Britain by
HQ, an imprint of HarperCollins*Publishers* Ltd 2019

HB ISBN: 978-0-00-824071-4
TPB ISBN: 978-0-00-824072-1

MIX
Paper from
responsible sources
FSC™ C007454

This book is produced from independently certified FSC™ paper
to ensure responsible forest management.

For more information visit: www.harpercollins.co.uk/green

This book is set in 10.6/15.5 pt. Minion

Printed and bound in Great Britain by
CPI Group (UK) Ltd, Croydon, CR0 4YY

For my father, who I miss every day.

FRIDAY

Rosa, 2 p.m.

Rosa Feldman stood at the door of her Brick Lane newsagent's, staring out at the street she'd known since she was four. She couldn't shake the feeling that something was wrong. It was the shop opposite, run by the young Lithuanian couple. Since first thing this morning, the lights had been off and the shutters down. Initially, she was relieved that for once, the ugly neon sign, with its air of Margate or Blackpool, wasn't flashing outside her bedroom window, but as the morning progressed, she felt increasingly uneasy.

It wasn't like them at all.

She couldn't recall ever seeing the shop closed in the daytime.

A tap on the glass snapped Rosa back into the afternoon. It was Mr Walker from the off-licence a few doors down. He shouted a cheery greeting and waved as he passed the window. Regular as clockwork, off to get chips for tea. Rosa raised her hand to return the gesture, but the pain in her wrists and knuckles bit again. Damned arthritis.

Mr Walker's knock was usually her reminder to think about their meal. Today was Friday after all. But without Józef, the Sabbath meal wasn't the same and she didn't bother with the rituals any more. In the last year, she'd lost weight and clothes hung off her spare frame. What was the point of lighting candles when there was only one of you? She'd steam a plate of yesterday's chicken and potatoes. That would do her. Fortunately, she didn't have to go far to get home, just upstairs to the flat, even if it was still freezing at this time of year.

Over the dusty window display, two men were putting a new shop sign up where Rosenberg's jewellers used to be. Work had been going on for weeks, and it looked like the place was nearly ready to open. *Alchemia*, it said. A swanky new Polish bar by the looks of it, slap bang next-door to Mr Hamid's curry house. He wasn't going to be happy. So much had changed in Brick Lane since she and her family had arrived, and life moved so fast on the other side of the window, it made Rosa dizzy. The pace was relentless and the change uncompromising. Inside the shop, though, she felt safe. Change there was slow and predictable. Above her head, by the door, the fan heater droned noisily and made little impact on the chilly air, but she didn't mind. It had always done that. And she barely noticed the crumbling plaster of the ground floor walls, or the mildew which clung to ceiling corners like a nasty rash.

Her thoughts slid back to the shop over the road. The place was usually open all hours of the day and night, selling its fancy five-quid soups to whoever could afford them. She had no objection to people earning a living, but her parents would be turning in their graves. They'd survived the Ghetto on two hundred calories a day. When they left Warsaw, and arrived in London, it was the handouts from the Jewish soup kitchen in Brune Street that kept them alive. It was extraordinary to think that what had been humble subsistence for many families was now a fad-food. She'd been over for a spy at the menu, of course, when they were shut. Apart from some matzo ball soup, she couldn't find much she fancied and didn't know what most of it was, let alone how to pronounce it. Keen-war, or something, a youth with a bicycle and a dog had told Rosa.

She sighed. She missed her old neighbours. Those were Sabbath meals to look forward to. They were exactly how her mother described Warsaw before the war. Mrs Blum from the bagel shop would make the *challah*. Rich, eggy and sweet. It had been ages since Rosa had felt one of those in her hands, soft and warm, in its pretty braid shape. The Altmans would bring the wine. The Posners, candles. And the Rosenbergs, the jewellers, always came with freshly made *kugel*.

But now her parents were dead, and all her Jewish neighbours were either dead too or had moved away.

Except Rosa.

And there was that feeling again, a gnawing emptiness, a sense that life had moved on without her. It was so unsettling. Every fibre of her being was exhausted by the continual need to think about whether to follow her compatriots out of the East End and into the London suburbs.

The sound of voices jolted her back into the present.

Yelling.

Music.

Outside in the street, a thumping bass beat started up. Tremors vibrated through the shop, and a booming noise invaded the silence of her thoughts. Yobbos, probably, spitting everywhere and pumping out music from one of those dreadful sound-systems. They'd pass in a minute.

But they didn't.

The music got louder and louder, and – oh, typical – the group had stopped outside Rosa's shop. All guffaws, swearing, floppy hair and hoodies. More voices, bellowing and cheering, and one by one, people were joining them. What on earth was going on? On a Friday afternoon, from lunchtime onwards, she was used to the steady trickle of people down Brick Lane, getting ready for a night on the tiles and a curry, but it was unusual to see so many people together. She edged over to the corner of the shop window to get a better view. The music had changed, and one by one people pulled black bandanas into masks, over their mouths and noses, and were dancing, if jabbing a finger in the air and screaming counted as dancing these days. Teenagers, by the look of them. Some younger. She wasn't very good at judging age, and they all wore such similar clothes, but she'd put money on some of them not being a day over ten.

Rosa pressed her nose against the pane of glass. Outside, the street hummed with joy. There was an innocence to their dancing, even if the masks were a bit scary. And they weren't doing any harm, were they? She couldn't believe what she was seeing. She used to know all the kids round here; knew their families by name, but none of this lot were familiar. There were at least ten of them, dancing in the street, throwing themselves about like acrobats, bending, leaping, twirling each other around. For a moment, Rosa was reminded of the tea room dances she and Józef used to go to before Agnieszka and Tomasz were born. They'd save for weeks, get dolled up in their best clothes. Oh, how much fun they'd been.

There were more than twenty of them now, maybe thirty. Someone was lighting sparklers and passing them round for the kids. She adored sparklers. And before she knew it, her fingers pulled the door handle and she was outside, the bell dinging shut behind her. The sulphurous smell set light to her dulled senses and she felt the day's irritation shake itself from her shoulders. She was a kid again, at crisp November bonfires and balmy mid-summer street parties, with people passing sparklers round.

Rosa cleared her throat.

Coughed.

Her lungs weren't good these days, weakened by years of a poorly heated flat, the damp shop walls, and Józef's cigarette smoke.

She joined the throng of passers-by who were huddled, mesmerised by the dancing. Was it a student gathering? She was puzzled. Who was in charge? She couldn't see any organisers or anyone giving instructions, and had no idea where the music was coming from. People were merging with the group of their own accord and encouraging others to do the same. They all looked so carefree.

The music brought a smile to Rosa's cold lips. Her heel began to tap and she was lost to nostalgia. It was such a relief to forget the pain and drudgery of the last year. To forget her arthritis and money worries. Was that Lulu and 'Shout'? Her heart leaped. Many a time she and Józef had danced to that tune. Her mind was flooded with memories of all the occasions when they'd danced together, his warm hand in the small of her back, guiding her forwards, the other clasping hers, keeping her safe. She felt a lump in her throat. They were glorious memories, even if they were now tainted by the agony of loss. It had only been a year and she still missed him so much.

A waltz kicked in, floaty and dramatic. Initially, it had been youngsters dancing but now it was people of all ages, lured over by the infectious atmosphere of Brick Lane on a chilly April afternoon. Hearing the waltz start, a Sikh man checked his turban and, with a huge grin, he clasped the hands of a woman in a navy-blue trench coat. She was giggling like a schoolgirl, a small flat bag diagonally across her body, her head tilted back, carefree and stunned, as though she hadn't had so much fun in ages. Rosa guessed the woman was about her age. Perhaps she was a widow too?

Rosa's hips started to sway, and she was tempted to go over and join in. What was she thinking? She was being silly. She couldn't. Who would mind the shop while she was cavorting in the street?

Another crowd of youths piled in, hee-hawing and smoking, in their thin cotton clothing and baseball shoes. Some with their bottoms hanging out of their trousers, others in drainpipe jeans. Didn't they feel the cold? Several more children were in tow. Why weren't they all at school? Before Rosa knew it, one of them had taken her hand and led her towards the group. Elvis' crooning tones wafted down the street and once again Rosa's spirits soared. The teenagers looked so funny, impersonating the rock 'n' roll moves of 'All Shook Up'. It was the most fun she'd had on a Friday afternoon since . . .

Józef would have enjoyed this. 'Come on, Rosa,' he would have said in his calm, decisive voice, and he'd have locked the shop, led her out into the street and begun whirling her around with that boyish grin of his.

A quick head count told her there were about fifty people dancing now and a good twenty more hanging around. The street whiffed of whacky-backy. Rosa had forgotten her nagging joints and aching legs; the grimy shelves with mounting dust; the delivery boxes she couldn't carry. For a few sweet moments, she'd stopped feeling sick to death of the damn shop, of book-keeping and fretting over decisions. She didn't care about any of it anymore. All she wanted was—

A loud splitting sound tore through the air, followed by a series of cracks and bangs. Rosa gasped as orange flames burst out of the top floor windows of the shop opposite, and billowed upwards. Swirling streams of black smoke inked the pale sky. Fire raged behind the first-floor windows, and the ground floor shop was filled with smoke and flames. She cried out in pain as acrid fumes hit her lungs, forcing her to clamp her hand over her mouth. Everyone was shouting and running for cover as burning timber peeled away from windows. Screams pierced the air as lengths of wood and red-hot embers rained down on the crowd below. Rosa's legs were like jelly and she felt dizzy. She stumbled over something on the ground in front of her and lurched forwards. She made out a woman, clutching her arm.

'*Help*,' came the agonised cry at Rosa's feet. 'Please help me.'

Panic engulfed Rosa, and she was transported back to the sensory onslaught of the Warsaw Ghetto, to primitive memories of endless screaming, to the cacophony of bombs and blasts and gunshots. From behind, someone shoved her out of the way and she stumbled forwards. All around her, people were coughing, retching and staggering, scarves and hands clasped over their mouths, desperate to escape the blaze. The air was cloying. Putrid. She was plunged into blind terror, realising she could die. This wasn't Poland, and it wasn't the end of the war, but she had to get away from the fire and ring 999 before someone died.

As the blaze ripped through the roof, smoke continued to spiral upwards into the sky. Rosa staggered blindly towards the blue door of her shop, to the step and doorway, arms groping ahead for something to grab. The fumes bit at her lungs and she was gasping for air so much she was retching. Finally, her hands grabbed the handle. She used all her weight to heave the door open and stumbled inside, pushing it shut behind her as quickly as she could.

She sucked in some air.

It was like breathing through needles.

She had to get to the phone in the back room. Stands and magazine racks flashed past her as she lurched towards the till, gasping for breath and snatching for a hold. She hauled her way round the counter, head spinning, and grabbed the phone receiver from the wall. Her eyes were streaming.

Keep blinking, she told herself.

Breathe.

She tried to calm herself; to rub away the tears that the fumes

9

had produced; to steady her shaking hands and press the buttons. What should she say? Was it terrorists? Had there been an explosion?

Just say FIRE.

Rosa felt her head starting to spin. Lights flashed, dots appeared and she went floppy. Her mind slipped sideways and everything stopped.

Maya, 2.30 p.m.

I scraped my scruffy hair into a ponytail and took a deep breath. It was the first moment's peace in the MIT room since seven this morning. I opened the email app on my phone and scrolled down to the one from Forensic Services with 'Mr K A Rahman' in the subject line. The message had dropped into my private inbox moments earlier. My finger was poised, ready to click, when Dougie's advice popped into my mind. 'If you're going to do this, you need to be prepared for all possible outcomes,' he'd said.

Was I?

I wasn't sure.

I'd given up trying to find out what had happened to Dad. We'd all accepted he was dead, until a year ago when Mum started saying he'd visited her. And now it seemed like he might be alive after all.

'Emergency services have been on the blower, eh.' Dan's Australian accent cut through my thoughts. Never one to enter a room slowly, he lobbed his keys on the desk, curved his athletic frame down on the seat next to me and whacked the space bar on his computer. The impact made my desk shake.

I grunted my disapproval and tucked my phone back in my pocket. 'What about?' After eighteen months of working with Dan, I still found some of his behaviour—

'If you stop texting your boyfriend, I'll tell you.' He faced me, his hazel eyes red-rimmed and puffy. 'Listen to this. First response has flagged up the smell of accelerant.' He pressed 'play' on the recording on his phone.

'Poleece?' The woman's voice was shrill. A heavy accent. 'My husband is in the fire in Brick Lane. I think someone's tried to kill him.' Her words came out in snatches. There was a female voice in the background. It sounded like the person was prompting her. 'I think someone's murdered him.'

'Shit.' I searched Dan's face for a reaction, but it was its standard pallid hue. 'Do we know who made the call?'

'Can't trace it. Cell site data places the phone in East Ham but it's an unregistered mobile. Goes straight to voicemail and there's no personalised message.'

'Is there a fire in Brick Lane?'

'Yeah. Massive one. Uniform are there now with the fire brigade. Here.' He passed me a transcript of the call. 'No CID yet though.'

'"My husband is in the fire" and "I think someone has tried to kill him"? We'd better get over there. I'll tell Superintendent Campbell we're going to check it out. What's the shop?'

'New place.' Dan checked the incident log. 'The Brick Lane Soup Company.'

'You're kidding?' I stared at him. 'That's where the Jewish bagel shop used to be. Developers bought it a couple of years ago. There was a real hoo-ha.' I could vividly picture the freshly cooked salt beef and bagels that had once sat in the window. I grabbed my jacket. 'Come on. Let's get over there.'

Minutes later, we were zig-zagging along the A13 from Limehouse, in the clank and clatter of the afternoon traffic. Lorries and red buses belched out choking fumes into the watery April sunlight.

In Brick Lane now, and on foot, the blue lights from the emergency services vehicles barely cut through the black smog which hung over the area. As we approached the street, heading north, discombobulated voices echoed through the haze. Two motorcycle responders tore past us, sirens blaring and blue lights flashing. Dan's stride quickened, and I broke into a jog to keep up, past the takeaways of my childhood, the barber's and money shops.

Up ahead, it was a scene of devastation. Smoke caught in my throat and I fished in my pocket for a tissue to cover my mouth and nose. I made out a terrace of three-storey buildings. Here, parts of the roof hung precariously over the shop I'd known since I was a child. Torrents of water were gushing down the street, and spray and fizz had sent puffs of steam into the atmosphere.

A few yards away, the liveried news crew vans were in a cluster, and their staff were frantically assembling satellite dishes, gangly tripods, panels of bright lights, video cameras and sound equipment. The BBC, Sky and ITV reporters were shouting into microphones over the noise of the water pump.

Carly, one of the Sky reporters, had just begun live broadcasting.

' . . . here in Brick Lane, it's a scene of utter carnage. Earlier this afternoon, at around two thirty, emergency services were inundated with calls about a fire in the shop behind me.' She stopped and pointed. 'Many callers mentioned music and people dancing in the street before the blaze began. Locals are worried that this might be a tragic case of arson.' Carly paused. 'Unusually, it appears that the shop was closed today and . . . '

We'd arrived at the red and white fire tape now. Outside the cordon, I counted four ambulances. Blue-light staff were escorting people with injuries and burns away from the fumes and into a mobile phone repair shop. Here, paramedics and ambulance staff were triaging care needs, dispensing first aid and carrying out emergency treatments. In the Indian restaurant next-door, uniformed officers were collecting contact details from passers-by and had begun basic interviews.

Dan and I hurried over to the uniformed police officer who was guarding the scene. 'I'm DI Rahman. This is DS Maguire. Limehouse.' While he added our names to the log, I told him about the woman's call to 999. 'She thinks her husband's been murdered in the fire. Sounds extremely scared.'

He pointed at a thick-set man with a shaved head, who was standing inside the cordon next to a digger, giving orders to a team of fluorescent-jacketed men with brooms and shovels. 'Simon Chapel is the fire crew manager. You'll have to speak to him.'

Dan and I made our way over. An army of personnel had cleared people away and begun conducting operations. Uniformed police, fire-fighters, fire investigation officers and CSIs all weaved around each other. A high-volume pump was in front of the shop, and a water management unit and aerial platform were standing by. Firefighters were a mass of blue uniforms, and their yellow stripes and helmets stood out like beacons. Some were transporting ladders and breathing apparatus. Others were holding jets and unravelling reels. A few charred window frames were still in place. One small pane remained, jagged and angry. Black and white tendrils of smoke were still seeping out of openings, but it was hard to tell whether these were fumes or steam. Water streaked the walls of the building, staining the yellow brickwork.

I introduced Dan and myself to Simon, and told him about the woman's phone call.

He groaned. 'Someone knew what they were doing, I can tell you that, but I hope she's wrong.' The man's tone was clipped and the veins on his face and scalp bulged with concern, knowing he held

14

people's lives in his hands, and that his decisions were critical. 'As soon as the building's safe, we'll get someone in.'

'Any signs of anyone in there?' The woman on the recording had sounded terrified. Not a bit like a crank caller.

'We can't get close enough to see. The speed the flames tore through the floors, and the fumes in there . . . ' He was shaking his head. 'If anyone was inside, they won't have survived those temperatures or the smoke. They had an extraction system on the ground floor. Add timber flooring to that, wooden joists, lathe and plaster, and it's all increased the speed the fire spread. Not seen a blaze like this for several months.'

'Any indication it was deliberate?' A sinking feeling was stealing over me. The caller had refused to give the emergency services operator her name, so we couldn't be certain she was connected to the premises.

'Can't say for definite yet but we're pretty sure accelerant was involved. Whoever poured it couldn't have lit it from inside. Or if they did, we'll be finding their body too.' His phone buzzed and he checked the screen. 'Excuse me. I need to take this.' He clamped the phone to his ear. 'Chapel.'

Around us, debris had been shovelled into huge piles for the council to remove. Strips of drenched, charred wood smelled bitter. Glass shards glinted threateningly in the light. Curtains and blinds had blown out into the street. Human traces were littered around the pavement: clothes, drink cans, food wrappers, a baseball hat, a couple of rucksacks, all drenched and abandoned.

Simon rang off. 'That was the building inspector,' he said to Dan and me. 'He's on his way. We aren't sure whether the fire is completely out in the centre of the building. It's still too hot to get in there. Our thermal imaging cameras can only reach so far.' He gave me an apologetic smile. 'I'll call you the moment we get news or can get in.'

'Thank you.' I turned to Dan. 'Let's find out what witnesses we've got before they all clear off.'

We left the cordoned area and headed up the street to the phone repair shop where casualties had been ushered for treatment. When we arrived, the interior of the shop was a mass of people who'd been injured, display cabinets and product racks. A Sikh man was stretched out on his back on the floor with an oxygen mask over his face. Teenagers were huddled against the wall, looking pale and scared. Others were sitting on the floor, cuts and burns on their faces and arms. A lady with a blue-rinse hairdo was sitting on a plastic chair, clutching her arm, her entire demeanour one of shell-shock. Her hair was dishevelled and flecked with ash and dust, and she was clinging to her bag as though she was scared for her life. Beside the door, a paramedic was trying to attend to a lanky boy who had a large gash on his forehead. The young lad seemed unsteady on his feet and was muttering in Arabic.

Amidst the bodies, I spotted Dougie. As crime scene manager, his job was to talk me through the evidence and forensics. As soon as he saw us, he hurried over to the shop entrance. His large frame filled the doorway. He had a smear of blood on his cheek and ash had lodged in his hair and eyebrows, making his eyes seem greyer than usual.

'Practising your First Aid?' I smiled at him.

'It's been mayhem.' He turned away from the shop so we were out of earshot. 'I had a feeling you'd turn up when you heard it was the old bagel shop.' Affection creased the corners of his mouth before he switched into professional mode. 'Uniform have begun eyewitness interviews, including some of the teenagers from the flash mob. The woman with the sling was on her way to visit her mum and someone pulled her into the crowd. She fell on her wrist. The young lad by the door is anxious to get moving – something about his parents being worried. His English isn't great so it's hard to figure out exactly what he saw, but the priority is to get stitches over that cut before he gets a nasty infection. He's already feeling dizzy. Rima's on her way to interpret.'

I was absorbing the details. 'A flash mob *and* arson?' I frowned the question.

The three of us began walking towards the burnt building.

'It is a bit of a coincidence,' Dougie replied.

My mind was spinning.

Dougie wiped his blackened face with the sleeve of his jacket. 'The fire investigators think the blaze started on the ground floor. Probably at the foot of the stairs. It would then have spread quickly upwards, building in intensity, and then blown out the windows. The top floor has collapsed under the weight of the water.'

'In that case, I'll get the H-2-H teams started so we don't waste time.' I glanced ahead. A neon sign lay on the ground. Over the front of the shop, smoke-charred in places, I made out 'SOUP'. I turned to face the shop opposite the fire and felt nostalgic momentarily.

FELDMAN'S NEWSAGENT.

'Dad often brought us here. He and Mr Feldman were pals.'

Suddenly, I heard something. Faint and weak, but its distress gnawed through the air. 'What's that? I can hear someone.' I wheeled round, trying to locate the source. 'It's coming from one of the shops.' There it was. 'It's the newsagent's. Someone's calling for help.'

I dashed over to the shop; pushed the door open and entered the shop alone. 'Hello? It's the police.'

A different smell greeted me. Musty. Less of the acrid smoke, and the water-drenched tarmac and masonry; this was damp timber and plaster. It reminded me of our first flat. In the dim light, it was like stepping back in time. It was as if the whole place hadn't been touched for thirty years, and suddenly I was a child again, in here with my brother and sister, choosing sweets.

'Help, help,' came the voice, followed by a series of rasping coughs.

'Hello? Help's arrived.' I scoured the room for signs of movement or noise. Around me, white MDF shelves were thin on stock. Tea bags, tins of soup and jars of coffee lay in rows, collecting dust. A central aisle housed packets of envelopes and writing paper. 'Can you tell me where you are?'

The paintwork was a nicotine-stained ochre, and had a sheen to it, as if the place hadn't been painted for decades. By the till, a barely touched drink sat in a cup and saucer. Behind the counter, folding doors were drawn over a cabinet with a lock in the middle. The closer I got to the back room, the stronger the damp smell got. Years of living in unheated flats had tuned my nose.

'Mrs Feldman? Is that you?'

'Here,' came a croaky voice from behind the counter. She was flat on the floor, cheek to the ground and lying on one arm.

'It's OK. Don't try and move. Have you hurt yourself?' She was an older version of the one I remembered but it was definitely her.

She cleared her throat. Once, twice. Then wheezing coughs erupted.

I was about to dial 999 when Mrs Feldman began spluttering and gurgling again. She was gasping for breath – and failing. If she didn't get help quickly, she was going to die. 'Emergency in Feldman's Newsagent's,' I shouted down the phone at Dan. 'Get one of the paramedics and bring them in. Behind the counter. The shopkeeper is having trouble breathing.' I took in her grey features, the rasping breath, and her bloodshot eyes. 'Hurry. We're losing her.'

Maya, 3.30 p.m.

Back on Brick Lane, the air was damp, and a bitter nip was creeping in. The paramedics stretchered Rosa Feldman into an ambulance, their faces worry-streaked. Her body was barely a bump beneath the blanket and an oxygen mask was clamped over her tiny face.

My phone rang. I took in the news and conveyed it to Dan. 'The soup shop belongs to a young Lithuanian couple. Simas Gudelis and Indra Ulbiene. Uniform have spoken to Indra. She's been out all day, visiting her sister in Upton Park. They closed the shop because Simas wasn't feeling well. He was going to dose himself up and try and sleep it off.'

Dan's expression mirrored mine and I wondered if he was thinking about the fire investigation officer's warning when we arrived.

'She *is* the person who rang emergency services earlier. Someone told her about the fire. As far as she knows, Simas was at home in bed today. She'll be here any minute.'

'Has she heard from him since the fire?'

'No. She said his mobile goes straight to answerphone.' An awful thought occurred to me. I'd seen the bodies of people who had been in fires, including my brother's, still as vivid now as when I'd seen it in the Sylhet mosque eighteen months ago. Laid out on a shroud, Sabbir had looked like a bag of greasy bones. 'If Indra's husband is in there, I don't want her arriving just as we are hoisting his body out.' There was a practical concern too: fire victims often lost their skin and tissue, and this made DNA analysis and formal identification a slow and frustrating process.

'Let's hope that no-one else was in the building then.'

I gathered my thoughts. I needed to update Simon, the fire crew manager, and joined him and Dougie. 'One of the shop owners has confirmed that her husband *was* in the building. He was in bed, ill. Are we any closer to getting someone inside?' I sensed from their expressions that it wasn't good news.

'Not at the moment.' Simon's voice was unequivocal. 'It's still not safe to enter. We are waiting for a taller aerial platform to arrive from Bethnal Green station.' He pointed at the building's height. 'That should enable us to lift an officer up the outside.' He paused. 'We're pretty sure the fire is out but we're waiting for a structural engineer. He'll be able to conduct a more sophisticated assessment of the building's strength. If he says it's OK to lower someone in, we can do it, but until then we cannot risk it, I'm sorry.'

'Alright.'

Dan joined us. 'I've just spoken to Indra. She's in a cab on her way here. Their bedroom is on the top floor, at the front. She's asking about her husband.'

It was always difficult to know what to tell the families of victims on the phone. In training they told us to say as little as possible, that face to face was best, but there was also an argument for preparing people for bad news, so it wasn't such a shock. 'OK, thanks.' It was hard to imagine a worse outcome for Indra than her husband having burnt to death in his bed, but something told me that her world had changed irrevocably this morning when she left the shop to meet her sister.

Maya, 3.45 p.m.

Dan and I were in the mobile phone shop, helping uniform to interview the people who needed medical treatment. Rima, an interpreter I'd met before, was perching on a stool next to the Syrian boy with the gash on his forehead. She had a bag at her feet and was filling out a form on an iPad. Her patient features conveyed her caring, professional manner as she spoke to him in Arabic.

'Thanks for coming, Rima. It's—'

'Scared the life out of me, it did.' The interruption came from a woman who was sitting nearby. 'I hope no-one was in there.'

I introduced myself, and tried to reassure her. 'While we've got the interpreter here,' I said to her, 'can I speak to this young lad? If you go with DS Maguire, he'll ask you a few questions.'

'If you like, dear,' she said, looking mildly put out for a second before beaming at Dan's youthful, squaddie appearance and running her hand over her hair.

I gestured Dan over and shifted my attention to the boy who had been sitting next to her. 'What's your name?'

'Ali.' He shrugged. 'I need go.'

Dougie was right about him being nervous. Shock from the fire and the gash, probably. The cut had been stitched, and traces of congealed blood were smeared over his childlike features. 'I'm Maya. Rima is going to translate, OK?'

His nod was fast. He was chewing at the skin round his finger nails. 'My parent be worry. I need go.'

'I'll be as quick as I can.'

Rima translated.

'Were you already here when the flash mob started?'

He shook his head. From his height and build I guessed he was about ten, but the expression in his eyes could have put him at three times that age. He pulled himself up straight as though wanting to shake off the fear he knew I'd seen.

'You aren't in any trouble.' I kept my voice as gentle as I could and waited for him to relax. 'Can you tell me what you saw?'

His face held its silence but his eyes didn't. He stared at Rima as though he was hoping she'd understand something. 'Was just bit fun.' He didn't wait for the translation. He fixed dark eyes on me, and it hit me how vulnerable he seemed. 'Dance. Music. Is all.' He pointed his nose away from me, dismissive and disinterested.

The burnt-out building was a mere shell, the damage self-evident. I wanted to say that it wasn't fun for the people who'd been hurt and lost their livelihoods, but he was just a kid, and I needed to focus on getting what key information I could. 'What was the flash mob about?'

Rima spoke gently.

Ali shifted forward so that his feet were on the ground, and pawed at the laminate flooring with his scruffy trainer. He gabbled in Arabic, and gestured pleadingly to Rima with his eyes.

'He says he doesn't know anything about the flash mob. He was there. It started up. That's it.' Rima's frown suggested she wasn't convinced.

'Who brought the speakers?'

Rima translated.

'He doesn't know.' He was avoiding my gaze, and his spindly leg was jigging up and down. His white trainers had broken laces, and were covered in scuff marks, and he wasn't wearing any socks.

'How old are you?'

He cleared his throat and straightened his back again. Spoke for longer than it would take to give his age.

'He says he's nearly eleven,' said Rima.

'D'you live round here?'

'York Square.' He looked up at me through a thick forelock of almost-black hair. 'My parent wait me there.'

'In Limehouse?'

'Yes.'

'Who asked you to come here for the flash mob?' I posed the question slowly, as I suspected he'd understand, and I wanted to gauge his reactions.

He waved his arms in the air, angrily, muttering in Arabic.

'He says it wasn't a flash mob. It was just a few people, dancing and playing music. He was here with a friend.'

He clenched a fist. Gabbled to Rima again.

'He says they weren't doing anything. Just passing time. They were bored. He says they're The Street Rats.'

Ali laughed, pretending to be cocky. 'Yeah. We are Street Rat.' He winced as the movement tugged at the stitches in his forehead.

'Is that a gang name?'

He jutted his jaw, defiance blazing in his eyes.

'Do you need Rima to call your parents?'

'Is OK. They wait me already.'

I needed to revisit a question. 'We believe the flash mob was deliberately organised. Where did you hear about it?'

'He can't remember,' said Rima.

'We suspect that the fire at the shop was also caused deliberately. If that's true, it's a very serious offence.' I softened my tone. 'Especially if anyone has died.'

Ali looked at me now, and for the first time I noticed how black his eyes were. His shoulders were hunched, and he was jabbing at the floor with the heel of his shoe. I realised I felt scared for him. 'Where did you hear about the flash mob?'

He began a lengthy explanation.

Rima translated as he spoke. 'There's a website that posts about upcoming events . . . some are flash mobs . . . the website tells you the date . . . and the rough location . . . you register your email or cell phone number . . . it's called London for All. LfA, for short.'

'And is the website public?' A sinking feeling stole over me.

'Yes, but they have a private discussion board,' said Rima.

The news filled me with dread. Discussion forums were the bane of the police. 'Do you know who runs the forum?'

He shook his head and spoke further.

'A guy called Frazer,' Rima translated, ' . . . posts the messages . . . but it's never him that comes to the events . . . and no one knows who he is . . . it's a different person . . . who comes along . . . and no one uses their real names on the forum.'

'And what's your username?' I asked.

'He says it's "cookiemonster".'

Ali blushed, and for a few moments, vulnerability betrayed his desire to look older.

The police technicians would be able to track down the site host and administrators. With any luck, the cyber-crime unit might already have data on LfA. 'Did the posts say what the purpose was of today's flash mob?'

He'd said no but I wasn't convinced.

'He says they didn't care,' said Rima. 'But from how he describes it, it sounds like it was something to do with anti-gentrification.'

'Yes. Genti-thingy.' He pointed at the street and lapsed back into Arabic.

'Was any incentive offered to turn up?'

'He doesn't want to get anyone into trouble. They were told not to tell anyone.'

'Tell anyone what?' I looked from Rima to Ali.

Ali was silent.

'Who told them not to say anything?'

'Frazer.' Rima emphasised the name and raised her eyebrows. I got the impression she was trying to check I'd taken note.

'What was the payment?' Please, God, may it not have been drugs.

'Sometimes he gave them a bit of money or some food,' said Rima. 'And masks.'

'What sort of masks?'

Ali and Rima talked in Arabic. 'Black bandanas with the LfA logo on them,' she said.

This was news. 'And drugs?'

'NO.' Ali was on his feet now. His eyes were flashing with fear, and for a moment I wondered if he was about to make a dash, but his body swayed and rocked. He put his hand out and sunk back down onto his seat. 'Not drug.'

'OK.' I changed tack. 'Today – who brought the speakers?'

'He says they were there when they arrived.'

'They?'

'He came with his brother and his brother's girlfriend.'

'What are their names?'

'Riad.'

'How old's he?'

'Nearly sixteen.'

'And Sophie,' Rima said. 'She's doing A-levels at New City College.'

'Does Riad live with you in York Square?'

'Yes.'

'What number in York Square?'

'Twenty-eight. Opposite the entrance to the park.'

'Where are Riad and Sophie now?'

Fear filled Ali's eyes and he covered his mouth with his hand.

'He doesn't know. They got separated . . . When the fire started . . . they ran for cover and . . . Riad's not answering his phone. He says he's scared.'

'Which direction did they run in?'

'That way and left.' He pointed.

'That way?' I gestured. 'That's right.'

'*Ach.*' He punched his leg, as though he felt stupid. He turned to Rima and spoke to her.

'Down there and right,' she said. 'He says his brother will turn up. He's probably dropped his phone or they've gone to get some chips.'

'Ali. Are you sure neither of them entered the building before it went on fire?'

'They were both with him.'

'We'll need their descriptions . . . and a formal statement, Rima, if you can translate, please? Ali, if you hear from your brother or Sophie, please inform us straightaway.' I summoned a uniformed officer and began briefing him.

Dan, 3.45 p.m.

Mrs Jones, the blue-rinse lady who'd hurt her wrist, was shivering and fidgety, so Dan settled her on a fold-out chair in the stock room at the back of the mobile phone shop and went to fetch her a cuppa. As he returned with it, she made a point of checking her watch and sighing loudly.

'You got a hot date to get to?' he asked, grinning mischievously.

Mrs Jones gave a giggle. 'My old mum will be wondering where I've got to. She'll have seen all this on the news and will be fretting. She doesn't do mobile phones and neither do I.'

'Thanks for waiting,' Dan said. 'Have a swig of this.' He passed her the cup of sweet tea and squatted down next to her. 'It'll soon get you warmed up, eh.'

She was trembling, but her expression relaxed a few notches and she sipped the tea.

'Can you take me through what you saw when you arrived?'

She nudged smeared glasses up the bridge of her nose with a shaky finger. 'I was walking that way.' She pointed in the direction of Whitechapel. 'My mum lives on White Church Lane. Out of the blue, music started up behind me. Gave me a real fright, it did.' She clamped her hand to her chest. 'When I turned round, I saw people dancing in the street.'

Dan guessed Mrs Jones was around his mum's age: late sixties.

Too much energy to do nothing, she always told him. 'Who was in charge?'

'No-one as far as I could see. Everyone was encouraging everyone to join in. D'you know what I mean?'

Dan had seen flash mobs in Sydney and knew how quickly they snowballed. 'Yes, I do. And the music?'

She pursed her lips while she tried to remember. 'The tracks were quite short. Prepared, ready, like those cassette tape things we used to make. The songs changed every couple of minutes.' She looked as though she was enjoying having someone listen to her. 'Those masks though. They were a bit sinister.'

Maya, 4 p.m.

In the afternoon light, Dan's ginger hair was glowing through his military buzz-cut. His usually pale skin was flushed with excitement as he strode the few metres along Brick Lane towards me. I could tell there'd been a development.

'The kids at the flash mob were wearing—'

'. . . masks. Yeah.' I conveyed what Ali had told me.

'London for All?' He repeated the name back. 'That certainly fits with anti-gentrification.'

'Exactly. Let's walk back to the cordon. Indra has just arrived. She's asking if her husband is alive and I haven't spoken to her yet.' I told Dan about the man called Frazer. 'I've forwarded the LfA link to the technicians and the cyber-crime unit. Told them it's urgent. Screenshot some of the content in case it's deleted.'

'Woah. Get you, Ms Suddenly Tech Savvy.'

'Suddenly? Cheeky bugger. I expect it comes from working with someone who's on the internet all the time.'

We both laughed, relieved to have a bit of banter.

'Let's hope they shut that bastard site down.' Dan's words came out in an angry whisper. 'A lot of these kids don't know how to keep themselves safe online.'

'The kid with the gash is only ten.' I gestured to the two shops. 'What the hell's he doing, roaming the streets with these older boys?'

Dan's manner was sombre. 'I agree. It worries me about my

two girls. Kids are growing up so quickly these days. They don't understand how careful they need to be.' He was shaking his head. 'At least it sounds like that young Syrian lad's got his parents and brother to look after him.'

Back at the scene, Simon Chapel gave me a thumbs-up. A second aerial platform was manoeuvring itself into position outside the shop.

A uniformed officer was standing with two women at the cordon. From behind, they had similar frames. Both tall and slim. One had a curtain of blonde hair down her back, and wore a khaki parka with a furry hood, jeans and trainers. The woman she was talking to had dark brown hair in a ponytail, knee-high leather boots. I guessed they were Indra and her sister. I went straight over to them. 'DI Rahman. You must be—'

'Is my husband dead?' The blonde woman's voice quaked with fear. She had mascara smears round her eyes.

'I'm sorry. We don't know what the situation is yet,' I said. 'I think it's only fair to warn you that if he was in the fire, it's unlikely he will have survived.' It was an awful thing to have to tell her, and I paused for her to absorb the news. 'We should know more once the platform lifts a fire officer into the room where your husband is.' I turned to the dark-haired woman. 'Are you Indra's sister?'

'Taip. Marta.' Her tone was as expressionless as her face.

'I want to see Simas. I want to go up there.' Indra kept covering her face with her hands and lapsing into her mother tongue. She took two paces to the left, then two back again. 'Please can I—'

'I'm afraid that's not possible. It may be several hours before they can bring any victims out. As soon as we know anything, we will let you know. Would you like to go and get warm somewhere and we can ring you? It may not be until tomorrow.'

'No. I want to stay here.' Anguish was contorting her features, pulling the skin tight around her eyes and mouth. 'Everything. My life is in that—'

'Inspector?' Simon Chapel shouted. 'We're going up now.'

The lift was finally in place beside the shop.

'Excuse me,' I said to Indra and hurried over to join Chapel, where a fire officer, in protective clothing and breathing apparatus, was being lifted up the outside of the building on the aerial platform.

'He's got a mic so he can tell us what he sees.' Chapel was repeating the man's commentary aloud to Dan and I. 'Floor almost completely collapsed in the room on the left . . . some of the ceiling is down . . . nothing much in there . . . going to use binoculars . . . a few remnants of furniture . . . no-one alive in there . . . no signs of a corpse.' He stopped. 'We need to shift the lift over to the room on the right.'

A few agonising minutes later, the vehicle had moved and the crane was in place. The fire officers repeated the commentary procedure.

'Floor intact in this room . . . what looks like a bed . . . a bump . . . bedding around the bump . . . yep, the body's in there. He can smell it.' Simon turned away from us to speak into his radio to his ground personnel. 'Right, get the lift down and get him checked over. Someone chase up the structural engineer. If he can't get here, get another one. We need to get that body out and that means getting in.'

I turned to look for Indra, to tell her that we had found a body, but she and her sister were nowhere to be seen.

Maya, 4.30 p.m.

While we waited for the engineer to arrive, I walked a couple of buildings away to make some calls. Dan was trying to get hold of Indra, so I rang the Royal London Hospital to inquire about Rosa Feldman. The news wasn't good. With her asthma, and years of living with Józef's cigarette smoke, the fumes she'd inhaled in the street had ripped through the lining of her lungs, the ward sister told me, and Rosa was still having difficulty breathing.

'She's on steroids and has been hallucinating,' the nurse said. 'She's convinced she's in the Warsaw Ghetto at the end of the war.'

We would have to hope she pulled through.

'One thing,' the nurse said. 'She keeps mentioning masks. Black masks. Does that mean anything to you?'

*

Half an hour later, with so much soot in the sky, the light was fading fast. Floodlights shone over the crime scene and made it look as though it was the film set for a horror or disaster movie. The fire service engineer, Terry Dixon, had arrived. He confirmed within minutes that the building was not structurally safe to enter from the ground. To get Simas's body out, we would ideally need to go through the windows, using support structures, but that would mean a further delay while we waited for those to arrive. Another option was for an enclosed cage – with a fire officer inside it – to be lowered through the hole in the collapsed roof from above.

'We did something similar at that warehouse fire in Shoreditch a few months back.' Terry was showing Simon the images on his phone. 'D'you remember?'

'OK,' Simon said, his voice heavy with resignation and apprehension. 'Let's do it.'

Fifteen minutes later, and after careful manoeuvring by the lift operator, the fire officer was finally able to see into the room at the top of the house where he'd seen a body. I held my breath as he was lowered from above, where the roof had been. They had to move the lift at a painfully slow pace so that the cage and crane arm did not disturb the building structure. There was nothing above him to fall, but the walls were difficult to assess. Other than the instructions of Simon Chapel, the site was quiet. Until—

'Hey,' a voice shouted. 'Why is he looking at that side of the building?'

We all turned and saw Indra, rake thin and ashen.

'Our bedroom is on the left,' she shouted. 'Not that side.' She bolted over to Chapel. 'He's got the wrong room. Simas isn't in that room. Our bedroom is this one.' She was pointing, jabbing the air urgently, her arms stick-like in the parka.

I followed her over to Chapel and relayed what the officer had seen when he looked through their bedroom window.

'The floor collapsed? Where is he then?' She glanced from me to Dan, and I could tell that the realisation was dawning that something wasn't right. 'Why would he be in the spare room?'

I was racking my brain for things to say. I wasn't sure why Indra was bothered which room her husband was in. 'Perhaps Simas went

33

next door to sleep? Maybe he went in there to fetch something and got trapped by the fire?' I could see Indra wasn't convinced.

'He never sleeps in there.' She began gabbling in Lithuanian to her sister.

'Hold it.' Chapel put his hand up to signal that the medical officer was relaying some news to him via a headset.

'He's coming out. He says he can see—' Chapel broke off abruptly. His face fell. 'Inspector, can you . . . ?' He took hold of my elbow and steered me away from Indra to the side of the building. 'Bad news, I'm afraid.' His voice was hushed. 'Andy says there are two bodies in there.'

'Two?' I was absorbing the implications. 'Can he see whether they are male or female?'

He was nodding. 'One's definitely male. The other one looks like it's female.' His eyes communicated possible interpretations of what they'd found.

Shit. Poor Indra. 'Is he sure?'

'We're trying to check, but he's pretty certain. The time on Andy's breathing apparatus runs out in a few minutes so he's got to come out, but we're going to lower Bill in next. If we're lucky, he can grab a few samples, but everything depends on the temperature.'

'Do whatever you can, please. We have to find out who's responsible for this. Rosa Feldman nearly died. Now we've now got two confirmed deaths and—'

'What's going on?' Indra was striding towards us, yelling. 'What's he found? Is my husband in there?'

'I'm sorry. I can't confirm anything until we've made a formal ID.'

'But someone is definitely dead?' Her green eyes were pools of tears. 'It's Simas, isn't it? I knew it as soon as I got the call.' Her hand was clasped over her mouth as she stifled sobs. 'Was it the gas?' Suddenly, Indra winced with pain and clamped her hand to her belly. 'We had cylinders . . . in the . . . ' She grabbed hold of her sister's arm, let out an agonised scream and fell to the ground like a dropped towel.

'*Help,*' Marta shouted. 'Paramedics. Over here.'

Indra lay on the pavement, her slender frame writhing in agony, her face a deathly white.

Marta was kneeling at her sister's side, leaning over, her hand on Indra's forehead. 'Hurry. She's pregnant.'

Maya, 5.30 p.m.

Minutes later, Indra was in an ambulance. The vehicle rattled out of Brick Lane, siren shrieking into the evening air, blue lights slicing through the darkness.

'I hope she's OK.' I was standing with Dan and Simon.

'*And* the baby,' Dan added as I marched over to Chapel. I had to fill him in on what Indra had said about gas cylinders in the shop.

His demeanour tightened. 'Did she say where?'

'No. Just "we had gas cylinders". That was it.'

'Shit. That means we could have an explosion. Oh Christ. The whole street could go up.' He grabbed hold of his radio and sprang into action. 'Right. Emergency procedures.' Chapel pointed away from the soup shop. 'Both of you,' he said to Dan and me, 'start moving people back. We need to extend the cordon a further five shops. Tell everyone who isn't family to go home as soon as they've spoken to the police.' He began shouting clipped instructions into his radio to the lift operator. 'Gas alert. Get Andy down from the platform and over to us as quick as you can. Repeat. Get Andy down.' He switched channels on his radio. 'All crew. All crew. Gas alert. All crew away from the building. Repeat. Gas alert. All crew to me at the front of the barber's shop. Prepare for emergency evacuation procedures. Over.'

Within seconds, fire officers reported in to their crew leader and Simon filled them in.

'We don't know the details or whether the cylinders have already gone up. We need to evacuate everyone three shops each side. Tell them to go to family, friends or a hotel until we give the all-clear.' Simon fixed his gaze on each of his officers in turn and issued instructions.

The team burst into action and the fire officers each marched towards the premises they'd been allocated.

'Gas emergency. Clear the area, please,' Simon shouted at the emergency services staff who were still hanging around to the left of the soup shop. He checked progress with the lift and made sure the cordon had been widened adequately.

People streamed out of shops, onto the street, wide-eyed and terrified, and were herded to beyond the new cordon. The lift lowered Andy onto the pavement. The operator jumped out of his cab to meet him and steered him towards the cordon as quickly as he could. Here, we were waiting.

Andy began removing his breathing apparatus and climbed out of his protective clothing and head gear. 'It's definitely a man and a woman in there,' he said. 'They're curled round each other on what looks like a bed.'

'Did you manage to get any photographs?'

He nodded. 'Let me grab a swig of water.' He was laying his kit out as he removed it. Mask, oxygen cylinders, thermal suit, thermal imaging camera. Dust and debris flew everywhere. For a moment it made me think of the way people lay out bodies after disasters.

'Poor Indra,' I said to Dan. Thank goodness she had her sister with her. Losing her husband and business were awful enough.

'Yes,' he replied. 'Things are going to get even worse for her when she finds out about the other body.'

'You know what the media are like. As soon as they get hold of the story, they'll splash her personal life all over the TV. It'll be on the internet and in all the papers. It's going to be awful for her. And when we broadcast a public appeal for information on the woman, it's going to increase speculation further.' While Andy removed his gear, I was turning over in my mind who the best person would be to tell us – in Indra's absence – whether the man in the photographs was Simas Gudelis. A reliable ID would depend on how burned the body was. Hopefully, we could identify the victims from the images the medical officer had taken and wouldn't have to rely on dental records or DNA analysis. A thought occurred to me. 'Dan, can you see if there's an image of Simas online? A mug shot that we can use as a temporary reference point?'

He swiped his phone into life. 'Here we go. The soup shop has a website.' Dan was clicking through the website pages. 'Simas Gudelis and Indra Ulbiene. Lithuanian. Both from Vilnius originally. They've lived in Tower Hamlets for three years, and before that they lived in Cambridgeshire for two years.'

'Doing what?'

'Agricultural labourers on various farm camps.'

He showed me an image of the two of them, outside their shop. They stood at their blue front door. The man was shaking a bottle of champagne and the woman was cutting a piece of yellow tape. She was recognisable as the one we had just met, although her build and muscle tone were heftier then and her hair was darker. Simas was taller than Indra. A brown line clung to his jawline and top lip, and he had thick eyebrows. At least we had something to go on.

Andy was rubbing his unmasked face as though wanting to shake off the things he'd seen. 'Extremely unpleasant in there.'

'I bet. Could we look through the photographs on your camera? We need to ID the bodies.'

'Sure.' He fetched it from the ground and passed it over.

With Dan looking on, I flicked through the camera's memory card. The images showed two bodies, lying on a surface with their arms round each other. The pose – the man curled round the woman like a spoon – was a peaceful one but their melted, greasy appearance and the fire-charred room was a vision of agony.

'Jeez.' Unless they'd grabbed hold of each other out of terror, it suggested they'd been curled up in bed together when the fumes and flames got to them.

'If it's any consolation,' Andy said, 'the two people in that room would have become unconscious extremely quickly and died within minutes. The accelerant was focussed on the hall and staircase. The fire will have ripped through the centre of the building.'

In the image, the man's face was shiny and burned back to tissues and fat, but his cheeks and the area around his mouth was much darker, which could be from having a beard and moustache.

Dan lined his phone up with the camera so that one of the internet images was next to the shot. 'Looks like him, doesn't it?'

'There are definitely similarities but it's hard to be sure from these images.' It was frustrating. Facial profiling might help but it wasn't a reliable method on its own. 'We need to find out from Indra if she has anything of Simas' which might have his DNA on.'

'And whether he had any identifying marks,' said Dan. 'The sister might be able to help too.'

I glanced at the images again. 'We can't be certain it's Simas, but it seems probable. Let's hope someone has reported the woman missing.'

'I'll get Alexej to check the MisPer Register.' Dan began to dial on his mobile.

I faced Andy again. 'Can we take a copy of a few of these photographs as an interim?'

'Sure.'

It took Dan a couple of moments to copy a few of the images into secure cloud storage and we made our way off the crime scene.

Just as we reached the car, a tall, mousey-haired man strode towards us. 'Hey. Police. Wait a moment.' It was a clipped, East London accent. His black, military-style trench-coat flapped with each stride and his eyes were darting around the scene.

The voice was familiar.

Maya, 6 p.m.

'Someone said my mother's been taken to hospital.' The man was peering through the window of the newsagent's and looking over at the wreckage of the soup shop.

Of course. That's why he was familiar. It was Tomasz Feldman. The man in front of me was tall, a couple of years older than I was – but last time I'd seen him, he'd been a teenager.

'Is Mum OK? Where is she?' He took in the scene of devastation. 'Why's the street being evacuated?'

'Your mother has been taken to the Royal London Hospital.' Perhaps he didn't recognise me?

'Christ. She's asthmatic.'

'She's inhaled smoke and was in a bad way. I gather her condition is stable now. She was in the street when the fire broke out and must've struggled back into the newsagent's. I found her on the floor behind the counter.'

'Thank you so much. Sounds like you saved her life.' He had the same kind manner as when we were kids. 'I'll get down to the hospital and see if she needs anything.'

'I don't know if you remember me. I'm Maya Rahman. My sister and I used to—?'

His face softened. 'Oh, I remember you two. The pick-n-mix,' he said with a note of amused affection. 'I was sorry to read about your brother. Dreadful thing to happen.'

'Thank you.' I paused to recalibrate and tell him about the gas in the soup shop. 'The reason we've evac—'

'It's very damp in your mother's shop.' Dan's interruption broke my train of thought. 'Couldn't you help her to get the heating updated?'

I shot Dan an unimpressed look. 'Er – this is my sergeant, DS Maguire.'

'I've been trying, believe me,' Tomasz replied. 'Spent the last ten years trying to get Dad to sort it out. Even offered to organise and pay for the work myself but the old man wouldn't hear of it. Said the place was fine.' He raised his hand in a baffled gesture. 'Everyone can see it's been neglected for years. With Dad, unfortunately, I think it was pride.' He focused his gaze on me. 'But it's created an impasse as Mum seems to feel some misguided sense of loyalty now that Dad's dead, and she won't agree to work being done either. I've offered to put her up in one of my properties while the work is done but she won't hear of it. I've run out of ideas.'

'What's your line of business?' I wasn't surprised that he hadn't followed his parents into running the newsagent's. He'd always seemed ambitious.

'I own some property and I have a bar.'

'Around here?'

'A bit further towards Shoreditch.' He gestured behind him with his thumb.

Dan was already on his phone. He seemed to have taken a dislike to Rosa's son.

'Do you live up there too?' I asked.

'Yes. When my sister and I left home, she moved out to Newham and I stayed in Tower Hamlets. She had a family and when Dad got sick, it was easier for me to keep an eye on Mum when I was up the road.'

'Are you in touch with your sister much?' She'd been a few years younger than me I'd never got to know her.

'Agnieszka? Oh, yes. We both do what we can to help Mum. Especially now Dad's not around.' He paused, as though he was deciding what to say. 'It isn't easy. I don't think they make them like her anymore.' He gave a small, frustrated laugh. 'Perhaps it's a generational thing: being born at the end of the war and emigrating . . . ? It must have been hard. She's fiercely independent and not good at asking for help. The old man was extremely proud. He didn't like help either.' His smile creased the corners of his mouth, and the obvious affection made his thoughtful brown eyes shine.

His comments reminded me of my own mother, and I wondered how she would have coped, slogging away in a shop, organising orders and deliveries, and doing business accounts at the age of seventy-five, after losing her husband months earlier.

'Agnieszka and I both told them to give up the shop years ago. Things have changed round here. All the people Mum and Dad knew have moved out of Brick Lane.' He pointed, first at *Alchemia*, with its new glitzy shopfront, and then at his mother's newsagent. 'It's sounds harsh but no-one needs Basildon Bond envelopes and jars of instant coffee when we are surrounded by espresso bars and supermarkets.' He checked his watch. 'I'd better shoot. I want to get to the hospital and make sure she's OK.'

'Before you dash off, we'll need your contact details.' I signalled for one of the uniformed officers. 'When did you last see your mother?'

'First thing this morning.' The frown clouded his features briefly and I noticed that his hair was scattered with grey at the temples.

'I helped her with a delivery. The boxes were far too heavy for her and the driver dumped them in the street.'

'Did you see any activity over the road at the soup shop?'

'I saw Indra leave around nine. The shop was shut up. That's extremely unusual for them.'

Maya, 6.15 p.m.

As Dan and I walked away from the crime scene, my thoughts shifted from Rosa Feldman. It was clear that the fire was arson, so we now had a double murder and two people in hospital, both extremely ill. I'd need to report in to Superintendent Campbell and request she appoint me SIO. Questions were swirling in my mind, and I was determined that whoever was responsible would be brought to justice.

I dialled the hospital and asked to be put through to the ward. Rosa was much better but was refusing to go and stay with her daughter. 'Rosa has been having more nightmares,' I told Dan once I'd rung off. 'She's waking up screaming, convinced she's back in Warsaw.'

'Poor lady. If she was born at the end of the war, the German army razed the city to the ground. The Soviet troops finished it off a year later. I'm not surprised the fire has triggered traumatic memories.'

'Once she's awake she knows she's not back in Poland, but she insists that the only place she feels safe is at the newsagent's . . . '

'. . . which may be true but isn't necessarily what's best for her.'

'How on earth can she return to the shop after inhaling all that smoke?' I asked.

Dan was pensive. 'I'm sure her kids will see her right. Tomasz has gone to the hospital, so he'll find out about the dreams. It sounds like he's got property to put her up in.'

As we walked away, a gaggle of reporters swarmed towards us, clutching microphones and filming equipment, and shouting questions. Cameras flashed in my face, blinding me temporarily. I blinked and recognised a slim figure in a full-length coat at the front of the group. Her usual long black tresses had been pulled up into a faux-casual top-knot, and she was wearing her trademark four-inch heels.

'Inspector Rahman.' Suzie James' rasping voice was unmistakeable. 'What can you tell us about the fire?'

I took a deep breath and gathered my thoughts. At this stage of the investigation, I couldn't afford to antagonise the press or get into a skirmish with Suzie.

'Has anyone been killed and was it arson?' Another reporter shouted and shoved a microphone at me.

I stopped and prepared to address the group. 'I'm Detective Inspector Maya Rahman. An investigation is underway following the fire at the Brick Lane Soup Company this afternoon. The fire is being treated as deliberate, and my team and I are working hard to piece together the sequence of events and to apprehend whoever may be responsible.' I paused, wanting to emphasise our request for help from the community. 'We are appealing for a number of critical pieces of information. Firstly, we want to hear from anyone who was at the flash mob or in the shop area this morning. If you saw anyone acting suspiciously, or have smartphone video footage, please contact us. Secondly, anyone who has been unable to contact a friend or loved one since the fire, please call us. At the moment, we have two fatalities, and we need help identifying one of these. We are keen to hear about anyone who is missing or from anyone who cannot contact a female friend, sister, mother or daughter. Any information, no matter how insignificant it may seem, please contact the incident room at Limehouse Police Station. Thank you.' I checked my watch. 'I'll take a few quick questions.'

A cacophony of voices broke out.

'Where is the shopkeeper, Mr Gudelis?' a local journalist shouted.

'We are trying to establish his whereabouts,' I replied.

'Is this a hate crime?' shouted a reporter for *The Messenger*.

'We have no evidence of that.'

'You're not ruling it out though?'

'We are pursuing a number of lines of enquiry.'

'We've seen Mrs Gudelis. Who is the other fire victim?'

'We're waiting for a formal ID.'

'Are we likely to see a wave of arson attacks in East London? Copycat flash mobs and property torching? Bit like the way the London riots spread.'

The man's question hit me like a smack in the face. Tony was a reporter who'd worked for the *City Eye* for as long as I could remember. He was famous for his sensationalist headlines.

'We have no reason to believe that's going to happen and would urge you not to scaremonger, Tony, please. We want to encourage people to come forward with information, not send the city into panic.'

'That's a yes, then.'

I gritted my teeth.

'Does this case have personal involvement for you too, Inspector?' Suzie's question purred through a beautifully lipsticked mouth, and I'm sure I wasn't the only one to catch her jeer.

I glanced over at Dan who rolled his eyes. We both knew Suzie James of old. 'I've lived in this area for thirty-seven years, Suzie. It's all personal to me. Thank you. No further questions.'

'Well done.' Dan spoke softly.

'Thanks,' I said wearily. 'Right. Back to the nick for briefing and let's get cracking.' And added, 'I dread to think what the headlines are going to be.'

6.30 p.m.

When the girl woke up, she lay where she was, allowing her eyes to adjust to the dark. She knew something was wrong when she saw the ceiling. Her stars had gone. She tried to sit up. The mattress was slippery and smelled funny and didn't have a sheet. Her head was spinning, like when she was poorly sometimes. She lay down on her side, trying to figure out where she was. Two windows. In a corner of one, black plastic was peeling away from the frame, and slivers of light fell on the carpet and walls. No posters. No lamp. Her bedroom at home had a blind and a fluffy rug.

While she was sleeping, she'd thought she'd heard footsteps. They'd stopped at the end of the bed. And voices. She must've been dreaming.

She listened now.

Nothing.

'Mummy?' She spoke quietly in the dark, but no-one heard.

Thirsty. Her mouth was dry.

She sat up again, and slid her legs off the edge of the mattress and onto the floor. She'd sit here for a while, until her head stopped spinning. Beneath her toes, the thick carpet felt soft and squishy. She liked it. She liked being in a warm room with a lovely carpet, but she wanted Mummy. Mummy would bring her a drink and Mummy would know where the stars were and the slippy mattress with a drink . . . dizzy . . . and the stars in the shiny . . .

Maya, 7.30 p.m.

Back in the MIT room, the team were poised for our first briefing. The first twenty-four hours of the investigation were critical. We all knew that. Around the room, the boards were up and important information had been plastered over all available surfaces. Maps showed locations and routes. Shops had been plotted on a street plan. Facts and questions stood out in coloured board markers. We'd all examined the mug shots and got to grips with the key names.

'Let's get started, everyone,' I said. 'First, good news. The fire brigade has inspected the soup shop through the openings where the windows were, and only found one gas cylinder. It has already exploded, which probably contributed to the ferocity of the blaze, but it means we no longer have an explosion risk.'

A wave of relief swept through the team.

'We have a tentative ID on the male victim. Simas Gudelis, age forty-two, originally from Lithuania. He was co-owner of the shop with his wife, who says he was ill in bed.' I paused for breath. 'We have no ID for the woman, who isn't his wife.'

The next board had 'VICTIMS' as its heading. Here, we had multiple image sources for Simas: social media, the shop website and the ones from the fire officer. We only had the low-resolution photographs of the female.

'We need to prioritise identifying the woman so we can notify her next of kin and consider who may have wished her harm. Have we had any calls?' I'd only just briefed the media but I couldn't help hoping we'd had news.

'Nothing yet. And no matches on the MisPer register.' I saw the concern on Dan's face. 'She could live alone or work away a lot? Sometimes it takes a while to realise someone's missing.'

'True. Another possibility is that she has dependents at home. This could help our chances of someone calling in or it could create additional risk factors.' A terrible thought occurred to me. 'If she's got someone old or young at home, they might not be able to look after themselves. That bumps the need for her ID even higher up the order of priority.' My brain was snatching at possible solutions. 'What's the situation with the facial profiler?'

'She can't make much progress because of the lack of detail on the photographs.' Dan spoke quietly.

'OK. Our other priority needs to be getting the bodies out of the building. That'll be done the moment the building is deemed safe to enter. Then we can get better quality images, do a more specific media appeal, process DNA samples and search dental records.' I approached the board and took in the woman's wax-like features. It was impossible not to be reminded of my brother's appearance after the fire that killed him, although our victim had more flesh intact than Sabbir's charred bones. I swallowed down the dull thud of pain which the memory stirred, and took the cap off one of the marker pens to jot on the board.

Victim 2 (UnSub)
-Lives alone?
-Homeless?
-No family vs. dependents?

-Asylum seeker?
-MisPer?

'Dan, I think you've got information on motives?'

Dan zapped on the overhead projector and stepped in front of the team. The light on the board exaggerated his Irish colouring. 'Let's consider why might someone might want to set fire to the soup shop. The key arson motives are crime concealment, financial gain and boredom.' His iPad projected each motive as a bullet point on the board.

An angry mutter bobbed round the room at the mention of 'boredom'.

'We also need to consider extremism, jealousy and revenge. The intention is always criminal damage or endangering life, sometimes both.' He faced us now. 'With those in mind, what should our working hypotheses be?'

'An insurance job by Indra?' Alexej offered, looking up from his monitor. 'I'm checking whether Simas and Indra had the building insured, and whether Simas had a life insurance policy.'

'Yes,' said Dan. 'What else?'

'Who might not have liked the soup shop being in Brick Lane?' Alexej pointed at the street plans and photos. 'We know ethnic groups stick together. There's also an element of immigrant kinship and turf-orientation, but when it comes down to business, people's loyalties are to themselves.'

The atmosphere tightened.

'Thanks, buddy,' Dan said. 'I agree. Other ideas?'

'Maybe someone has their eye on the building?' Shen had been listening to Alexej carefully. 'A developer, perhaps?' She had a small, delicate frame and her voice was quiet at first. 'I often walk up Brick

Lane to visit my brother. The shops change hands quickly and businesses move from one premises to another.' She checked her notes. 'The shop was gutted before the Brick Lane Soup Company opened. Perhaps the arsonist was targeting the freeholder rather than Simas Gudelis?'

'Who is their freeholder? They'll have the building insured.' I tapped at the image of the shop on the board, as though encouraging it to speak to me.

'Man called Solomon Stein. He owns a few freeholds in Brick Lane.' Shen pointed to her notepad. 'Seems legit but I'm doing a few more checks.'

'It's possible the arsonist was targeting the woman.' Dan was typing the additional points into his list. 'It's difficult to assess until we know who she was.' He was rubbing his chin thoughtfully. 'I want to know what bad blood exists between Indra and Simas, and between them and other people.'

'If Indra knew Simas was having an affair, she might want revenge?' Shen suggested. 'Or perhaps we are looking for the partner of the woman in the fire?'

'Yes, Indra has to be a suspect.' I tucked my hair behind my ears, feeling the weight and scope of the task ahead. 'If the woman's partner is responsible, surely they'd have reported her missing so as not to arouse suspicion?'

Dan was in front of the board again. 'I agree with both those possibilities. My gut feeling is that we can rule out extremism, but I think we need to consider that it may have been a racist attack.'

I gestured to the board. 'OK, until we know what or who the targets of the arson were, we will need to consider all of these hypotheses. What else do we need to know?'

'Was the flash mob a distraction so that the arsonists could start the fire?' A familiar voice echoed through the room. 'In other words, are we looking at organised crime?'

'Jackie?' I said, incredulous. 'What are you doing here?'

Maya, 7.45 p.m.

'Surely the grapevine hasn't stopped working?' Jackie chuckled as she cruised in confidently and surveyed the incident room.

The team were transfixed.

'Hello, everyone. I'm DCI Jackie Lawson. I'll be covering your DCI post until a permanent appointment is made. If you're nice to me, you might get stuck with me. I'm looking for a cushy number.' She peered at me and grinned, and I couldn't help noticing that a curiosity-induced pink filter had slid over Dan's usual white face. 'I'm not here to be SIO, Maya. Don't worry.'

'The last I heard you'd moved from the Met to the North-West,' I said.

'Correct. I've been leading a new team there as part of the Serious Organised Crime Strategy. Masses of it in the North-West, lots in the South-East. The hotspot is in London. I'm going to be based here at Limehouse, but my brief is to monitor all ongoing Met investigations for elements of organised crime.'

The room was silent. All eyes were on the woman who was the epitome of smart-casual in her black jeans and white cotton shirt. It was clear she hadn't gone soft. Jackie Lawson was known for her mischievous sense of humour and was one of the sharpest and toughest cops in the service. 'It's great to see you. I had no idea you were coming here.' I'd only checked my email ten minutes earlier and there'd been no mention of Jackie joining the team. 'We'll catch up after briefing, yes?' I faced the room again. 'Dan, add DCI Lawson's question to the board, please, and let's continue. Who's next?'

'The analysts are working on a number of significant eyewitness statements,' Shen said. 'Their initial report is due any moment.'

'And we've made a start on the CCTV,' Alexej said. 'The fire took hold so quickly, and produced so much smoke, it's difficult to see much but if there's anything useful, we'll find it. I'm still calling security operators for footage from the hours prior to the flash mob and the fire.'

'Good,' I said. 'That should help us with identifying timescales and routes, and hopefully suspects. Someone may have seen the arsonist entering the shop.' I paused. 'We need to check dog walkers, postmen, joggers, road sweepers, people going to work, people coming home from night shifts and nights out. A lot of those people may not live locally so we'll need to ring-fence mobiles and send ping-outs on social media.' I tried not to look too obviously at Jackie who'd need to agree budgets. 'What's the latest with LfA?'

Alexej waved a print-out. 'I've got the technicians' report. The website lists the objective of the flash mob as taking back control of the streets. It says: "Young people can't afford to rent a place in E1, and shopkeepers are losing their businesses because greedy landlords are hiking rents. Let's take back control of the streets from the capitalists and opportunist entrepreneurs."'

'Perhaps the fire was about gentrification too?' Dan eyed us all.

'If I can chip in here . . . ?' Jackie said, and I could tell from her tone that things were about to get a lot more complicated. 'I'm not saying gentrification isn't a genuine issue, but it's possible that it was a front for both the flash mob and the arson.' She spoke quietly but her voice conveyed authority. She joined Dan and I at the front of the room. 'It's the Trojan horse model of sneaking something under the radar. If you want to create a distraction, you pick a theme which is guaranteed to stir people up. That way, you maximise the chances of getting a big crowd.'

'From what I see as a newcomer, it's definitely the cost of living that bothers Londoners most,' said Dan.

'And the more faces and bodies you can gather,' Jackie continued, 'especially when they dress the same, the more difficult it is to see what's going on.'

'The masks?' It was obvious now.

'Precisely,' she said, gauging the reaction to her words. 'Masks aren't just about group identity. They render people faceless. Group dynamics quickly shift from the inter-personal to a mob.'

'Do we know whether LfA simply publicises these flash mobs or whether they're the organisers?' Shen asked.

'We don't know.' I felt frustration bite. 'Some of the kids mentioned a man called Frazer. Hopefully the technicians can find out what his role is.' I took stock. 'Moving on to evidence. Alexej, can you summarise?'

'The exhibits are all catalogued. Loads of personal items.' He clicked his screen into life and read off it. 'Bags. Clothing. Phones. Keys. The speakers.' He turned to face me. 'Dougie's sent through a list of the top priority ones. Any chance of the lab fast-tracking these?'

Jackie must've caught his sideways glance. 'I can see that the scope of this investigation is vast,' she said, adopting a cautious tone of voice, 'but I've literally just got off the DLR. Maya, I'll need you to bring me up to speed on budgets, PDQ.'

'Sure. Let me run through the main lines of enquiry and who's doing what later.'

Jackie nodded her agreement.

'Until evidence tells us otherwise, I'm going to suggest that Indra is our prime suspect. Anyone disagree?'

The room was quiet.

'Right. Shen, can you assess the H-2-H reports? Check alibis and if anyone was seen entering the shop. We need background information on Simas and Indra. Bank and phone records. And insurance details for the shop.'

Shen leaped into an empty seat.

'Alexej, the CCTV. There wasn't any smoke when the arsonist entered the shop. It's a small window of time but let's find it. And keep checking for anything that'll help ID our UnSub.'

'Sure.' He wheeled round on his chair.

'Dan, can you chase the fire investigation engineer on when we can get the bodies out?'

'Gotcha.'

'I'll ask Indra for a list of people who had beef with them or their business.' We had more questions than answers, but at least we had a plan of action. 'Let's get some sleep and I'll see you all bright and early tomorrow.' I turned to Jackie. 'Shall we nip up to the Morgan Arms? We can grab a bite to eat and I'll bring you up to speed.'

'You read my mind.' Her tone shifted and she smiled warmly. 'Tell me to mind my own business,' she lowered her voice, 'but I'm pleased Dougie is still around. I hope you two are still . . . ?'

I chuckled. It was so 'Jackie' to make a comment like this, moments after joining the team. 'We are.'

She began gathering up her bag and jacket, then stood still for a moment. 'I was sorry to hear about your brother last year.'

'Thank you. At the time, his suicide was a terrible shock for all of us. Particularly Mum.' I felt my eyes filling up and my throat tighten. This wasn't like me. Was it Jackie's kindness?

'Maya, I know how much you cared about him and—'

'. . . It's Mum I worry about. She's never recovered from Dad leaving. It's like a huge black cloud rolled in front of her and she can't seem to emerge from behind it.' Mentioning Dad reminded me that I still hadn't opened the forensic results. 'When Sabbir moved back to Bangladesh, she took it personally, as though it was another betrayal and he was leaving her rather than a life that wasn't the right shape for him.'

Jackie was nodding gently, and I appreciated her not churning out comments about 'sympathising' and 'time healing'.

'. . . She was never going to understand Sabbir committing suicide. Do you know the really sad thing though?' I wiped my eyes on my sleeve and looked at Jackie. 'It shouldn't have been a shock to any of us. All the warning signs had been there for years. We just didn't see them.' I paused. 'The truth is, I can't stand on Brick Lane without remembering him and wondering whether I could have done things differently.'

Brick Lane, 1984 – Maya

Jasmina holds the packet of Love Hearts to her nose and sniffs. 'You have a go.' Her giggle rings out in the enclosed space of the shop. She stuffs the packet at my face. 'It's like breathing in *luuuurve*.' She makes her voice go all dreamy and breathy as she says the last word, and pulls a silly face.

'Urgh. They're too sickly.' I push her hand away, grabbing several Cough Candies instead.

'Come on, you two.' Sabbir's frustrated plea falls on deaf ears as usual. He's at the door, flicking through a magazine which he's already paid for. 'Dad's waiting.'

'I wouldn't worry,' Mrs Feldman whispers to Jasmina and I conspiratorially, and it sends me into giggles because she's deliberately made her voice loud enough for Sabbir to catch. 'If I know them, your father will be having a good chinwag with my husband.'

Sabbir's demeanour relaxes and he returns his attention to his magazine.

Jaz peers at the contents of my paper bag. 'I don't like Cough Candy. They cut the roof of my mouth. You always get Parma Violets. How can you say that Love Hearts are too sweet and like them?' She chuckles.

Coming to Mrs Feldman's shop is such a treat. Dad came home in a good mood and announced that he was taking us out.

'The wholesaler delivered some new sweets this morning,' Mrs

Feldman says. 'My son put the order through and only told me when they arrived. Shall I get him to bring them out for you?'

Jasmina and I beam at her.

'Thanks, Mrs F,' says Jaz.

'Knowing him, he's probably putting through a few more orders while his father's not looking.' She chuckles, as though she's secretly proud of Tomasz's interest in the shop. She disappears out the back and begins calling. 'Tomasz? Tomasz, love, could you bring the new sweets through for the Rahman girls?'

A few moments later, she arrives back with a mousey-haired boy in tow. He's about Sabbir's age but taller. I've seen him in the shop before. He's carrying two boxes with an air of cool about him.

'Here you go, girls,' Tomasz says. 'Lemon Sherbets and Black Jacks.' He places the two boxes on the glass counter and his smile warms the room. 'Bet you haven't had them before.' He gives a friendly chuckle. Rips open a black and white packet and offers us a wrapped cube.

'My Agnieszka loves the Black Jacks. Soft and chewy, she says, but they make your tongue go black.' Mrs Feldman looks a little worried.

'Chill, Mum. They're only sweets. No-one's going to die.'

'Cheeky wretch.'

Sabbir's face softens and he joins us at the counter. 'Alright, mate,' he says to Tomasz.

'Thanks, Thomas,' Jasmina says, and it makes me giggle, because she's said his name wrong. I catch the way she avoids eye contact with him, and blushes when he speaks.

'Thank you,' I say and don't even try to say his name. 'What else shall I have?' I wonder aloud. 'I need to add up what it comes to. We could get some Aniseed Balls and share them?'

Jasmina isn't listening. She's pretending to count her sweets but I can see her, watching Tomasz Feldman out of the corner of her eye.

61

'What about Gob Stoppers? Shall we get some of them?' I elbow her. 'Or some rhubarbrhubarbrhubarbrhu . . . ?'

She hasn't realised I've stopped talking.

'You're dribbling,' I whisper.

'Am not.' She elbows me, recovers her poise and smooths her hair.

'I'm off now, Mum.' Tomasz glides towards the door of the shop. 'I said I'd pick Agnieszka up from Brownies.' He sees us watching him. 'Definitely the Aniseed Balls,' he says and gives us a huge wink, and I honestly think I'm about to burst.

SATURDAY

Maya, 7 a.m.

First thing the next morning, I grabbed a shower and steeled myself to check the media coverage of the arson. I hoped it would be reported responsibly but experience told me it was too good a click-bait opportunity to pass up.

From the lounge, I heard the soft burble of the television news. Dougie had stayed over, so I made a fresh cafetière of coffee and took it in with a couple of mugs. 'On a scale of one to ten, with ten as perfectly hideous, where are we?' I slid the tray onto the coffee table and sank onto the sofa next to him.

'Eleven.' He picked up the cafetière and began pouring.

'Shit.'

'I've screenshot them for you.' He passed me his iPad.

The *City Eye* headline said: LOCALS FEAR COPY-CAT ARSON ATTACKS.

'Tony couldn't resist, could he?' I swiped at the images on the screen. The broadsheets were benign. *The Messenger* had taken ethnicity as their angle: IMMIGRANTS' SHOP BURNT TO THE GROUND IN RACIST ATTACK.

'Scumbags.' I took a swig of coffee. 'What about the news channels?'

'BBC News seems to be sticking to the facts.'

'That's a relief.' I continued to scroll through Dougie's screenshots. 'WHO IS THE MYSTERY WOMAN IN THE FIRE? Blimey.

I hadn't expected that from Sky. Who's told the press there was a woman in the fire? Media Liaison haven't released the information yet and I didn't mention it.'

'Someone must've been blabbing.' Dougie didn't sound surprised and continued checking his emails.

'Anything from Suzie?' She'd be hard pressed to come up with anything worse than the *City Eye* or *The Messenger*, but milking national concerns wasn't Suzie's style. Her penchant was to go for people, personally, and her favourite target was me.

'Nothing on their website yet.'

*

Dan was joining me at the hospital. Hopefully, as well as asking Indra some questions, we could persuade Rosa to stay on the ward or go home with her daughter and spend a few days in East Ham.

When I walked in through the entrance doors, I was greeted in the lobby by a solemn-faced Shen.

'Bad news, Ma'am, I'm afraid,' she said. 'Indra Ulbiene was ten weeks pregnant and she's had a miscarriage.'

Shit. The poor woman. 'So, her husband is dead and it looks like he might have been having an affair. And now she's lost her baby?' I kicked at the linoleum. Occasionally, the news we had to convey was good but most of the time it wasn't. 'Where's the silver lining in this situation?'

'I know, Ma'am.'

'Is she conscious?' Questions were circling in my mind. 'Does she know she's lost the baby?'

'Yes, the medical staff have told her. We've not said anything to her about her husband yet. I think she knows he's dead but we were waiting for you. She's extremely distressed. They've got her sedated. She was asleep when I left the ward a few minutes ago.'

'Thanks, Shen. I'll speak to Rosa Feldman first then. Give Indra a bit of space. It's the least we can do to help her.'

*

When I arrived on the ward, colour had returned to Rosa's cheeks and her facial expression was resolute. She was sipping a mug of tea, and a half-eaten breakfast tray was on the side table.

'You look better than when I last saw you,' I said. 'Thought we were going to lose you. How are you?'

'Fit as a fiddle and ready to go home.'

I recognised the determination in her voice.

'Those stock boxes won't unpack themselves and all the while the shop's closed, I'm losing customers.'

I wanted to steer Rosa away from the shop so I asked her about the flash mob.

'When everyone began dancing, it took me back to the tea dances Józef and I used to go to after the war.' Her eyes glistened as tears formed.

It felt uncaring to cut off her reminiscences, and whisk her onto interview questions, so I listened for a few moments while she talked, mentally noting anything that might be relevant to the investigation.

'There are hardly any Jewish families left in Brick Lane now. The Blums, from the bagel shop, were the last to move out. Golders Green, Józef said.'

Aware that Rosa could tire quickly, I directed her attention to the arson. 'Thinking back to the last few days, have you noticed anything suspicious or unusual? People you didn't recognise?'

'I don't think so.'

'Anyone acting suspiciously or anything out of the ordinary?'

'No. But to be honest, I'm so busy in the shop, the days shoot by and I don't notice much. Just boxes of stock and dust.'

'What about arguments? Anyone been rowing recently? Neighbours had fallouts?'

She paused to think back. 'Sorry. I'm not much help, am I?'

'Did you recognise anyone in the street or at the flash mob?' Having lived in the area for so long, if anyone would recognise locals, it was Rosa.

'No.'

'The ward sister said you've mentioned black masks. Can you tell me about these?'

'They all had them. Black bandana things. Tied round their neck, and when they joined the dancing, they pulled them up over their nose to just beneath their eyes.' She shuddered. 'They looked really sinister.'

'How well do you know Simas and Indra?'

'Only to say hello to. I try to be neighbourly.' Rosa was pensive, nodding gently, as though she was sifting through her experiences and opinions. 'Actually, now you mention it, they had rows. I'd often hear one of them shouting and slamming the front door.' She seemed distressed by the memory. 'But it's not my business and you can't get involved in other people's lives.' A wistful look spread over her features. 'I can't believe the husband was in the . . .' Her voice croaked and broke off.

'Sorry to upset you. Can we call anyone for you? Get someone to help with the shop?' Uniform had told us that Tomasz and Agnieszka had come to the hospital.

She shook her head, her fingers under her nose as if she was holding back a floodgate.

'Tomasz arrived at the shop earlier. He was very worried about you. Would you consider staying with him until you're back on your feet again?'

'He's very kind. Always has been. I'm very lucky with both my children. But Bethnal Green's too far away.' She sighed. 'And I don't want to put anyone out. My children have their own lives.'

'If your son wants to help, why not let him?' I voiced the question gently, realising that it was a sensitive subject.

Rosa shook her head. Determined. 'He's extremely busy . . . '

I paused, trying to decide whether to press her. I got the impression that not wanting to put people out wasn't the real reason.

'I'll be right as rain in a day or two.' She smiled bravely.

'What about your daughter? Would you consider staying with her?'

'Oh, no. It's all arranged. She's popping back later to take me home to the shop.'

'Is that wise? You've had a nasty scare.'

She shook her head. 'Agnieszka and Olaf have a tiny terraced house and three children. They don't have room for an old lady. I've made my mind up. I'm going home to the shop.'

There was pride in her features, and a reluctance to ask for help. I recognised it from Mum. A dogged refusal to accept limitations and change, and the need for help. But it was hard to know when pride became stubbornness. 'Are you sure the shop is the best place though? It's so damp and cold.'

She sighed. 'I know but it's my home. All my memories are there and it's where I feel safe.'

Her face took on a wistful look and I felt desperately sad for her. 'Would you mind if we contacted your daughter?'

She frowned, then shrugged in resignation. 'If you want to.'

She was trembling now. 'For years I had nightmares. My mother was pregnant with me when the Nazis resumed deportations from Warsaw to Treblinka. The Jews in the Ghetto mounted an armed resistance. There were twenty-seven days of bombs, blasts and gunfire while they fought the Germans. My brother was eight. He made the mistake of smiling at an SS officer, who ordered one of the *Judenrat* officials to shoot him. When the man refused, the SS officer shot him and my brother straight through the head.'

'Oh, Rosa . . . ' I gasped.

'My mother nearly miscarried, but I made it and was born in 1944, the year of the Warsaw Uprising. It was when Christian Poles rose up against the Germans. My parents escaped from the Ghetto, and we lived outside the city with a Polish family that Dad knew from his old shop. They say you remember things from in the womb. Sounds, words, voices. For me, it's blasts and gunfire.' The expression in her eyes was haunted. 'And my mother's sobbing.' She looked away for a few moments. 'I used to have the dreams regularly, even when the war was over and when we arrived here. Once we settled into life in Brick Lane, they receded. I haven't had them for years, apart from the occasional one. The fire at the soup shop yesterday . . . ' she was shaking her head, ' . . . brought it all back.' She coughed, and I heard her chest wheeze. 'There was a woman on the ground in front of me. The cracks and bangs were so loud, I tripped over her.'

Much as she seemed to want to explain, I could see it was distressing her, talking about Poland, and I wanted to move the conversation onto happier times. 'When did you come to live in Brick Lane?'

'Nineteen forty-eight. I was four.' She released a sigh. 'My family moved back to central Warsaw after the war, but life under communism wasn't easy, and my parents found it impossible to settle amongst such horrible memories.' Her expression changed again as

70

the recollections came alive. 'At that time, Józef and his family were already living in Brick Lane. His parents owned the newsagent's. He worked for his father when he was at school, doing a paper round, and then helping with deliveries and putting stock out. The two of them worked alongside each other for twenty-five years. He took the shop over when his father died, and then he and I ran it together. I'd known him since I was four.' Her mouth flickered a tiny smile and it was one of the saddest things I'd ever seen.

The arrival of a staff member prevented Rosa from saying anything further. 'Time for your meds, Mrs Feldman,' the nurse said cheerily, and she poured out fresh water.

I waved to indicate I was off. 'I'll leave you in peace.' My phone had been vibrating in my pocket, so I took the opportunity to check my messages.

It was a text from Shen.

Indra had woken up and was extremely agitated. She wanted to speak to me.

Maya, 8.30 a.m.

Dan and I were in the lift at the Royal London Hospital, on our way to interview Indra on the ward.

'Rosa is adamant she's going back to the shop,' I told him, and pressed the lift button. 'I've asked Shen to speak to the consultant. She's a determined lady. I've got visions of her discharging herself, flagging a black cab down in her hospital gown and then falling down the stairs at the shop.'

'Good idea.'

'Given what Indra's gone through, I'd have preferred to leave it a day or two before broaching the subject of money and murder motives, but we have to consider her a suspect.'

'I hope for her sake the shop was well insured. Not just the building but their income and business.'

'I was thinking the same thing.' The lift dinged and I followed Dan out.

'I want to know why she told the police she thought Simas had been murdered. Don't you?'

'I guess it'll depend whether she knew about her husband's infidelities. If that's his body in their shop, and he was messing around with another woman . . . ' The thought was upsetting. 'I'm hoping there will be an innocent explanation for the woman being there. Perhaps the two of them huddled together to escape the fumes?' One thing was sure, the interview was going to require careful handling.

When we arrived at Indra's ward, rows of narrow beds greeted us. Nylon curtains hung on rails round each unit. It was hardly private. Marta was sitting beside her sister's bed on the visitors' chair, holding Indra's frail hand. It was bruised, and Marta held it carefully so as not to aggravate the place where the cannula entered the vein.

Indra's blonde hair lay around her head like a nest, and her eyes looked huge in her gaunt features.

'I'm sorry for your loss, Mrs Ulbiene. We all are.'

'*Ačiū.*'

I pulled up a chair and gathered my thoughts. 'Would you like your sister to stay with you?'

'*Taip.*' I knew this meant yes. Beside the bed, the drip stand held a bag of clear fluid.

'I'll keep it as brief as I can. They aren't tactful questions, I'm afraid.'

She didn't react.

'Is your shop insured?'

'*Taip.*'

'Building and contents cover?'

'*Taip, žinoma.*'

'Are you OK to speak English or do you need an interpreter?'

'I speak English.'

I smiled an acknowledgement. 'Do you remember the name of the insurers?'

'My husband deals with that side of the business. The paperwork is in the flat and . . . ' Her arm flailed in the air because the rest was obvious. Hopefully, she'd have details of their insurers in an email account.

'Did your husband have a life insurance policy?'

'*Žinoma, ne.*'

'Does your husband have any family in the UK?'

'A brother in Bethnal Green.'

'What's his name?'

'Artem Gudelis.'

Dan opened his phone browser.

'Were they close?'

'Of course.'

Dan shifted his gaze from his mobile to Indra in the bed. 'Does Artem run the club COCO?'

'*Taip.*'

'Get hold of him,' I whispered to Dan. 'Tell him we need to speak to him in person, ASAP.'

Dan slid away from Indra's bedside and marched towards the ward exit with his mobile already clamped to his ear.

'Mrs Ulbiene, did you speak to your husband yesterday?'

'*Taip.*'

'Are these questions necessary?' Marta stroked her sister's forehead soothingly. 'You can see she —'

'They are,' I said to Marta. 'What did your conversation entail?'

'It was short. We'd just arrived at the hospital and the security man told me I'd need to switch my phone off when we reached the ward.'

'Was your husband home all day?'

'As far as I know.' Indra shielded her face with her hand.

'What were you doing?'

'I had . . . *ultragarsu* at the hospital in the morning for the baby. After that, Marta and I went for lunch to celebrate, then to a salon for facials and *masažas.*'

74

'What time did you leave home to meet your sister?'

'Nine-ish?' She glanced at Marta for confirmation.

'Were you with Marta the whole time until you came to Brick Lane?' This would mean they were each other's alibis.

'*Taip.*' She let out a heavy sigh. 'Am I a suspect? Is that what these questions are about?'

'I'm sorry. We do need to know whether you were involved with the arson, yes.' I winced as I said it. It was horrible to think Indra could have been responsible, and even worse to have to raise it so soon after she'd lost her baby.

'*Kristus.*' Indra raised her arm in irritation and let it fall back on the bed. 'Why would I kill my husband? And set fire to my own business? We've worked our arses off trying to get it off the ground. We wanted to expand.'

'Which day do you normally close the shop?'

'We never close in the daytime. Neither of us has had a day off in two years. We work seven days a week. We were trying to build up the business so we could open another shop. Maybe set up *franšizės* around London.'

'Has your husband ever suggested closing the shop before today?'

'*Ne.*'

'When you spoke to him, did he mention having any visitors at all?'

'*Ne.*'

'He didn't say that anyone had called round to see him or that he'd arranged for someone to come round? Your GP? Or a friend?'

'He was sick. I told you. He called me. Said he was in bed with a fever. That was it.'

'Was he in your bedroom? The left-hand room at the front of the house?' I gestured with my left hand to make sure there was no misunderstanding.

'Of course.' She frowned. 'Where else would he be?'

'I have to ask this, I'm afraid. Can you think of anyone who might wish your husband harm?'

Anguish spread over Indra's face, and she looked at her sister and then me. 'No. I cannot.' No Lithuanian this time.

'You told the 999 operator that you thought someone had tried to kill your husband. Why did you think that?'

She blushed.

'Mrs Ulbiene?'

Dan had joined us again. He gave me a subtle thumbs-up.

'If I remembered saying it, I'd say.' Indra's tone of voice told me she knew exactly what she'd done and why, but something was stopping her from saying.

'Are you saying you don't remember calling 999 or you don't remember saying it?'

Marta sucked a breath in through her teeth.

'Calls to 999 are recorded and this one was traced to your mobile.'

'She said she doesn't remember.' Marta's expression was mutinous.

Dan played the recording on his phone.

'Poleece? My husband is in the fire in Brick Lane. I think someone's tried to kill him.' In the background, a female voice was talking. 'I think someone's murdered him.'

'I take it that's you, Mrs Ulbiene?'

'*Taip.*'

'Is that you in the background?' I watched Marta.

She groaned. 'Yes.'

'Why did you think someone had tried to kill your husband, Mrs Ulbiene?'

'Things are difficult.' Indra seemed annoyed with herself, as though she'd given away something she hadn't intended, or was hiding something.

'In what way are they difficult?'

'*Detektyva*, we are immigrants.' She raised her fist in frustration, and dropped it back on the bed. 'We work long hours. We're in a lot of debt because we had to borrow money to set up the business and haven't paid the loans off yet. Because we are foreigners, we didn't get the best interest rates. Banks see a Lithuanian passport and immediately see you as high risk.'

I picked up the bitterness in her reply and my heart went out to Indra again. It had been the same for my parents when we arrived in the UK. It'd taken a good ten years for Dad to establish himself, earn enough money for us to live off and gain respect. 'I understand that. My family were immigrants too, but I don't see how that relates to you thinking your husband was murdered. Can you fill me in?'

Indra rolled her eyes.

She was a smart woman. Given she'd asked to speak to us, she must've known we'd ask her about the call to emergency services. There was something she wasn't telling us. I was sure of it. 'Did you think he'd been murdered because you heard that the fire was arson or because you suspected that someone might want to kill him?'

Marta muttered to her sister in Lithuanian.

Indra gabbled a reply and they had a heated exchange. Marta's speech became faster and louder, and her hands gesticulated in agitation.

'I don't remember what I thought,' Indra said finally. 'I was in shock when I heard about the fire. I was scared for my husband, and the business is our livelihood.'

I suspected she was going to say something like this. 'Of course.

It must've been upsetting news to receive.' I waited a few moments for her to regain her composure. 'Who told you about the fire?'

'Pardon?'

I repeated the question.

'Tomasz Feldman.'

That was a surprise. 'Why did Tomasz Feldman tell you about the fire? Do you know him?'

Maya, 8.45 a.m.

I was keen to hear Indra's response to my question about Tomasz Feldman.

'I don't understand—' Indra said, her voice weary.

'Is Mr Feldman connected to your shop in some way?' I was wondering why he had Indra's phone number.

She muttered to Marta again, then spoke to me. 'No. We are neighbours. He knows everyone round here.'

Dan raised his eyebrows at me.

'OK. Last few questions – did your husband have any arguments recently?'

'*Ne.*'

'Anyone unhappy about you two opening the soup shop?' She'd dodged my question about how things had been difficult for them recently.

Marta spoke to her sister in a low voice. Then to me, she said, 'She can't think of anyone. If she does, we'll call you.'

'I've almost finished. Mrs Ulbiene? It's very important. Who might want to harm your husband or your business?'

Indra glanced at her sister for a cue. Marta was shaking her head from side to side.

'I've answered. I don't know.'

I didn't believe her but there was something else I needed to ask before she clammed up. 'OK. This is the last question. I'm so sorry.

There's no easy way to tell you this. We found a woman with your husband. They were curled round each other on what looks like was a bed. Do you know who the woman might have been?'

'No idea,' came her quick response.

Shock was written all over Marta's face.

'I don't want to answer any more questions. I'm tired. Could you leave me now, please?' Indra flashed me an angry expression. 'Nurse. *Nurse.*'

'Of course.' I bundled my notepad into my bag. 'An officer will come later today to take a formal statement from you. You will be asked to provide details of all the people your husband had fall-outs with, and anyone you think might want to harm him or you, or your business.' I placed my contact card on the bedside table. 'I'm sorry, but you will also be asked about the woman in the fire. If you remember why you rang 999, please call me. I hope you feel stronger soon.' I turned to Marta and said gently, 'Could I have a word, please?' I gestured for her to follow me towards the ward exit and the lobby area where the lifts were.

Marta placed her hand reassuringly on her sister's arm for a moment. '*Nebus ilgas.*' She tailed me across the ward, dragging her boots on the linoleum and tutting loudly, in case we hadn't got the message that she was pissed off with us.

Once we were out of earshot, I turned and faced her. 'I understand that you're concerned about your sister, but two people are dead, and you were hindering a murder investigation back there. Given you brought things to a halt, perhaps you can help us with the information we need? Do you know who might have had it in for your sister and brother-in-law?'

'No.'

'How about just Simas?'

She snorted contemptuously and her eyes narrowed a fraction. 'That's a completely different question. Lots of people. Simas was a piece of shit but love is blind – and my sister has always loved him.'

'"Piece of shit" in what sense?'

She did an unzipping gesture at the level of the flies on her jeans, and I felt my heart sink.

'Do you know who the woman in the fire is?'

She opened her hands wide. 'Could be anyone. If he burnt in that place, it's what that bastard deserved.'

'Has he been unfaithful to your sister before?'

Disgust forced air out of Marta's mouth. 'Many times. She should have left him but it's not easy when you're from a country like ours. This shop, and the baby, were supposed to be their "new start".' She made a quotation mark gesture with her fingers as though she never believed it was going to happen, and they were empty words.

'We have some photographs of the bodies in the fire. Could you look at them for me, please? I'm afraid they aren't pleasant, or particularly good quality, but until we can see Artem, or persuade Indra to look at them, you're the best person to identify them.' On my phone, I brought up a cropped image of the man lying cupped round another person, and showed it to her. 'Is this your brother-in-law?'

'Jēzus Kristus.' She turned away, doubling over, her hand over her mouth in revulsion. 'Tai virsta.' She staggered away from me. 'Yes, that's him. That bastard. I'm glad he's dead. Except my sister will continue to suffer because of him.' She lurched and stumbled around the lobby area and beat her fist on the lift door several times, muttering agitatedly in Lithuanian.

'Marta, are you certain that's Simas in the image?'

She spun round. 'Yes. I recognise the stud in his ear and the watch. Indra gave them to him for Christmas. Spent far more on him than he was worth.' She took her phone from her jeans pocket and swiped it into life. 'Here. Look. This was at Christmas.' She scrolled through the images and showed me a photo of Indra and Simas around a table, plates loaded with food. Crackers and wrapping littered the tablecloth. They both wore paper hats, and he had his arm round his wife's shoulders. The watch was clearly visible. She scrolled to another image, one that showed Simas' face and ear. 'See. It's white gold with a diamond.'

'Are those images date stamped?'

'Yes. Look.' Beneath the images, location, time and date were shown.

'Could I get copies of them, please?'

'If you'll let my sister have a bit of time to come to terms with losing everything before you show her these.' There was an edge to her voice, as though she was used to having to negotiate.

I felt the pressure in her words and let it float for a moment. 'Marta, I can't commit to a timeframe, but I give you my word that we won't put Indra through any unnecessary distress. It's in your sister's interests that the murders are solved. She can't claim on her insurance until the investigation is over.'

'People always promise us things.' She said it in a sarcastic, sing-song-y way and disengaged her glance. ' . . . and they're always lies.'

I'd seen the wariness in Marta's eyes when we were on the ward, but this wasn't just that. Beneath the sarcasm was a quiet rage. And beneath that, something else lay, like a rumble of distant thunder. 'Is there a reason why your brother-in-law might have been sleeping in the spare room rather than his own bedroom?'

She used the back of her hand to blot the tears from her eyes. 'The spare room is his way of pretending it didn't matter. He could shag whoever he liked as long as he didn't do it in their bed.'

I was absorbing what she was telling me. 'Was Indra OK with that?'

'Of course not.' She flashed an angry glance. 'He promised he wouldn't do it anymore, and then did it again and again.' She muttered now. 'Some men should have their dicks cut off at birth.'

'Marta, do you recognise the woman in the photo? Or have any idea who it might be?'

She glanced at the image again and quickly shook her head. 'I don't recognise her but he could've just met her. Indra knows how I feel about Simas, and when they decided to make a fresh start in Brick Lane, she said she wasn't going to discuss him with me anymore.'

'OK. I appreciate that you may not feel sympathetic towards the woman in the fire, but someone is likely to be searching for her. Indra may know who she is. If either of you do, we can inform the woman's next of kin. Also, her identity may provide vital clues on who might want to set the shop on fire, and why.'

'I get that.'

'Good. And to be clear – when my officer comes, we will need to interview your sister alone.'

She opened her mouth to protest and clamped it shut.

'We will need you to give a statement too.' She'd no doubt want to stay at the hospital. 'I'll ask the officer to take yours after Indra's. The sooner we can find the person responsible for the fire, the sooner your sister can make an insurance claim and move on.' I gave her my contact card. 'Can you email me those photographs of Indra and Simas?'

'OK.' This time she met my eyes, and I sensed she was trying to decide whether she could trust me. 'I will talk to my sister.'

'I'm really sorry about what's happened. I know how hard these questions are to answer. I can't promise that it's going to be easy for anyone, but I give you my word that I will not rest until we find out who did this.'

She acknowledged the comment with a curt nod and closed her eyes, as though she couldn't believe what had happened.

'A few final things – back on the ward, why was Indra looking to you to tell her what to say?'

Marta fiddled with her cigarettes and lighter.

'It was the same when she called 999. You were in the background.'

'My sister is much nicer than me, but she isn't as strong as me. Living with Simas ground her down. She works all day, every day, and she's been doing language classes. You can see how thin she is. Everyone thinks immigrants are lazy and can't be bothered to learn English, and Indra was determined to prove them wrong.' She paused. 'I'm her big sister so now it's my turn to look after her.'

I took in Marta's explanation. What was bothering me was whether Indra had any inkling what her husband was going to get up to when she'd left for her sister's yesterday. Did she believe they'd made a fresh start and that Simas had changed his ways? What a horrible mess.

'Why did Indra phone 999 and say she thought someone had murdered her husband?'

'I don't know. I told her not to. It's what we were arguing about. If you get someone to translate, what you will hear in the background is me asking her what the hell she's doing.'

I recalled something that Indra had mentioned. 'Why didn't Simas accompany Indra to the hospital for her scan?'

'Because he's an asshole.'

'Did he know that his wife was pregnant?'

Maya, 9.15 a.m.

I was at the hospital reception, still taking in the implications of Marta's answer.

Dan was talking on his phone. 'We'll go straight there,' he said into his receiver. 'Tell him not to leave the premises.' He ended the call. 'Alexej has spoken to Artem Gudelis and arranged for us to interview him at his club. Shall we go?'

'Where's Rosa?'

'She's gone to her daughter's. She got the consultant to discharge her. I managed to have a word with him about the state of the shop and the damp, and he knew about the dreams and her asthma, so he only agreed to let her go home if she promised to stay at Agnieszka's for at least a week. I've just put her in a black cab.'

'Phew. At least she'll be safe there.' We discussed recent developments as we walked towards the exit.

'Ten weeks pregnant and Simas didn't know? Jeez.' Dan stared at me in disbelief. 'Did Marta say why Indra hadn't told him?'

'Apparently, Simas was adamant he didn't want children.'

'Meaning what? Indra hoped he'd change his mind and was building up to telling him? She was waiting 'til she was past the three-month mark? Simas wasn't the father?'

'Marta swore she didn't know why. All she said was she and Indra don't discuss Simas any more.'

Dan tutted. 'That's convenient.'

'Actually, I believe her. She clearly has a low opinion of her brother-in-law. Perhaps she found it easiest, and kindest, not to talk about him.' Mum flashed through my mind. Had this been why she hadn't wanted to talk about Dad?

'I wonder what Artem will say about his brother's philandering.' Dan pulled a face. 'I'd put money on two things. He'll be on the defensive and he'll take Simas' side.'

At the exit, as the glass doors swung back, a swarm of reporters surged towards us, firing out questions and wanting their pound of flesh.

'Inspector, is it true that the other person in the fire was a woman?' asked one.

'Keep walking,' I hissed at Dan, blinking amidst the blinding flash lights.

'Given the woman in the fire wasn't the shopkeeper's wife, who was it?' another shouted.

'Inspector, what precautions have you taken to keep the capital safe in the face of fears about copy-cat fires?' It was Tony from the *City Eye* again.

Something slid round the back of my hair and ear. I turned to see a microphone below my chin, and it was then stuffed towards my mouth.

'Can you confirm reports that a child was in the fire?' The beefy hulk of a journo bellowed at me, practically spitting in my face.

'A what?' Damn. I'd responded before I could stop myself. I pushed his mic away from my face and addressed the gaggle. 'There have been NO reports of a child in the fire. No further questions for now. All communication will go through the usual channels. Thanks.'

*

Half an hour later, Dan and I were outside a large glass-fronted business premises in Bethnal Green. Silver lettering twinkled in the morning sunlight and showed the name COCO. Two shiny-suited security guards stood outside, wearing headsets and attitude, next to a roped-off section on the pavement. One of the bouncers lumbered towards us, tight-faced and suspicious.

'We're here to see Artem Gudelis,' I said, and we showed our warrants.

The security guard didn't acknowledge what I said but immediately started to speak into his headset in Lithuanian, and then turned to his colleague and made a comment to him. They both sniggered at whatever he'd said. It was hard not to wonder if they were indicative of what their boss might be like.

The man snapped, 'Come,' and marched inside the building.

We followed him up a set of steps. The lights were low. The carpets were thick and grey, and the walls were lined with floor-to-ceiling mirrors. Cashier staff were arriving and getting ready for the customers, who would be buying payment chips in an hour or so and hurrying to the lap-dance booths.

Downstairs, it was a warren of corridors with subdued lighting, and this was where Artem had his office. As we entered, I gave the lavish basement room the once-over. In one corner, two plush sofas lay in an L-shape. In another corner, behind a giant desk, the sort you might expect to find in a multi-national oil company, sat a stocky man with thinning hair. He had proud, heavy features and metal-framed glasses, and looked far from delighted to see us. Had I not known differently, he could easily have been Simas' uncle.

'Come in, detectives.' He spoke quietly and made no attempt to get up from his chair. 'I gather you want to talk to me about my brother.' His voice was monotonous and only just audible.

His manner reminded me of someone who was no stranger to dominance. This was a man who was used to getting exactly what he wanted.

I left Dan to observe and approached Artem's desk. All the while he remained motionless in his chair, watching my every step. Calm and in control, or so he wanted us to think. In turn, I made sure he saw that I'd clocked the well-stocked drinks cabinet and the framed prints on the walls of grinning Z-list celebrities. This was a man who felt well-connected, even if he wasn't, and we were about to test his self-importance. 'We'd like to ask you some questions in relation to the blaze at your brother's shop yesterday.'

'If it's quick.'

'We now know that it was arson, and sadly we've found two bodies in the burnt-out building.'

'Simas and Indra, presumably?' The set of his mouth was hard, and he showed no emotion.

'It's interesting that you assume that. We are fairly sure that one of them is Simas. We need a family member to formally identify his body. Can you do this for us, please?'

'I suppose I'll have to given Indra is—'

'The other body is female but *isn't* Indra.'

'Oh?' His expression fell a fraction before he caught it. 'Who is it then?'

'We don't know yet.' I felt his eyes scrutinising me. He clearly wasn't relieved Indra was alive. 'Indra isn't up to coming to the mortuary. She's is in hospital, recovering from miscarrying your brother's child.' I let the news float and waited for him to comment.

'I'm sorry to hear that. I had no idea she was pregnant.'

There was still no emotion visible on Artem's features. He was smart. It was a pragmatic response. Maybe none of it was news.

88

It was hard to tell. 'In the interim, perhaps you can help us with identification?' I showed him Marta's photos and an image of the two bodies.

'He did have that watch and earring. If it helps, I can confirm that.' He held my gaze defiantly. 'So, what else can I do for you? My accountant is due shortly and I need to go over some figures.'

'We will need you to come to the mortuary to ID the body in person.'

He gave a sharp nod.

'There are a number of things we need to ask you about, so we'll take it in stages, if that's OK.' I had no intention of leaving before I'd covered everything we needed to know. 'First of all, do you have any idea who the woman in the fire might have been?'

'No.' He shook his head, as though he was surprised to see his brother with another woman.

'Are you sure?'

'Perfectly.'

'Was your brother having an affair?'

'I have no idea.'

'Do you know any of the women he has had affairs with?'

'It's none of my business.' It was a clever answer but he hadn't denied his brother's infidelity.

'That wasn't what I asked you. We need to know who might wish your brother harm and who might have a grudge against him?'

'How long have you got?' He lounged back in his leather bucket chair and rested both hands behind his head, arms wide. His suit cuffs rose up, and I caught a glimpse of his gold watch, gleaming in the subdued lighting.

'I'm not here to play games, Mr Gudelis. Arson is a very serious offence and two people are dead.' I took two steps closer. 'If you know anything that could help us find your brother's killer, we'd appreciate you telling us.'

He let out a sigh. 'You're Bangladeshi, right?'

I folded my arms. 'Is this relevant?'

'Did you grow up round here? If you did, you'll know that things are changing in Brick Lane.'

'They're continually changing. Everywhere is. When my family moved here, it was still quite Jewish. The Bangladeshis were trying to establish themselves.'

'My point is that some people were not happy about Simas and Indra opening their soup shop. Some of the local business owners and residents thought they were trying to push out the Bangladeshis. Others claim their soups and salads were pretentious, hipster food. You've seen their menu, right?'

'Of course.'

'They sold soups made from a base of lentils, quinoa, freekeh and teff. They're healthy, nutritious and offer good profit potential. For some, their food was over-priced.'

'Given that thousands of people owe their lives to the handouts from the Jewish Soup Kitchen in Brune Street, you can understand why.'

'Quite,' he said, and I wasn't sure what he was agreeing with. 'There have been numerous anti-gentrification campaigns targeting businesses in Shoreditch and Brick Lane. The bad feeling is worse where people are marking up products which are cheap to buy or make. People believe they're ripping off consumers.' He paused. 'The owners of the vintage clothing shops, for example, often buy up charity stock for a few quid and sell the items for hundreds of pounds. One of them was targeted a while back.'

'We know about the attack on Pick Your Vintage. But no-one

makes people shop in Brick Lane.' Was there disapproval in his comments? 'Are you suggesting your brother's soup business was in the same category?'

'You asked me what I thought and I'm telling you.'

'If people want vintage clothing, posh coffee and soup, and can afford them, what's the problem? Can everyone afford to come into your club and pay for a lap dance?'

'No, they can't. And that's my point. People claim that businesses like mine and my brother's change the fabric of an area. They attract people who can afford them and push out those who can't. As wealthier people move in, the mix of businesses changes.'

'You mean gentrification?'

'Exactly. When I set up this club, there were already loads of bars in the area. The Brick Lane Soup Company is another business which isn't in keeping with what many people want for the area.' He flicked his hand dismissively. 'Personally, I think people need to move with the times and stop whingeing. There are several shops in Brick Lane which are way past their sell-by date.'

I pricked up my ears. 'Such as?'

'The off-licence a few doors down from my brother's place. The newsagent's opposite. Pre-historic that place is, and its owner.' His words dripped with contempt and it was hard to contain my irritation.

'So, they're supposed to give up their livelihoods because you can think of a preferable business for their location?'

'It's basic economics.' He tossed his biro onto his mouse-mat. 'Anyhow, it's their look-out, but they need to be careful. That's all I'm saying. Sooner or later, things get taken out of people's hands.'

I sensed that Artem was no stranger to violence. He reminded me of a piranha, lurking in the safety of the shallows while he waited for his next victim. 'Like someone torching their business, you mean?'

Dan had joined me in front of Artem's desk.

'It's perfectly possible, isn't it?'

It was a confident response, but I noticed Artem easing his chair back a few inches.

'Did Simas receive any aggravation about the shop?' I asked.

'Oh yes. Mainly passive-aggressive stuff. People phoning through fake orders. That sort of thing. But they had their car vandalised twice and the shop windows smashed several times.'

'We will need details from you of all the episodes you know about, and as many names as you can remember.'

His gaze didn't flicker.

'Who else might have had it in for your brother?' I asked.

'How about all the husbands and boyfriends of the women he shagged?' He spat his words out as though they gave him pleasure.

I bit back my disdain. He was trying to test or shock, and I wasn't prepared to give him the satisfaction of reacting. 'I need names. Your brother has been murdered. If I may say so, you don't seem upset or surprised.'

'I'm not surprised, no. My brother was a risk taker all his life. He thrived on it. I told him to be more discreet, but he was a stubborn man, and he always had more energy than me.'

I let his last comment go. 'Nevertheless, I'm sure that you want to see whoever murdered him brought to justice?' I watched him. 'It's easy to look down on your brother's business but in reality he sold soup and you sell naked women.'

Artem cackled. 'This place might not be everyone's idea of a good business, but I know the market and I know my clientele, and I make a good living. I wouldn't have opened this club in the part of Brick Lane where Simas opened the soup place, for example.'

I needed to think about what Artem was saying, and talk it

through with the team. Were the murders about economics? Turf? Ethnicities? Religion? Or were they personal? I walked to the edge of the room, surveyed the awards and certificates on the walls, the beaming faces of his celebrity clientele. I got the distinct impression that these two brothers were very different, and I sensed tension between them. I made a mental note to get the team to do a background check on Artem. 'Do you have a family, Mr Gudelis?'

'I do.'

'Doesn't your wife mind you running a strip club?'

'I don't hear her complaining too much when we are flying business class to the Caribbean, or when she's booking spa treatments and personal shoppers at Selfridges.'

I stifled a groan. In many an idle moment, I'd wondered what it must be like to be married to a man like this. 'Children?'

'A boy and a girl. One's at prep school and the other is home-educated. He has special needs.'

'Were you and your brother close?'

'There was a ten-year age gap between us, and we didn't agree about everything, but we have always been close.'

'What didn't you agree about?'

He cackled again but didn't answer. It was a horrible, dirty sound.

'Mr Gudelis?'

Maya, 10 a.m.

'What did you and your brother disagree about?' I repeated my question to Artem.

'Women, for a start.'

'Oh?' I faced him. 'Would you care to elaborate?'

'*Indra.*'

As soon as he said it, I realised it didn't surprise me. 'What about her?'

'I warned him about her.'

'You warned him about what?'

'They were both as bad as each other. The baby . . . ? If you ask me, it could be anyone's. He probably didn't even know about it. It's a good job she miscarried. Least this way she won't be bringing some bastard baby into the world.'

This corroborated what Marta had said: that Simas hadn't known about the baby. 'Did you warn Indra about your brother?' It was hard to keep the irritation from my voice.

Artem shot me a dirty look, his expression full of contempt.

'Is it your opinion that they were both unfaithful or do you know this for a fact?'

'Listen,' he snorted, 'she even hit on me a few times.'

'I suppose it's what you expect from a slapper like her, eh? Or perhaps she was getting even with your brother? I'm sure you politely turned her down.' This time I didn't bother trying to hide my disgust. 'Is that true about Indra or are you making it up?'

'I suggest you ask her.'

'I intend to, but this is a double murder investigation and I'm not prepared to have you turn it into cheap score-settling. I appreciate you sharing your views but where one person has their story, so do others.' This was one of those investigations where everyone hinted at things and referred us on to someone else. 'One thing.' I put on my innocent face. 'If you had to place a bet, who do you reckon lit that fire?'

'I would bet my club on it being Indra.' As he spoke, he covered his desk with a fine spray of spit. He sat forward and clambered to his feet. 'Or that psycho sister of hers.' He pointed at his temples in case I hadn't got the message. 'Hard as bloody nails, she is.'

I nodded. Pretended I agreed and that his words hadn't shocked me. Artem might have hoped he was about to shoo us out, but we had a surprise in store for him. 'DS Maguire?' It was time to wind Artem up.

Dan was still in front of Artem's desk. I shuffled back a few steps, allowing him to position himself right in front of Artem. Dan stood there with his legs apart, his left arm across his body, the right stroking his chin mock-pensively. 'I see you have a record for arson, Mr Gudelis.' His voice was quiet.

Artem stared at Dan then me, and I saw fury fill his small eyes. Good. We'd got a reaction.

'Setting fire to a shed in 2009,' Dan said. 'Did you know it had animals in it when you torched it?' He waited for a response.

Artem's right hand clenched into a fist. 'What's that got to do with anything? It was an accident and it was ten years ago.' He batted his computer mouse away.

I watched his tells. Listened to every word for nuances and implications.

Dan was nodding, as if he was unsure of what to say. I'd seen him play dumb and he was good at it. 'Arson can be habit-forming. Addictive, even.'

'I'm not sure what you're getting at. Are you implying that I set fire to my brother's shop?'

'Did you?'

Artem's eyes blazed. 'Of course I didn't. The idea that I've become some sort of pyromaniac is absurd.' He stared at me. 'Do you agree with this joker, Inspector?'

I switched on the falsest smile I could conjure. 'As a matter of fact, I do.'

'What reason would I have for burning down my brother's business?'

'You tell us, buddy.' Dan locked his eyes on Artem's. 'Perhaps you want Indra for yourself?'

Artem's fist came crashing down on the desk. 'I am *not* your buddy.' His head was tilted back in annoyance. He opened a bottle of water which was on his desk; took a few gulps and screwed the top back up.

A beefy security guard had arrived now and Artem oozed relief. 'Sergei, these two officers are leaving. Kindly escort them off the premises, and make sure they are not shown in again without my authorisation.'

Sergei held out his arm to herd us out of the room.

Dan was still by the desk. 'You know, you were lucky not to have got a custodial sentence, mate. You would have done in Australia.'

Artem's face was a picture. Pink and puffed-up with indignation. 'I said get out. Sergei, get these officers out of my sight.'

'Don't forget, we need that list and a statement,' Dan added, as we were escorted out of Artem's office. 'Otherwise, we'll be back.'

We had hit a few raw nerves.

10.30 a.m.

She woke again, needing the toilet. Her head was still fuzzy. Kind of floaty.

She'd had the dream again. Someone came in while she was asleep, but she couldn't remember who it was. She tried to get her brain to think but it felt heavy. It hadn't been Mummy. Mummy would've brought her fish-fingers and some juice and Snuggabear. 'Mummy? I don't feel well.'

The room gobbled up her words, as though it held a terrible secret.

She lay still, waiting to hear her mum's voice, but nothing came back. Just a dog whining, and a telly down low and a funny smell. Perhaps she was at an uncle's and Mummy had gone out? Except – when she did that, Mummy always brought Snuggabear and left her a biscuit and something to drink. Here, it was just the dog and shouting and guns on the telly.

She slid off the bed and padded towards the door. Mummy must be watching telly in the lounge. That's why she hadn't left the light on. She pressed the handle and pulled the door.

But it was stiff.

Or stuck.

She tried again, pushed this time. The handle went down but the door wouldn't move. Something was wrong. 'Mum? Mummy? I'm scared.' She tried the door again. Rattled the handle as hard as she could. Last time this happened, Mummy'd gone out, and she'd locked her in to keep her safe. But that was at home, and it didn't matter because Mummy gave her a kiss.

'Mummy? I don't like this. I'm scared and I'm thirsty.' A single tear crept bravely down her pale cheek. Then her eyes filled up and very quietly, in the dark room, she began to sob.

Dan, 11 a.m.

Dan and Maya were in Brick Lane to gather information on what might have motivated the arson. Overhead, a giant crane boom swung its red jib across the rooftops and plunged its bucket into a semi-demolished building. Dan had never seen so many tradies in one spot. No matter which direction he cast his eye, builders were standing around in huddles of testosterone. In their high-viz jackets, hard hats and work boots, they bellowed in an array of languages as they slurped tea and rolled fags.

The two of them passed barber's, saree shops, fabric outlets, halal butcher's and money transfer shops.

'Dad used to send money home to relatives,' Maya shouted over the beeping of a reversing digger. 'Took ten years for him to be able to afford to, I think, but after that he did it every week.'

'Were your folks planning to go home eventually?' Dan asked.

'I honestly don't know.' She frowned, as though the idea was out of reach. 'Dad liked it here and Mum has always wanted to go home to Bangladesh, but I don't recall it being discussed.'

Dan knew Maya's father had left them when they were kids. 'She must've been even keener when your dad left. Imagine how different your life would've been if she'd taken you guys with her.'

A shadow fell over Maya's face.

'Sorry, I didn't mean to pry.' Dan cursed his tactlessness. It was obvious how much Maya's family situation affected her still.

'You weren't.'

Dan wasn't sure if she was going to say any more.

'There's been a *development*.' She made it sound like a case.

'Couldn't you be a bit more cryptic?' he joked.

'Sorry. Habit.' Maya laughed. 'We all assumed Dad was dead, but it seems he may be alive after all.' She told him about the visits their mother reported to her residential home; the times Maya had thought someone was watching her; the battered iPhone that mysteriously appeared with a radio app installed. 'I have a feeling the shit is about to hit the fan. I've sent fingerprints off for testing. From the mobile.'

'*And?*'

Any response Maya was about to make was prevented by the loud voice of a tout as they passed an Indian restaurant. 'Very good price, all fresh,' the man said through a tired perma-smile. 'Special menu,' he said, pointing at the laminated double A4 sheet in the window.

Ahead, an enclosed brick bridge straddled the street. An eagle insignia lay above the word TRUMAN. Underneath this, it said, 'A Black Eagle Brewery.' A tall chimney rose high above the top of the bridge.

Maya tapped his arm and pointed at a restaurant on the corner of Woodseer Street. 'See that place. City Spice. When we arrived here in 1982, the top floor of that corner building was our first home. No-one had double glazing then so even with the windows shut, the flat permanently smelled of hops being boiled.' Her eyes shone as though the memory warmed her. 'We had two rooms up in the eaves. One was an open plan living room and kitchen, and the other was the bedroom.'

'One bedroom for five of you?'

'Mum and Dad slept in the front room.' She pointed at a small sash window which now had a container on the sill outside, filled with bobbing yellow tulips. 'Jasmina, Sabbir and I slept in the bedroom at the side, and we shared an outside toilet with loads of other families. Jaz and I hated having to go downstairs in the dark, and out into the yard at the back.' She shuddered. 'A couple of times a week we'd go to the public baths to get a shower. Depressing to think that lots of people are still living in conditions like these, and worse.'

Dan was aware that Maya had used the interruption to dodge his question. She must've been going through hell these last few months. 'Maya, the *fingerprints*. What did the lab find?'

'I haven't read the report yet.' Her face was solemn. Haunted. 'I was about to yesterday afternoon when some gobby Australian bloke rocked up and told me there was a fire.'

It was funny hearing Maya use an Aussie expression. It was also typical of her to deflect and make a joke to cover her pain. 'That told me,' he jested, feigning an offended face. 'Tell you what. I'll hold your hand later. You can open it then.'

A slow smile warmed her features. 'Let me think about it.' Her tone of voice was final, and she lengthened her stride to indicate the conversation was over.

They passed under the Truman Brewery bridge towards the area where the soup shop was based. Here, the landscape had a completely different vibe. The Indian restaurants were replaced by vintage clothing shops, record stores, bars, and posh cafés selling speciality coffees. They passed one bar after another, licensed cafés, clubs, nouvelle cuisine restaurants and trendy health food outlets. Pumped male bouncers stood threateningly, Bluetooth earpieces inserted. Their tight charcoal suits made their biceps look like they'd been shrink-wrapped.

'With those prices you'd think the rent-a-muscle would be herding the public in, not trying to keep people out.'

Maya laughed. 'Reverse psychology, I think. They want to give the impression of exclusivity.'

They walked past a place selling second-hand coats. 'All vintage,' said a guy with the teeniest goatee Dan had ever seen. He was wearing a calf-length black coat with a purple velvet trim, presumably one of his bargains.

'There are more and more hipster joints, slick bars and late-night clubs,' Maya said. 'If the landlords can command a higher rent from those, the Bangladeshis will be forced to sell up or to change the sorts of businesses they run.' She kicked at some decaying leaves in the gutter. Stood still for a moment and gestured to a shop with dressed manikins in the window. 'That place, Pick Your Vintage, was targeted by demonstrators a few years ago. A load of people wearing masks set on the place. They had fire torches and lobbed paint over the shop front.' Maya was shaking her head.

'What was it about?'

'Buying up clothes cheaply from charity shops, hiking the prices and selling them as vintage. A shop that appeals to the well-off rather than one that everyone can afford to . . .'

The deafening sound of a pneumatic drill drowned out her reply. The whole street shuddered and shook: pavements, the road, all the shops and buildings on Brick Lane. Dan could feel the vibration in his body. It was like his brain was being rattled about inside his head.

'Five days that bloody racket's been going on for.' A young guy had stopped at a graffiti-sprayed door. He placed a LIDL bag at his feet while he fished in his pockets for his keys. 'They're drilling through concrete and laying the foundations for a new ten-storey development on the old school playing fields. Bloody penthouse flats with a private gym in the basement and a roof-terrace.' Ripped drainpipe jeans and a grubby jacket clung to a skinny frame. He pointed behind the shops, then pushed the flat door open. 'You're Old Bill, aren't you? I saw you at the fire yesterday.'

Dan gave a cool smile and got out his warrant. 'Did you know the people who ran the soup shop?'

'Nah. Their gear was way out of my budget.' He waved his hand dismissively and lifted his LIDL bag.

'Did you see the flash mob?'

'Not really. My front room looks out over the street. I had a quick look when I heard the music start and all the shouting. I can catch the corner of their shop from my gaff.'

'What's your name, buddy?'

'Matt.'

'Surname?'

'Barker.'

'We've got officers doing house-to-house inquiries. Have they interviewed you?'

'Saw them coming, didn't I? Didn't answer the door.' He grinned, pleased with himself.

As had lots of residents no doubt. 'Did you see anyone going into the soup shop in the morning? Or leaving?'

Matt shook his head. 'I don't get up 'til late. I do a lot of my work at night.'

'Seen anything suspicious or out-of-the-usual the last few days?'

'Nah.'

'Would you tell me if you had?'

'Probably not.' He grinned again.

Dan gave him a steely stare. 'Well, aren't you the epitome of neighbourly good feeling? Two people died in that fire. The owners have lost their livelihood, and two residents were taken to hospital in a critical condition.'

'Oh. Right . . . ' The glee disappeared from his face.

'You heard of a website called LfA?'

'Course. Everyone has.'

Dan threw him a dirty look. 'What do you know about them?'

'They organise street events. Flash mobs, pavement painting and stuff like that. Know what I mean?' He winked.

'No, buddy, I don't. Care to fill me in?'

'Look, I don't want to get anyone in trouble or spread slander. I'm not sure they're legit, that's all. I've seen their guys hanging round youth clubs, chatting to the kids. Might be kosher but I don't get that feeling.'

Dan saw that Maya's antennae had zoomed in on the twenty-something lad. 'Do they sell drugs?'

'Bit of weed, maybe.' Then added hastily, 'Don't know for sure, like.'

'Do you know the names of any of the LfA guys?'

'The one everyone knows is Frazer but he doesn't go out recruiting. He gets his dogs to do that. Frazer just posts on the forum. Keyboard warrior, innit?'

Dan got out his notepad and wrote down the house number. 'Matt Barker, you said. Contact details?'

*

Ten minutes later, they'd reached Sclater Street on the left. The building site that Matt was referring to was like bomb-wreckage. Buildings had been flattened. Red brick and render rubble lay in heaps. 'I've never seen so much construction work.' Dan's head was on a permanent swivel.

They carried on walking.

Dan cast his eye up and down the street. All around them, cranes loomed like long-armed monsters stretching across the koala-grey Shoreditch skies. In every direction high-end flats were springing up, offered to anyone who could afford them, despite the fact that what the area desperately needed was affordable housing.

'Shall we grab a cuppa?' Maya pointed at Brick Lane Coffee, the tiny slit of a shop with tables outside. 'This noise is doing my head in.'

Sitting outside, talking to himself and with a roll-up on the go, was an old guy in a sheepskin jacket.

Dan followed Maya over to the coffee shop. A few minutes later, they were inside the café, sitting down, and they began discussing the attack on Pick Your Vintage again.

'The protest organisers claimed that the business owners were making an obscene profit on the clothes they bought and were depleting affordable stocks at charity shops.' Maya sipped her coffee. 'They've got a point.'

'Sorry to butt in. I heard you talking about the street mob and the vintage shop. You don't think there's going to be another attack, do you? You're police officers, right?' A young mum had a pram with a sleeping toddler in it and a boy of about four in tow. She was chewing her lip. 'I was in that shop with my kids when the protesters started on it. Hundreds of them in the street, throwing paint at the windows, and twenty or so trying to kick the door in.' She patted her chest to soothe herself. 'The owners barricaded us all in. We were terrified that they were going to torch the place.' Her eyes were wide with alarm. 'My toddler still has nightmares about men in masks, carrying fire torches.' She tucked a blanket over the youngster who was asleep in the buggy.

'We certainly hope not,' Maya replied.

The woman was shaking her head in disbelief. 'They weren't all working class people demonstrating about inequality. I heard a load of posh youngsters and university students boasting about signing up to join the protest because it would be a laugh and—'

'Hold on a sec.' Maya's eyes shone with excitement. 'At the time of the protest, did you hear anyone mention a website or a forum called LfA?'

The woman's eyes popped in shock and her hand rose to her mouth. 'No, but lots of them were wearing masks with an LfA logo.'

Maya, midday

Still in Brick Lane, Dan and I headed towards a clothing shop and went in. It had a sumptuous, funky window display. Inside, there were rows and rows of fashionable clothes.

'They're all made locally, in Old Street,' a glamorous young woman said, walking to meet us with a warm smile. She had cherry red lipstick, matching hair and a black-and-white polka dot dress, probably late twenties. 'And all made ethically.' She smiled and offered her hand to shake. 'I'm Natassja. It's my shop.' Her English was perfect but heavily accented.

'We're police officers,' I said. 'Investigating the arson attack at the—'

'. . . Soup shop. Yeah. I heard.' She straightened some of the stock and picked up a dress which had fallen on the floor.

'Do you know anything about it?'

'A lot of people round here think the wife did it.' There was no self-consciousness to her statement.

'How d'you know that?'

'People talk.' She shrugged dismissively.

'Were you not a fan of Mrs Ulbiene?'

She shrugged. 'I don't know her. She came charging in here one day, screaming at me because she thought I was having an affair with her husband. Accusing me. Calling me all sorts of names. Can't say I was too thrilled about that.'

'What happened?'

'I told her I'd never even spoken to him, but she wouldn't believe me.' She brushed some dust off a jacket and straightened another on a hanger. 'Turned out he had some woman on the go and she'd got it into her head that it was me.'

'How did you find that out?'

'She came back in and apologised.' Natassja's expression was furtive. 'I'll give it to her. I felt right sorry for her. She was in pieces. Said she was pregnant.'

'Did you get an idea of who the woman was?' I was thinking about our UnSub in the fire.

'No, but she knows. She said she'd found out who it was and confronted him.' She paused. Seemed to reflect. 'Poor cow. Her life can't have been a barrel of laughs, living with him.' She tapped her fingers on her chin, and I got the impression there was something else she wanted to say. 'There was a journo in here earlier, asking all sorts. Said something about "blowing the story wide open".' She flashed an apologetic smile. 'I'm really sorry. She caught me on the hop and I'd just had a double espresso. I think I told her a bit too much.'

I stifled a groan. 'Who was it?'

'The woman from the local paper. You'll know her. Black hair. High heels.'

I opened the internet browser on my phone and pulled up the *Stepney Gazette*'s website. On the front page, posted twenty-one minutes ago, was a piece by Suzie James, with the headline: 'SERIAL ADULTERER DIES IN FIRE – was the person with him one of his many mistresses?'

The article text went on to say:

'With his pregnant wife out, local womaniser, Simas Gudelis, is thought to be the man who died in the arson at the old bagel shop yesterday . . . '

'Do you realise his wife is in hospital?' I asked Natassja. 'If she clicks on this website, thanks to you, she will read things that she doesn't know and which may not be true.' I made sure my eyes locked on hers while she absorbed my words. 'If any more reporters ask you questions, please don't tell them anything.' Then, to Dan, I said, 'Let's go.'

*

Five minutes later, we were on our way, walking down Brick Lane towards Whitechapel. When we passed Fournier Street, a group of kids came hurtling round the corner towards us, shouting and running full pelt. None of them a day over ten.

'Hurry up,' one of them yelled over his shoulder to his mates. 'They'll catch us.' He lengthened his stride and the gang powered down the street, seemingly not bothered that they were on a collision course with the two of us and several other pedestrians.

'Woah. Look where you're going, fellas,' Dan told them, his hand raised to indicate they needed to slow down.

'Sod off, Grandad,' the boy snarled, wild-eyed. His accent was familiar. He spat on the pavement when he approached Dan, narrowly missing his shoes.

As he passed us, I caught the glint of metal as he slid a knife out from his jacket sleeve. 'Dan, *leave it*,' I hissed. 'He's got a blade.'

Several boys were behind him, slapping each other on the back, eyes popping and jaws twitching. At the rear, four younger boys were sprinting to keep up. One of them was Ali, the boy from the flash mob, but he seemed completely different. Hyper and out of control. A few metres past us, he stopped dead and his three pals crashed into him.

'It's finish,' Ali shouted back to them. 'They got us block off. Look.' He pointed. 'Is that psycho, Kyle. He's going to kill us. *Run.*'

'Ali?' His lip was bleeding and the stitches on his forehead had burst. 'What's happened?' His trousers were ripped at the knee.

For a fleeting moment, his face softened when he saw me, and relief flooded over it, but before I could say any more, the leader of the group of boys took off down an alley, yelling at the others to follow him. Within seconds, they'd scaled a wall into someone's back garden.

Dan punched the air in frustration.

'I wonder who Kyle is?' I asked.

Dan shrugged. 'Ali said, "He's going to kill us." Whatever it's about, I suspect it's a bit more than a couple of kids wagging school.' He took his phone out and started dialling.

Maya, 12.30 p.m.

'We've found some ID in one of the bags we recovered at the Brick Lane crime scene.' Dougie was on loudspeaker in the car. 'Belongs to a student called Sophie Williams. She's doing A-levels at New City College.'

'Any more detail?'

'She's seventeen and lives in Bow. Place is registered to a Mrs Williams. It's 162, Saxon Court. Massive block on Hamlets Way, the ones that are being developed. Huge contractor banner outside.'

'Thanks.'

'Luckily for us, the bag was water-resistant. Bit of damage at the seams and pockets, but the technicians have dried out her phone. They've begun accessing her comms data.'

'Hallelujah.' I grinned at Dan.

'Have you seen Suzie's article?' Dougie asked.

'Yeah. We've just interviewed the shopkeeper she got her gossip from.'

'She cannot resist, can she?' Dougie knew better than anyone how much grief Suzie had caused me over the years, and how she delighted in dredging up the most personal information in people's lives.

'Listen, was there literally *nothing* on the premises that could give us a clue to the woman's ID?'

'Nope. I'd have told you.'

112

'No child's hair grip or toy? I can't get out of my head that she may have an elderly relative or kid at home.'

'Sorry.'

'OK. Speak later.' I rung off and turned to Dan. 'Let's get over there, shall we?'

'Do you think Sophie's a significant witness?' Dan asked.

'Hmm. Don't know. I'm curious about her relationship with these two lads. Particularly since one's so young.'

Ten minutes later we arrived at Sophie Williams' address. As Dougie had suggested, she lived in a vast block. The building stretched the length of the entire road and had five identical entrances at the front, on the street. A large scaffolding clung to the outside of the property with a green net suspended from the roof to the ground, to stop debris falling. We didn't need to ring the buzzer as the door to the block was propped open and builders were traipsing in and out.

Sophie's flat was on the third floor. The door was yanked open seconds after I rang the bell.

'Where the hell have you—?' A ghost of a face was staring at me, with a scruffy top-knot of strawberry-blonde hair.

A large black dog pushed its nose round the teenager's legs.

'Sophie Williams?' I asked.

'That's me.'

'DI Rahman and DS Maguire.'

Her face fell.

'Were you expecting someone?'

'Oh, my mum. It's probably nothing . . . ' Her words drifted off.

'Could we come in? We'd like to ask you a few questions about yesterday's flash mob.'

Sophie's cheeks flushed with colour and she froze momentarily before pulling the dog away from the door and showing us into a sparsely furnished lounge. The spacious room had no carpet, just board with paint splatters and stains, and underlay remnants all over it. A threadbare two-seater sofa and matching armchair took pride of place in the centre of the room, both of which faced a boxy, old-fashioned TV set, which was propped up by a pile of text books.

Sophie was in the first year of her A-levels, she told us. Politics, history and law. 'Mum and Dad got divorced last year and it's been a nightmare. Mum's had to go back to work and she's really struggling.' Sophie's teenage features seemed younger than seventeen. 'Dad's got a new family and he's taken my sister to live with him.' Her sentence oozed with hurt. 'There wasn't room for me though.' She gestured to the bare floor and the sagging sofa and the crappy telly.

Dan was sizing up the room while Sophie was speaking but the distress in her voice must've pulled him up too, as he turned his attention to her.

'Sorry to hear that,' I said. 'I know how difficult it can be when someone isn't around anymore.' Sophie wasn't to know quite how intimately I understood this.

'We only moved in here four months ago and now we've got to find somewhere else because the block is being sold for development. Mum had to buy furniture 'cause Dad needs ours for his new family . . .' Her sentence petered out as she began to cry.

I felt sorry for Sophie and her mother, and wondered why she was telling us all this when I'd asked her about the flash mob. Either something was wrong, or she'd learnt deflection skills early in life. 'What are you worried about? Is it your mum?'

'She's started drinking again.' I detected shame in Sophie's voice. 'It's why Dad left us . . . and left *me* to look after her. Last night she didn't come home at all. I've rung her mobile but it goes straight to voicemail, and I'm starting to get scared.'

'When did you see her last?'

'Yesterday morning. Before I left for college.'

'Did you speak to her in the day?'

'No. I rang her to say I was going to Brick Lane, but she didn't answer.'

This wasn't what we'd come about but Sophie was still a minor and we had to refer on the fact her mother had been missing for thirty-six hours. More worryingly, it occurred to me that Sophie's mother might be the woman in the fire. 'Have any of her friends heard from her? Or anyone else in the family?'

'I've rung everyone I can think of, including Dad. Nothing.'

'We'll need her full name, description, a recent photograph, work details and where she goes drinking, please. Plus her mobile number, and your dad's contact details too. Can you do that?'

Sophie set about collecting together the information we'd requested, and it gave me the chance to check in with Dan, whose face was the mirror of mine.

'Could be in the right age range,' he whispered. 'Missing since yesterday, mobile going to voicemail?'

I nodded.

Having got the information we needed, we returned to the subject of the arson attack.

'How did you get involved with the flash mob?' I asked her.

'Oh yeah. Have you got my bag? It's got loads of my uni stuff in it, and my phone.'

I explained about the forensic tests and that we'd let her have the returnable items as soon as we could. 'We understand you've had some dealings with a website called LfA. Is that where you learnt about the flash mob?'

She called the dog over and began petting him. 'A guy at college told me about LfA. John's his name. I think he's a mate of Riad and Ali's. He said that LfA organises flash mobs and protests and sometimes you get food or a bit of cash.' Something zipped across her face. 'They post the date and venue on the forum, and say whether it's going to be morning, afternoon or evening. You go on the website and enter your details, and they WhatsApp or text the location and time on the day.'

'Did you know what the events were about?' I asked.

'He did tell us but, to be honest, I just thought it would be a good way to make a bit of cash and have a laugh.'

'Can you remember who you communicated with?'

'It's always a guy called Frazer who posts on the forum, then someone else gets in contact.' She gave a sheepish smile and stroked the dog's ears.

'What were you told you were going to do?'

'To dance in the street for half an hour.' She laughed and fiddled with her top-knot.

Something felt off. I thought carefully about what to say. 'Were any other elements described?'

She frowned. Confused. 'He said something about gentrification, but it went right over my head. We were just there for a laugh.'

'Anything criminal?'

She shook her head furiously. 'God, no. If I got involved in anything like that my dad would kill me. It was just a laugh. When that fire broke out, we were all shocked.' She looked from me to Dan.

'Who else did you know there?'

'Just Riad. He's my boyfriend. His younger brother, Ali, and the guy called John that I told you about. I don't really know him. I didn't know half the people there. I recognised a few faces from other flash mobs, but no-one by name.'

'Is John from New City College too?'

'Yeah. I think Riad said he's doing one of the new BTECs. Digital Technologies or something. He's around fifteen.' She screwed up her nose.

'How do you know Riad and Ali?'

'We met doing the climbing wall at the youth club.' Her eyes danced with excitement. 'It's lots of fun. Have you ever done it?' She giggled nervously.

'Have you wondered whether the flash mob and the fire were linked?'

Her hands went to her face. 'Oh my God, you don't think . . . ?'

I studied her body language. Was she a good actress or genuinely naïve? 'We think it's very possible.'

'Please don't tell my dad that. He'll kill me.'

'Sophie, please be honest with us. This is important. Did anyone at the flash mob mention the fire?'

'I swear, no. I did think it was a coincidence that the flash mob gathered outside a shop which then burst into flames, but that wasn't because anyone said anything.'

'What did Riad and John think?'

'I haven't seen either of them and you've got my phone.'

'Didn't you all leave together?'

'No. We were terrified. Everyone scarpered.'

'Have you been back onto the website since the fire?'

She began chewing at the skin round her nails.

'Sophie, the arson caused two deaths,' said Dan. 'The fire was deliberate. That's murder. If you know anything, we need you to tell us.'

'Will you tell my mum?' The question shot out.

'It depends,' Dan replied. 'Only if we think she needs to know.' He paused. Made his voice softer. 'Did you get drugs for attending the flash mob?'

Wet blobs fell from her eyes and landed on her hands and lap. She buried her face in the dog. 'Please don't tell Mum. Or Dad. I swear, they'll go mad.'

'What sort of drugs?' I chipped in.

'We could choose. Weed or E.' She sat up. 'And they said they'd give us a tenner.'

'Who was giving people their money?'

'I didn't see. I got there a bit late, so I never got mine.'

'When you arrived, was anyone greeting you? Giving instructions?'

'No, it was supposed to be a spontaneous thing.'

'And who was responsible for the music?'

'Dunno. I went to college then my job. When I got there, the music was already playing. Riad and Ali arrived with John, I think, and I met them there.'

'We will need their names and contact details.'

'They're in my phone. I don't know any of their addresses, sorry.' She picked up a pencil, scribbled on a Nando's receipt, and passed it to me.

Riad Farzat
Ali Kousa
John

'You don't know John's surname?'

'Sorry, no.'

'Do you have any photos of them on your phone?'

'Yeah. Loads. The four of us and everyone.' Her expression became panicky. 'But we were probably pissed, and a bit . . . '

'We won't worry about that now. When you were dancing, did you see anyone go into the soup shop?'

'No. But to be honest, we weren't looking. Someone had made a playlist and the tracks changed quickly, and we were all dancing. For a while, until the fire, it was fun. It helped to take my mind off my mum and dad.' She looked worried again. 'You won't tell the olds about the drugs, will you?'

*

Back in the car, outside Sophie's block, I called in the details of her mother's disappearance while Dan ran Riad, Ali and Sophie's names through the PNC. John would have to wait until we had a surname for him.

I couldn't stop thinking about the conversation that Jackie and I'd had yesterday evening in the Morgan Arms. 'Jackie's just finished an investigation in Manchester. Criminal gangs are using eleven, twelve and thirteen year-olds there to deliver drugs and collect money. What if those kids we met in Brick Lane earlier are involved with something similar?' The implications filled my mind. 'How the hell are we meant to protect them? Homelessness is off the scale in London, and so is child poverty.'

'Sadly, I think there are going to be a load more kids in that situation,' Dan added. 'Every day, there are more people needing asylum, and more vulnerable kids. I guess we can start with these jokers.' He gestured to the block where Sophie lived. 'I'll chase the technicians for Sophie's comms data. I have a feeling that's going to be interesting.'

But something else was worrying me. 'That poor girl hasn't a clue what she's getting mixed up in. She's so upset about her parents' divorce, and so worried about her mum, she's going anywhere there's drugs and booze.' I turned to Dan. 'I really hope it wasn't her mother in the fire with Simas. She's not coping as it is, and it doesn't sound like Daddy wants to know.'

Maya, 1 p.m.

Now in daylight, and without the enhanced reality of artificial floodlights, the arson scene was grey and drab. The ambulances, fire engines and two aerial platforms had returned to base. The building carcass was still water-drenched, and debris had been pushed into piles. The remaining apertures had smoke-stained gashes round them. The entire roof had caved in and two new forensic tents stood at either side of the shop.

Something had happened.

Dougie met Dan and I at the cordon. 'We've had engineers working through the night to try and strengthen the rooms where the floors and ceilings collapsed,' Dougie told us. 'Unfortunately, they've had to demolish what remained of the top floor as it simply wasn't safe. The ceiling collapsed just after I spoke to you.'

I groaned. 'That'll mean limited forensics from that section then.'

'Unfortunately. The two bodies came down with the ceiling.' He pointed at the tents. 'Dr Clark has just left, and the CSIs are preserving evidence.'

I surveyed the scene. 'I hope this speeds up identification of the woman.'

'Should do. The bodies had quite a fall though, and a load of debris came crashing down on top of them so that's going to work against us.'

'Any idea when we can get them over to the mortuary for PM?'

'They will be taken over any minute now. I don't want the bodies exposed to the elements any longer than necessary. We've already lost twenty-four hours.' He hesitated. 'Do you want to see them?' He paused. 'They aren't pretty.'

'Have we got close-up photographs?'

'I made sure Cathy uploaded several of each body onto PCloud.'

'In that case, I'll pass.' I shuddered. 'Bit close to home.' An image of Sabbir's remains flashed before my eyes. 'I'll call Dr Clark for a verbal.'

Shen was arriving, and I walked over to meet her at the Portakabin.

'Any developments?' I asked her.

'We've got some useful leads. The analysts have reported on the eyewitness data, and intelligence is coming in from smartphone users following the social media ping-outs.' She had really taken to her new role and was shaping up as a valuable team member. She took out her notebook and mentioned several things that confirmed what Dan and I had learnt. 'Mixed feeling about Simas and Indra . . . everyone says they were polite and hard-working . . . local shopkeepers in competition with each other. And . . . '

My ears pricked up.

'. . . several people mentioned that Simas Gudelis had lady visitors when his wife was out.'

This corroborated what Marta, and the shopkeeper, Natassja, had told us. 'Any descriptions?'

'A few people mentioned a tall woman with a black bob and a silver BMW. She used to park it round the back of the shop. Someone else mentioned a fair-haired woman with a nose-stud, and pink tufts in her hair.'

'Did no-one recognise either of them?' Everyone knew everyone round here. Even if certain groups didn't actively mix, they still knew what was going on and who everyone was.

Shen shook her head.

'It's possible they don't want to say.' I was processing the information. 'Any other eyewitness data?'

'Two further teenagers mentioned Frazer and LfA. A Somalian boy said that a guy called John had been at his youth club – it's the one on Shandy Street . . . '

'Arbour Youth Centre? I know it. Busy place.'

'That's the one. Apparently, this John encouraged lots of the kids there to join the forum. Told them it was a laugh and he'd make it "worth their time" if they came along to protests. And something about masks.'

I felt a flurry of excitement. With so many people mentioning Frazer and John, I sensed we were onto something, along with reports of masks with logos. 'Sophie Williams has just mentioned a guy called John. He's a student at New City College. She knows him from their youth club.'

She nodded. 'No-one seems to know his surname.'

'I'll drop in at the Arbour place. Someone has to know where he lives.' I was thinking aloud. 'Can you get onto the registry at New City College and ask them for the full names and addresses of all students called John?' With such a common name, it was going to be like looking for a needle in a haystack, but we had to try.

'Sure.'

'Dougie said the garden isn't secure behind the soup shop,' I told Shen. 'The gate barely shuts, the posts are wobbly, and the entrance is from an alley which runs behind all these shops, parallel to Brick Lane. The CSIs are still processing the forensic evidence from that area.'

Shen was still leafing through her notebook. 'A female eyewitness said she heard about the flash mob on Facebook. The analysts say there's an LfA Facebook page, as well as a website, and Frazer posted there last week about the protest in Brick Lane.' Shen paused. 'There's more.' She pointed out of the Portakabin window at a restaurant, two doors along from Rosa Feldman's newsagent's, in the other direction from *Alchemia*. 'See the Raj, over there. One of the chefs told H-2-H that he saw a group of teenagers arrive on Friday with speakers. They set them down, switched on the music and started dancing. He was out the front, having a cigarette. Commented on how young some of the kids were. We showed him the photograph from Ali's witness statement, and he's identified one of the boys as Ali Kousa.'

'That's interesting. Sophie Williams told us that Ali, Riad and John arrived at the flash mob together, but Ali denied having anything to do with the music.'

Shen passed me the chef's name and address.

Iqbal Chowdhury
247a Raleigh House
Sclater Street

I shuddered at the mention of Raleigh House. 'That place is a blast from the past. It's on the Gunthorpe Estate.' Memories flooded into my mind. 'Have any of the witnesses said they knew the flash mob's theme was anti-gentrification?'

'Some did. Some claim they didn't.' Shen rolled her eyes.

'Did none of them think to question how a dance in the street to music was going to do anything about gentrification?'

'Reading between the lines, I think lots of them didn't bother to ask.'

'Ali is ten, for goodness' sake.' I cursed under my breath. 'Who the hell are LfA? Is no-one checking how old these kids are? It's so irresponsible.'

'I haven't seen any mention of age checks, Boss.'

Jackie was right. 'These bloody websites and protest groups are luring kids into stuff they're too young to understand.' I kicked at the floor of the cabin and it sent a rattle through the entire space. 'For kids who are bored or hacked off, a mixed-gender event with music, booze and drugs might seem like a good laugh, but they don't seem to realise they're vulnerable to exploitation.' I thought about the London riots in 2011, where youngsters were recruited into illegal activities simply because they were bored, angry and fed up with their lives.

'Have any of our witnesses actually met Frazer? Any idea of his age, background? Is he even male?'

Shen screwed up her nose. 'We asked each witness.'

Of course, it was possible that no such person existed. The internet created so many opportunities for anonymity and un-traceability. I needed to speak to Jackie. Get her input. 'It's time to put out another public appeal. Get onto the media liaison officer and Megan in PR right away. We need to get the message out to everyone who saw the fire start that their eyewitness accounts are vital.'

I left the Portakabin with my mind racing.

As I stood facing the debris from the fire, I developed a creeping feeling that someone was watching me from behind. Just as I wheeled round, a net curtain dropped into place in one of the windows above Rosa's shop, and a light was clearly on in the room beyond. Then a hand drew both curtains. That was strange. Burglars didn't tend to put lights on if they could be seen through net curtains. And if Rosa had gone to Agnieszka's, who was in the flat above the shop?

Maya, 1.30 p.m.

'She's not at Tomasz's either?' I was on the phone to Rosa's daughter. 'I think I know where she is in that case.' I told Agnieszka about the light I'd seen in her mother's flat. 'I'll give her a quick knock and make sure she's OK.'

When Rosa appeared at the shop door a few minutes later, she was back in her own clothes and had managed a thin smear of lipstick. 'Oh, hello, Inspector.'

'For some reason you don't seem surprised to see me,' I said, teasing her.

'I know they mean well but I don't need nurse-maiding. I'm looking forward to sleeping in my own bed tonight.' Her tone was triumphant. 'That's if my daughter doesn't arrive in a few minutes and cart me off. I'm guessing you told her I was here?'

'I saw the light on and had to call her to ask if you were there. Everything alright up there?'

'Perfectly, thank you.'

Her determination made me chuckle. 'You take care now. OK?'

I was soon on Ben Jonson Road, heading back to the office. The traffic was at a standstill while a bulldozer and a bus tried to pass each other in a narrow street with cars parked on either side.

My phone rang. I switched the loudspeaker on. 'Hi, Doc. What's the news from the lab?'

'As we suspected, both bodies were badly burned. I've taken

dental samples and sent the woman's for fast-track analysis. If she has records, those should enable an ID. The forensic scientists aren't sure if they'll be able to extract enough DNA strands from the samples I took. She had a lean frame and there's very little tissue on her bones. We'll have to keep our fingers crossed. It might just be family details, I'm afraid.'

'That's fine. It's more than we have currently.'

'Righto.'

'Someone must be missing her and know where she lives.' I heard the frustration in my voice. 'We can use reconstructive identity when we've got more facial details. Until then it's fingers crossed the forensic odontology and DNA analysis turn something up.'

*

Ten minutes later I arrived back at the office. There was a buzz of activity in the incident room.

Alexej met me at the boards, waving a print-out. 'We've got a match on one of the sets of prints from the speakers at the flash mob. Guy called Kenny Hayes. Last known address was in Manchester. Before that, he was in Scotland. Currently no fixed abode, and heavily involved with Class A.' He paused. 'There were other prints but the CSIs don't have a match for them.'

Dan joined us. 'Is he a dealer?'

'Big-time. At one point the police knew he was dealing but he was clever enough not to sell directly himself, and they couldn't catch him.' Alexej was in full flow. 'Had an army of worker bees who did his dirty work for him. Most of them were illegal immigrants and asylum seekers who were desperate for money while their applications and appeals were going through.'

'What a scumbag. So, this is what Jackie was talking about. Any idea how he's involved in the flash mob?' I felt a rush of blood to my head. 'Those cases in Glasgow and Manchester. What if this is what Kenny Hayes is up to?'

'I checked his record,' Alexej continued. 'He's a nasty piece of work. Possession of Class A. Several arrests for physical violence: common assault, assault on a prison officer, assault on a constable in the execution of his duty, ABH and GBH.'

'Perhaps it's what Jackie said – he's involved with social action around anti-gentrification as a front for criminality? You got a mugshot?'

Alexej turned his monitor round so we could see.

'Check out the scar beside his eye.' Dan pointed at the screen. 'Much closer and he'd have been screwed. Doesn't do much for his looks, does it?'

It was a face that would give anyone nightmares.

'I've distributed his photograph.' Alexej showed us the range of shots. 'He's pretty adept at changing his appearance, but we'll get him. He can't alter his height or his DNA.'

'Any links with LfA?'

'Not so far.'

'This is good timing, actually,' I said. 'I've asked Shen to set up a press conference. We can appeal to the public for information on Hayes too.'

Alexej was still at his computer. 'I've set up google alerts for all flash mobs in the UK, and have set up a dummy account on the LfA forum. I'm about to log in. D'you want to have a look?'

I checked my watch. 'Sure.' I pulled out a chair and folded down onto it. Leaned over to see the screen.

Alexej keyed in the username he'd created, 'LP5', and had a click round the site. It used an old-fashioned, basic template, and was hosted with a cheap company in Canada. There were large blocks of plain colour and text, interspersed with a few generic skyline images. The menu was a string of topics to click on. 'There's no mission statement, no biographical information about key people.' He looked at me. 'The technicians are checking who the website is registered to.'

'Very clever. The lack of biographical information makes it harder to find out who's behind the site.'

Alexej signed into the forum. In LP5's profile, several unopened envelopes indicated that we had correspondence. He clicked on the 'welcome' message and scrolled down to site rules.

'Look.' Alexej highlighted the text. 'No mention of age.'

Another message asked us to sign up to a newsletter, and to enter an email address and mobile phone number.

'I can't believe people are willingly giving out this information.' He was shaking his head.

Two messages were greetings from other users, and one was a reply to a message that Alexej had sent, asking about forthcoming flash mobs in London. It was from a user called 's10s' and simply said: 'yes very soon watch forum.'

From there, Alexej clicked through some of the discussion threads. A week before the fire, 'Frazer' had posted a notification of a flash mob gathering in Brick Lane. It gave the date of the event and stated 'afternoon'. Ali had mentioned some brief information about anti-gentrification. However, no details about the protest's aims were given, just a prompt to enter your contract details in another box. It was probably sent out via the follow-up once people had registered interest. It was the foot-in-the-door technique of asking for increasing commitment.

'Sign up. See what happens.'

Alexej clicked on the link.

Too late, comrades!
Watch and listen
We need u

'That's interesting.' I turned to Dan. 'It looks basic but they've got it plugged into dates and times.'

A scan through some of the other discussion threads revealed three interesting facts. There were no posts from 'Frazer' since the day of the flash mob and fire. Ali and Sophie Williams were regular forum users. There was one new post:

s10s: who's got stereo from 5/4 it's mine

user9: feds

'Post a reply. Say you have the stereo.'

Alexej typed:

'It aint wiv feds i have it safe message me bro.'

'Look,' I said. 'These forums are the contemporary equivalent of back-room meetings. They're the perfect breeding ground for criminal activities. User-names are nonsense. Most people have non-human avatars.'

'Yes. It's always possible to exchange information if people want to badly enough.' Alexej faced me. 'It looks anonymous and a lot of these people think they can't be traced. But every click can be monitored. And if they're targeting kids, it could be mine one day.' He pointed at the photograph frame on his desk of his wife and two children. 'I intend to make sure that doesn't happen.'

Alexej's computer dinged.

'Here we go,' he said, 's10s has just posted. There's another flash mob in London a week from today.' He clicked into the 'sign up here' screen and entered the details for our dummy account, including the Gmail address and mobile phone number that Alexej had set up. Immediately, his Gmail account issued a message notification. 'Bingo.'

'Let's make our voices heard. Working class areas of London are becoming the domain of the privileged. Join next week's protest. Let's bring dance to the streets of Limehouse and show the men in suits, the non-dom wankers and oligarchs that London doesn't belong to them. We don't want plush apartments, gastro-pubs and mindfulness classes. We want libraries, community centres and proper pubs. Most importantly, we want affordable housing.'

Underneath the post, there was a question.

mac: was last one invlvd with fire?

Alexej quickly screenshot mac's question in case it got deleted, and clicked on the user's profile. The forum offered the option to send private messages. Alexej typed one to mac: 'u go to that one m8? proper scary.'

'That's enough for today.' He logged out. 'The analysts will be monitoring the forum. Too much activity looks suspicious.'

I checked the office clock. The press conference was in twenty minutes. I needed to decide how to phrase things to get the public on board.

Dan, 2.30 p.m.

Dan switched on the plasma screen in the office. 'Here we go, team. Grab your popcorn. She's on.'

'... am Suzanne Innes from the BBC,' said the smiley reporter, 'and we are live from Limehouse Police Station where there are developments on the recent arson investigation in East London. I'm here with Detective Inspector Maya Rahman from the Metropolitan Police who is about to release a statement.'

'Thanks, Suzanne,' Maya said. 'Yes, we have some worrying developments and urgently need the public's help with these.' Maya looked straight into the camera. 'Yesterday's fire in Brick Lane was caused deliberately, and resulted in the death of two members of our community. This is now a double murder investigation. It is vital that we speak to anyone who has information about who might be responsible, but hasn't yet come forward. I would also like to appeal again to anyone who captured video footage of the flash mob or the arson attack. If that's you, please get in touch.' The screen displayed the contact details for the incident room. 'We also need to speak to anyone who has recently been approached about joining local protests or flash mobs, either online or at local youth clubs and community centres. We know that people have been offered masks with logos like these.'

The screen showed a computer artist's representation of the black masks with the LfA logo.

'It's important to stress that some of these protests are made to sound innocent and fun, but we strongly suspect that some of them are a front for very serious crimes, and we need your help to keep you and your children safe.' Maya paused. 'We wish to speak to this man in connection with the arson and need help with finding him.'

At the bottom of the screen, portrait and profile shots of Kenny Hayes appeared.

'Kenny Hayes is British, approximately forty years old, six feet three, thin build, and has a distinctive tattoo on his neck. Mr Hayes' last known address was in Manchester and he has connections in Scotland. He has a string of convictions and arrests for violent offences and is believed to be extremely dangerous. We are appealing to the public for information as we strongly suspect he is involving children as young as ten in serious criminal offences.'

The screen showed a bullet point summary of the key request areas and the segment closed with the police contact numbers.

'Nice one,' Dan said, and rubbed his hands together. Maya wasn't the sort to give up easily and he respected that. 'Let's hope those phones start ringing.'

Dan, 3 p.m.

It was early afternoon when Dan and Maya arrived in Limehouse to speak to Ali.

'Rima's either here or on her way.' Dan checked the time on his phone. 'It certainly makes me suspicious that Sophie Williams contradicted Ali's account of when he arrived. Shall we knock? Maybe Rima's gone in.'

A stocky, middle-aged man opened the front door of the Georgian house, and Vivaldi bounced into pretty York Square. Concern shot over the man's face when he saw Dan and Maya, and he held the door close to his body.

'G'day, Sir. I'm Detective Maguire. This is DI Rahman. Sorry to knock you up like this . . . ' Dan smelled cooking. 'We're looking for Ali Kousa. Are you his—?'

'Who?' His accent was English. As he frowned, his round spectacles bobbed down and then up again.

'Ali Kousa. He's a ten-year-old Syrian boy. Gave this as his address. Said he lived here with his brother, Riad.' Dan double checked the house number. 'Twenty-eight, York Square?'

'That's us. There are no children here though.' The man was shaking his head. 'I think you've been run up the garden path, Detective. It's just my wife and I here. She's in the kitchen. We're a bit late having lunch today. You're welcome to come in and look around, if you want to check.' He stepped back and motioned for them to enter. 'Darling?' he yelled over his shoulder. 'The police are here.'

Maya, 3.30 p.m.

Having found no Ali to interview at the address he'd given us, Dan and I reached Rosa's newsagent's sooner than expected.

Agnieszka opened the flat door in tracksuit bottoms and a baggy jumper. 'Come in.' A smile warmed her features. 'Mum's upstairs. I've just put the baby down.' She spoke over her shoulder in Polish to her children before returning her attention to us. 'I've taken the day off to make sure she's OK. I'm still trying to persuade her to come back to ours.' She led us upstairs into the lounge.

Rosa looked ten years younger. Colour had returned to her cheeks, she'd stopped coughing and was more perky. She was installed on a worn but cosy-looking sofa, surrounded by her family. She had one granddaughter beside her and another on the floor by her feet. Photographs covered the carpet. Mainly black and white. Tatty, dog-eared and time-bleached.

'OK, you two, I'd like you out of your school uniforms, please,' Agnieszka stated firmly in their direction. 'Come in. Have a seat,' she said to Dan and I. 'The girls have just got home from school and Mum's showing them some of the pictures of when she and her parents came to live in London.' She stopped and smiled. 'None of us have seen them in ages.'

'How are you, Mrs Feldman?' I asked.

'You got me into trouble, you know,' Dan added. 'Going walka-bout like that.'

Her expression lifted, and a guilty grin spread over her features. 'Sorry about that, Sergeant. I rather thought I was due for a telling off. I got halfway to East Ham and realised I wanted to come home. Much as I love my daughter and grandchildren, my life is here.'

Agnieszka looked at me and gave a gentle roll of her eyes. She was tidying toys away and had her back to her mother. 'There's always room for you with us, Mum,' she said, in the sort of affectionate, sing-song-y way that suggested they'd had this conversation a few times already. 'I keep telling you.'

'I was showing the girls the photographs of the soup kitchen in Brune Street,' Agnieszka said. She held the image out to me. 'Four days a week they would give soup, bread, margarine and sardines. No questions asked. At one point, they had over four thousand people pass through the doors, according to Mum.'

What she said made me feel sad. It was often hard to look back on times gone by, especially when you'd lost people. Even if those times weren't good, hindsight seemed to weave a rosy glow round the memories, making them seem as if they were somehow better. Particularly if the present was unsatisfactory; if it was haunted with ghosts and memories, the past could be such a cruel tormenter.

I took the black-and-white image from Rosa's daughter. The old red brick building seemed so solid and proud. On its steps, people were queuing, thin as coat hangers inside their threadbare clothes, their skin stretched tight with hunger and desperation over protruding cheekbones.

'Neska says the soup kitchen has been sold now. Converted into luxury flats. How much did you say, love?'

'There was a one-bedroom penthouse apartment for sale on Rightmove for one and a half million pounds. No garden, no parking. It's gone now. Sold. Snapped up no doubt by someone with more money than sense.'

Rosa was tutting irritatedly. 'It's wrong. That's what it is.' She took her spectacles off and tucked them into a case. 'That building was enormous. Several floors. The equivalent of two or three shops in width. Imagine how much profit they must've made from that development.'

'So much has changed.' Agnieszka looked wistful. 'Makes me furious. I grew up in this flat, but Olaf and I can't afford to live in Tower Hamlets.' She closed the living room door behind the children. 'It's people like Mum I'm worried about. People who have lived in Brick Lane for years.' She paused, seemed to think about what she wanted to say. 'Why don't you let them have the shop, Mum? Buy somewhere near us and make a new life for yourself?'

Rosa sighed.

'They keep pressuring you to leave. Why not give them what they want? It would make your life so much easier. Or take Tomasz's help.'

'Your father would turn in his grave. I can't let those opportunist whatsits cash in on this place. Your father's parents ran the shop before we took it over. It's part of our family history. I feel like I'd be letting them all down. They fought so hard for the place.'

Agnieszka fidgeted and sighed as she picked up the array of photos which covered the floor. She passed me one. 'Look. That's the four of us. Mum, Dad, Tomasz and I. Opposite the newsagent's, in the Jewish bakery. We loved their bagels.'

I studied the photo. It was exactly as I recalled it all those years ago when we used to go as kids. The glass display cabinet with all the bagels on trays. The racks of mouth-watering loaves. The sweet smell of baking. 'It's such a shame.'

Her face clouded over and her whole energy shifted, tightened, as though something had prodded her into a different mental space. 'Mum was telling me about the flash mob. It sounds frightening. Was it connected to the fire?'

'Almost certainly. It's partly what I wanted to ask your mother about.'

'The young couple who ran the soup shop were kind to Mum. I met them a few times. Mum has had a few emergencies. The electricity went off once. It's so damp downstairs, the fuse board keeps tripping when she uses the sockets. Another time, she got locked out. The husband came straight over and helped her. When she lost her keys, they took her into their flat and gave her soup.'

'He was *very* charming,' Rosa added.

My thoughts slipped back to Agnieszka's comment about someone pressurising her mother. 'Who wants you to give up the shop, Mrs Feldman?'

Rosa began humming, pretending she hadn't heard me.

'Mrs Feldman?'

'Hmm?' she said, feigning absent-mindedness. I recognised the signs of denial from Mum. Clearly it was a conversation Rosa had had many a time with her daughter, and didn't want to repeat.

'The freeholders, of course,' Agnieszka blurted out. 'They're complete shits—'

'Agnieszka.'

'*Na litość Boską*. They are and you know it. They're leaving this place to get more and more unpleasant for you so you're desperate, and agree to hand it back to them cheap. Even Tomasz can't get them to see sense. They'll get you out and do exactly what they've done with that stupid soup place: give it an upgrade and flog it to some trendy outfit. You wait. We'll have brioche-bakers selling a loaf full of sugar and butter for four quid. Or another vintage clothes shop.'

Rosa was squirming in her seat, and her lips were moving, as though protests were forming and falling away.

'They should fix the damp and install proper heating for you,' Agnieszka continued. 'It's Dickensian. I mean it, Mum. Enough's enough. Either let Tomasz help you, or sell up and move out. It's what everyone else has done.'

I was taking this exchange in. Rosa was nodding. She seemed to agree with her daughter but feel conflicted. 'You said your brother has tried to help your mum . . . ?' I looked at Agnieszka.

She shook her head. Perplexed. 'Dad and Tomasz had some weird father-son clash. Tomasz had loads of ideas for the shop, but Dad was infuriated by anything he suggested. He tried for years to get Dad to sort out the damp. When the freeholders were difficult, he said he'd send his guys in to fix it, but Dad wouldn't hear of it. I think it was pride.' She rolled her eyes and lowered her voice to a whisper.

It was what Tomasz had told me.

'Mum wanted the work done and kept saying so, but since Dad died, Mum's loyalties have become more complex. She seems to feel that if she doesn't stick to Dad's wishes, she's dishonouring his memory.'

I pictured Tomasz Feldman with his snappy clothes, his intense energy and generosity. Theoretically, Rosa was free to do what she wanted now. Except – I knew from my own mother that it often wasn't as simple as that. The tentacles of the past often reached into the present.

'She's still grieving, and we all get that. But she's in her seventies and this place is making her ill.'

'You can talk about me all you like. I can hear you. I'm not deaf, you know.'

'I *want* you to hear me, Mum,' Agnieszka said, now even louder.

'Someone needs to make you see sense. Tomasz has given up, and I don't blame him. You know what I think about this stupid shop. It's a millstone round your neck. If you're not careful, your stubbornness will be the death of you.' She picked up a pair of children's shoes and put them by the wall. 'What gets me is that Mum wants to be here even after the fire.'

I got the impression that Agnieszka wanted me to agree with her in front of Rosa, to persuade her mother to see sense. But I also felt her mother's helplessness, her fear and frustration. And for a moment, I felt torn. What should I say? It wasn't my business but if it were Mum, would I want her grafting away in a cold, damp shop, surrounded by memories and determined to continue to be independent? I could relate to the stubbornness that Rosa exhibited. Like Mum, it came from strength of character and having had to overcome some dreadful experiences in life, and I was sure it was keeping the two women alive. 'I can understand your concerns but . . . ' I frowned an apology.

'Oh sorry, Inspector. It's not your problem at all. I'm just desperate to get Mum out of here and am being indiscreet and unfair.' Agnieszka's cheeks flushed pink. 'Can I get you a cup of tea? You said you needed to talk to Mum about the flash mob?'

'Thank you, yes. Don't worry about the tea though.' I smiled appreciatively and turned to Rosa, hoping Agnieszka would now go. 'Mrs Feldman, did you see Indra leave the shop yesterday?'

She was pensive. Eyes screwed up, head cocked to the side. 'Yes. I was opening up. Would've been around nine o'clock.'

'Did she go back in at any point?'

'Not that I noticed. But I wasn't at the window all the time. I was trying to put some of the new stock out.'

'Anyone else go in? Or Mr Gudelis leave?'

'I don't think so.'

'What were you doing in the morning? Can you think back?' I didn't want to lead Rosa.

'I had a delivery. Tomasz came and carried the boxes for me and I began unpacking them. But I was cold, and I had out-of-date stock which I needed to dispose of. Ah. That's it. The husband came into the shop. He asked for Lemsip and Nurofen. Said he had flu and was going to go to bed and sleep it off.'

'What did you say?' That was interesting. I didn't know whether Simas had actually been ill yesterday, or whether the flu remedies were a cover.

'Nothing.' She opened her hands wide. 'I sold him the remedies. I wasn't sure why he was telling me what he was going to do. It wasn't as if we knew each other that well.' She frowned. Confused. 'Does that mean I was the last person to see him alive?'

'I'd imagine that was the person he was with.'

'Golly, that's a relief. It would feel a bit strange otherwise. The last person to see him before he was killed?' She shuddered. 'I feel stupid now for being duped. Cavorting around in the street like an idiot while someone was setting light to their shop.' She was trembling.

'If you were duped, you weren't the only one. And we have a feeling that was the intention. The people who set up these flash mobs know exactly what they're doing. Don't give yourself a hard time. You weren't to know.' I tried to give her a reassuring smile.

Dan was beside me now. He was holding out his phone screen so I could read an email he'd just received. Indra Gudelis had been rushed back into hospital with internal bleeding.

'OK,' I said to him. Poor Indra. It'd been one thing after another. 'Mrs Feldman, we'll be off now.'

'OK, dear. Neska, the detectives are leaving,' Rosa shouted to her daughter. 'We'll see you out.'

'You don't need to—'

'Nonsense. I won't hear of it.'

Dan chuckled behind me as we all filed down the narrow stairs and through the shop to the street.

As soon as we were outside, I turned to Rosa. 'You go in, back in the warm.'

But she wasn't listening.

Her attention was fixed on the front of her shop and she was studying a patch of masonry above the door. With the lights on inside, the brickwork seemed lighter than I'd seen previously, and a Star of David was clearly illuminated, etched into the surface with a sharp instrument.

'I thought anti-Semitism was on the wane,' said Rosa. 'Look. They've scratched it into the brick.' She was shaking her head in horror and disbelief, and pointing at the symbol. 'I hope this doesn't mean we're going to have the windows smashed again.' She put her hand out to steady herself. 'I don't think I can cope with much more.'

The star was the height of one brick, so not huge, but it was visible and striking. I certainly hadn't seen it before. 'Is this the first time you've noticed it?'

'I think so.' She looked over her shoulder at me. 'But I don't tend to stand out the front and face the entrance. My mind's usually on the till or I'm carrying a heavy load, so generally I'm rushing in or out. I'm not usually looking that high up.'

'I haven't seen it either, but Mum's not been here for a couple of days.' Agnieszka had followed us downstairs and overheard. 'Maybe someone did it then? When I arrived with the kids earlier, I let us in and bundled them upstairs. I didn't notice it, but we were in a hurry to get inside.' Concern pulled at the muscles round her eyes. 'I know you're Jewish, Mum, but why would someone suddenly decide to scratch a Star of David outside the shop?'

'Anti-Semitism.' Rosa's voice was a whisper. 'We had it for years before you and Tomasz were born. It came in waves. Several spates of it when you two were kids. Your father wouldn't have it. He scrubbed it off. But it was often a sign of things to come.'

Agnieszka glanced at me and I caught the worry in her eyes. 'It's probably just bored kids mucking about. Thinking they're clever.' She adopted a calming tone. 'I'm sure it's nothing, Mum. We can—' She broke off, as though something had dawned on her. 'Hang on. Wasn't there something in the newspaper recently about people marking premises when they plan to steal a dog?'

'But I haven't got a dog.'

'I know. People do similar recces for places to burgle. They mark them to come back to. Maybe that's what this is.' She turned to me. 'What do you think?'

'I'm not sure.' The scratched symbol looked new. 'It could be any of those things or a coincidence.' As I heard the words leave my mouth, I was aware I didn't believe them.

Rosa's laugh feigned courage and although she was trying to make out she'd recovered her composure, she was trembling. 'They won't find much worth stealing in there but I'm not keen on being bashed over the head or having my precious photographs damaged. They're all I've got left of your father.'

'I don't like you living here on your own, Mum. Thank goodness we're staying with you.' Agnieszka faced her mother, as though she was hoping she'd realise something. 'But we can't stay forever.' She gestured to the upstairs bedrooms. 'The kids need more space and

Olaf misses them. I do wish you'd come and live with us for a bit. Sell this bloody shop.'

My thoughts were spinning. I didn't know what to make of the star. Hopefully Rosa was safe with her daughter staying for now, and this was family business. I needed to leave them to it. But as Dan and I walked away, I couldn't shift the nagging suspicion that there was more to the symbol than a few kids messing around.

Maya, 4.30 p.m.

'Yes, it's neighbourly to call Indra and tell her the shop's on fire, but something feels off,' I said to Dan.

We were in Shoreditch to interview Tomasz Feldman.

'He doesn't really know her or Simas. How has he got her number? And why?'

'You're the one that knows him,' Dan replied.

Trendy and upmarket, this part of London was packed with clubs and bars. Whereas many places were struggling to get customers through the door, Tomasz's champagne bar, restaurant and night-club clearly wasn't having difficulty attracting customers. A string of affluent trendies was filing into the building's plush entrance.

As we entered the premises, I immediately noticed how different the atmosphere was from Artem's strip club. Here, security cameras were attached at different vantage points, all extremely high-tech. Walls were spotless in brilliant white. The front desk was made of black marble. There was no glass or mirrors, just a huge expanse of black and white with low lighting at various angles. The floors had been stripped, sanded smooth and painted. The combination of natural wood surfaces and white walls lent the place a sense of elegance and sophistication.

'Could you tell Mr Feldman the police are here?' I said.

The girl on the front desk was coiffed and manicured, and she spoke in Polish through plump lips covered with frosted pink lip gloss. '*Policja jest w recepcji*,' she said into her headset with a bored expression. Then, to us she said, 'He's in a meeting. I'll show you into the bar. He'll collect you from there.' She led us across the lobby, down carpeted steps and through double doors into a vast room.

The space was divided up into bar and seating areas, a restaurant and a stage. The interior, with white walls and modern furniture, wasn't warm or feminine but it was a high-end design with an extremely stylish finish. Men and women, ranging from spotty twenty-year-olds to tubby middle-aged men, stood around in huddles at the various tall bars, their pink faces glowing under the lights, dousing oysters with tabasco and vinegar and chucking them down their throats. Dotted at intervals on the shiny bar surface, bottles of champagne arrived in buckets of ice, and were drained and replaced. In a corner, a gaggle of girls sipped cocktails, already half cut and doubled-over in giggles. Towards the end of the main bar was a large silver-service restaurant which was almost fully occupied. With main courses at twenty-five quid, and the cheapest bottle of wine a bit more than that, Tomasz Feldman had clearly pitched his establishment at the upper end of the market.

The girl led us to a table. 'Mr Feldman won't be long,' she said, and left us.

'Jeez.' Dan gestured to the Cristal champagne on the bar. 'That stuff is big bucks. They're getting through it like water.'

My eyes raked the room.

'I've checked their licence and record.' Dan kept his voice low. 'Nothing about drugs. Seems Mr Feldman runs a clean business.'

'That or he's got systems in place. Are you telling me none of these people go to the loo to sniff a line of coke or pop a pill?'

Dan shrugged. 'I'm sure they do. I'm simply saying that I can't see any record of drugs being reported here, and . . . ' He broke off as Tomasz came into view, striding towards us.

'Detectives. Sorry to keep you waiting.' Tomasz straightened his jacket and gave us a welcoming smile. 'Please come with me.'

We followed him across the room.

Once in his office, he walked over to a cluster of chairs by his desk and sank into one. 'Please. Have a seat. Mum hasn't gone walkabout again, has she?'

'No, no. She's at the shop with your sister.' I sat down, leaving Dan by the door.

'I've offered to put her up in one of my flats but she won't hear of it. At least Agnieszka can keep an eye on her there and she's not going to toddle off. I've been running out of ideas for how to help her. It's distressing to see her struggle needlessly.' An air of unease had come over him. 'So, how can I help?'

'We're here to get some background information.' It was strange seeing the boy I'd known from the newsagent's. It was as though we were back there, and I was someone different from the person I've become.

He looked at me properly for the first time. The hair at his temples was sprinkled with grey, and I caught a glimpse of the same kindness and patience in his eyes I recalled.

He laughed. 'I remember you asking lots of questions. I'm not surprised you became a cop.' He looked embarrassed briefly.

'Do you mind explaining why you called Indra about the fire at the soup shop? Is there a connection between the two of you?'

Tomasz shook his head. 'Someone rang and told me, so I wanted to let them know. I was at Mum's yesterday morning and noticed the shop was shut. I tried Simas' phone and it went straight to voicemail. It made sense to ring Indra and Marta.'

What he said was plausible, but it occurred to me that I didn't know if Tomasz was married, and if something was going on between him and Indra . . . 'You just happened to have her number?'

He laughed. 'I have Indra and Simas' numbers because their shop is opposite Mum's. It's useful to be able to contact them sometimes if I can't get hold of her. I've got lots of her neighbours' numbers. I have Marta's because she works in the bar here.' He hesitated, as though he had forgotten something, or thought perhaps I had. 'It's how Brick Lane works.' He held my gaze fleetingly. 'Or – it *was*.'

Maya, 5.30 p.m.

Dan and I were back in the street outside Tomasz Feldman's bar. Black cabs and double-deckers thundered along the bus lane on Hackney Road, while lorries and cars sniffed each other's bumpers and waited for a gap to jump ahead.

'D'you think we need to consider Tomasz a suspect?' I was trying to reconcile the man of today with the boy I knew growing up. I'd left the bar feeling more confused than when we arrived.

'I can't see what motivation he'd have for setting light to the soup shop,' said Dan. 'Like I said, I've checked his record. He's clean.'

'I can't either.' I watched a group of twenty-somethings bundle out of a cab, all well-oiled and chatting loudly about their recent deals. Advertising executives, probably. Brokers at a push. 'When we were growing up, my sister and I had a crush on him. He seemed so cool. And whenever we went into Rosa's newsagent's, he was always friendly and . . . nice.'

'You're kidding?' Dan spun round. 'You had a crush on him? You wait 'til I tell the team.'

I laughed. 'It was a long time ago. I'd forgotten all about him until yesterday. Jasmina and I didn't think of it like that at the time, but I guess that's what it was. We were younger than him but he never seemed to look down on us.'

'It's interesting that Rosa has maintained a Jewish identity and lifestyle,' Dan said. 'I wonder how she feels about that not mattering to either of her children.'

I told him about Rosa's parents being helped to escape from the Warsaw Ghetto by Christian Poles.

'Ah. That makes sense,' he said. 'What about Tomasz though?'

'Rosa seems to have adapted to life here. Maybe she doesn't mind?' I couldn't help thinking about Mum and the difficulty she'd had adjusting when we arrived over from Sylhet in the eighties. How she'd clung, all her life, to Bangladeshi customs, to her mother tongue, and how anglicised she found me. 'From what I see, it's pretty common for things to change from one generation to the next. It depends on who people mix with and marry.'

We'd stopped now to get a takeaway coffee from a stand.

Dan passed a tenner to the barista and we shuffled along the pavement to wait for our drinks.

Mum was still on my mind. She'd barely changed since living in the UK. 'I wonder why some people adapt and others don't.' I remembered the times Jasmina and I came home from school and found her in a ball on the floor, in the dark, beside the sofa. It was an image which had lodged in the folds of my memory. 'My mother still doesn't speak English. Key words but nothing more.'

Dan seemed surprised. He collected our drinks. 'What about your dad?'

The question caught me unprepared. Dan knew that Dad had left us when we were kids. The truth was I had no idea what he was like now. 'Dad's English was always better than Mum's, and when we arrived in the UK he kept saying how important it was for us to become bilingual.' I felt the knot tightening in my stomach. I cleared my throat, keen to change the subject. 'I think we have to consider

Marta a suspect, don't you?' I hoped Dan would pick up on my cue. 'She's certainly got a motive for removing Simas from Indra's—'

The vibrating of my mobile interrupted our conversation. It was Alexej.

'OK,' I said, once he'd briefed me. 'We're on our way back.'

Dan's eyes were on me.

'LfA has claimed responsibility for organising the flash mob.' I lobbed my coffee into a bin, hoping that this would be a productive lead. 'And the tech team have traced the owner of the domain address. Have a guess who LfA was founded by?'

Dan, 6 p.m.

'Any previous?' Maya asked as they walked up the front path of Agnieszka and Olaf's terraced house in East Ham.

'Nothing,' Dan replied, thinking back to the information he'd read about Agnieszka's husband. 'Strozyk came to the UK in 1985. School in Plaistow. Tower Hamlets College after that. Studied accountancy here, and runs his own business in Upton Park.'

A dumped couch sat on its haunches against the garden wall, rusty springs protruding and a gaping burn hole in the seat.

Olaf opened the front door within seconds of Maya ringing the bell. 'You made me jump. I've just got home.' He clocked their warrants and his face flushed pink. 'Has something happened?' He had a strong Polish accent.

Maya introduced them. 'We need to ask you a few questions about LfA. Can we come in, please?'

'Wow. That's a blast from the past.' His expression shifted to relief, and he stepped backwards to let them in. 'Of course. I was just about to head over to the shop to visit Agnieszka and the kids.' He led them along the hall, loosening his tie as he walked.

It was a family home, with all the things Dan missed. Underneath the adult coats, each of their three children had a peg for their clothes and bags, and a plastic box for their shoes. In the lounge, Dan began sizing up the room. Last night's dinner. Lever arch files all over the coffee tables. This wasn't children's mess.

Someone had created a system, a place for everything. Another was ignoring it.

'We understand you set up LfA.' Maya was watching Olaf closely.

'A long time ago, yes. When I was at university.' He waved his hand dismissively.

'And the website, LfA.com?'

'Yup.'

'Are you still involved with it?'

'Fat chance.' He snorted. 'Look at me.' He patted his belly and, as he moved, Dan noticed the sweat under his arms. 'Do I look like a man who's got time to do campaign work? I work long hours and I've got three kids. I haven't got time to wash my car let alone organise demonstrations and rallies.' He snorted at the idea.

'Who runs it now then?'

'No-one. I let the payments lapse on the website.'

'When was that?'

'Several years ago.' His face clouded over and his posture tensed. 'Can't remember exactly but I should have the details in my email somewhere. What's this about?'

'Someone called the police today,' Maya explained, 'and said that LfA was responsible for the flash mob in Brick Lane yesterday. Do you know who that might have been?'

'No. *Co ten pierdolić?*' His gaze was loose for a moment.

Dan wondered if he was trying to make sense of the news or prepare excuses.

'How can they be responsible? LfA was a socialist organisation not a . . . a . . . I don't know what.' Olaf unbuttoned his cuffs and began rolling his sleeves up. 'Did this person say the flash mob or the fire?'

'We were hoping you might tell us.' Dan's kept his tone solemn.

'I'm not sure what you're insinuating, Sergeant. I don't know anything about the flash mob, or the fire, other than what I've seen on the news. I was at work all day yesterday until 6 p.m. and I certainly haven't been making phone calls to the police.' He fished in his trouser pocket for his mobile and swiped at the screen. 'I should have the renewal failure email in my Gmail. *Gówno*. Bloody phone. Battery's dead.' He cursed under his breath. 'Do you want to come through to the kitchen and I'll plug it in?' He strode past them and out into the hall.

The kitchen was wall-to-wall white cabinets, leaving little room to move. Fitted at floor and eye level, so as to provide maximum storage, they covered the entire circumference of the room. Each child had their weekly activity timetable stuck to the fridge-freezer.

Olaf plugged his phone into a mains charger. 'My laptop's at the office. I'll be able to start it up in a minute or two.' He glanced round the kitchen as though he didn't know what to do. 'I'm trying to get my head round all this. Someone from LfA has claimed responsibility for the flash mob? That's preposterous. Or a hoax. LfA doesn't exist anymore.'

'We're going to need to see that email, buddy,' said Dan.

Olaf thumbed at his screen which still didn't seem to be responding. '*Jezusa Chrystusa*.' He flung the mobile back on the worktop.

'While we're waiting for your phone, can anyone vouch for you being in the office all day yesterday?' Dan leaned against the worktop.

Something flashed across Olaf's face. 'You mean, do I have an alibi?'

'If you like.'

'Yes. My PA, Sara Baranska.'

'We'll need her address.'

'Of course. Ah, here we go. Bloody thing's starting up at last.'

While they were waiting, Dan continued to assess their surroundings. On the worktop by the microwave, crayons and pens were stacked neatly, and colourful drawings clustered above the timetables. Plastic containers of cereal sat in rows next to the toaster, and a toddler's drinking beaker was on the draining board.

Across the room, Olaf was fiddling with his phone.

'You sure you let the payments lapse?'

'Of course I'm sure,' snapped Olaf. 'I've got the email. I know I have. It's just that I've got so much spam in my inbox, it's a nightmare finding anything.' Several minutes passed while he continued to swipe at his phone screen. 'Would you like me to forward it onto you? No point wasting time.'

'Who was the site hosted with? That's got to be the easiest way of searching.' Dan was itching to take the man's mobile and do it himself.

'Oh, it was only a cheap one. Got it on special offer. Web4U, I think it was. Something like that. Paid ten upfront. Here we are. Oh. No, that's not it.' Olaf pushed the phone away from him to get a better view. 'That's strange . . . ' He repeated the gesture. 'I can't seem to . . . I must've deleted them when I ran out of space on my Gmail account. I can't find any emails from Web4U.'

'That's a coincidence.' Dan knew his voice was impatient. 'Because your website is still active and has been promoting all sorts of criminal activities. As things stand, it's still currently registered to you. How do you explain that?'

Olaf's face froze.

Maya, 6.45 p.m.

Back at the station, Dan and I hurried to the incident room for briefing. The office stank of leftover pizza and stale coffee. On the large plasma screen, Carly, the Sky News reporter, was standing outside a large red brick building, facing a camera. It was the converted Synagogue in Belvedere Street, and children and teens were trailing in and out as she spoke. Above her head, a large Star of David had been carved into a strip of cream stone.

'I'm here at the busy Coley Youth Centre in Brick Lane . . .' she said into her microphone.

I paused to listen briefly, hoping the coverage would be helpful.

' . . . where there's increasing concern amongst parents and volunteers about children being groomed into taking part in flash mobs. The police say these gatherings, which typically involve spontaneous music and dancing, may conceal criminal acts, and are involving children as young as ten.'

'Bloody pond-life,' Dan muttered.

'We've long been familiar with the idea of grooming being something which paedophiles do,' Carly continued, 'but the police tell us that the same behaviour is being used in places like this,' she gestured to the building behind her, 'to lure children and vulnerable adults into breaking the law.'

'Let's hope this helps to get the message across,' I said.

I left the broadcast and approached the board.

Alexej had written up the key developments.

- UnSub
- Kenny, Artem, Indra & Marta
- LfA
- Who are Frazer & John?
- Ali's address

'Jackie's on her way and said to start without her.' I pointed at LfA on the board. 'Let's begin with Agnieszka's husband, Olaf Strozyk. Does his alibi check out for Friday?'

'Yes.' Dan got in first, his face tight with determination. 'His PA confirms he was in the office all day and was still working when she left at six.'

'What I don't understand is, the fire was yesterday. Why wait a day and then call in?' The photos of the burnt-out shop stared back at me from the board. Two lives had been snuffed out with the strike of a match. 'The analysts still can't identify the caller so there's nothing to suggest whether the person actually represents LfA, or whether they're trying to drop LfA in it.'

'Is there no cell site data from the phone call?' Shen's eyes shone with hope.

'No.' Alexej had been following this up. 'The voice sounds female but whoever made the call used voice distortion software and put it through a router so that the location bounced every few seconds.'

'That's not an amateur.' I felt my heart sinking. 'That's someone who knows their technology.' Olaf had been hopeless with his phone when we interviewed him, and hardly fell into the tech-savvy category. 'I can't see why Olaf would make the call himself when it drops him in it.'

'The thing is, most people use anonymous usernames on the internet, so it's hard to establish who's responsible for what.' Alexej was checking his screens. 'Going on their company records, LfA seemed legitimate when Olaf was in charge. "Based on socialist principles . . . peaceful protests . . . affordable housing for everyone" . . .' He was reading off his monitor. 'They didn't oppose all development, just gentrification.' He was shaking his head. 'I know people behave recklessly at university but given Olaf was planning to train as an accountant, he'd have been a bit silly to have got involved with anything criminal, surely?'

'I agree.' Dan was jabbing his finger at the image of Rosa's son-in-law. 'And people hijack group names and identities all the time, so someone could be organising criminal activities and using LfA as a shield and Olaf Strozyk as a fall guy. Once we've received confirmation that he let the website lapse, we can rule him out, I think.'

'What about Artem?' I asked. 'We know he has form for arson.' I put my mug down. 'There's a difference between setting fire to a tumble-down shed at the bottom of someone's garden and burning down a three-storey shop though, and it was ten years ago. Is that enough to make him a suspect for setting light to the soup shop?'

'It was still arson.' Dan's tone was unequivocal.

I faced the team. 'I think we have to consider him a possible suspect but not our prime one. I don't see him as a pyromaniac and he's not stupid enough to risk his livelihood.' The female fire victim was bothering me. 'I'm pleased the public has taken our appeal for information to heart. Any news on our UnSub?'

'No,' Alexej replied. 'Not good news about Sophie Williams, unfortunately, either. We haven't traced her mother yet so we can't rule her out as our UnSub. I've spoken to the lab. The UnSub's dental records don't match with any on the database, and because her body was so badly burned, they're still having trouble extracting enough DNA strands.' He stopped. 'On the positive side, they've got her corpse now so they're continuing to take samples and test.'

It was what Dr Clark had warned about.

'We need to speak to Indra again,' Dan said. 'If she knows who one of the women was that her husband was having sex with – as the shop-keeper told us – this woman could be our UnSub. Do we know when the doctors will let us speak to her?'

Alexej looked up from his email. 'As soon as they've got her bleeding under control.'

'I feel sorry for Indra,' I said. 'She's having a dreadful time.'

'There has to be a number of people queuing up to take a swipe at Simas, surely?' Shen curled a disapproving look. 'Including Indra. I can't say I'd blame her either. Although a quick chat and a good kicking would have been less drastic.' She paused, as though she was re-thinking her comment, and was beginning to realise how difficult it was to navigete the complexities and darkness of CID.

'I didn't have you down as violent.' Dan nudged Shen, his tone playful.

'I'm not.' She eyeballed him. 'Unless provoked by a stupid man who can't keep his dick in his pants.'

Alexej laughed. 'Let's hope no-one cheats on you then.'

We were all relieved to release some tension.

'Before we move on,' I said, 'I'm still concerned that our UnSub may have dependents. Someone has got to be missing a daughter or a sister or a friend, surely?' I took in the images of her waxy, blackened corpse on the board. 'If she has an elderly relative at home or a kid, they may not be able to look after themselves or call for help.' I felt the atmosphere change in the room and knew I'd hit a nerve with the team. 'We've got to keep appealing to the public for information.' We'd all done First Aid courses and knew how crucial hydration was. 'It's been two days now. Forget food. Without water, if she's got anyone at home, relying on her, they could be close to death. We're running out of time.'

For a few moments, everyone was still and there was a deathly quiet in the room.

'If they rely on medication, even worse,' Dan added, and the disturbing reality ricocheted around us.

Shen plonked her elbows on the desk and rested her chin in her hands. 'Where now, Boss?' Her voice was down-beat.

It was up to me to motivate the team and lead the way; to make sense of the mass of information and leads. But all we had was the next few steps, and an ever-increasing pile of questions. 'Have we learned anything new about Hayes?'

'Nope. We haven't had one call about him,' Alexej said. 'I'm wondering if he's changed his appearance again.' He was pointing at the images we had for him. 'Alternatively, he could be doing time. The analysts are checking prisons.'

'What if he's gone abroad?' Shen's face was pinched.

'I hope not.' Jackie had just arrived. 'I've just come off the phone with Manchester. We've had Kenny Hayes in our sights for several years. He's a ruthless scumbag who will stop at nothing. His convictions are a drop in the ocean compared with what we suspect he's been involved with.'

Her words sent a chill through the room.

'I've got a list here of the aliases he's used most frequently. He seems to like "Jimmy" and "Kieran", and uses the surnames "Cox" and "Moore". But he could be using anything.'

'Uniform are taking Hayes' mugshot out to some of the key flash mob witnesses and places where he might be lurking.' Alexej told us.

'With any luck, someone will recognise him and perhaps someone knows who Frazer is.'

I checked the clock. 'I suggest we view Indra and Marta as our key suspects.' I did a sweep of everyone's faces. 'Tomorrow's tasks . . .'

Everyone in the team braced themselves.

'We'll have to wait until we can see Indra. Shen, can you monitor incoming data on Kenny Hayes and John, please? And chase the analysts for the key messages from the H-2-H data?'

Shen gathered up her printouts and highlighter.

There was still a mass of film to view. 'I'll get some ops to help with the CCTV. Alexej, can you liaise with them, please? Dig up all the dirt you can on Artem Gudelis. Girlfriends, employees, fall-outs, the shed fire. Has anything happened between him and Simas?' I paused. 'Run a full check on Olaf too.'

'Sure.' Alexej spun his chair back to face his computer screens.

'I'll make sure the lab is prioritising the ID of our UnSub.' It was seven fifteen. We still needed to know why Ali Kousa had lied about his arrival time at the flash mob. The analysts had found an address for him and Riad in Sophie Williams' comms data. 'Ali has to be at home now, surely?' I said to Dan. 'Shall we see what he's got to say? This time I'll tell Rima we'll give her a call when we know we've got the right address.'

Maya, 7.30 p.m.

'How much did this lot cost then?' Dan pointed at the recently landscaped gardens and new wooden benches.

We'd arrived at Stepney's Ocean Estate, to interview Ali Kousa.

'Twenty-two million. It's won design awards. Been all over the news.'

Dan whistled. 'Very nice.'

'It needed the investment. Been one of the most deprived estates in the country for years. When Dougie and I were training, we'd have a call-out here practically every day.'

'I'm impressed. It's often cheaper to flatten the lot and start again. Looks like they've added a health centre over there, and some shops and a job centre.'

'Duckett House is this way. It's very different.' I pointed at the looming tower block and a few moments later, we were in front of a derelict building. Sheets of metal covered ground floor windows. Others were smashed and gaping. On the dull concrete fascia, chalky water deposits told tales of leaking gutters and downpipes. A boy, around Ali's age, was repeatedly kicking a ball – bang, bang, bang – against a wall while his two mates looked on.

'Jeez. What happened? Why'd this place get left off the development schedule?'

'The council ran out of money.'

Dan approached the boys. 'Any idea where 286a is, fellas?'

'You feds?' One of the boys asked.

'Uh-huh.'

'That one over there.' He pointed at a ground floor flat, one with boarded windows.

Dan's gaze met mine.

'I hope they're winding us up.' I kept my voice low.

'It may be a lot better inside than it looks from here.' Dan scoped the block. 'I'd guess the main entrance is that one with the knackered CCTV.' He pointed, and began striding towards a set of metal double-doors.

The three boys had gathered in a scrum and were whispering. Nudging and pointing.

I checked my watch. Under normal circumstances, a ten-year-old boy would be on his way to bed, but I somehow doubted this was what we were going to find. I pressed the buzzer for the flat.

'It's bust,' the boy yelled. 'Just pull the door.'

'Thanks.' I yanked the handle and entered the building, Dan behind me. The lobby was in darkness, except for a weak light which seemed to be flickering from a doorway along a short corridor. I switched on the torch on my phone, aware that we should probably call for back-up, and wait for it to arrive. But we'd wasted so much time already, I pushed the thought from my mind. 'Flat 286a must be where the light's coming from,' I said to Dan over my shoulder. 'It corresponds with where that kid pointed.' As we made our way along the corridor, the stench of filth and skunk hit me.

The flat door was loose on its hinges and was propped open by a broken chair. The doorway opened onto a tiny hall, and beyond that, there was a room which had been stripped and had no electricity. Inside, black bin liners had been taped over the windows to keep out the draught. Concrete floors were partially covered with board, and several people were sitting on the floor. It had probably been someone's lounge. Now it was a squat.

Dan and I entered the room.

'We're looking for Ali Kousa,' I said.

'He ain't here.' A tall figure on the floor growled the words. His voice was older than the boys outside, and his attention was glued to the screen of a mobile phone.

My eyes were struggling to make out who was where. 'How about you boys help us out? No-one's going anywhere. Back-up is waiting for the word from me.'

'Hey, Paki. It's you they're after so you speak to them.' The tall youth on the floor stood up and hauled a boy to his feet. It was Ali. He shoved him in my direction. 'And piss off out of here. Bringing them filthy feds here.' He slumped back down to the ground.

I grabbed hold of Ali. 'You're not going anywhere. Where's your brother?'

'Who?'

Hadn't Sophie said that Riad's surname was 'Farzat'? 'He's not your brother, is he?'

No answer.

'Ali, who's that?' I gestured to the youth on the ground, who was muttering, swearing and fidgeting, presumably off his head on something.

'Come on, buddy.' Dan was beside Ali now. 'Do yourself a favour and answer the question.' He was eyeballing the chap on the floor.

'Ali?' I spoke gently, aware that Dan's Australian accent and booming male voice sounded intimidating.

'Let me go,' Ali shouted. 'He kill me if I talk to you. He fucking kill me. And all of us.'

'Who?'

He pointed at the guy on the ground, who had put his phone away. 'Him. Or him crazy brother, Kyle.'

My grip relaxed slightly as I felt Ali's body tremble and realised he was crying.

Ali must've sensed my momentary loss of concentration. With one almighty yank, he took a flying leap, and launched himself past Dan towards the doorway from the lounge into the corridor. Dan lost his balance and fell on his side. Moments later, I heard the front door of the building bang shut. Before I knew it, the wiry body was up from the floor. The youth plunged after Ali, out of the squat, and began sprinting along the corridor towards the exit.

'*Bugger*,' Dan yelled, as he scrambled to his feet. 'We well and truly screwed that up.' He turned to me, his eyes blazing. 'Right. Time to call it in. Let's get this shithole cleared before any more of these kids nick off. They need to be in foster homes where they're safe and we can keep an eye on them.' He took out his mobile.

Dan was right. We'd assumed we were visiting a home and had been foolish to go inside without back-up. I'd allowed impatience to cloud my judgement. 'I'd better alert Jackie. She's going to be furious.'

'Good idea. I'll start putting calls out about Ali and the other boy. Somehow I don't think Ali was joking about Kyle.'

Through the dim light of the squat, I caught Dan's expression and knew he felt as scared for Ali as I did.

Maya, 8.30 p.m.

As we left the estate, the sequence of events at the squat were playing on a constant loop in my mind. I couldn't escape the fact we'd cocked up. Ali had run off. He seemed sure that someone called Kyle was going to kill him, and that meant we'd exposed him to even greater danger. What the hell were these kids mixed up in? I was sure about one thing: I had to find Ali.

And that meant going looking for him.

From the squat, I drove straight to Brick Lane.

At night, it always took on a different quality from the daytime. This evening, the brightly coloured neon strips seemed to jump out at me from the shops. Vandalised street lights plunged me in and out of darkness, and shadows lurked beside every vehicle and wheelie bin. Each street corner was filled with menace. I kept my eyes peeled for anyone of Ali's age, scouring doorways and alleys for a scrawny kid with black hair and white trainers.

Suddenly, I caught a movement between the rows of jackets in a leather shop and then saw Mr Bashir's bald head pop up. I strode past Sclater Street and continued walking towards Bethnal Green Road. Ahead, the crumbling remains of the soup shop were a sad sight behind vast hoardings. I signalled to the uniformed officer who was guarding the crime scene and ducked under the cordon. 'Hi, Gary. Everything OK?'

'Evening, Ma'am. Nothing to report.'

'You haven't seen a ten-year-old boy, have you?' I described Ali.

'No, Ma'am.'

I knew it was a long shot but couldn't help hoping. 'Let me know if you do, please.'

'Will do.'

The water from the pumps had drained away now but even in the dim light, above the hoardings, I could see the white scars that water residue had left on the once pretty fascia. Where the windows had been, smoke charring hooded the masonry over every aperture like black eyelids. The gaping holes yawned into the darkness behind. It looked as though the building had had its teeth knocked out.

To the left of the soup shop, the glass-fronted barber's was still open, and through the window, gowned men sat in chrome chairs having their hair cut and beards trimmed. It reminded me of how much Dad had loved popping in there in the evening, as much for a chat as for a haircut. I suddenly felt nostalgic for my childhood, and a life which was more innocent.

'S'cuse me, love.' Behind me, a discombobulated voice penetrated my mind. 'Can you ring her bell? I've got a delivery here and eight more to do after this one.'

I turned and saw a Waitrose delivery driver, holding a plastic crate of shopping.

'Who's it for?'

'Mrs Feldman.' He strode towards the door of the newsagent. 'It's her regular order.'

'It's OK. Leave it there. I'll take it in for her.'

The puffer-jacketed driver didn't seem bothered who I was, or need any further encouragement. He yanked the shopping bags from the box and stacked them against the shop front. 'Cheers, darlin'.'

I rang the bell.

A few moments later, Agnieszka came down and opened the door.

'Your mum's Waitrose delivery has just arrived.' I pointed at the bags. 'I told the guy to leave—'

'Come in. Come in. You've saved me. Mum's got all Dad's photographs out. I've seen them a million times, but she wants to show me each one again.' She grabbed a couple of carrier bags.

Her good humour made me wonder whether she knew that we'd interviewed Olaf. 'I'll give you a hand.'

'Thanks. Tomasz orders it for her every month. He even gets her Jewish food.' She pushed the door open with her foot. 'Olaf's busy so I've sent the girls home with his parents. I don't feel safe having them here, but I can't leave Mum on her own. She's scared stiff but too bloody stubborn to admit it. That Star of David business has shaken her.'

There was no awkwardness when Agnieszka mentioned her husband. Had he really not told her about LfA and the flash mob?

'Olaf's working,' she said. 'Someone's forgotten their tax return and needs some accounts done quickly.'

That wasn't a good sign. 'Has your husband spoken to you about an organisation called LfA?'

She frowned. 'Doesn't ring a bell.'

'They campaign against gentrification.'

Confusion spread over her face. 'Olaf?'

I followed her through the shop towards the stairs. 'I take it you didn't know?'

'I don't think so. Why? He probably belongs to lots of organisations for his job.'

'Could you stop a minute?' I didn't want to discuss my concerns in front of Rosa.

She turned on the stairs. Put the bags down. 'What's this about?'

'This group, LfA, may have been responsible for the flash mob. We received an anonymous call from someone purporting to be from them. We haven't been able to trace its source or authenticity. Your husband denies any current involvement with the group, but its website is registered to him.' I waited for her to absorb the news.

She sank down onto one of the steps. 'Christ.' She held her head between her palms. 'There's got to be some mistake. What does Olaf say?'

'That he ceased involvement with LfA years ago.'

Agnieszka let out a deep sigh of relief.

'However – he hasn't been able to provide any evidence to support that.'

She stared down at the stairs as she absorbed the implications of what I'd said. 'There must be some mistake. Surely?'

'We hope so,' I said gently.

'Why didn't he tell me? I need to speak to him.' She got up and continued carrying her mum's shopping upstairs and I followed her, aware that I'd dropped a bomb on her world.

Upstairs, Agnieszka quickly dumped the shopping on the landing and scurried off towards one of the bedrooms. 'Say hello to Mum if you like,' she said over her shoulder as she padded across the carpet. 'She'll be upset if she knows you came but didn't say hi.'

*

Along the corridor, Rosa was in her bedroom, sorting through what I assumed were Józef's belongings. From the side, her slender frame made her look vulnerable. Her elbows were clenched against her body and she was holding an item to her nose and drinking in its smell. Away from the ground-floor walls, the room felt less damp but didn't have proper heating, just an electric bar heater. On the outside wall, the wood-chip wallpaper was peeling away from the plaster around the window, where a pipe or gutter had been leaking. This wasn't a year of poor maintenance. Had the decline been so gradual over the years that it hadn't registered? Or had Rosa really not realised how bad things had got? 'Knock, knock,' I said.

'Hello, Maya, love.' She was perching on the edge of the bed, on a floral counterpane, kneading a man's shirt and staring at it, as though she couldn't quite believe that its owner wasn't going to wear it again.

'Oh, Mrs Feldman.' It was a heart-breaking sight.

'I keep expecting him to walk through the door. To hear his whistle. Smell his clothes when he'd been smoking. Hear him calling up the stairs. It's been a year, but I still can't believe I'm not going to see him again.'

I swallowed, not wanting to burden her with my own grief by saying I knew exactly what she meant.

She placed the shirt on the bed next to a cluster of photographs and her hand lingered for a moment on the cloth. 'These are from when we got married.' She picked one up, in a polished silver multi-frame. 'In over forty years of marriage, we were best friends.' There were no tears in Rosa's eyes, none streaming down her face, but the sunken eye sockets and dark bags under them suggested she was resigned to her losses, and had been crushed by them.

I took the battered frame, eager not to say anything which would upset Rosa further. In one of the photos, a bright-eyed couple beamed at each other in spring sunshine. Guests cheered as Rosa got ready to launch her bouquet into the crowd. 'What a lovely picture. And precious memories.'

'There are more there beneath the glass.' She pointed at the wooden dressing table by the wall. 'There are a few of Józef with some of his friends from the tennis club, and Agnieszka and Tomasz when they were babies.'

I glided over to the antique dresser and my gaze fell on the pictures. They'd all faded and gone brown. It seemed insensitive to whisk Rosa through her memories and dash off. I removed the mirror, her hairbrush, the perfume; lifted the glass carefully and slid out the delicate images. They curled in my hand. I studied each one before passing them over. Józef Feldman with an older man, outside the shop. 'Was this his father?'

'That's right.'

In another, Józef stood proudly holding a tennis racquet. Time and sunlight hadn't dulled the huge grin on his face.

I chuckled. 'He was sporty, then?'

Rosa nodded.

In another, Józef was in Brick Lane with three other men. They were outside the barber's, all wearing suits, and laughing and smoking while they chatted amiably. 'I wonder what they were laughing at. I looked closer and – 'Oh my gosh.' I peered again. 'That's . . . ' I turned to Rosa in disbelief. Looked at the image again. 'That's Dad.'

'Show me,' Rosa said, her eyes shimmering with excitement.

The room stood still. I drank in the familiar image; let my eyes feast on every pixel of his face, his hair, his kind eyes. My thoughts were spinning with the shock of seeing his photograph. I handed the image to Rosa.

'The one smoking the roll-up? That's right.' She paused. 'How silly of me. Things have been so hectic, I must've forgotten. Now what was his name? Kass? Kaz?'

'Kazi, people called him. Kazol Rahman.'

'That's it. *Kazi Rahman*.' She chuckled, as though memories were trickling into her mind, warming her. 'He and Józef met over there at the barber's. He always enjoyed your father's company. Said he told good stories.' She chuckled.

A smile stretched over my face. 'He did. Sadly, he . . . he left us. In 1990.' The familiar pain knifed at my insides before the automatic response emerged. 'He popped out to get candles during a power cut and didn't come back. We've never seen him since.' I heard the words leave my mouth and it was as though someone else had said them, as if in the intervening years of trying to cut myself off from the pain of Dad's disappearance, it was someone else's father who had left and never come back.

'Oh, Maya, love. I am sorry.' Rosa was trembling, one hand clasped to her mouth. 'Now you mention it, I remember something about that. I think we all thought he'd died.' Her voice was a whisper. 'And you never found out what happened?'

I shook my head, keenly aware of how many times I'd been asked the same question in the last twenty-nine years.

'Or whether he's even alive?'

I bit back a gulp. 'Until recently, nothing.' I still hadn't had the courage to read the fingerprint analysis from the lab. So much depended on the results. 'Mum's struggled . . . and never wanted to talk about it.' Talking to Rosa felt different from the nosey questions of peers and strangers. 'We've never been able to find out what prompted it. One moment he was there and then he'd gone.' I remembered opening the door that evening when the flat bell rang, expecting Dad to be there. But he hadn't been. Just the . . . 'Oh my God. The *smell*.' I stared at Rosa. 'I hadn't registered the tobacco smell on the landing that night. Someone left candles and four bagels in a bag at the front door. My sister and I always thought it was Dad – but we've never known for certain. If the landing smelled of his tobacco, it must've been him.' I felt elated. Seeing the picture of him, and talking to someone who knew him, must've loosened the memories. It made me hungry for more information. For the stuff I didn't know. 'Did Józef see much of Dad?' Recollections were stirring at the edges of my consciousness.

'Oh, yes. They were great friends for many years. They belonged to a few of the same clubs and would spend hours discussing politics and religion.' A warm laugh bounced around the room. It was heartening to see a smile on her aching features. 'Your father was interested in finding out about Judaism and Józef had never met a Sufi before. They both found each other—'

'Was Dad a Sufi?' It was a minor detail and only bothered me because it was something else I'd forgotten about him.

She looked puzzled. 'I'm sure that's what Józef said.' She paused to review what she knew. 'I don't want to talk out of turn.' Her fingers were pulling at her lip. 'Yes, he did.' She frowned. 'I suppose you must've been young when he left.'

'I was twelve.' I still remembered it vividly. The tense atmosphere when he came home from work. The sharp words between Mum and Dad, and then him leaving. The candles and bagels. 'It was a long time ago.' I was walking up and down Rosa's bedroom, scouring my memory for any hints or mentions of Dad having been a Sufi.

Rosa was still looking thoughtful. 'Józef had a nickname for your dad because he was always reading verse.' She smiled. 'What was it now?' She tapped her lips gently.

I was eager for this new piece of information.

'Ba . . .' She broke off. Looked at the photograph again. 'Baba. That was it. He called him Baba.'

The name rang a bell. Something to do with Dad telling Jasmina and I about whirling dervishes once in our old flat in Sylhet. My head was thick with thoughts. 'Who are the other two?'

'Let me see.' She put her glasses back on. 'This one is Ody. That's what Józef called him. Can't remember his surname but I'm sure he was from Uganda. The other one is Cyril. He was born in Bow.'

'I remember them now. They were often at your shop. Can I take a picture of this? Jasmina would love to see it.'

'Take it. There are lots more somewhere. If only I could find things in this darn pl—'

'Oh, no, I couldn't take it.' I snapped a couple of photos on my phone and gave it back to her. 'This'll do fine. Thank you.' And then I realised that I had simply come to say hello and I'd got lost in reverie about my father. 'I'm so sorry. I hadn't meant to talk about my family. It was a shock seeing Dad like that.' I was looking round the room for an anchor. 'Could I nip to your loo?'

'Of course, dear. It's at the end of landing.'

Along the corridor, in the bathroom, I was relieved to feel the cold air on my face and be alone. It had been an odd conversation, and my mind was aflutter with thoughts of Dad. The vivid memories of the night he left, and our abject confusion. The harsh words with Mum in gabbled Sylheti; him telling us to be good for our mother; Mum's sickening scream once he'd shut the door behind him. And once again I felt the pain of the two questions which had been ghosts for Jasmina, Sabbir and I ever since that day: whether the person who left candles and bagels on the doorstep was Dad, and what Mum knew about him leaving.

*

Ten minutes later, Rosa and Agnieszka were seeing me out when voices caught my attention over at *Alchemia*, the new Polish bar which was two doors along from the arson site. The building's slick black fascia and smoky glass stood out amongst the dated decor of the other businesses. The shop door was open, and the lights were on, giving a glimpse of a black bar with chrome stools. In the doorway, a small woman in an apron was cleaning the windows in the dark.

Dan had arrived and was walking over to us. 'Thought I might find you here.' He grinned at me. 'Any sign of Ali?'

I shook my head.

'That's the Posners' old place,' said Rosa, behind me. 'Do you remember, Agnieszka?' Nostalgia had crept over Rosa's features again and she was watching the woman clean. 'So, we've lost our shoemaker and got another bar.'

'I've been spying on her from upstairs while you and Mum were chatting,' Agnieszka said. 'She and her hubby are acquaintances of Olaf's. He does their accounts.' She turned to her mother. 'Anyway, let's get you back in the warm, Mum. Thanks for your help with the bags, Inspector.'

'It's no trouble.' My mind was buzzing with questions, including why the bar owners hadn't come up in the H-2-H inquiries or mobile phone ring-fencing.

Agnieszka and Rosa clattered through the shop, and back up to the flat, and Dan walked over to speak to the crime scene guard. It was then that the turmoil of the day hit me. I stood outside the newsagent's, facing the street, taking in the cool evening air. What an awful day it had been. The squat, Ali, the UnSub. And now this stuff with Dad.

I sank to the ground and perched on the shop step for a few moments, my back against the door. How I wished Jasmina had been with me to see the photos of Dad with Józef and the other two men. Had she forgotten things about Dad too? I stood up, wanting to see Rosa's shop as I had as a child. I turned and looked up at the glass-panelled door. The CLOSED sign. The window displays.

And there it was, above the door frame, the Star of David that Rosa had seen earlier, etched into the brickwork.

And I couldn't shake the uneasy feeling I'd had when I first saw it. In fact, the more I thought about it, the more certain I was that we were missing something. What if it wasn't a despicable act of anti-Semitism, but a missing link in our case?

Dan, 9.30 p.m.

'What d'you think it means?' Maya asked him, and pointed at the Star of David outside the newsagent's. She'd called Dan over to look at it again, and he could feel her studying his reactions.

'Definitely looks new.' He shone his torch on the brickwork and stepped back to get a longer view. 'Could be kids. Most people will know Rosa's a Jew. Maybe anti-Semitism . . . ?'

Dan caught Maya's worried expression.

'On the other hand,' he looked over at the remains of the soup shop, '. . . it could be those low-lifes leaving us a message that they've got their sights on Rosa's shop too?'

'Which d'you reckon is most likely?'

Dan sucked air in through his teeth. 'That's a tough call. But having her windows smashed is a lot less serious than having her shop set light to.' He glanced at Maya. 'What's your take on it? You're usually Ms Instinct.'

'Same as you. If the fire at the soup shop wasn't intended to be serious, and got out of control quicker than they expected, these scum-bags could have the same plan for Rosa's place. The star could be the arsonists leaving us a message that Rosa's shop is the next to be torched.' She craned her neck to get a good look at *Alchemia*. 'Isn't that a CCTV camera over there? It looks like one of those high-spec rotating ones. If it is, it might have some film of Rosa's shop when

178

she was in hospital. Let's go and see what the shopkeeper can tell us. See if she'll let us view their CCTV.'

As they approached *Alchemia*, the woman they'd seen was replacing the COMING SOON sign in the shop window with OPENING NEXT WEEK. The tinted glass was even darker than it had looked, and the charcoal-grey interior gave a disconcerting impression.

'They've transformed this place in the last twenty-four hours,' Dan muttered. 'They must've had half the local tradies on their job.'

They showed their warrants and Maya introduced themselves. 'Are you the owner?'

'Yes. Monika Waglowa.' She had a pleasant manner and a cheerful face.

'You're working late.'

'Tell me about it,' she said wearily. 'We lost so much time yesterday and we're opening soon.'

'That's what we'd like to speak to you about,' Maya said. 'Our records show that the house-to-house teams didn't manage to speak to you after the fire at the soup shop yesterday. Weren't you around?'

'I was at home all day, looking after my dad.' She continued to buff the glass as she spoke. 'He had a hip replacement last week and has moved in with us for a few weeks. The first I heard about the fire was when the fire brigade called me around two.'

'Where is home?'

'West Ham.'

'Was anyone working here on Friday?' Maya was peering through the window.

'Until the fire officers switched off the electricity.'

'What happened then?'

'I rang my husband and he locked the shop up.'

'One more thing.' Maya pointed at the CCTV camera and Dan could see her assessing viewing angles.

His phone vibrated.

'Does your system at the front reach the newsagent's?' she asked.

'Yes, it covers two premises either side of this one, on both sides of the street. You're welcome to have a look at it, but I'll have to get my husband over. I haven't a clue how to work it.'

Dan's phone vibrated again. He scanned his messages and felt his spirits rise. This was what they'd been waiting for. Indra Ulbiene had been discharged from hospital. Hopefully now she'd tell them who the woman was that Simas had been having an affair with.

Maya, 10 p.m.

It took several knocks to rouse Indra, and her pretty face was bleached of colour when she finally opened the door of her sister's flat in Upton Park. A white hospital wrist-band stuck out of the arm of a fluffy silver dressing gown.

'I'm sorry it's so late.' I smiled apologetically. 'I know you've only just got home but I need to ask you a couple of urgent questions. Could I come in?'

Indra groaned loudly, and I didn't blame her. She turned slowly, as though it was uncomfortable to move, and led me inside. A waft of something floral greeted me. Despite her surgery, her movements were agile and graceful, as if she'd had dance training.

A pang of guilt jabbed at me for descending on her so quickly after her discharge. I'd keep it as brief as possible so she could get some rest.

'Marta's at work. I'd just got into bed when you knocked.' Her speech was flat, and I got the feeling that the last couple of days had squeezed almost every trace of life out of her.

I followed her into the kitchen.

'My sister left some food out for me but I'm not hungry.' She stood at the worktop, coat-hanger thin in the baggy gown. Next to a pot of multi-vitamins and the microwave, cling-film lay over a plate of chicken and potatoes. 'I don't know how to tell her, but I don't want this food. Or vitamins. *Or* bloody lavender oil.' She sounded exhausted. 'I just want to lie down and sleep.'

I took a gulp. 'Why don't you pop it in the fridge? You might fancy it tomorrow.' I paused while she got her bearings, then gestured to the table. 'Shall we sit down?' I pulled a chair out for her and got myself settled. 'As you know, we've been fairly certain from the start that the male body in the fire is your husband's, and we've had DNA confirmation of that.'

She didn't comment, just nodded her head up and down in large sweeps. 'And the woman?'

'That's what I need to ask you about. We still don't know who she is.' This was going to be a hard question to ask, but we had to know. 'I realise you might not feel sympathetic towards her, and I'd probably feel the same, but we'd really appreciate your help. She will have relatives who will be wondering where she is.' I paused again to see how my request was landing. 'She may have dependents who are relying on her.'

Indra faced me, pools for eyes.

I swallowed hard. 'If you have any idea who she might be, please tell us.'

Indra's hands were shaking and she lowered her gaze.

'At the moment, we don't know who or what was the target of the fire.' I spoke gently. 'As long as we only have your husband's ID, we only have half the information we need to find out who did this.'

She looked up now and fixed her eyes on mine. They were deep, dark green. 'You might think so, but the truth is I have no idea. When Simas and I moved to Brick Lane, and bought the shop, we said we'd make a fresh start.' She stopped, as if she wanted to check whether she was sure about what she was going to say. 'We made a pact. He'd stop shagging other women and I'd stop being suspicious. I wasn't convinced, but eventually I let Simas persuade me.'

I knew what was coming.

'Unfortunately, only one of us kept our word.'

'I'm sorry to hear that. I know it must be incredibly painful to talk about and it's rubbish timing after . . . ' I couldn't say it. 'We spoke to a shopkeeper who told us you'd accused her of having an affair with Simas. She said you apologised, and admitted that you'd made a mistake. Now, that's none of our business except that she said that you know who the woman is.'

Indra's eyes narrowed.

'Who is she?'

'She's lying.'

'Are you sure you don't know?' I asked gently. 'If it was her in the fire, she may have parents somewhere who are out of their mind with worry. What if she's got a child at home?' I thought of the Polish woman at *Alchemia*, looking after her dad. 'Or an elderly relative?'

'She's making it up. She'll just be saying it to make herself look like a victim.' Her mouth contorted as the words came out. 'I bet it was that red-haired woman who sells clothes? Natassja?'

The force of Indra's anger hit me, and I stood up and took a deep breath. I understood how betrayed she must feel and knew her anger wasn't directed at me. I kneeled in front of the wooden table where Indra was sitting, and spoke gently. 'If you know the names of any of the women your husband had relationships with, Mrs Ulbiene, please tell us so that we can find out who is responsible for his death.'

She was silent, and I hoped she was weighing up what I'd said. I was going to have to mention children to a woman who'd just lost her child and her husband, and found out that he'd been cheating. It seemed so cruel. 'If the woman in the fire has young children at home, they might not be able to get water or know how to get help.' I paused again to let her absorb the information. 'At best, they may be scared stiff. But if they've been without water since first thing yesterday, that's two days already. A young child, or one's who's sick, might not last much longer. If you know something, please —'

'OK, OK.' She raised her hand to silence me. 'Enough of the emotional blackmail.' Despair threaded through her delicate features. 'What Natassja said is true. I do know who she is but I don't know her name or much about her. She lives over in Essex and has a child.'

Finally.

The news was bitter-sweet but at least we had a bit more to go on, and the team could check for Missing Persons in Essex.

'How do you know that?'

'I overheard Simas on the phone one day. He didn't know I was there. He said something like, "Get the kid sorted and I'll come over to Essex later."'

'You didn't catch a name? Any more details?'

She shook her head. 'He rang off after that and I froze. I didn't want him to know that I'd overheard. I also found some restaurant receipts from Essex.'

I paused to recalibrate; to decide what else I needed to ask her. 'Can we go back to yesterday for a moment? When you left the shop to go to your sister's, did you believe your husband when he said he wasn't feeling well?'

'*Taip*. Inspector, I don't know if you've ever had a partner who's cheated on you but it's difficult to move on. The . . . *abejonių* . . . what's the word? Doubt?'

'Yes.'

'Doubt eats away at you like a cancer. Once a lover has been unfaithful, you become suspicious of everything they do. I told Simas I wanted a divorce. He begged me not to leave him. We made an agreement. The rest is as I've told you.'

I got the picture. I admired her. What she had done was brave. 'Without wishing to pry too much, why did you decide to stay with your husband?'

'We are immigrants. We are from a country no-one has heard of and we speak a language no-one understands except us. Other than my *sesuo*, I have no family here. Simas was my family for six years. I forgave him because I hoped he'd be different. That way, I would have no regrets.'

It was an extraordinarily brave attitude and I admired her courage. She was going to need it to sustain her. 'Did you get any antagonism from any residents or shopkeepers in the area?'

'Of course. Brick Lane is very cliquey, but I think that's the way immigrants end up living, you know? When we move, we form cliques with other people like us.'

'If you had to put money on who might have wanted Simas dead, who would that be?' I was hoping she would mention why, when she rang 999, she'd said she thought someone had murdered her husband.

Indra shifted in her seat and winced as the movement in her abdomen caused her pain. She got up and went over to the kettle. Shook it and flicked it on to boil. 'When you live like Simas, taking what you want and not caring about the people you hurt, there will always be people who want you dead. When Tomasz told me about the fire, it was my first thought. I can't really explain why – just that it's something I've been scared about the whole time Simas and I have been together.' She switched the kettle off again and took a bottle of vodka from a cupboard. 'In lots of ways I made excuses for him. I told myself he wasn't a bad person, not like Artem. He couldn't help it. That, despite the other women, he loved me. I tried to make myself believe all of it because I was scared to think otherwise.' Her eyes flinched with pain as she glugged vodka into a glass.

It was a story I'd heard on many occasions, yet each time it was slightly different, and it shocked me anew. I was relieved she'd explained, as it meant I hadn't needed to force the issue.

'Also,' she said, and then took a gulp of vodka, 'when Tomasz called,' she swallowed it and coughed, 'I can't remember exactly what he said, but I think he asked if anyone was in the shop. I know now that it was just because he was worried about us, but his call sent me into a panic.' Her face was distraught. 'As for who might have wanted Simas out of the picture, I gave you a list of all the people I could think of. There will be many more I've forgotten.'

I took a deep breath. 'How did your sister get on with Simas?'

A guffaw spilled out of Indra's mouth. 'She hated him. And I don't blame her.'

'Could she have wanted him dead?'

'In her head, yes. Most of the time. But as for murdering him? I doubt it very much.' She returned to the table and sat back down. 'Look, my sister had a very bad time when she first came to the UK and she's still – how should I put it? – pretty crazy from it. When you go through something like that, your ideal of normal changes. When you need money, you don't ask questions. You snatch it and run.' There was a look in her eye which told me that she had been in this situation herself; that life hadn't ever been rosy with Simas, even in the honeymoon stage of their relationship. 'My sister isn't forgiving, and I don't blame her one bit.'

'Did anyone know that your husband was going to be in the shop yesterday?'

She shrugged. 'We didn't announce it, if that's what you mean. We closed the shop because Simas had *gripas*. I had a hospital appointment for the baby, so I left him to it.'

'Didn't you want your husband to come to the hospital with you?'

She shook her head. 'Simas didn't want children.'

It wasn't what I'd asked. 'We spoke to your brother-in-law, Artem. How did you get on with him?'

She laughed. It was an irritated cackle. 'If you spoke to him, you'll know. Artem likes to make my life as difficult as he can, and that's included causing trouble with Simas. He tried to kiss me twice when my husband was working and had the cheek to tell Simas that I tried to kiss him. I suppose because I rejected his advances, he's hated me ever since. He laughs at me, like I'm stupid, saying that Simas still screws other women so why don't I join his game?'

'And did you?' I was remembering the things that Artem had said about the baby's father being anybody.

'No, I didn't. He's a liar. He bad-mouths me to everyone. He's either a bit of a psycho or he's jealous.'

'How did Simas and Artem get on?'

Here her face changed. 'They were close. Brothers, you know? They watched each other's backs. But something between them has always caused friction. I don't know what it was.'

'Did you tell your husband about Artem's advances toward you?'

'*Taip*. Simas was really angry. He didn't want to believe me. He went to see Artem, who told him that I'd hit on him. Artem knew that his brother would believe him over me, and he did.' She shrugged. Defeated. 'Simas went to see Artem feeling furious with him and came home angry with me. *Jis visiškai bastard*. Artem has no respect for women. Not me. Not his wife. Not his kids.' Her eyes closed as though thinking about the situation was painful, and she wanted to block it out.

I was trying to put myself in her shoes. It was easy to say that you wouldn't put up with a cheating partner but until you were in the situation, it was speculation. What did you do if you were madly in love with that person? Or were financially dependent on them? Indra struck me as a resourceful woman. Her sister had got a job in Tomasz' club, and I was sure that Indra could have done something similar if she had chosen to leave Simas. 'Have you thought about what you will do now?'

She shook her head. 'Wait a while. Start again.' She stared into space. 'I won't go back to Lithuania. Marta needs me and, to be honest, I need her right now.'

A few of the little things that Indra had said about Marta were niggling at the back of my mind. I was aware that they were both each other's alibis. Neither of them was above suspicion and both had motives for killing Simas and his mistress. I'd discuss it with the team. We needed to corroborate their stories – or dismiss them. What struck me was that, underneath the bravery of Indra's words, I sensed bitterness, and not unfairly. She was a survivor, I felt sure of that but, having had a miscarriage, she was vulnerable and needed to get her strength back. Against all the odds, Indra's story was starting to stack up. Then, something occurred to me. 'Did Simas know about the baby?'

Indra looked at me, blinking while she gathered her thoughts. 'No.' She paused. 'I told you; he didn't want children. I got pregnant by accident and I planned to tell him when I passed the first three months.'

'I need to ask you something a bit delicate. Was it Simas' baby?'

'*Žinoma.*' She looked confused. 'Ah. Artem's been telling you I'm a whore?' She rolled her eyes and looked to the heavens. '*Jēzus Kristus.*'

Our conversation was interrupted by the sound of voices and the front door closing. Giggles and squeals tinkled down the hall. Indra's sister was home.

And she wasn't alone.

Maya, 10.45 p.m.

I left Indra with my thoughts spiralling. It had been a long, exhausting day and part of me wanted to go home and collapse into bed, but my mind wouldn't settle until I'd told Dan about Simas' mistress, and found out whether we'd received news on Ali.

Questions were tumbling over in my mind when I arrived back at the MIT offices, and I hurried over to see if Dan was still here. For once, the office was quiet, and children's giggles and shrieks rang out in the incident room. Dan was still at his desk, captivated by whatever was on his screen, and didn't seem to hear me approach. An empty sandwich box sat next to his mug, and his planner showed a page-view of the months in 2020. The full-screen view on his monitor showed his two daughters, Kiara and Sharna. One was spooning breakfast cereal into her mouth while the other plaited her sister's hair.

'You've been saying that for ages,' Sharna's voice was thick with disappointment.

I froze.

'Can you come for my party, Daddy?' Kiara joined in. 'Please say you will.'

'Very soon, I promise.' Dan's voice was gentle. 'It depends on my job here, you see.' He was trying to sound cheerful, but I caught the despondency in his tone. 'And Mummy's been offered a new job outside Sydney, so we're still figuring out how to arrange things.'

'But Daddy, Christmas was ages ago. Like, months and months . . .'

Dan was massaging his neck muscles and rotating his head. 'I know, sweetheart, but these things take time, and . . . *Kiara, eat properly.* You've dropped milk on your uniform and Mummy . . .'

I decided to pop to the loo and give them a bit of space.

In the toilets, I perched on a plastic chair and dumped my jacket down. Dougie would be at home, so I gave him a quick ring and checked my emails for developments. When I stood up, my reflection in the mirror made me chuckle: hair everywhere and barely a scrap of make-up remaining from this morning – but I didn't care.

When I got back to our cluster of desks, Dan was off Skype. He was hunched over the desk, with his head resting on folded arms.

'Phew,' I said loudly to announce my arrival. 'What a day.' I dumped my bag down and realised I'd left my jacket in the loo.

'You can say that again,' he grunted towards the floor.

'There's a cuppa here for you.'

He sat up. 'Think I need something stronger than that.' I'd rarely seen Dan cry but his eyes were pink and bloodshot.

'What's up?' I hoped he hadn't heard me come in a few minutes ago.

'I thought Aroona was coming round to the idea of moving over here but she's been offered a job in the outback. It's a one-year contract to start with, and she's just told me she wants to take it.'

Everyone in the team knew how much Dan struggled with being apart from his family. 'Oh, Dan. I'm so sorry. I know how much you miss them.' Presumably it would mean the girls going with her, but I didn't like to ask.

'It's just . . . oh, never mind.'

'A year will pass in no time.' I wasn't sure if this was helpful or not but was grappling for what to say.

'Maybe. Maybe not. The girls would love the outback, and short-term it would be a fabulous experience for them. It wasn't what I signed up for though. I agreed to the fast-track post here on the understanding that Aroona and the girls would follow me over, not move even further away.' He scrunched his sandwich box into a ball and lobbed it into the bin. 'I know Aroona. This means she's changed her mind.'

'Why don't you knock off? Grab a pint somewhere.'

He brushed crumbs off his desk and shook his head. 'Nah. I really don't fancy being on my own right now.' He closed the Skype tab. 'How'd you go with Indra? Any developments?'

I updated him on what had happened. On the board, the image of the female fire victim taunted me, and I added 'Essex' and 'child' to what we knew about her.

'Do you think Marta and Tomasz are an item?' He began bustling about, as though he was relieved for the distraction.

'They weren't employer-employee giggles. Put it that way. When they saw me, they reined it in, but it looked like they'd been drinking together.'

Dan straightened his back and rolled his neck again. 'While I was waiting for you I had a read of the update log. According to the police database, Marta Ulbiene first came to London six years ago on a deal from Lithuania which was described as "helping girls to study in Britain", but which turned out to be a trafficking scheme.' Dan angled his monitor so I could see the record.

'Christ. Poor Marta.' I remembered the impression I'd had when I'd talked to her at the hospital, and what Indra had just told me about her not being forgiving.

'She and six other girls ended up in a prostitution ring run by fellow Lithuanians in Beckton in a council flat.' Dan was paraphrasing. 'She was lucky to survive, by the sounds of it. One of the girls died of a heroin overdose and one was beaten to death by the men running the girls. Indra came over to the UK to look for her, reported her missing, and eventually the police busted the ring and Marta was saved. Indra stayed here to look after her sister, who was in a bad way. That was when Indra met Simas, and they got married soon after.'

'No wonder Marta's angry. The trafficking thing is bad enough but to be betrayed by fellow Lithuanians?' What an awful time the two of them had had. 'Is there any link with Tomasz Feldman?'

'At the moment, no, apart from the fact he's her employer. What happened at the flat when they arrived?'

'There was some hurried talking between the two sisters in Lithuanian. Tomasz clocked me, made out it was a common occurrence that he dropped Marta home, and made a swift departure.'

'Definitely an item then.' Dan laughed.

'Back in a sec.' I nipped over to the toilets to fetch my jacket and was carrying it back when I saw that Dan was waving the landline receiver in the air.

'Maya, quick,' he bellowed across the office. 'Someone on the blower. Insists on speaking to you.'

'Who is it?' I dumped my jacket down.

'Someone's found a petrol can and a bag in their back garden. She's seen you on the appeals.'

I felt a lurch of excitement. 'Can you track the call?'

'I'll have a go.'

'What's her name?'

'She wouldn't say. Husband found them.'

I had to be quick before she rang off. I grabbed the receiver, took a deep breath to calm my voice and released the mute button. 'You're through to the incident room at Limehouse Police Station, DI Rahman speaking. I gather you've found something in your garden?'

'Yes, um . . . hello.' The woman's voice was shaky. 'I saw the press thingy on the news earlier. It's about the fire at the old bagel place in Brick Lane. . . Well, I think it might be.'

I tucked the receiver under my ear and reached for my notepad. Looked at Dan to see how he was getting on. 'Go on.'

'It might be nothing, but my Sid's just locked up the shop and was having a smoke in the back garden. He spotted one of them jerry cans. Stinks of petrol, he says. We're on the same side of the road as the soup place, three shops along. The off-licence. There's a bag too, one of them canvas hold-all things. It's all over-grown with weeds and whatnot out back, so we didn't see them before now. He reckons someone must've lobbed them over the fence. D'you think it's got anything to do with the fire?'

*

Fifteen minutes later, Dan and I were back in Brick Lane, on tenter-hooks in the alley behind the shops while the CSI team picked over every inch of the Walkers' back garden for evidence.

'You don't have to stay,' I said to Dan. 'There's no point us both being shattered tomorrow.' My body ached with exhaustion.

'Nah. You're alright. They might need someone to deliver samples to the lab. Speed things up.'

'I know it's not a case priority, but I can't stop thinking about Ali. Uniform kindly agreed to pop into some of the youth centres on their patrols. Hopefully someone will have seen him.'

Dan shook his head. 'After what he said about Kyle, he's probably gone to ground.'

'In another filthy squat?' It felt wrong. 'With another load of druggies and criminals?'

'I know you won't want to hear it but whenever I've seen a kid look that scared, it's rarely ended well.' He scratched the stubble on his chin. 'I'm worried about you, Maya. Don't get too involved. It won't help anyone. Plus – the ID of the woman in the fire is more urgent than Ali. Nothing has happened to him yet.'

I rolled my eyes in protest although I knew what he was saying was right. 'Thanks for the pep talk, Guv.' I forced a laugh to conceal my reaction. 'While you were on HOLMES earlier, is there anything new on Kenny?'

He shook his head. 'His sort are good at keeping their identities concealed. This is his area of expertise to a tee.'

'Do you think that Kenny might be Frazer from the forum?'

'It's possible.' He kicked a can and sent it flying. 'It's what's so frustrating. There are so many strands to the investigation, it's difficult to know who's a person of interest and who's a suspect.' He turned to face me. 'What was your impression of Indra when you interviewed her? Do you think she's a contender for the arson still?'

'She certainly has a motive with her husband's infidelity. Simas didn't have a life insurance policy but the business is well-insured. She's understandably angry but she doesn't seem particularly upset about losing her husband.' I stopped. I knew that people felt and expressed emotion differently. 'She seems genuinely broken by the news that he was still having affairs, and by losing the baby, but I'm not convinced by her alibi or Marta's. They've both used each other which is rather convenient.' If Indra had loved Simas, even if she was angry with him, wouldn't she have been more upset? Perhaps Simas had been simply a means of security or maybe she'd finally fallen out of love with him? That might have made it easier for her to have put up with his cheating, turn the other cheek, pretend to be bothered by it while all the time getting on with her own life. Particularly when she found out that she was pregnant. Perhaps she was planning to leave him all along? 'What about Marta? Indra told me that the trafficking had left her full of rage. She said Marta's idea of what was "normal" had gone awry. She also said that Marta hated Simas and she "hoped" Marta hadn't killed him.'

'Not that she definitely hadn't?' Dan seemed to have read my mind.

'No.' I recalled Indra's face when she said it. 'She didn't seem certain at all. She also told me that Simas didn't want children and that she hadn't told him she was pregnant. She said he was definitely the father of the baby, but Artem told us that he wasn't so sure.'

'Ah. Don't kill me. With Mrs Walker's phone call, I forgot to tell you. Alexej checked who was listed as the baby's father on the hospital records.' Dan put his arms up, pretending that I was going to hit him. 'I'll bet you a tenner you can't guess who it is.'

'Spill.' I made as though I was going to clip him round the ear.

Shouts from Dougie interrupted me. 'Maya. *Maya*. We've found something.'

I felt hope soar.

'Stay there. I'll bring it out.'

Dan reached the gate before me.

'There's petrol on the inside of the hold-all so I reckon it was used to transport the can,' Dougie told us. 'But this . . . ? Looks like a burner to me.' He held up an evidence bag with a mobile phone in it and handed it to me. 'I'll get the hold-all processed. We've got the prints we need, so your techs can get cracking on the comms data.'

'Cheers,' I said.

'With any luck,' Dougie added, 'they've been as careless with the phone as everything else.'

11.30 p.m.

When the girl opened her eyes, her head was spinning.

Click, clack. Click, clack.

Someone was sitting at the end of the bed, playing with beads. A dark figure, like on the telly. And wearing a hood.

'Thirsty,' she mumbled. 'Please may I—?'

A gloved hand loomed towards her and everything went black.

Maya, 11.30 p.m.

'For God's sake, don't keep me in suspense any longer', I said. 'Who's the father of Indra's baby?'

Dan and I had the burner and were on our way back to the office. 'It's Tomasz Feldman.'

'Tomasz? That's a bit messy, if we're right that he's seeing Marta now. And I only spoke to Indra a few hours ago. She told me she'd been faithful to Simas, and that he was definitely the baby's father.'

'That's another lie she's told us,' Dan said knowingly. 'Doesn't make her word seem reliable, does it?'

'I agree.' The dashboard clock said eleven thirty. 'Tomasz' bar has a late licence at weekends and will still be open. Let's pay him a visit and find out what's going on. If Tomasz and Indra were having an affair, that might increase Indra's motive and give Tomasz one too.'

Once we arrived back at Limehouse Police Station, I waited in the car outside while Dan delivered the mobile phone to the technicians. I reviewed the day's events. It had been full of nasty surprises, and I doubted it was about to get much better.

*

A quarter of an hour later, we arrived at Tomasz's bar. The two bouncers were outside, under the awning, looking as off-putting as they had the day before. One of them led us inside and escorted us along the corridor to the boss' office. The door was ajar and from inside, we could hear Rosa's son, bellowing into what I guessed was the phone.

'Of course it matters,' Tomasz yelled. 'Find out what the hell happened and get back to me ASAP.'

Above the door, another state-of-the-art CCTV camera quickly positioned itself to capture our arrival.

The knuckle-faced security guard rapped on the oak door and the conversation stopped immediately.

'Come.' Tomasz was behind his desk, sitting in a large high-backed chair. As soon as he saw us, he got to his feet. The phone call had obviously been of a tense nature and this was reflected in his body language: his brow was crunched into an irritated frown; his lips were pursed and the expression in his eyes was hard, as though he'd had to concentrate on the conversation and now needed to calm down and prepare himself for whatever was to come.

'Everything alright?' I asked.

'Oh, staff, that's all. Nothing serious.' He forced a smile. 'That'll be all, thanks, Aliasj.'

The bouncer left.

'What can I help you with?' He gestured to the seats in front of his desk. 'Rather late, isn't it?'

I preferred to stand. 'What's your relationship with Indra Gudelis?'

'I know her through their shop, opposite Mum's.'

'And her sister?'

'She works for me.'

'Did you know Indra was pregnant?'

'Of course.' He frowned suspiciously. 'She lost the baby when she fell in the street the other day. Marta took her to have her scan at the hospital. She asked if she could swap shifts so she could accompany her sister.'

'Did Indra tell you who the father was?' I studied his tells.

'Why would she?'

'Because *you* were.' I looked straight at him, watching every muscle in his face.

He sank back down on his enormous leather chair, his face drained of colour. 'I assume you aren't joking?' His cheek was twitching.

'The hospital confirmed it earlier. It's on the baby's records.' For a moment, I felt sorry for him. Unless he was an accomplished actor, the news was obviously a shock, but we had to assume it might not be. If he'd known, it gave him a possible motive for wanting Simas out of the way.

He closed his eyes slowly and placed his palms over his face, gently shaking his head from side to side.

Dan was tapping into his phone.

'Would you like to tell us what your relationship is with Indra and Marta?'

'I don't have a relationship with Indra. We slept together a couple of times around three months ago. She was wanting company and – how can I put it without sounding like a heartless bastard? – attention. I'd seen her a few times when I visited Mum and she'd made it obvious she liked me. On one occasion, she'd had a row with a local shopkeeper who she thought her husband was . . . Let's just say she was upset about her husband's infidelity and either wanted to get even, or was bored. I don't know, and I didn't ask.' He opened a bottle of water and took a large swig. 'I had no idea she'd got pregnant. She told me she was on the pill. Christ, what a mess.'

'And her sister?'

'Yeah. We are . . . not seeing each other yet but . . . ' He rubbed at the back of his neck while he thought what to say. 'Oh, hell.' He slammed his fist down on the table and stared at us both. 'I don't know if Marta knows that Indra and I slept together. Have you told her? You really aren't shitting me about this, are you?'

I shook my head. 'You can check with the hospital, I'm sure, or with Indra. As for Marta, I don't know what she knows, I'm afraid.' I wasn't about to start moralising. He'd said that he regarded himself as single. 'What is the situation with Marta?'

'I really like her. She and I only got together in the last couple of weeks. It might sound sordid, both sisters and all that, but nothing's happened with Marta and I don't want it to until all this is over and Indra is back on her feet again.' He blushed. 'Marta and I have had a couple of kisses and a bit of flirting. I'm assuming you've checked her background? The trafficking and—?'

'We have.' Dan's tone was solemn.

'I've been trying to persuade Marta to go out with me for a couple of months. I didn't tell her that I'd had a stupid fling with her sister because Marta was always teasing me about being a "lad", and I was worried that this would be proof and stop Marta and I getting together permanently. What a bloody idiot. I like Indra but not like that. It meant nothing. And now . . . now—'

'Are you sure Marta doesn't already know?'

Horror ran over his face. 'Shit. No. God, I really hope not. I need to go. I need to speak to Indra and find out what she's told her sister.' He grabbed up his phone.

'Hold on a moment,' I said firmly. 'With you being the baby's father, it might give you a motive for wanting Simas out of the way. Are you sure you don't have feelings for Indra?' It occurred to me that Marta could be his alibi.

'Of course I'm sure.' He looked indignant. 'I had no idea Indra had got pregnant.' He stuffed his keys in his jacket pocket. 'Why on earth would I want Simas and his girlfriend dead if I wanted to get together with Marta? It's hardly going to help, is it?' With that, he dashed past us and out of the room.

Maya, midnight

Beneath a cloudy sky, the streets of Whitechapel were full of shadows. Each time I moved, a shape appeared from a doorway or an alley, and the darkness seemed to swirl around me. The rain was a fine drizzle, the sort that made its way into your hair, ears and eyes, and drenched your clothing in minutes.

Under a thick coat, the stab-proof vest was tight, and the rain had already begun seeping through at the seams.

'Please. You have change?' A thin voice asked from the pavement. It was a teenage girl with deadened eyes, wrapped in a ripped tarpaulin, hair caked with dirt and despair.

I felt for some coins in my pocket and dropped them in her bowl. Was Ali here? Crashing in doorways and eating from bins?

My gloved hand went to my bag. I had to plough on for another hour, and keep distributing the photographs we had of Kenny Hayes and Ali. Once that was done, I wanted to get back home. It was time to read the Forensics report on the fingerprints on Mum's phone. If Dad was alive, I *had* to know – even if it turned my world upside down.

SUNDAY

Rosa, 7 a.m.

'It would help if you put the flipping light on. I can't see a thing.' Agnieszka's tone was snappy.

She and Rosa were in the garden at the back of the newsagent's. Once a much-loved family space, these days it was a mass of brambles and nettles.

'Here. Let me do it.' Agnieszka leant inside the ramshackle shed that had once housed the outside loo, and flicked the switch, but nothing happened. 'Great. The bulb's gone. What exactly are we looking for?' It was the second time she'd asked.

'Photographs of the funeral. I *told* you.' Rosa was impatient. She'd been awake most of the night, unable to stop thinking about Maya and her family.

'You got me out of bed at 7 a.m. to hunt for photos? Are you mad?'

Rosa yanked the handle on the rickety wooden door, trying to open it wider to let more light in. 'Oww. Stupid fingers.' She shook her hand and blew on it.

'Let me do it before you do yourself any more damage.'

'I'm sure I put a box of them in here after the funeral. I couldn't bear to keep seeing them. Try at the back.' She cupped her left hand round the aching fingers.

'Shift over then.'

Rosa shuffled out of Agnieszka's way. 'I've checked under the stairs and they aren't there. There may be some in the loft, but before either us gets up that dreadful ladder your father put up, I want to check the privy.' Rosa had been without Józef for a year and every day had been almost unbearable. Maya's anguish last night had moved her. For their father to have left, and for the family to have never found out whether he was dead or alive, they must have lived a daily hell.

Agnieszka got the shed door properly open and began rummaging. 'This needs a bloody good tidy.' She stopped. 'Can't we do this a bit later? Let me get dressed, and grab a coffee, and I'll clear it out for you. What's so urgent that we've got to find the photos now?'

'They're for DI Rahman.' Rosa told her daughter what Maya had said about Kazi.

'I think I remember something about that. They never found out what happened?'

'That's what she said. The thing is, I woke up this morning and remembered that Kazi came to your dad's funeral. Kazi, Ody and Cyril. I saw them there, as clear as day.' Rosa put her hand to her forehead. 'But now I'm wondering if I imagined it and I don't want to tell her unless I'm absolutely—'

'He *did*. He was there. They all were. I remember because Mr Rahman was telling the girls about the canal.' Agnieszka stopped. 'Given he was at Dad's funeral, most likely he's still alive. She must realise, surely?'

Rosa shook her head. 'It's why I don't want to tell her unless I'm sure.'

Agnieszka pushed the shed door shut and flicked the latch. 'C'mon. Let's go inside. I'll find the photos in a minute, even if it means getting up that bloody ladder.' She placed her hands on her mother's shoulders and gently guided her towards the back door of the shop. 'I've probably got some snaps of the funeral on my old phone. If I haven't, I doubt it matters. The local paper covered the funeral. They'll have loads of photographs. They're bound to have one of Mr Rahman.'

Brick Lane, 1984 – Maya

I can smell the sweetness of the dough as it cooks in the enormous ovens, and I yank my hand free of Jasmina's, and skip into the bagel shop. Behind us, even Sabbir is excited about the prospect of a warm, chewy bagel.

'Where's Dad gone?' I shout over my shoulder.

'Next door, to get a haircut,' Jasmina replies.

It's the weekend and we've left Mum at home to have a lie-in, and have come out early to enjoy the sun. We stand behind rows of hungry people, and peer at the bagels in the glass cabinets, mulling over the many choices before ordering the same as always. The smell of warm salt beef and pickles wafts through the shop, making my stomach rumble.

'Here you go.' Sabbir hands over the money and takes the paper bag, knowing that Jasmina and I will try to snatch ours from him before we've left the shop.

Back on the bustling street, we wait for Dad to emerge from the barber's next door. Over the road, the shopkeeper is arranging the window display at the newsagent's, and people are queuing at Posner's to get their shoes mended.

I've finished my bagel, and ease myself up onto tiptoes to see into the barber's. 'He's not here.' I turn to my brother.

'He'll be out in a minute.' Sabbir hands me a thin serviette. 'Here, wipe your mouth.'

I dab at my face half-heartedly and hand it back to him. Contort myself again to see into the shop. 'Can't see him.'

Jasmina's still eating her bagel. Far more ladylike than me, she savours each mouthful, enjoying the taste of the dough on her tongue.

At the window, my eyes search the build and clothes of each of the customers, my greasy fingers on the pane. A sharp rap on the glass sends me leaping backwards, and when I find my feet and glance up, a man's face is glowering at me, his finger wagging disapprovingly.

'Maya. Get away from the glass. It's just been cleaned.' Sabbir grabs hold of my hand and yanks me away, waving apologetically at the shopkeeper.

'Can't leave you alone for a minute without you causing havoc.' The familiar, warm voice is behind me.

I spin round. 'Dad.' And I fall into his smile.

He waves at the man in the barber's and mouths 'sorry' at him.

I fling my arms round Dad's waist, drinking in his smell, aware it's altered slightly.

'Oh, child. I've been gone all of five minutes.' He ruffles my hair, peels my arms off him and leads us off into the summer sunshine.

As we shuffle along, I scour his features from the side. No signs of a shave or haircut. 'Where did you go?'

'Hakim couldn't fit me in at the barber's,' he says, and he's looking at me in a strange way. For a moment, everything stops and the street goes still. 'So, I popped to see a friend.' He ruffles my hair again, knowing full well I hate it and that it will distract me. 'Nothing for you to worry about.'

'Who?' I seek out his eyes, and the caramel pools, which always tell the truth, are narrower than usual and darker.

'No-one you know, Miss Nosey-Parker.' He gives a small laugh, but it sounds hollow and tight.

'You told us you were going for a haircut.' I pull my hand from his and race back over to the barber's, unsure why Dad has said the place was busy.

'I changed my mind, darling. I had to attend to a bit of business. That's all.' He softens his voice and smiles warmly. 'There's nothing to worry about. Honestly. Let's catch up with your sister.' He turns to check where she is, and I catch sight of a waxy red mark on his neck and one on his cheek. Sabbir has gone ahead and is chatting to a friend but Jasmina is level with us now. I nudge her.

'What are they, Dad?' I point at the two round marks. 'On your neck and . . . '

Dad blushes and blindly rubs at his skin, where he thinks I mean.

'They've gone now,' I say, and I'm trying to push down the feelings which are bubbling up.

He's facing Jasmina and me. 'There's no need to tell your mother about this. OK? We don't want to upset her.'

His words make me angry and scared, and I don't understand why, except that it feels like a secret and I don't like secrets. 'I s'pose,' I reply begrudgingly, and I stomp away from him, thoughts crashing in my ears like waves on the seashore. All I can think of is that I want to yell at him, and ask him why he lied and where he went.

Maya, 8.30 a.m.

'Here you go.' The familiar voice broke into my sleep.

'Hmm?' I opened my eyes. 'What time is it?' I tried to orient myself. Kitchen cabinets. Notice boards. The news on low. And Dougie's face, smiling at me.

'Half eight,' he said.

I was in the staff rest area at the station. 'The couch was a bad idea.' I rotated my neck and kneaded it to ease the stiffness. 'I was dreaming about Dad and the fingerprint report and – *Wait*. Have we found Ali?'

'Not yet. But Sophie Williams' mother turned up this morning. She's been on a bender.'

I sighed. That was good news for Sophie, but it meant we were even further from identifying our UnSub. For every step we took forward, we were taking two back.

Dougie pulled up a spare chair and placed a mug on it. 'Here. I got you a packet of bourbons from the machine.' He handed them to me. 'Don't ever accuse me of being unromantic.'

I smiled a thank you. 'The fingerprints on Mum's mobile are likely to be Dad's. I read the report last night.'

'Talk about bad timing.' Dougie crouched down next to the couch. 'How do you feel about that?'

'God knows. I can't take it in.'

The television report broke into my thoughts.

'All I can think about is Ali and where he slept after running off, poor kid. I dreamt about that awful squat too . . . and a young girl—'

'Hold on. One thing at a time.' Dougie's voice was soft. 'First, Jackie's on the war-path.'

'I knew she would be.'

'And the media are all over the squat story.' He turned the volume up on the plasma screen on the wall.

The reporter continued:

'. . . where distressing details are emerging from Duckett House on Stepney's infamous Ocean Estate.' Behind him, a dingy housing block looked like a wall of miniature flats. Scaffolding clung to part of the outside, and windows were covered with metal plates. 'The place has been derelict for three years and no residents have been registered to live here for that time. There's a demolition order on part of it. The squat has been cleared overnight. We understand that four minors were living here with two men, thought to be in their late teens or early twenties, and a number of casual sleepers.' The reporter turned away from the scene. His words were factual, but anguish leaked into his tone. 'At the moment, we have no information on how long they've been living at the squat, and residents and councillors are demanding answers from the Mayor of Tower Hamlets. Local MP, Cherry Smith, is demanding to know how this situation has been allowed to happen.' He took a breath. 'Two of the minors escaped from the police last night and their whereabouts are unknown. The other minors are receiving emergency medical treatment and will be going into foster care while their circumstances are investigated, and family contacted. Two of them are thought to be aged ten and . . . ' The reporter's voice wobbled with emotion. He swallowed. Covered his mouth with his hand and cleared his throat. 'Excuse me, I'm . . .' He coughed into his fist. 'The other is aged twelve. One of the boys told the police that they originate from Syria and entered the country as asylum-seekers in a lorry at Dover, after several months travelling through Europe. The boy says he cannot remember when they arrived or how long their passage was. The police would like to hear from anyone with information on the squat or on any of the boys who were staying there.' A graphic flashed up contact details for Limehouse Police Station. 'The flats in this block have been vacant while developers tried to agree the details of the regeneration work with the council.'

The screen displayed a photograph of Duckett House's current state of decay, alongside an artist's impression of what it could look like.

'State of that place. It's a bloody disgrace,' Dougie snarled. 'If they got their finger out and finished the development of those blocks, those kids wouldn't be in this situation.'

'When officers searched the address,' continued the reporter, 'they found a handgun and a stash of ammunition, and large quantities of Class A drugs.'

'I agree about the estate,' I replied to Dougie, 'but those kids are obviously homeless. I dread to think what might have happened to them if they hadn't been able to squat there.' I bundled the blanket into a ball. 'Makes my blood boil. How can so many youngsters be fending for themselves like this? Dealing drugs in exchange for a floor to doss down on?' I lobbed the blanket on the sofa. 'Where the hell is Ali?'

Dougie shook his head. 'A piece of good news though – we've got a lead. It's what I came to tell you. The tech guys have downloaded the comms data on the burner. There's an SMS from an unregistered mobile. Here.' He reached into his pocket and gave me the print-out.

the shop on right wiv a star above a blue front door

A star? I couldn't help thinking of the Star of David that Rosa had found outside the newsagent's . . . and a terrible realisation hit me. 'Hold on.' I swiped my mobile into life and googled the Brick Lane Soup Company. Clicked on images and . . . 'Look.' I showed him the photograph. Simas and Indra stood together, beaming with pride in front of a blue door. Above the frame, carved by a mason into a block of stone, the way I'd seen on numerous Jewish buildings, was a Star of David. 'I know Rosa's door is blue too because she told me yesterday that it was one of the last things that Józef did before he died.'

'I doubt we'll get any viable prints off her brickwork, but whoever did it may have touched the wood frames. It hasn't rained. And there may be some transfer materials.'

'I really hope so. Because this could mean that Rosa's newsagent's isn't next to be torched.' I looked at Dougie to see if his deduction was the same as mine. 'It could mean that it was the *intended* target last Friday, and somehow the arsonist made a mistake.' I jumped to my feet. 'If that's the case—' I let out a scream of frustration '—we've spent two days investigating a crime that was never meant to happen.'

9 a.m.

This time, the girl was awake when they came. She heard the floor-boards creak on the other side of the door, the key in the lock, the whispered voices. Saw the slice of light as the door opened.

The footsteps came to a sudden halt beside the bed.

She wanted to turn away and curl into a ball, to bury her face in the pillow. But she was scared to move. She lay still, eyes closed.

And the shadow fell.

Maya, 9.30 a.m.

'Just the person I was looking for.' Jackie nabbed me as I was heading into the locker room, towel in one hand, shower gel in the other. 'Luckily, though, we've had some news this morning which has tempered my mood.'

'I know, I know. Reckless. Dangerous. Against procedures.'

'Those are some of the things I—'

'Could we get the briefing over and then you can bollock me?' I elbowed the door open, curious as to whether Jackie was going to follow me in. I knew I was being cheeky. 'If I don't get in the shower pretty soon, I'm going to stink the office out.'

The door closed behind me and there was no sign of Jackie.

After a two-minute shower, I was back in the MIT office. The atmosphere was heavy in the briefing room. We all stared at the familiar images on the investigation boards. Layers of facts and details had been added over the last two days to build up a picture of our investigation, like paint on a canvas.

On the new board, Dan had pinned images of the soup shop and the newsagent. Both buildings had blue doors, and both had a Star of David above their entrance. Next to them, I pinned the print-out Dougie had given me of the SMS from the burner.

'OK, everyone,' I said. 'We've had some critical developments overnight and we've got a long day ahead.'

'If the arsonists *did* get the wrong shop, are we back at square one?' Shen's question probably summed up what the whole team were thinking.

Everyone looked at me for confirmation.

'Yes and no. There has been a crime at the soup shop. Thank goodness we've found out that it might not have been what was intended, as it obviously changes things, but we didn't miss any clues. We followed the ones we had. Without the petrol can and the burner, we couldn't have known the arsonists might have got the wrong premises. We will have to continue to investigate the arson at the soup shop and pursue this new lead.' I parsed the cascade of faces in front of me. Disillusionment was evident on each of them, and it was my job to galvanise us all. 'On the plus side, we can use a lot of what we've learnt about Brick Lane, the forum, the flash mob and soup shop crime to help us to identify who might want to target Rosa's shop. If my theory is correct, this will be the person responsible for the soup shop arson.' I made my tone upbeat. 'Moving on, we have some tentative leads already. The mobile which sent the SMS is unregistered, but the technicians can still access the cell site data.' I waited to deliver the news. 'At the moment, it's switched off. They may have ditched it, but as soon as it's turned on the technicians will get a notification.'

Weak cheers ricocheted around the room and the atmosphere lifted a notch.

The team had accepted the positives and that we all had to focus on those. 'I suggest we decide which of our persons of interest on the soup shop arson might also have a motive for torching Rosa Feldman's newsagent's. It's going to be a bit unusual because Rosa's place hasn't been set on fire, but we need to investigate almost as if it had. Establishing motives for torching the soup shop won't help us if it wasn't the real target.'

'It's a stupidly easy mistake to make,' Dan said. 'Depending on which way you approach the two shops, they're technically both on the right-hand side of the street, and the person who sent that SMS can't have checked whether there was another shop with a Star of David over the door. A bit careless in an area that was predominantly Jewish for fifty years. And they aren't very helpful instructions, are they? They're different blues but how many shops have blue doors? What a dork.'

'That's useful information in itself. If this is organised crime, it's not very professional. It's a costly mistake to burn down the wrong premises, and they'll know that. It tells me that someone in this chain is an amateur or isn't thinking clearly.' I gathered my thoughts. 'Two further things. The English in the SMS is typical text-speak but my hunch is that the sender isn't the same person as whoever writes about gentrification on LfA.'

Heads were nodding in agreement.

'Also, I hope I'm wrong, but I suspect someone is going to pay for this mistake, so we need to bear that in mind too. Plus, of course, we still have a dead woman who we haven't identified, and still don't know if she has anyone at home who might be relying on her. Sophie Williams' mother has turned up, so it's not her.'

Dan peered at the image of Rosa's shop. 'Speaking of risks, what's the likelihood of the arsonists torching Rosa's place now?'

'I've been thinking about this. It's hard to gauge. I've compiled a list of reasons why Rosa's shop may still be in danger, and reasons why the arsonists may have abandoned the idea. I'd value your input and Jackie and I will make a decision.' I took the cap off a board marker. 'Why might they may skip the newsagent's now?'

'If it was a contract job, they may have to pay for a second hit, and may not want to or have the money,' Dan said.

'Yup.' I wrote it on the board.

'And returning to the scene of the crime will increase their risk of getting caught.'

'Thanks, Alexej. Any more?'

The room was quiet.

'Reasons why they may still target Rosa's newsagent's?'

'Whatever the motive was, it still exists.' Shen spoke with conviction. 'Going back to what Dan said, whoever wanted it done may be putting the arsonists under pressure. Plus, whoever torched the soup shop may not have been paid and may need to hit the right target to get their cash.'

'Yes. This is my fear. Whoever issued the instructions is likely to be furious, and may use the mistake as a reason to get out of coughing up. It's what makes me suspect that whoever made the cock-up is going to pay. Quite possibly with their life.'

'I'd echo that,' Jackie chipped in from the back of the room. 'I've seen this happen many times. These people are ruthless, even towards their own. They have no loyalties. You screw up, you're dead. It's as simple as that.'

'It also means that Rosa's place could still be at risk.' I surveyed the room. 'We don't have the resources to put an officer outside her place twenty-four-seven, but we have a duty of care towards her. There's no way we'll persuade her to shift, so I'll take her through the warning procedures.'

'The woman at *Alchemia*, Monika Waglowa, has asked her husband to send their front CCTV over. Hopefully, that'll show who scored the Star of David outside Rosa's shop.' Dan was studying the image of the soup shop in all its glory on opening day. Blue tape to match the door. Cake. A huddle of friends and family, all laughing and smiling. Indra and Simas were shaking a bottle of fizz, faces glowing with pride. 'Are we to take it that Simas and Indra are Jewish?'

'I've wondered that,' I said. 'A quick call to Indra will confirm one way or the other. I'd assumed they were Catholic. Most of the Jewish communities which survived the Holocaust suffered dreadfully under Soviet atheist policy. But Indra and Simas are from Vilnius, and there's been a re-birth of Judaism there.'

'And the Star of David above their shop?'

'It's a confident statement, isn't it? It was previously a Jewish shop, so they may have left it in place. If they put it up, my guess is they're Jewish and proud of it.' I was adding to my list of tasks as we spoke. 'OK. Going back to the fire on the soup shop, might any of our suspects have a motive for torching Rosa's newsagent's?' I pointed to the board we'd used so extensively the last few days.

'I can only think of motives, Boss, not people,' Shen piped up. 'Maybe someone wants to get their hands on the shop lease for development. Didn't Rosa say her freeholders were pressurising her to sell to them?'

'Yes, she did.' I wrote Solomon Stein's name on the board.

'Racism?' Alexej took the board marker from my hand and created a second list for motives. 'Anti-Semitism?'

'Definitely possible – although that could apply equally to the soup shop.'

'It's hard to see how Rosa's shop competes with anyone's business. Her turnover must be very low.' Shen had grabbed hold of the new focus and I appreciated her positivity.

'I don't think competition is likely either,' said Dan. 'But she must be struggling to cover her bills, let's face it. What if she wanted the shop damaged so she can claim on her insurance?'

I looked at the images of Rosa's newsagent's. Sifted through what

I knew and remembered about her: determined not to give the shop up; adamant she wouldn't go and stay with Agnieszka or Tomasz; feeling safest at the shop. 'Personally, I can't see that but I'm happy to ask her about it when I go round there. I don't think she cares about the business much any more, but I do think she cares about the building. It's where all her memories are, and they're all she's got. At the moment, she hasn't forged a link with her future. She's a bright lady. She'll know that getting someone to start a fire in her shop could go badly wrong.'

'Assuming the flash mob was still a distraction, we know that Kenny Hayes' prints were on the speakers. We need to keep him in our sights. Otherwise, what about people who would benefit financially from getting their hands on the shop, or Rosa's savings and any insurances she may have?' He faced us. 'Agnieszka and her family live in a pretty small house. What about her or Olaf?'

'I know we decided it was unlikely that Olaf is still involved with LfA,' said Dan. 'But he does seem like a man under pressure.'

'And then there's Tomasz,' Alexej said. 'He's clearly a shrewd businessman.'

'He's also loaded so what would he gain?' The images of Indra and Simas reminded me of Artem's comments. 'We also need to consider Artem. He thinks that shops like Rosa's have become redundant. In fact, he even named her business and the Walkers' off-licence.' His comments had sent shivers down my spine. 'He could have a number of motives.' I added his name to the board. 'What else do we know that might help us?'

Alexej's head shot up from his monitor. 'An update has just been added from last night. An eyewitness saw our appeal and called in.' He was reading off HOLMES. 'Chap works nights and uses the alley as a short-cut. Says he's seen a man hanging about at the rear of Rosa Feldman's newsagent's several times in the last fortnight.'

'Can we get a description from him?'

'I'm on it. His phone's switched off. He's probably asleep.' He checked the clock. 'I've already begun calling in the CCTV that covers the alley behind Rosa's shop. It's mainly all private but people are on edge after the fire and will want to help, I'm sure.'

I was taking stock. 'Well done, everyone. I'm fully confident that we can find out who meant to target the newsagent's but hit the soup shop instead.' I paused. 'Right. Our priorities are still to identify our UnSub; to investigate the people we've identified as having a potential motive; to follow up those with information; and to find Ali.'

I heard a muttered grumble but couldn't place whose it was.

'Alexej, can you chase *Alchemia* for their CCTV and continue calling in footage from the alley? And interview Solomon Stein about Rosa Feldman's lease.' I felt my shoulders relax, knowing we'd made a start. 'And keep chasing the lab for DNA results on the woman. If they can't narrow results to an individual, family details are better than the nothing we've had for the last three days.'

He gave a thumbs-up.

'Shen, can you check with Indra about their religion, please, and whether they put the Star of David up outside their shop? And chase the analysts on the MisPer register and Simas' mistress in Essex with a kid. Without any other leads, she has to be our prime UnSub candidate.'

'Sure thing, Boss.'

'Dan, can you interview Agnieszka and Olaf, and Tomasz?' I felt uneasy at the prospect of Rosa's children wanting to take advantage of her, but Olaf wasn't a blood relation. 'I'll pay Artem another visit, then brief Rosa on safety.' I recalled how frail she'd looked when she left hospital; how we'd nearly lost her after the arson; how crushed she seemed without Józef. There were various strands to the conversation I needed to have with her, and I wasn't looking forward to bringing her more bad news.

However, there was a more immediate matter. What was I going to tell the press about the new development?

And before that, I had to front up to Jackie.

Maya, 11 a.m.

'Let's start with reckless, dangerous and against procedures, shall we?'

I looked up from my keyboard. Jackie was standing by my desk wearing her no-nonsense face. I wasn't going to get away with fobbing her off again. 'Sorry, Jackie. I didn't mean to be rude earlier. I was—'

She fixed her steely gaze on mine. 'What the hell were you and Dan doing, entering the squat without adequate protection?' Her voice was getting louder. 'You know the correct procedure is to wait for back-up and wear a stab vest. You also know that preservation of life is paramount, and you have a duty not to put yourself in danger. Don't you?'

She was right. 'I'm not going to argue with you.'

'Are you sure about that?'

'With hindsight, we shouldn't have gone in. It's my fault. I let impatience get the better of me.' I cursed my stupidity. 'Ali had given us a false address first time around, and from the outside of the block, when we arrived, we thought he might be dossing there. He was – but we only realised it was a junkie squat once we were inside.' This was what had happened, but I wondered what Dan had told her.

I could see Jackie was thinking.

'In addition to the danger aspects,' she continued, 'the outcome is that we have now lost a significant witness.'

'I'll find Ali.'

'That is not the point, Maya, and you know it.'

'No, but it'll get our witness back and make sure he's safe, won't it?'

'Listen to me, Maya. You're a first-rate detective. What makes you different is that you really care. We all have the utmost respect for you. But you are not to put yourself, or any of your officers, in danger for a personal crusade. Do I make myself clear?'

I nodded. Resigned.

'Follow procedures in future, and that means waiting for back-up and wearing protective clothing.'

'OK. Sorry.'

'You don't need to apologise. I'm sure you thought you were doing the right thing. But your judgement slipped, and it could've ended badly.'

*

Jackie's words echoed in my ears as I made my way towards Stepney Green to see Rosa at the shop in Brick Lane. For once, the traffic was light, and I was half-way up Bromley Street when an urgent call-out came over the in-car radio.

'Control to DI Rahman. Immediate attendance required in Stepney. Over.'

I stifled a curse. 'Go ahead, Control. What've we got?'

'A suspicious death. Male body found at the Manor House development. First responders say it's linked to the fire in Brick Lane. DCI McLean wants you to attend, Ma'am. Immediate attendance, over.'

'Can you get hold of DS Maguire, please, and tell him to meet me there? I'm on my way. Over.' My thoughts rushed to whoever had torched the wrong shop. Was this going to be their body? I checked the SatNav. A red light was flashing to show a traffic incident on Commercial Road. I flicked on the blue lights, checked my mirrors and stuck my foot on the accelerator.

*

I reached the Manor House site before Dan. It was a half-finished development. Luxury apartments, penthouse suite and gym, and not something the locals were happy about. While I was waiting for the foreman to meet me, I rang Alexej for an update on the arson investigation. Indra had confirmed that she and Simas were Jewish, and they'd left the bagel shop's Star of David in place as they liked it. Alexej had questioned Solomon Stein about the freehold on Rosa's newsagent's.

'What's Stein like?'

'It's Solomon Stein junior. His father bought the freehold. Dead now. Junior's all about the money, but he says he's got clauses in his contracts saying he can sell the freeholds. He doesn't need to torch any of them.'

'Sounds like we can rule him out then.' There was still no sign of the foreman. 'Dan and I will be here for a while so can you and Shen question Agnieszka and her husband? Make sure Agnieszka stays with her mum afterwards. Jackie's going to interview Artem. Shake him up a bit.'

'Sure.'

'Before I go, any developments on our UnSub or Ali?'

'Negative.'

'OK. Dan's arriving now. Keep me posted.' I rang off and walked along Stepney Green Road where Dan was getting out of the car.

We talked as we approached the site entrance.

'I got Shen to pull up some research on the Manor House,' he said. 'It seemed a bizarre place to have a farm until I read the history.'

'My niece adored Stepney Farm when she was younger.' It was a neighbourhood I knew well, only a few miles east of where I'd grown up. 'Such a shame that they've plonked the development here though.' I took in the pretty village church of St Dunstan's, and the local secondary school, Sir John Cass Redcoat. 'When they floated the plans for these apartments, lots of locals were furious.' We'd arrived at the site entrance now. 'I wonder why the killer decided to leave the body here?'

Dan was paraphrasing from his email, momentarily oblivious of my question. '. . . built on the grounds of an old Tudor manor house . . . some of the farm-land wasn't being used . . . so presumably developers spotted an opportunity?'

One implication of working with a detail-obsessed newcomer to London was that he filled in all my knowledge gaps, whether I wanted it or not. I surveyed the red cranes, the hoardings, the high-tech machinery and warehouses, and said loudly, 'This place is crawling with CCTV. Isn't it?'

'Sorry. Yes.' Dan stuffed his mobile in his pocket. 'That should make our lives easier.'

'Thank God there's no media yet.' I knew we had minutes before they arrived. 'The red tops are going to have a field day with this.'

Outside the hoardings, at the crime scene perimeter, a uniformed officer was guarding the site. A man in a fluorescent jacket was charging towards us at the entrance. Beneath his hard hat, he was red in the face and veins bulged in his neck. 'How long is this going to take?' He addressed his question to Dan. 'We've got equipment arriving today.'

'As long as it takes, I'm afraid,' I said quietly. 'DI Rahman, Senior Investigating Officer. This is DS Maguire.' I watched him absorb his faux pas and we both showed him our warrants.

'You are?'

'Robert Johnson, the site foreman. The architects are due from Sweden. We've got millions of pounds worth of equipment arriving today and—'

'*And* a man is dead. The site will be closed for at least twenty-four hours. After that, areas may be released in stages or the whole thing.'

He tutted. Took out a packet of tobacco and papers from his trouser pocket and began rolling.

'My officers will need to see your CCTV. Could you organise that, please?'

He looked up. Lit his roll-up and nodded.

'Who found the body?'

'Young lad. Chris Thomas. Was doing an early morning site check. He's in the Portakabin over there with one of your officers. Badly shaken.' He pointed. 'By all accounts it's not pretty, I'll warn you now.' He gestured to his mouth.

'We'll take it from here.'

'Chris says it's one of our guys. Patrick Ryan. He recognised the work boots and his tattoo.'

'Why did he think it's related to the fire?'

'You'll see.'

Dougie joined us, two white forensic suits and protective wear in his arms. 'Dr Clark has just arrived.' He passed us protective clothing.

We pulled the suits over our clothes, and the shoe covers on, and followed Dougie through the outer cordon, round various items of machinery, diggers and concrete churners, and onto the crime scene via the common approach path.

'The team are still taking photographs.' Dougie was filling us in as we walked. 'We've got the elements to contend with, but the crime scene has a few characteristics I think you'll be interested in.'

His intonation reminded me of the foreman's gesture. 'Like what?'

'The—'

'Morning, Maya.' It was Dr Clark, our regular pathologist.

'Morning, Doc. What've we got?' I smiled an apology at Dougie.

'Most unusual, actually.' Dr Clark was standing over the body, his cheeks flushed pink with excitement. A man's body lay on its back on the ground. His arms were spread-eagled. In the middle of his chest, there was a cluster of bullet holes. The clothes had diluted blood on them. A black bandana had been tied over his nose and mouth, with the LfA logo clearly visible.

'Shit.' I leaned over him and the fumes hit me. 'So, he's been shot, had a scarf tied over him *and* been doused with petrol?' I turned to Dougie. 'Is that why uniform said it was linked to the fire?'

'Er—'

'Must be a good canister of petrol there.' Dan interrupted. 'Pain in the arse as it'll have washed off some of the blood pattern and GSR.'

'There's more,' said Dr Clark. Using gloved fingers, he carefully lifted the mask. The victim's mouth was open, and where his tongue should have been, there was a gaping black hole.

It was a sickening sight.

'The tongue's got to be a statement.' I looked at Dan, who was the other side of the body.

'Someone's keen to link him with LfA.' He pointed at the mask. 'The arson too?'

'What if this *is* our arsonist? Someone knew what he did and shot him. It's a possibility, isn't it?'

Other than what the body was lying in, there wasn't any blood spatter around the corpse.

'Presumably he wasn't killed here?' I asked Dr Clark.

'My guess is he was killed elsewhere and brought on site. It would be too much of a risk to shoot him here and cut out his tongue. I'm sure Dougie's team and ballistics will be able to add to that, and I'll leave you to establish why the body was left here.'

'What about the tongue? There's not much blood around his face and neck, so presumably that was done post-mortem?'

'Subject to the PM, I'd agree.'

'Do we have the tongue?'

'Sadly, not.'

Ideas coursed through my mind. Had the killer taken it as a souvenir? My thoughts turned to the victim's family. 'Right. Someone tell Chris Thomas to keep schtum about Ryan's ID. Last thing we want is it getting in the media before we've had time to notify next-of-kin.' I turned to Dr Clark. 'Have you got a slot for the PM?'

'I'll get it done later today.'

'I wonder what the petrol's about. D'you suppose they were planning to set him alight or is it hinting at the fire on Friday?'

'Impossible to say,' Dr Clark replied.

'Fortunately, it's dry so if he's been brought here from another location, there may still be transfer materials on him.' I surveyed the scene.

'Speaking of transfer materials, his body is covered with what looks like dog hair.' Dr Clark pointed.

'Oh, yes. I can see them.' Medium-length dark hairs had collected in the fibre of his clothing and speckled his skin.

'As soon as I give the go-ahead to move him, the CSIs can start on the body's forensics.' Dr Clark was recording measurements.

'Cheers, Doc.'

Dan had gone to speak to Chris Thomas, so I left the crime scene area and pulled off the white suit and shoe covers.

Back on the street, the site foreman, Robert Johnson, was leaning up against the wooden hoardings around the development, bellowing into his mobile and pacing up and down. When he saw me, he cut his call and tucked his mobile in his pocket. 'Sorry about earlier. Behaving like a dick.' He looked sheepish. 'Working in this kind of environment, the alpha male thing becomes a habit after a while.'

I smiled. It can't have been an easy thing to admit. 'I would appreciate it if you would tell your guys not to discuss the man's identity with anyone. We don't want it leaking into the media until we've notified his next-of-kin.' Suzie came to mind. No doubt she'd be sniffing around any moment. 'Was Patrick Ryan scheduled to work today?'

'Uh-huh.'

'Was he in yesterday?'

'His shift finished at 6 p.m.' He began rolling another cigarette. 'Manor House HQ is at Canary Wharf, if you need them. Patrick was a nice bloke. This is awful. He had a daughter similar in age to mine.'

I caught the anguish in his voice.

'He used to show me photos of her, and I could tell how much he loved her.' He coughed to cover his sniff, and turned away from me. 'The Manor House bosses are shouting about delays. Time. Money. It's a billion-pound project with massive penalties for late completion of works. No excuse. And all I can think about is that Patrick's kid is going to grow up without a dad.' He kicked at the kerb with his boot. 'I don't know what the police is like as an employer but people in my world aren't interested in human factors. They shake them down the line. Make sure that we all feel responsible.' He snorted. 'Over-sodding-responsible, more like.'

I knew what he meant. It was how the police worked too. 'We will release the crime scene as quickly as we can.'

'I appreciate that.' His eyes were bloodshot. 'I'm lucky. I've still got my missus. After all he's been through, Patrick has done amazingly. I can't believe this has happened to him.'

'What do you mean?'

'It's not really my place to tell you. His ex will fill you in, I'm sure. Nice lady.'

I was curious. 'I'll ask her. Did Ryan have any enemies at work? Recent fall-outs?'

'Not that I know of. He was a popular staff member. A people-person, you know? He got on well with the labourers and the bosses. Not everyone can do that.' He shook his head and started to make the next phone call.

Dan re-appeared at the site entrance, out of breath from running. He clocked the foreman, so I walked to meet him. 'Just talked to Chris Thomas. Ryan has a tattoo on his arm, saying "Amanda". It's his daughter's name.'

'Has Chris told anyone who the victim is?'

'He says he hasn't but he was pretty cagey. I've just rung the personnel office. Ryan was divorced. His wife has re-married, and lives in Mile End with their daughter. Ryan lived in a shared house in Bromley-by-Bow. I've sent a uniformed officer round to his ex-wife to notify her of the death, and a team is on its way to search Ryan's home address.'

'Good. I can't see any of us getting any sleep over the next few days. We'll have to plough on with investigating Rosa's newsagent and crack on with this investigation. Can you interview his ex-wife and then get over to the Strozyk's and Tomasz?'

'Sure. Except—'

'I'll stop off at Bromley-by-Bow and see if the search of Ryan's home address turns up anything useful.'

'Maya, hold up.' Dan stood still, legs apart, as though he wasn't going anywhere until he'd said what he wanted. 'You aren't going to like this, but I think you need to put finding Ali on the back-burner. I know you feel guilty for him running off, and so do I, but we've got a hell of a lot on, and we can't watch out for every kid that's in trouble.' He paused. 'Also – we run the risk of screwing up again if we try to spread ourselves too thin.'

I absorbed his words and felt my determination galvanise. 'No way.'

'It's not fair on the team.'

'Since when did you speak for everyone?' I heard my voice rise.

'I'm not. I'm saying how I feel. I'm part of your team.'

The mumbled comment back at the station must've been Dan.

'You heard what Ali said. Kyle's going to kill him. He's homeless, for Christ's sake.'

'I know that. I still think we need to prioritise solving crimes that have *actually* happened, not ones that haven't but may. Our resources are stretched as it is.'

'Rosa's shop hasn't been torched and we are investigating that.'

'It's not the same, Maya, and you know it. We are investigating an arson attack and two deaths, all of which occurred because the culprit got the wrong shop. We need to know who might want to target Rosa's newsagent's in order to find out who set fire to the soup shop.'

'Fine.' I caught the sulky tone in my voice but couldn't help it. 'I'll look for Ali in my own time then. Thanks for your support, buddy.' And with that, I left Dan standing there and stomped off.

Dan, 12.30 p.m.

In the watery afternoon sunlight, Dan entered the gated community where Patrick Ryan's ex-missus lived. It was a new development, overlooking the canal behind Mile End park. After the barney with Maya, the neatly trimmed hedges and immaculate lawns irritated him. He wondered how Aroona would enjoy living somewhere like this, with gardeners and visitor parking bays and swanky wrought iron electric gates.

He parked the car and hurried up the manicured path to the main entrance, his warm breath billowing in the chilly air. He rang on the entry-com system. 'It's the police.'

'Second floor,' came a posh-sounding woman's voice, and he was buzzed in.

Dan took the stairs. There were no blood stains here, no empty dope bags or graffiti. The walls were papered and painted – belt and braces – and their surfaces gleamed. A thick cream carpet made the stairs springy under his shoes.

The second floor had a view out over the canal and lock. A woman was waiting for him, the flat door open. In jeans and a jumper, she was drying her hands on a tea-towel.

'Mrs Grant? I'm Detective Maguire. Could I speak to you about your ex-husband?'

She nodded solemnly, and led him into the flat, past neat rows of coats and along a spotless hall. There wasn't a scooter or toy in sight. The lounge was similarly immaculate with a large crate in the corner where games and toys were neatly stacked.

Dan thought about his girls, and how frustrated Aroona got at the continually scattered toys in their apartment at home. He felt a pang of homesickness. How he wished his life here had the cushion of a family to return home to, something permanent which wasn't a part of him being a cop. 'We are all very sorry for your loss.' Dan let her settle.

She pulled her sleeves down over her wrists and shuffled over to a large red sofa.

'We will do everything we can to find the person that's responsible.'

'What happened?'

'He was found on the Manor House site first thing this morning. One of the workers was doing his rounds. We are treating it as a suspicious death.'

'That means you think he was murdered, right?'

'We suspect that's the case but can't say any more at the moment. His identity will be given in the media. I've arranged for a family liaison officer to come over shortly.'

Nicola was bent over with her arms round her knees, looking at the carpet. 'I knew something like this would happen. I knew it. I told him over and over, you go back to that stuff and you'll end up dead. I really thought he'd changed.' Her voice creaked with anger.

'Can your husband keep you company for a couple of days? It's bound to be a dreadful shock.' Dan was interested in why she feared Patrick would end up dead, but wanted to give her time to take the news in.

'Alan will be back later.' She had her hand clamped over her mouth. Wide, staring eyes were fixed on the floor in front of her as she rattled off a succession of questions and statements. 'What am I going to tell Amanda? She's going to be devastated. She adores her dad. Always has. It hit her hard when he and I split up. This is going to break her.' Her eyes bulged with anguish. 'How do you tell your daughter that her dad's been murdered?'

Dan swallowed. 'I'm so sorry.' It was impossible not to feel her pain. 'I have daughters myself and I honestly don't know. I'm sure the family liaison officer will be able to help with what to tell your daughter, and how to talk to her about it. And we can put you in touch with specialist counsellors too.' He thought about Kiara and Sharna, and shuddered as he tried to imagine what Aroona would tell them if he was killed. 'I do have to warn you, though. It is going to be on the national news, and your daughter's mates will see it even if she doesn't.'

'They're both at school. Alan and I have a daughter too. I'll have to tell them, won't I?'

He nodded gently. 'When you're ready.'

She dabbed at her cheeks with a tissue and rested her head on the back of the sofa. 'Amanda's just started her GCSE subjects. It's going to disrupt her education all over again.'

'You don't need to explain.'

'I don't want you to think I'm not upset about Patrick. I am. But . . . ' She stared at the ceiling as though she was searching for the words to express what she wanted to say. '. . . what I feel for my ex-husband is . . . ' She broke off again. Looked around the room and seemed to gather muster. 'Our relationship got very complicated and so did my feelings for him. It's been hard not to be angry. I am angry. I'm bloody angry.' The words came out in a splutter.

'Can I get you anything? Cuppa? Some water?' Dan often found this the most challenging part of his job. For some, it was the dead bodies and blood. But to Dan, the victim's suffering was over then. For relatives, their nightmare was only just beginning.

Nicola pulled at her bottom lip. 'Underneath all the hurt and the anger and the disappointment, I still love him.' The distress was evident in her eyes. 'Amanda hoped that one day we'd get back together, and I think that was probably what I wanted too. But not all the while there was a possibility he'd go back to the drugs. And I always suspected he would.'

It was a sad story and Dan sensed there was more to it than that.

She sniffed. Blew her nose and rocked gently, as though she was preparing to explain something important but couldn't put the words together. 'Patrick and I split up seven years ago. We were married young and had Amanda. He was working in the city as a trader. The hours and company he kept lured him into lifestyle which ruined our relationship. When we divorced I barely recognised him. If you take cocaine regularly, it changes you. It turns you nasty and manic, and makes you paranoid. And eventually it takes your life over. People think they can control it – Patrick did – and they often can for a while, but eventually it gets you in its grip.'

Dan was thinking about what she was saying. He'd known loads of people who'd got into the coke scene in Sydney. School mates, colleagues, family. Very few managed to keep it recreational. 'I'm sorry to ask this but was he involved with anything illegal? Now or in the past?'

Her face fell. 'It depends what you call "illegal".'

'I'm a police officer so my definition is anything that breaks the law.' He wasn't being patronising. His sense was that her question was more along the lines of, how much do you want to know? 'It's likely that his death is related to the arson in Brick Lane so please tell us anything you can.'

She snatched a breath. 'When Patrick worked in the city, he was a high-flyer and he took a lot of risks. It's part of the job. He had an eye for the markets, and had split-second timing. He earned a lot of money very quickly and made many of the bank's clients very rich. But he also pissed people off. Some of his colleagues were envious of his deals and abilities, and there was some back-stabbing. Occasionally, something unpredictable happened and people lost money. For a long time, luck seemed to ride with him and then it deserted him. Whether that coincided with the cocaine getting its teeth in, I don't know, because he denied taking it, but his judgement seemed to waver. You need keen attention to work the markets. You need to be able to spot patterns, relationships, warning signs. Some of the risks paid off and some didn't. It's the way that world works. He didn't tell me the details of all his deals, but I know that many of them involved speculating on unstable markets in the Middle East and central Europe. He had customers from all round the world.'

'How'd that pan out?'

'He was barely sleeping, partly due to the coke and partly because somewhere in the world a market is open, twenty-four-seven. He began having psychotic episodes and symptoms of mania, and became very paranoid. It's truly awful to witness this happening to someone you love. Someone you've had a child with. They literally disintegrate in front of you. Eventually, he had a breakdown and landed up in a psychiatric hospital. The coke well and truly messed his brain up. I didn't trust him around Amanda, and I didn't feel safe around him myself. His rage was extremely unpredictable and scary.'

'I have to ask. Did he ever hurt you or your daughter?'

'Physically, no. Never. But, on many occasions, he was completely out of control of himself. Babbling and ranting, and we were all scared. It was the drugs. It wasn't him. When we met, Patrick was the nicest person in the world. I wouldn't have married him otherwise.' Her voice had got higher. 'Very few people can work in that city environment for long without it turning their head and dragging them into . . . well, I've told you.' She looked up from her hands. 'Did he suffer? How was he killed?'

'It would have been quick.' No-one wanted to know that their loved one had died an agonising death and been mutilated.

She smiled in appreciation. It was clear that Nicola Grant had cared deeply about her ex-husband, and still did. And that she had obviously been through some extremely challenging times with him. 'When did you see him last? Were you in touch?'

'Patrick didn't cope well with hospital. The drugs they put him on, the attempts at getting him to engage with therapy. They just made him more manic and more determined to self-medicate. He was discharged far too soon. The service had insufficient beds, and they said they had patients with greater needs than him – although that's hard to fathom. So, he ended up on the streets and never kicked the drugs. He was terrified, sleeping rough. I completely understand. I wouldn't survive one night. Unfortunately, from cocaine he got into heroin and began mixing it with cheap alcohol. He hadn't solved his original cocaine addiction and he was self-medicating to cope with living rough. Taking anything he could get hold of. He nearly died. He was lucky to survive and not contract any diseases. Slowly, he got back on his feet, got work at the Old Manor House and worked his way up to sub-foreman. Which is why this . . . this is such a bloody tragedy.' She let out a sob.

'How did he get the job there?'

'He was determined the get off the gear. Took him a good two years but he decided to go cold turkey. After that he touted for a job as a labourer on various building sites. Said he'd work a day for no pay, and if they didn't want to pay him, they didn't have to. Manor House Developments offered him a job halfway through the day. He spent the next few years grafting, kept out of trouble, worked his way up, and earned people's respect and trust. When he got the sub-foreman job, he was really thrilled. He felt he'd finally managed to put the past behind him.'

'Is there any chance he was involved with anything illegal recently?'

'Personally, I think it's unlikely, but I can't say for definite. Last time I saw him, he was over the moon to have made a success of this job and he'd started some volunteering that he was enjoying. Youth centres round here are busy places, and he was giving talks at them about the dangers of drugs. I can't see him wanting to risk all that and end up where he was all over again. He said to me that you can't get much lower or desperate than being a coke and heroin addict and living on the streets. But – he also said that shit was only ever a snort, smoke or syringe away.' She looked towards the door and the stairs. 'Can I see him?'

'Of course. There will be a post-mortem first. We will let you know when that's possible.' He glanced round the room. 'We know that it wasn't suicide. Can you tell me whether Patrick had any enemies? Or whether he'd had any barneys with anyone recently?'

'Not that I know of but I'm not the best person to ask. He was very cagey with me. He knew how much distress he had caused us, and he was keen to see his daughter. She worshipped him. But it meant that there were things he didn't tell me.'

'A few final questions – did Patrick have any links with Brick Lane?'

'He knows the area. We all do. We'd go out there occasionally for a curry. I can't think of much more than that.'

'Did he know any people there?'

'Yeah. Of course. He knew people all over London.'

'Before I go, has anything unusual occurred in the last few weeks?' Dan focussed his attention on Nicola's face.

'Not that I can think of.'

'He didn't mention that anything was bothering him?'

She frowned. 'He did say there'd been some unpleasantness recently but as soon as he told me, he realised he'd freaked me out, and he clammed up.'

Dan felt sad about Patrick Ryan. It was a darn shame for him to have gone through such suffering and hardship, to have been so determined to get his life back on track and to end up dead just when it was all beginning to take shape again. He made a note in his phone to get the office to find out which youth clubs Ryan had been volunteering with. 'Does Patrick have any family alive other than your daughter? Parents, siblings?'

'Both his parents are still alive. They're in Kilburn.'

'What are their names?'

'Sinead and Gabriel.' She jotted his parents' address on a pad and handed it to him.

Dan nodded. 'Do you know if he was involved with any social action or community events?'

She frowned.

'For example, protests or flash mobs?'

Her face fell, and she looked scared. 'Is this about the arson in Brick Lane?'

'Yes.'

'I'll be honest: protests don't sound like him but he was certainly against gentrification, just as he was opposed to people pretending to be something they weren't. When Patrick worked at the bank, he earned a lot of money and suffered terrible imposter syndrome. He felt he'd betrayed his working-class roots and it made him feel guilty. He was a lot of things, but he wasn't a hypocrite – although he did change when he was working at the bank.' She paused. 'But – we obviously weren't as close in the last few years as we once were. It may be that stuff happened on the streets that I don't know about. You can't go through all that, the drugs, psychiatric hospital, and sleeping rough, without it changing you somehow.' She stopped again, as though there was something she wanted to add but wasn't sure about. 'I know he was angry about getting kicked out of hospital so quickly so maybe that changed his attitudes.'

'Can you explain how he changed?'

'He got hard when he was working in the city. He began not to give a shit about anyone. He worshipped at the altar of money and his mind was on the current deal and the markets. But it wasn't really who he was.' Her eyes ached with regret. 'That's probably partly why he started boozing and taking cocaine. The pressure, the weirdness of the environment, the hours, the imposter syndrome. Somewhere along the way he lost touch with who he was, and it was as though he despised himself for what he was doing. That led to more booze and drugs, and more self-loathing. Really, he was a classic example of a working-class boy who got a lucky break, found something that he was good at, made hundreds of thousands, and all the while felt unworthy of the success and guilty.'

Dan was processing what she was saying. Her ex-husband's experiences were tragic but weren't uncommon. If he felt unworthy, perhaps the labouring jobs had suited him better? Rather than being catapulted into success, he'd had to work his way up and earn the respect of his peers on the site.

And that made his murder all the sadder.

But it didn't help them with what was important, and that was finding out how Patrick Ryan's death was linked to the arson.

Maya, 12.30 p.m.

Having stormed off in a huff, it was a relief to be surrounded by strangers in Mile End Park, where I could gather my thoughts. I was annoyed with myself for getting into an argument with Dan, but I couldn't let go of the feeling that we had a duty of care towards Ali. As I walked towards the play area, dragging my heels in the grass, only patches of morning dew remained. Most had evaporated under the clear skies and dappled April sunlight.

At the bottom of the slide, a man was standing with a teenager. He looked relaxed and happy as he watched two girls. 'That's it,' he called over encouragingly to the young girl who was perching at the top of the slide, clinging onto the frame. 'We'll catch you.' He was wearing a quilted jacket in navy blue with a brown corduroy collar, and dark jeans. He wasn't my idea of handsome, but this was exactly how Nicola had described her ex-husband.

'Mr Grant? Alan Grant?'

He turned at the sound of his name, almost as if he'd been waiting for this moment.

'I'm DI Rahman. Could I speak to you for a moment, please?' I didn't want to mention Patrick Ryan by name, or the murder.

'Er, sure. Hold on.' He faced the teenager. 'Mand, honey, can you look after your sister for a few minutes? Maybe take her on the swings.' He waited 'til the young girl was down from the slide and watched Amanda install her sister safely on the seat.

I led him over to the trampoline where we could talk without being overheard. 'I'm leading the investigation into Patrick Ryan's death. My sergeant is talking to Nicola. Did you see much of Patrick?'

'Every couple of weeks. He would pick Amanda up from the flat when it was his turn to have her. Before that, he was often at the Saturday Soup thing that Nicola helps with, for the homeless. I usually drop her off there and collect her, especially when it's cold. Saw him there several times.'

'How were things between you and Patrick?'

He shrugged, and scratched his chin while he collected his thoughts. 'It wasn't an easy situation for any of us, but he was a decent bloke and we aren't the only ones to have a blended family.' He gave a sad shrug. 'You just have to get on with it.' He gestured in the direction of the girls on the swings. 'He never missed his turn to have Amanda, and she adores him. Which is all that matters, I guess.'

I sensed a *but*. 'Any niggles? Rows?'

'I may as well be frank. It did annoy me that he and Nicola were so close, and I suppose I felt a bit jealous.' He gathered his thoughts. 'She said it was over between them but I could see he still loved her.' He sat down beside me. 'And I loved her too, so I put up with it. The poor guy had been through hell, so I wasn't about to start making life more difficult for him.' He fiddled with a button on his jacket. 'But it's quite hard knowing you're the consolation prize.'

I nodded. Unless he was a good actor, his mixed feelings seemed genuine. But feeling sorry for a person didn't stop someone from killing them if there were other motivating factors. 'When did you last see Patrick?'

'Last weekend. He had Amanda.'

'Did your wife have any spats with him recently?'

He faced me. Pulled his hand through his hair while he considered the question. 'Not that I'm aware of. But he wasn't our favourite subject so you're best off asking her.' His gaze slipped back to the swings, and melancholy seemed to consume him. 'As far as I saw, they all got on really well.' He let out a sigh. 'Even Sally adored him.' The resentment in his voice was unmistakeable.

I couldn't help wondering whether Alan Grant might have wanted Patrick out of the way. And if he had, why on earth would he go to such lengths to link his death to the arson on Brick Lane?

Dan, 2.30 p.m.

It was early afternoon by the time Maya and Dan arrived in Kilburn to interview Patrick Ryan's parents. Sunday traffic had caught them at Old Street roundabout, Euston and Maida Vale. The journey had given him the chance to ask Maya if he could take some leave once the case was over, and despite the frostiness that lingered between them over Ali, she'd agreed. He was relieved – he desperately wanted to go home to Sydney and spend some time with Aroona and the girls, to see if they could sort out a way forward that would work for them all. The girls were best off with their mum, there was no doubt about that, so, much as he was tempted, he hadn't suggested that they come to the UK and live with him. He missed Aroona terribly. Her wise soul, her kindness and the way she kept him grounded. He missed being a husband, but more than anything, he wanted to be a dad again.

Gabriel and Sinead Ryan had a ground-floor flat in an ugly concrete block set back from the main road. The woman who opened the front door was barely an inch over five feet tall. She had hair the colour of sand, cut into a neat bob around what was still a pretty face. A baggy cardigan hung on her petite frame.

Dan showed his warrant. 'DS Maguire and DI Rahman. Could we speak to you about your son, please?'

Sinead wrapped the cardigan tighter about herself. 'Come in,' she said, clearly flustered. 'Nicola rang and told us about Patrick.'

She padded along the hall in socks, and led Dan and Maya into a spacious lounge where they'd been vegging out in front of the telly.

In the middle of the room, an archway opened onto a kitchen. At the other end, two black leather sofas lay opposite each other, with drinks tables dotted round the room. The floral wallpaper felt almost cheerful, but Dan got the impression that fun and laughter were commodities which were in short supply in the Ryan household. Gabriel was sitting, rock-still, in an armchair. His shirt wasn't tucked in and he hadn't shaved for days. Beside him, a small table was littered with medication packets, inhalers and tablets.

'Nicola didn't say much on the phone but then she rarely does.' Sinead's dull eyes conveyed a combination of frustration and resignation. 'My poor boy. What happened to him?'

The room echoed with the ghosts of dissatisfaction and Dan found it hard not to feel sorry for her. 'Our investigations are still ongoing. Nicola told us about some of the difficulties your son's had in the last few years. Can you give us your take on these?' He smiled at her, trying to be friendly. He was aware that they'd rocked up and begun asking questions, and he had no idea how much they knew about Patrick's lifestyle and addictions.

Sinead slid onto the other sofa and tucked her legs underneath her. 'Paddy was a good boy but that job at the bank turned his head. The money they earned, it was like toy money. We're retired now but, growing up, he's always seen his father and me struggle to get by, struggle to make ends meet. Oh, he was very generous – but it sent him dizzy. He went from being skint to earning thousands of pounds a week. He could afford anything. They were all drinking champagne and eating oysters. And then there were the drugs. He denied it of course but we knew. Nicola covered up for him for several years. I always said the drugs would get him, didn't I,

Gabriel?' She glanced over at her husband who seemed to be in his own world. 'When he came here to visit, he'd be off his head. Wild-eyed and sniffing, all twitchy and jumpy, saying that he'd got a cold or a bit of flu. And either snappy or deliriously happy.'

'It wasn't drugs which killed your son,' Maya said gently but straight to the point. It was something Dan admired about her. 'Didn't your daughter-in-law tell you?'

Her eyes popped with surprise. 'What was it then? Did you hear that, Gabriel?'

Gabriel still hadn't spoken.

'The forensic evidence suggests he was murdered.'

She gasped. 'Our Paddy?' She began fiddling with her wedding ring.

'I'm very sorry.' Maya kept quiet for a few moments. 'Have you had much contact with him in recent years?'

Dan had wanted to move Sinead on too.

'We phone him – don't we, Gabriel? – but he never phones us back.' She shot her husband an intense look of some kind, a meaningful frown, as if urging him to say something . . . or warning him not to. 'I think he's ashamed of his ma and da.' She gave a sniff and fanned her face with her hand.

Dan picked up on the anger in her words and tone. 'Why would he be?' Suddenly, the room felt heavy, and it made him wonder whether Patrick had known she thought this.

Sinead gave a tiny laugh, as though she didn't know how to respond to Dan's comments. 'I think it was when he got that job, working with all them high flyers. It was as if he'd forgotten his roots. Thought he'd climbed up the social ladder with all that money, you know?'

All the time Gabriel Ryan had been silent apart from continual wheezing as he breathed, and intermittent coughs. He was flicking through the TV channels, seemingly oblivious of the conversation which was going on around him. Dan wondered whether this was deliberate or caused by medication.

'Can you think of anyone who might have had a grudge against your son?' he asked.

She was silent for several seconds. 'We didn't know much about Paddy's life.'

'Did he ever mention to you that he was in trouble or had problems with anyone?' Dan carried on looking round their front room. It was pleasant, comfortable and clean, but he couldn't escape the feeling of unhappiness that clung to the air.

'No-o.'

'What about his ex-wife, Nicola?'

'What about her?' There was a tightening in her voice as she spoke.

A chesty, gurgle-y cough erupted from Mr Ryan.

'Weren't you keen on her?'

She gave an I-don't-want-to-say shrug.

'Is that a no?'

'She was much posher than him. We always felt that she put pressure on him to make all that money. To support her in a certain lifestyle. You know?'

'What made you think that?' Dan asked.

She shrugged and got up from the sofa. 'We suspected she clocked onto his earning potential from the off.' She shuffled over to the fireplace where she began rearranging objects on the mantelpiece.

For a moment Dan watched her, considering whether he had got Nicola wrong – but he didn't think so. People were often quick, when something turned out badly, to blame another person for having a bad influence.

'Maybe success and money were what your son wanted at the time.' Maya moved closer until she was beside Sinead at the hearth. 'Was he easily influenced?'

'Paddy? *Never.*' Her response couldn't have been more unequivocal.

Dan and Maya exchanged looks.

'Mrs Ryan,' Maya said gently, 'could you have a seat for a moment?' She gestured to the sofa where Sinead had been sitting, and waited for her to sit down. 'I'm sorry to say that your son was shot.'

She gasped. 'Shot?' Her hand went straight to her mouth.

Dan hoped Maya wasn't going to mention his tongue.

'What we don't know is why. Can you help us with that?'

She sat, frozen, as though she'd been stung. 'I haven't a clue.'

'Do you have any idea who might want to harm him?'

Sinead seemed paralysed. Hands still clasped over her nose and mouth, she continued to shake her head. This time she didn't ask her husband what he thought, and it was as though she'd given up expecting an answer from him.

'Can you think of any reason why someone might harm your son?' Maya asked.

It was a small sniff to start with. Then another and a wipe of the nose. Then she dabbed her eyes with the back of her hand. And then the sobs came full tilt. Huge, loud wracking sobs.

Maya waited for a few moments. 'Mrs Ryan, would you like a cup of tea? Can I get you some tissues?'

'Um . . . tissue, please.' She sniffed and swallowed and dabbed at her face.

Maya passed her a packet of tissues and sat down next to her on the sofa.

For several more minutes Sinead continued to sob and blow her nose.

When she stopped, Maya said, 'I have a feeling it's not just your son's death that's upsetting you. Can you tell us what it is?'

She took a loud breath in through her nostrils, her head moving back as she drew it in. 'I'm his ma. I should have known what was going on in his life. I don't blame him for wanting to better himself. We weren't always like this. We came to the UK forty years ago. Things weren't easy back home in Ireland and there was a labour shortage here. It was before the asbestos got to Gabriel. He was well then. Worked on the tools as a sparky. Now look at us. Stuck here in this dump.' She waved her hand at the walls and the furniture. 'If you'd had the opportunity to earn that sort of money, would you have taken it?' She locked eyes with Maya.

'I honestly don't know,' she replied. 'But I think a lot of people would have. And I certainly know about having to graft to make a successful career.'

'Why did he have to end up dead?' Sinead's face was streaked with blotches and her eyes were tiny. 'I never told him I loved him, and now it's too late.' Her regret lay in the room between them all.

'I'm so sorry. We will find the person who did this.'

Maya's words were interrupted by an email alert from first Dan's phone, then Maya's.

'Excuse me,' Dan said. He left Maya with the Ryans and crept over to the door. Clicked his browser open and read the message.

It was from Alexej.

Frazer was back.

And he'd posted on the forum.

Maya, 5 p.m.

Telling the Ryans about their son's death had been awful. It was always one of the worst parts of the job, and it had been made all the more poignant by the family's estrangement, and the regrets I knew Mrs Ryan would have to deal with alone. Once I got back to Tower Hamlets, I decided to duck in at the flat and grab a quick shower. It was a relief to turn my door-key and feel the deadlock: Dougie was at his place, and I could soak up fifteen minutes of silence and be alone with the events of the last few days. I switched the shower on full-blast and hoped the stream of hot water might rinse away some of the day's human devastation.

*

A while later, I was back in Brick Lane, in the front room above the newsagent's, with Rosa and her daughter sitting opposite me on the worn sofa. The flat was quiet except for voices on the TV. The front room seemed cosier and warmer than last time I'd been there, thanks to a halogen heater which I suspected Agnieszka had introduced.

I politely declined a cup of tea, all too aware that the conversation wasn't going to be an easy one. I'd prepared what I wanted to say on the way over, but now I was here, it felt wrong.

Rosa must've picked up on my preoccupation, as she said, 'What is it, dear? Has something happened?'

'I'm afraid I have some bad news which affects you both. It looks like the soup shop was targeted by the arsonists in error. We now believe that the intended target could have been this place, the newsagent's.' I ploughed on. 'That has a number of implications. For the police, it means refocussing our investigation. What we need to know is who might want to target you, Rosa, or the shop? Next, it means that the arsonists may still have plans to set fire to this place.'

'You're kidding?' Agnieszka's face paled in horror. '*Here?*'

'We think it's possible.' I explained that we didn't know whether the target was the shop or Rosa, but the outcome was the same: it would be best for her to move out until we'd concluded the investigation.

'Definitely not.' Rosa didn't waste a moment to state her position, and her look of defiance wasn't lost on her daughter. 'I'm not being chased out of my home.'

This was what I'd expected, so I took the two of them through safety precautions and explained the limitations of police support. 'Now, I need to ask who might want to harm you or the shop?' I fixed my attention on Rosa.

'Mum's freeholders are the most obvious candidates,' Agnieszka chipped in. 'They'd do anything to get Mum out of here.'

'That's preposterous,' came Rosa's response. 'You've been watching too much TV.'

I studied her facial expression and body language. Despite Rosa's bravado, I could see the news had unsettled her. 'Has anyone been threatening you recently? Any petty vandalism?' Again, I directed my question at Rosa.

She shook her head. 'Apart from the star.'

'Anyone complaining about the business?'

'No.'

'Either of you seen a tall, thin guy, hanging around?'

They both looked blank.

'This part's a bit delicate. Is the shop insured?'

'Of course.' Rosa's face was a mixture of indignation and anticipation. 'Mr Stein, the freeholder, organises the building insurance – which we then pay for – and Józef always did the contents.'

'Now, I have to ask this too. Did either of you decide to help things along? Get the shop burnt down maybe?' It was an unpleasant question to ask, and I had no idea how it would land.

Rosa snorted, as though the idea was ridiculous. 'I know I look doddery but I'm not daft. I've seen enough lives ruined by fires. There's no such thing as one that's safe. And if I wanted to claim on my insurance, why would I set fire to the soup shop?'

'I think she means did we *pay* anyone to do it, Mum?' Agnieszka's words had an icy tone.

'Did you?' This time I faced Agnieszka.

'Absolutely not. Unlike Mum, I don't care about this stupid building, but I do care about my mother. Do you think I'd risk her getting hurt? Are you asking Tomasz this too? And my husband?'

'Of course. We have to consider all possibilities.' I paused. 'But someone wanted to torch the place and I won't rest until we know who that was.' I was about to get up when I saw that Agnieszka was nudging her mum.

'*Tell her,*' Agnieszka whispered.

'The thing is . . .' Rosa broke off. Her voice sounded strange. Almost nervous.

'*Mum.* She needs to know.'

'The thing is, after you left the other day, I remembered something about your father.'

'What?'

'It was seeing them all together in that photograph,' said Rosa. 'Your father came to Józef's funeral. They all did. Kazi, Ody and Cyril.'

The news hit me like a slap in the face.

'I was worried that perhaps I'd imagined it,' Rosa said hurriedly, as if she was scared she'd lose her nerve. 'I know I've got photos somewhere, but I think they're in the loft. The ladder's riddled with woodworm and we daren't go up. I've asked Tomasz to fix it but he's busy and can't do it until tomorrow, and we thought you'd want to know.'

'Thanks. Yes.' I was absorbing the implications of her news.

'I'll leave you to . . . er . . . I mean, if he was alive a year ago—'

'Don't say that,' Agnieszka muttered, and mouthed 'sorry' at me.

'The funeral was a bit of a blur for me, but Agnieszka says the local paper covered the event and took lots of photos. One of the last Jewish processions in the East End, or something. You'll know the journalist. She's probably still got the images. Who was it, Agnieszka?'

'Suzie James.'

'I'll have a look,' I said. 'The article will probably still be online.'

Rosa was apologising and explaining and apologising some more, but her words were a blur. I wanted to be on my own. To sit down and think. I thanked them both, said goodbye as quickly as I could and told them I'd see myself out. As I clambered down the stairs, my legs felt weak and my body was shaking. This was a shock. What the hell did I do with the information? It had to mean Dad was alive, surely?

On the corner of the street, the pub lights beckoned. A window seat and a large gin were sorely tempting, but I had a task to complete. Dad would have to wait; I'd have a quick coffee and plough on.

Maya, 9 p.m.

We'd been searching for Ali in the dark for the last two hours. Under-the-radar doss spots, recreation grounds, car parks, we'd tried them all. Still there was no sign of him in the Brick Lane area. This was the sixth youth centre we'd been to.

Dougie pulled the door open. 'You'd better take me somewhere swanky.' He'd been teasing me all evening. 'Dragging me out like this.'

'Wherever you like, as long as you stop moaning and we find Ali.' I marched ahead.

'Ah, now that's sneaky. Talk about moving the goalposts. You only mentioned me coming with you, not a successful outcome or having to wear a bloody stab-vest.'

We entered a lobby. In overall appearance, it looked the same as the last one, and the four before that. Washable flooring, scuffed walls, strip lighting and plastic-coated notices. A faint babble of chatting trickled along the corridor.

The manager already had photos of Kenny, John, and Ali. 'Sorry, no,' he said. 'Ali hasn't been here all week, and I haven't seen the other two.'

Dougie and I retraced our steps, each time a little slower than the last.

'We need a plan,' I said when we got back outside. 'The youth clubs will be closing soon. I've already emailed Ali's photograph to all the local libraries, and asked the shopping centre managers to distribute them to their security guys. That leaves a few more stations, hundreds of bus stops and four more parks. We'll be more effective if we split up.'

'Only if I cover the parks. You'll get yourself killed, traipsing round like this at night.'

Dougie knew I was capable, but I appreciated his concern and was too knackered to argue. 'OK, you take the parks and I'll do the rail and bus stations. We'll have to leave bus stops for tonight. They're less likely anyway as they're open.' I handed him the list we'd compiled earlier over supper. 'Shall we meet for last orders at the Morgan Arms? I reckon I can shout you a pint to make that vest a bit tighter.'

'Good idea. I'll duck into Shoreditch nick and borrow some wheels. See you later. Be careful.'

'You too.' I got in the car, floored the accelerator and sped away.

It was so frustrating.

How could Ali have disappeared into thin air? As the days and hours rolled by, I began to wonder if we were ever going to see Ali alive again.

Feldman's Newsagent's,
Brick Lane, 1989 – Maya

I catch the urgency in Mum's voice as she makes the request. She hates it when Dad's home late.

'I'll go,' I say, relieved at the chance to get out of the flat. I don't get any competition from Jasmina, who's got her nose in a book, or Sabbir, who's been quiet again ever since he got in from work. It's the last week of the summer holidays and lots of my friends are dreading the new term, but I've been counting down the days until school starts.

Down the road, in Brick Lane, the shop door dings when I push it. Mrs Feldman is serving a customer, so I smile politely and wait until she's finished.

'Hello, dear,' she says once the customer has left.

'Is Dad here? Mum's sent me to get him.'

'They're out the back. I don't know what they're doing, but you're welcome to go through.'

In the garden at the back of the Feldmans' shop, tunes from next-door's radio jangle from a window ledge. The sun has bleached the grass to a creamy-white and it's bald in places where it's been trampled. Along the fence, and where trees cast shade, it's long and a lush green, and a broken hose dribbles water. A couple of bushes are brimming with late summer blackberries. The four men are seated around a cardboard-box table. In shirt-sleeves and shorts, their backsides on upside-down bottle crates, they seem oblivious to the whine of flies. I've seen this sight before. Dad, Mr Feldman, Mr Atyeno and Mr Merrick. Their elbows on their knees in the blistering afternoon sun, playing cards and sipping beer from bottles. Dad always says it's man's business.

Dad sees me arrive and beams. 'Ah, here she is. Won't be long, darling. We'll just finish this round. Come and sit with us.' He pats his leg, and sits back to make room for me on his lap. 'Say hello, Maya.'

I mumble a greeting and skip over. Wriggle onto Dad's lap, and lean into him, aware of his warmth behind and around me, the welcome familiar smell of him.

'What have you been up to today?' he mutters into my hair. 'Hmm?'

'Nothing much. Mum's not well again, so Jasmina and I made her some soup, and we went to the shops to get food.' We all heard them arguing last night. And Mum sobbing afterwards, but I don't want to say anything and especially not in front of Dad's friends. 'She asked if you can come home.'

'In a minute, sweetie,' he says dismissively and leans round me to lay a card on the make-shift table. 'Did she eat today?'

'Not really. She didn't like the soup we made.'

'I won't be long, then we'll go home and make sure she's OK.' He plants a kiss on my hair and throws out a light-hearted comment to his three friends. They all roar with laughter and Mum is forgotten.

I sink back into his warmth again and Dad's belly moves up and down as he chuckles and breathes. The movement is comforting, but as I soak up the sun on my face and arms, I realise that Dad doesn't want to go home at all. He prefers being here with Mr Feldman, Mr Atyeno and Mr Merrick. And I feel separate and strange and wonder if it's Mum he doesn't want to go home to or all of us. Perhaps I should go home without him?

MONDAY

8 a.m.

She opened her eyes and he was there again, a face above hers and a horrible smell. Her head was swimming and she couldn't move.

'A bit more,' the man shouted. 'She's nearly there.'

She was in a tunnel, with whooshing water, trying to crawl.

'One more dose,' said another voice. 'That'll do it.'

And right there, she knew.

She was going to die.

Maya, 8.30 a.m.

By the time briefing kicked off, my head was pounding from lack of sleep and the pace of events in the last three days. Dougie and I had been out looking for Ali until just before eleven last night, and we finally collapsed into bed around midnight. Six in the morning saw me back in the alleys where supermarkets and restaurants dumped their waste food – all to no avail. Dozens of people recognised my description of Ali, but no-one had seen him for several days.

I was finding it hard to suppress my growing unease, but right now, we had three murders to solve and adrenaline was my ally. 'Morning, everyone,' I said. 'We now have Ryan's murder to investigate alongside the refocussed arson investigation. Shen, I gather we've finally got news on our UnSub.' The intel had just come through, and Shen had picked it up.

Everyone's eyes fell on the youngest member of the team.

'No-one fitting her description has been reported missing in Essex,' she said. 'The lab still can't identify her individual DNA because none of the samples provided enough strands. However, there is a close enough match to a sample already on the database to suggest a family connection. A man called Barry Turner, currently in HMP Berwyn. He has a wife called Sharon, who lives in Romford.' Shen wrote Sharon and Barry's addresses on the board.

'So, where are we now?' I asked Shen.

'Still trying to contact the mum. There's a uniformed officer on his way to Wales to request an interview with the father. The daughter's name is Kelly, and she hasn't married or changed her surname.'

'Well done.' Relief soared in me, and I yanked the cap off a board-marker, rubbed 'UnSub' out with my thumb and wrote KELLY TURNER above her photograph. 'Finally, she has a name. Can you pass that on to the analysts? They'll check Kelly's social media. Registers, hospitals, social security. The lot.'

'Thanks, Boss. Will do.' She shone with pride. 'We've had a development from H-2-H too.'

'Go on.'

'An eyewitness saw a young woman climb into one of the back gardens on the soup shop side of the street at lunchtime on Friday. Old bloke called Arthur Monro. He's in his seventies and often walks his dog along the alley.' She checked her notepad. 'He isn't a hundred per cent sure it was the soup shop back garden, as they all have tall panel fences and wooden gates, and from a distance many of them look the same. He said he's seen her before. I'm following this up.'

'Maybe she's Kelly Turner?' Alexej's face was hopeful. 'I've got progress too. We've received the CCTV from *Alchemia* and the techs are looking for whoever carved the star on Rosa's shop, and we now have a description of the male that the shift-worker has seen in the alley behind Rosa's shop.' He pointed at an e-fit image on the board. 'IC1. Twenties, over six feet and thin.'

'That's definitely not Kenny. He's in his forties.' I caught the disappointment in Jackie's tone.

'No, but I do have an update on Kenny,' said Alexej. 'He's the person who's been posting on LfA as "s10s".'

'I bloody knew it,' Jackie screeched. 'I knew that low-life scumbag was involved in all this. We're going to get him. I can feel it.'

Hayes' surly features scowled from his mugshots on the board. Next to him, his teenage brother's face looked equally angry.

'They've tracked Kenny's username to an email address and regular internet activity.' He paused. 'There's been private messaging between Kenny and Frazer. Frazer is the person that people first have contact with and s10s is the person who provides the flash mob venue and time. We're still working on Frazer's email address. He's either extremely clever at masking his identity or knows someone who is. His email goes through a proxy system and three re-routers, one of which is via Columbia.'

Dan looked at the ceiling in frustration.

'It doesn't mean any connection with Columbia necessarily,' Alexej continued. 'There are various countries which people use to divert their ISPs to, and Columbia is one of them.' He took a breath. 'Unfortunately, people often share user profiles and log-ins on these forums. They know it makes it harder for their activity to be traced. Frazer's first post since before the arson, the one he put up yesterday, said this:

'"Stealth, my friends. This is how we will win. The deniers are after us, spreading their fake news and propaganda, but with your help, they won't stop us. Keep recruiting to the LfA family and ignore the lies. Gentrification is real. Social action is the law of the streets. Keep your eyes and ears peeled."'

'As much as that post is a load of bullshit, it's not written by someone illiterate,' I said. 'My guess is it was written by the same person who posted the other gentrification stuff.' I studied the images on the board. 'So, given s10s is Kenny, I reckon Frazer is his brother, John. Sophie Williams said John's doing a vocational course in Digital Technologies.'

'Putting his studies to good use, by the looks of it,' Jackie grunted.

'I agree. There's no way that gentrification stuff was written by Kenny Hayes.' Her tone was as unequivocal as her words. 'His writing is more like the SMS that was sent to the burner phone.'

'What if the tall bloke in the alley behind Rosa's is Kenny's brother, John?' I said. 'He's a bit younger but age is difficult to judge. He'd match that description.'

'Could be him,' said Jackie.

'My gut feeling is that Olaf Strozyk isn't involved with LfA *or* the arson,' Dan said. 'It's true that he's scraping by as an account-ant, and can't afford to employ more staff so he's working long hours. He also has no blood ties with Rosa but we've now received confirmation that he wasn't lying when he said LfA and the website aren't anything to do with him. Web4U have confirmed that his ten-year domain subscription ended, and the website was temporar-ily suspended.'

Dan's comments rang a bell. 'I agree. When we interviewed him, he denied reactivating the LfA website. Someone who's tech-savvy wouldn't have much difficulty making it look as though a website was registered to a different person, and once payments on a domain name discontinue, after a while, it can be sold again.'

'You mean someone could be setting Olaf up to take the flack?'

'Yeah. He might be a good accountant but he's a bit dozy, and naïve, and he's clearly over-worked. I don't see him as a criminal mastermind, though, do you? Perhaps, as Dan says, he really isn't involved with the group now, and didn't notice that his old website had been taken over by someone else?'

'So, we discount Olaf as a suspect?' Dan asked.

'I think so. Everything points towards LfA. With their knowl-edge, they could have used Olaf as a shield.' I shifted my attention to Jackie. 'What did Artem have to say?'

'He's a charmer, isn't he?' She was shaking her head in disbelief. 'He said it doesn't surprise him that someone intended to torch the newsagent's, and says – and I quote, he "wishes they had because it's completely redundant and his brother would still be alive".'

'Twat,' Dan muttered.

'He said if he'd wanted to target Rosa's shop, he'd have made damn sure he got the right one.' Jackie groaned.

'Thing is, that's potentially a clever bluff because it's hard to argue with.' I gathered my thoughts. 'For anyone who's interested, there's still no sign of Ali.' I tried not to give Dan a dirty look. 'I've been out searching whenever I've had a spare moment.' I checked the team's faces, remembering Dan's comments. 'Please ask your contacts to keep an eye out for him. We've got to find him. He may have crucial information. He's a minor and he's vulnerable, and we don't have the resources to launch a manhunt for him . . .'

'You *know* why that is.' The comment was Dan's, but his tone of voice had softened from when we'd argued. 'It upsets me just as much as you, Maya, but he's an illegal. Where the law's concerned, he doesn't count, and funding follows the law.'

I didn't want to argue in front of the team again.

Dan was on his feet, ready to update the suspect list on the board. 'Who are we looking at then? Kenny and Artem?'

I nodded, pleased he'd moved on.

'Who should we put at the top of the list?' Dan asked.

'*Kenny*,' came a loud chorus, and amongst the noise we missed the first few beeps from Alexej's laptop. Then the alerts got louder, and his phone started to ping.

'Hold up.' Alexej snatched his phone up and checked his

notifications. 'Someone's posted on LfA.' He wiggled his mouse. After a few clicks, his monitor displayed the forum. 'It's Frazer.'

'Oh, shit. What is it?' A knot of dread tightened in my stomach. We all clustered round Alexej's desk and craned our necks to see. Whatever he'd posted, it wasn't going to be good news.

Maya, 9 a.m.

Alexej clicked on the forum post. 'It's another flash mob. What if that means another arson?'

> **FLASH MOB – this afternoon, E1**
> Make your voice heard at St Katherine's Dock.
> Are the two marinas successful urban developments or
> gentrification? Who needs yachts, restaurants and luxury
> flats when we have a crisis in affordable housing?
> Sign up here and check your mob/email
> Exact time and venue TBA.
> Keep your eyes and ears peeled.

'Quick, Alexej,' I said. 'Sign up for it so we can get the time and location. We'll need to get a few officers over there.'

Once Alexej finished on LfA, we agreed our strategy for monitoring the flash mob, and then needed to return to the morning briefing.

'OK, everyone,' I said. 'Grab a cuppa, clear your heads, and let's resume in a couple of minutes to review lines of inquiry on Patrick Ryan's murder.'

While I was waiting, I scanned some of the reports that had been filed overnight. Dougie had sent over preliminary forensics and Dr Clark had managed to conduct his post-mortem yesterday, so the

PM report was on file. Cause of death was blood loss resulting from gunshot wounds. Tongue cut out post-mortem with a butcher's knife, by someone almost definitely left-handed. The forensic lab confirmed that the hairs came from a mixed breed dog, greyhound and collie cross, and there were traces of plastic on Ryan's clothing. So, Ryan had been wrapped in plastic at some point, and we were looking for someone who was left-handed and had a lurcher. The CSIs had preserved numerous sets of tyre marks and finger prints, but were having to eliminate those that belonged to site staff and vehicles before they could report.

Alexej and Dan were the first to return to the briefing room.

Dan handed me a mug of coffee, which I took gratefully. I was sure neither of us wanted tension in the team.

'I think Jackie's bunked off for a fag,' he said jokingly.

'I heard that, Sergeant,' came Jackie's mock-remonstrative voice, as she arrived with Shen and a few of the analysts and a technician.

'Right, let's make this brief so we can all get out there and find these bastards.' I filled the team in on Patrick Ryan's PM report, the dog hairs and CSI evidence. 'Alexej, where are we with Manor House CCTV?'

'It's a huge site, and there's so much of it, I've sent the film over to the Stratford viewing suite. I've got a mate who's a team leader over there. He owes me a favour, and he's put two of his guys on it. I've briefed them on the date and critical times, and he's going to report back to me as soon as they see something.'

'Good. Thanks. Shen, where are we with H-2-H and eyewitnesses?'

'Not great, Boss, I'm afraid. The co-ordinator says the area around the site isn't a regular residential street. There's the school, the church, the sixth form college, the farm. They've not found it easy to interview people, and currently there's nothing of interest to report.'

'So, hypotheses for Ryan's murder?' I reviewed the list I'd made on my pad. One, in particular, was concerning me.

'Given his death is linked to the arson, maybe he knew something about it?' Dan was flicking his biro. 'Or, as you mentioned, Maya, what if he's the person who bungled the arson and this is his punishment?'

'That's exactly what's bothering me. Someone clearly links his death with LfA and the fire at the soup shop, or they want us to make that connection. Unless it's a deliberate attempt to send us up the wrong path, I think we need to view his murder in that context.' I tried to get a gauge on the room. 'I've also been wondering why the killer chose to dump the body at the Manor House development. We know Ryan was killed elsewhere. Why not dump his body in a ditch?'

'That site must mean something to the killer,' Shen offered. 'It's too big a risk to take otherwise.'

'Or the killer thinks it symbolised something to Ryan,' said Dan.

'It did,' I replied. 'It symbolised him leaving his old life behind.'

'Perhaps that's it?' Dan asked. 'Perhaps the killer wanted to snuff out Ryan the person, and the new life that he created for himself? Make sure he ruined it all? Someone who's jealous maybe?'

'I think you may be onto something there.' My brain was buzzing with ideas. 'OK. Action points. For the arson, our number one priority is finding Kenny Hayes. I'm convinced the forum is the key. Alexej, tell the techs to prioritise finding his IP address.'

He gave a thumbs-up.

'Jackie, could you check whether your contacts in the North have anything new on Kenny, please? And whether Kenny is left- or right-handed.'

'Will do.'

'Dan, can you find out from uniform what Mr and Mrs Turner have told them, and get an address for Kelly, please? Try the prison governor but if you need to, get over to Berwyn.'

'Sweet,' said Dan.

'We need to chase up our two alley sightings. Shen, please.'

'For Ryan, we need to find out everything there is to know. Alexej, bank statements, mobile phone data, relationship history. And chase your mate for any sightings of the vehicle and perpetrators on the Manor House CCTV. I'm about to press the site foreman on a couple of aspects of Ryan's life. Dan, can you also speak to Manor House's HR? I'll get Dougie to fast-track the tyre data.' I switched off the projector. 'Thanks for your hard work, everyone. Let's get closure and justice for Simas, Kelly and Ryan, and their families. And let's make sure no-one else gets hurt.'

Dan, 10.30 a.m.

'Come through,' a drippy looking twenty-year-old simpered. With plaits and a short skirt, Dan thought she seemed about twelve. 'Tina will see you now. I'm Jennifer. Her PA.'

Dan had arrived at Manor House Developments' head office in the Docklands to speak to the HR Manager. He showed his warrant and followed Jennifer along a corridor. 'How's the Stepney project going?'

'We are on target to have everything up and running by the end of 2021. Well, we were . . .' She blushed and muttered to herself. Shot ahead and showed him into a spacious, bright office.

'Tina Sands. HR Manager.' A woman was waiting for him, matching grey jacket and skirt, her hand outstretched. She took her glasses off. 'You want to discuss Patrick Ryan, I believe.' She motioned to a cluster of faux-suede bucket chairs which looked like they'd come straight from Habitat. 'How can I help?'

Dan sat down. 'Are you aware of any recent disputes between Patrick and his colleagues?'

'I'm probably not the best person to ask about how he gets on with the guys on site. That would be the foreman there, Robert Johnson. We tend to only hear about issues once someone gets a bit physical or wants to make it formal.'

'And there haven't been any incidents of that with Mr Ryan?'

'No. I checked his record before you arrived. It's exemplary.'

She shook her head. 'He was doing a good job over there. A reliable sub-foreman.'

'What was his sick record like?'

'I'll check. Hold on a second.' She popped her glasses back on and wiggled her computer mouse. 'He's within the normal range for amount of sick days.' She was reading off a spreadsheet. 'Time-keeping fine. All seems good.' She looked up at Dan and smiled.

'What were his references like when he applied for his post with you?'

'Let me see.' A few more clicks. 'He started work with us in 2015. Applied for a position as a labourer. Clearly over-qualified—'

'Did he tell you what work he'd done before?'

Click, click. 'Trader in the City. I remember now. That's why he wasn't really a labourer. He'd had management experience.'

'Didn't you wonder why a city trader wanted a job as a labourer?'

She frowned. 'It's not my job to probe into people's pasts. As long as there's nothing there to worry about, we employ our staff on an equal opportunities basis.'

'Don't you ask them why they want to work for your company?'

'Of course.'

'And what did Mr Ryan say?'

'I have no idea, I'm afraid. I didn't interview him.'

Dan was trying to picture Ryan saying that he really wanted a job as a labourer. Or perhaps – after a spell in psychiatric hospital, and then on the streets as a heroin addict before he finally managed to kick the gear – that was what he had genuinely wanted. 'Who were his referees?'

She returned her attention to the monitor. 'One was Adrian Parry. The second was Mrs Nicola Grant.'

'Where is Mr Parry from? Is that a work reference?'

'From Zentralbank. He listed them as his last employer and Mr Parry as his manager there.'

'Wasn't Nicola Grant a personal referee?'

'Yes. His ex-wife. One of his referees declined to submit, so we needed another. Ordinarily, I wouldn't be allowed to give you this information but under the circumstan—'

'Of course. What's the name of the person who declined?'

'Nilufar Ahmed.'

'What grounds did she give?' Dan tapped her name into his phone.

'None. If you don't want to provide a reference, you simply decline. You don't have to say why.'

'Fair enough. What was her connection with him?'

'She was a Project Co-ordinator at Coley Lane youth centre. He'd been volunteering there.'

What had gone on there? Dan wondered. 'I'll need her contact details, please.'

Tina clicked a few keys and the printer clunked into action.

'Last question. This is important. Can you think of anything that might link Ryan to protests about gentrification? Did he ever make any comments about Tower Hamlets getting posh and too expensive for people to live?' He was looking at her perplexed face.

'Not that I know of. Perhaps someone at the site might know?'

'Nothing about Ryan and fire?'

Her eyes widened. 'Gosh, no.'

Dan gave her his contact card, but didn't feel very hopeful that Tina Sands could help them further. He hurried out of the building, humming with impatience because he had no signal on his phone. At ground level, it returned to four bars. He dialled the incident room. As he conveyed the news about Nilufar, he felt anticipation tickle.

You didn't refuse to give a reference without a good reason.

Maya, 10.30 a.m.

Overnight, elements of the media had gone to town on the Manor House murder, and Suzie James was at the front of the pack. She'd got wind of Ryan's drug problems and homelessness, and had written a vicious piece with the headline, LOCAL DRUG ADDICT MURDERED – IS HE THE BRICK LANE ARSONIST? The *City Eye* was leading with PANIC OVER CRIME WAVE.

When I arrived in Stepney, I was relieved to see that the crime scene was still cordoned off. Several metres back, reporters and journalists were jostling to interrogate a man with a poker face and a sharp suit. He had a heavy accent and was doing a good job of fielding questions with broken record responses.

Robert Johnson, the site foreman, was standing at the hoardings and seemed to be in a better frame of mind today. He wasn't shouting into his phone, but he still looked as if he was carrying the weight of the world on his shoulders. He gestured to the media. 'Some of them have been here all bloody night. It'll be a five-minute segment on the news, that's all, then onto the next person whose life has been ruined.'

'Yup.' I smiled in sympathy.

'One of them caught some of my lads in the Half Moon last night. Dredging around for gossip.' He shot the news crews a dirty look. 'I knew there'd be a feeding-frenzy once they got wind of the drugs and hospital stuff.'

Suzie, no doubt. 'I need to ask a few more questions about Patrick Ryan. Did he have any disagreements with anyone on site?'

Robert screwed his face up to think. 'Not that I'm aware of. He was a good sub-foreman. The lads respected him. Knew he wasn't from a construction background, but they liked him. It's a busy site. There are billions of pounds riding on this project. We all have the occasional spat, but I've been here all the time Patrick has, and I've never seen anything get any further than a bit of swearing when someone's knackered.'

My gut feeling was that he was telling the truth.

'How did he seem recently? Anything different?'

'He'd started helping out at some of the local youth clubs. Mentoring some of the kids and giving talks on drugs. Said he was pleased if his experiences could help them to stay safe.' He smiled. 'It was refreshing to see him buzzing.' Then Robert's face changed. 'A couple of times he seemed agitated though. I asked if he was OK, and he said something unpleasant had happened.'

This was what Nicola had told us. 'Did he say what?'

'A complaint, I think. He downplayed it, but the fact he mentioned it a few times, I could tell he was shaken.' He stared into the distance at the large crane underneath which the body had been dumped. 'What did he say now? Something about the past "rearing its head".'

'Did he say which clubs he'd been volunteering with?'

Robert shook his head. 'Sorry. There are so many round here. A lot of parents are struggling. It's amazing how youth clubs have reinvented themselves to fill the gaps. My kids love them.'

'That's OK. I'll ask about. Last thing – what are the night security arrangements here? Who's on site?'

'We have twenty-four-hour security. We have to. On a few

occasions we've had the place broken into. Idiots who are bored or off their heads. Youngsters' high jinks and showing off. We've had equipment vandalised. The cranes are a favourite with the urb-ex crowd, and we get graffiti on the hoardings at least once a week.' He pointed at the latest tags, sprayed in red, purple, black, green and blue aerosol paint. He glanced over at the media. 'On occasions, it's targeted crime.'

'Targeted by who?' I thought about the flash mob.

'Several groups have opposed the project from the start. 'Most of it's low-level. Placards. Loud-speakers. That sort of thing. The most vociferous are the ones who don't understand that private developments can help fund regeneration. They think all housing should be affordable.'

'Surely the issue is that there's no affordable provision here? It's all high-end.' I cast about for signs of vandalism. 'Wait. That tag on your hoardings.' I pointed at round letters sprayed in black aerosol. 'Is LfA one of the groups opposed to the development?'

The foreman followed my arm line. 'Too right.' His face clouded over. 'Nasty outfit they are too. If there's one group involved with criminal activity, it's them.'

Dan, 11.15 a.m.

On the drive over to Nicola Grant's flat in Mile End, Dan replayed in his head the conversation he'd just had with Shen. Nilufar Ahmed had sacked Patrick Ryan because a youth lodged a complaint about him. When she investigated the complaint, her colleagues said Ryan had become aggressive with the youth, and there had been mention of drugs. She hadn't cited the youth's name as 'John' but she had said he was tall and thin. If this was Kenny's brother John, it was evidence not just that they knew each other, but they'd had a serious falling out.

Nicola was in trackie dacks and a hoodie when Dan arrived, and had just got home. 'I nipped into Waitrose after yoga.' She had a couple of supermarket bags in her hands.

Dan followed her into the immaculate kitchen.

She plonked the shopping on a worktop and flicked the kettle on to boil.

'I wanted to ask a few more questions about Patrick.' Dan strained his ears for sounds of the girls. 'Are the kids at school?'

'Yes.'

'Do you know who Patrick got his drugs from?'

She let out a long sigh. 'It wasn't something he was open about, for obvious reasons, and he made sure the girls and I didn't meet the people involved. Twice, though, I did. On one occasion, some dodgy bloke with a cut on his face turned up at our house. The other was when we were out, having a pub meal, and a man approached us.'

'Someone came to the house?'

'Yes. Ordinary guy. Dirty hair. Off his head and ranting, claiming that Patrick owed him money. That was all I could make out. Patrick was at work and I had no idea how the man got our address. I was terrified. The cut on his face was gushing with blood, and it looked like he'd been in a fight and had his face slashed. Luckily, Amanda was staying with a friend overnight.' Nicola began unpacking the shopping. 'I was furious that this man had come to our home. I have no idea who he was or whether Patrick really owed him money. When you get caught up in the drug world, you never know who is telling the truth, and unpleasant things can happen any time.'

From the harrowed expression on her face, Dan could see she was speaking from experience. 'What happened?'

'I threatened to call the police and managed to persuade him to leave. Rang Patrick and told him what had happened. He came racing home about twenty minutes later and went straight out, presumably to find the guy. I asked him what the man wanted, and he refused to talk about it. Just said he wouldn't bother us again.' Nicola shrugged. 'After that, I learnt not to ask any questions. Our relationship wasn't sustainable, of course. Quite apart from how drugs affect a person's moods, living with someone who has a secret life means that you continually feel anxious.' Her elegant features looked haunted by memories. 'You are always waiting for that phone call, that knock on the door.' She paused, a tin of baked beans in her hand. 'We split up soon after that. I couldn't take it.' She shoved the tin in the cupboard and covered her face with splayed fingers.

It must've been awful for Nicola. Aroona would've gone apeshit if that had been him. 'And who was the other guy you encountered when you were out?'

'This was quite soon after we got together and before I learnt that Patrick had started taking coke. We were in a pub, having a meal one Saturday evening. We were eating, and this young chap sidled up to our table, asked Patrick if he had everything he needed for the weekend.'

'Asking if Patrick was looking to score, you mean?'

'Yeah. Or letting him know that he knew where to find us. And *me*.' Her eyes were wide with fear and it was obvious that the memory hadn't left her.

'That must've been scary.' Dan felt for Nicola, living under that sort of tension. Perhaps one of Patrick's old drug associates had killed him? 'Can you describe this fella?'

'He sounded pretty posh. Floppy hair on top, short at the sides. Public school accent. Not your average junkie.'

'What happened?'

'Patrick leaped up and steered the bloke away from our table and when he came back, he waffled on about him being some 'random' and not to worry about it. It wasn't until a few months later that I made the connection with drugs.' She switched the kettle on to boil again, having got distracted. 'Would you like a cup of tea?'

'Please.' Dan waited a moment. 'Can you think who might want to hurt Patrick?'

She was silent while she poured milk into the mugs and thought about the question. 'No. Sorry. I'm beginning to wonder if I knew much about his life recently. He was aware he'd hurt me, and he kept a lot of secrets. When he was on the streets, he must've come into contact with hundreds of people. Everyone's fighting to stay alive. Who knows who might have taken against him?'

Dan wasn't looking forward to asking his next two questions. 'We know that Patrick had a row with a fifteen-year-old guy at a youth club. This lad filed a formal complaint about him, and he lost his volunteer post. Do you know anything about this?' He was careful here not to mention the Hayes brothers.

She drummed her fingers on the worktop. 'He told me he was volunteering there and some weeks later said he'd been sacked. He was cagey about it, and it made me wonder whether he'd got back into drugs.'

'Drugs *were* mentioned, but Patrick strongly denied all the allegations.'

'Christ. It gets worse and worse.' She pulled a chair out from the kitchen table and thumped down on it. 'As if him being killed isn't bad enough. It's upsetting for his family to have all this crap dragged up again. Did you see what that bloody reporter wrote in the local paper?' She covered her face. 'Amanda saw it. Read every word.'

'I'm sorry.' He gave her a few moments, and then said, 'Did anything happen, or did he mention anything about drugs, that made you believe he'd got back into them?'

She was shaking her head, and through a voice thick with distress, said, 'That's what I don't understand. I kept asking him. Each time he said no, he was never going back.' She faced me now, tears streaming down her cheeks. 'And each time I believed him.'

Dan nodded. 'I've got a couple more questions, then I'll leave you in peace. Has Patrick ever been in trouble for starting a fire?'

She recoiled at the question. 'No-o.' Her tone was suspicious. Irritated. 'You don't think he was involved with the arson, do you?'

'We're pursuing a number of hypotheses.' They weren't going public with the mask and tongue elements of the crime yet so as to reduce the likelihood of copycat crimes and false confessions. 'Do you know if he had much to do with internet forums and social action?'

Nicola sipped her tea and muttered to herself. 'I'm finding this all rather upsetting. Fires. The internet. Flash mobs. None of them sound like the Patrick I knew, but he may have changed when he was homeless. Perhaps he used the internet for drugs? When we saw him, I didn't think he had changed fundamentally. He was always a decent person. But I did notice edges, little things. You know? He was less trusting, a bit more defensive, always watching over his shoulder. I don't think you can go through addiction, psychiatric hospital, homelessness and going cold turkey without it having a permanent effect on you. But he always was a bit of a revolutionary.' She passed Dan a mug and he caught the sorrow in her eyes. 'If he didn't think something was right, he would say so. He told me once that when he was on the streets, he saw a load of things which really upset him, and had wanted to step in, but he'd had to pretend he hadn't seen them, to avoid having the shit kicked out of him.' Her gaze was lowered now and her voice was a whisper. 'I can't imagine how hard he must've found that.'

Maya, 11.15 a.m.

'If your death wasn't connected to the arson, why would the murderer cut your tongue out, tie a mask over your mouth *and* pour petrol over you?' I was muttering to myself in front of the boards. 'And why leave you there?'

In the most recent photograph, Ryan was at the Old Manor House site in his hard hat and fluorescent jacket, surrounded by cranes and digging equipment, and fully focussed on the labourers he was briefing. His posture was confident, and his face had a warmth which suggested pride and trust. In the next image, Ryan was sitting on the sofa with Nicola, head thrown back in laughter while he tickled his daughter, Amanda. The third showed Ryan on the streets, dirt-clumped hair, greyed-out features and greasy clothes.

'I've heard of talking to yourself but having a chat with the dead is in another league.' Jackie handed me a doughnut in a paper bag, and gave me a knowing smile. 'How's it going?'

'It looks like Ryan knew Kenny Hayes and his brother.' I bit into the sugary dough.

'We've all been convinced Hayes is involved in this investigation somehow.'

'What I'm struggling to understand is what his motivation could be.' I stuffed another piece of doughnut in my mouth. 'Instinct tells me it's likely to be money—'

'It's always money with him. It's all he cares about.'

'I've double-checked that Hayes isn't doing time.' Alexej had overheard our conversation. 'There's no mention of him being in prison. He's not on benefits under that name, so no registered address is a possibility. With all the money he's made, I doubt he's actually homeless.' He pointed at the long list of previous addresses. 'This is the most recent mugshot of him. I'll print it.' He pointed at the image on his monitor of a tall, spindly man.

I picked up the photograph from the printer tray and pinned it to the board under his name. There were thin white scars on his scalp and a large tattoo of a woman screaming, naked and bleeding, stretched from his right ear down to his neckline. Part of the tattoo design had either faded or been hacked away at. Beneath a shaved head, pinched features and dead eyes were set into a small skull. 'He's not someone you'd forget meeting in a dark alley, is he? Even with a disguise, or changing his appearance, you wouldn't miss those eyes. And it'd be hard to cover the tattoo.' I turned to face Alexej. 'Any response from the public on him?'

'Not yet. But he operates in the shadows. I can't see him being skint, so my hunch is that he's lying low. He's probably living amongst families who have absolutely no idea what he's capable of.'

A shudder went down my spine.

'Hayes has been extremely lucky,' Jackie said. 'He was arrested in 2012 in Manchester for aggravated assault and GBH, but there wasn't enough evidence to charge him, and in 2015 he was thought to be involved in the beating of a prostitute who was part of a European trafficking ring in Salford. The girl was found in a public toilet, practically unconscious, head shoved down the loo pan. Someone had given her a beating, and slashed her face with a razor blade. She lost the sight in one eye as a result. Same thing happened: insufficient evidence to charge him. Grainy CCTV footage from the toilets, circumstantial evidence, the CPS said, and the girls involved were deemed to be unreliable witnesses.'

I groaned. What Jackie said didn't surprise me, but it was depressing. 'Another misogynist who sees women as dispensable commodities. Scumbag. I hope our hunch is right, and he is involved with these murders so that we can get him off the streets once and for all.' The tattoo was vile. 'Someone has to spot Hayes soon. I can't see him sitting still. He'll be out and about, checking up on people and keeping an eye out for kids and women who are vulnerable.'

'Thing is – he uses so many aliases, people might not know it's him,' said Jackie.

I stared at the photograph from when Ryan was homeless. 'Christ. Ryan looks half-dead in that picture of him at Waterloo.' He was on a bench with Nicola Grant. Filthy, ripped clothes. Sores speckled his dirty face and hopelessness seeped from every pore. 'Look at the difference between then and now. The Manor House job saved his life.'

'Then some arsehole took him out, and all that struggling and determination were for nothing.' Alexej thumped his fist on the desk, spilling tea from his mug. 'You know what gets me? I bet the one thing that helped him to stay alive was probably the desire to see his daughter grow up, to be a part of her life.' His voice faltered. 'And now . . . now he won't and she's going to grow up without her dad.'

His words hung in the air, like a spectre.

All murders were awful, but there was something even more tragic about someone having their life taken from them just as they'd turned it round.

Shen's voice snapped us back to the room. 'Boss, Dan's just rung. He's got Kelly Turner's address. The mum was pissed, and he couldn't get any sense out of her, but he managed to spot her address book. Kelly's got a four-year-old daughter, Abbie, and they live in Romford.' She passed me the message slip.

'I bloody well hope she got her kid looked after while she was over at the soup shop.' Alexej's voice was strident.

All eyes were on me as I read out the address. 'Flat 5, 257 Bridge Road, Romford. We can't take any risks. We'll need back-up to meet us at her place with an ambulance, and we'll need an enforcer in case no-one answers the door.'

It had been three days.

If Abbie wasn't already dead, she'd be a whisker away from it.

Maya, midday

Minutes later, I was in the car, scooting from Limehouse towards Romford, blue lights and siren on.

'There's no mention of Kelly living with anyone or having a partner.' Alexej was paraphrasing what we'd learnt about Kelly through the in-car radio.

When I arrived, Dan was standing by. Two officers from armed response were at the door of the flat, pressing the buzzer. The entrance was beside a café.

'No response, Ma'am,' said one of the armed officers. 'There's either no-one in or they're not answering.'

'Right. Ram the door,' I said. 'It's got a feeble Yale lock, so it won't take much.'

It took one ram with the enforcer and the latch gave way. Dan and I followed ARU in, clambering up the stairs into the cold flat. No cooking smells greeted us, and no recent heat. The stairs took us onto a bare landing with wood-chip magnolia walls. We split up and I went into the lounge at the front of the building. 'Nothing in here,' I yelled.

'All the rooms are empty,' one of the ARU officers said as she dashed into the lounge. 'No sign of the child anywhere here. The mother must've taken her somewhere.'

'Thanks, Phil. *Shit.*' I was gripped by a sense of foreboding. I'd naively hoped we would find her in the flat, safe and well. 'We'll need to search the place to find her address book. Anything with contacts in it for family, babysitters, friends. No phones were retrieved from the shop. I'll look in here.'

The six of us split up again.

A few moments later Dan yelled from the bedroom. 'In here. I've found something.'

We piled in.

He had a pink and mauve book in his hand and was fanning through the pages. 'It's the emptiest bloody address book I've ever seen.'

'Right, keep looking. Can you bag up her hairbrush for DNA analysis? I'll go downstairs to the café and ask what they know about Kelly and Abbie.' I took Kelly's photograph with me and hurried out onto the street and into the bustling café. Here, workmen were tucking into fry-ups and large mugs of milky tea. I spotted the boss, giving orders in broken English to his waiting staff.

'DI Rahman,' I said, and showed him my warrant. 'The little girl who lives upstairs? Abbie Turner. Could you tell me when you last saw her?'

'Not sure.'

'I need you to think back, please? Thursday, Friday, Saturday or yesterday?'

'Let me see. It was when the man come with roll and bread . . . so Friday.' He looked pleased with himself. 'I give the little girl a roll, see.'

'Was the girl with her mother?'

'Together. Yes.'

'What time was this on Friday?'

'Half eight? Something like that.'

'Have you ever seen this man with Kelly, or arriving to visit her?' I showed him a photograph of Simas Gudelis on my phone.

He took a quick look. 'Many time,' he replied without hesitation. 'And other men too.' He handed me a mug of tea. 'Sugar on tables.'

'Thank you.' I took the mug. 'Are you sure that no-one has been in or out of the flat in the last three days?'

'Nobody. We hear everything. Clomp, clomp. She has no carpet. Like elephant.'

'Do you know if she has any other regular visitors? Babysitters? Friends?'

He shook his head. 'I've seen her with many people but no-one I can tell who. She come here sometime for *pusryčiai*.'

'Does she talk to any of your customers?'

'No. Keep self to self. Best way.' He tapped his nose.

Dan was weaving between the café tables, waving a book in the air, so I handed the owner my contact card. 'Thank you. If you think of anything useful, please call us.'

'Let's go,' Dan said. His pale face looked strained and he was clutching a different address book. He turned me round and bundled me towards the door. Once we were on the street, and out of earshot of the café, he stopped. 'I've got several places to contact. Most of the names in her address book are men. She also has the numbers for half the cheap hotels in London.'

'As in she's an escort?' I said.

'Or masseuse. Something like that.'

'So, Simas Gudelis could have been a client?'

'Or even the baby's father.'

'Christ. Poor Indra. This is going to be an awful shock for her. So much for a fresh start for the two of them.' I was thinking about Abbie. 'Still no mention of the girl's father anywhere? Photos of her with a man?'

Dan shook his head, his expression a grimace. 'The analysts can go through Kelly's contacts more closely. I've got the numbers of everyone whose details seem linked to child care. There are two companies and four babysitters. I'm going to start ringing round as soon as we are in the car.'

'Right, I'm calling it,' I said. 'We need to launch a manhunt. The clock's been ticking since Friday and we're running out of time.'

Maya, 1 p.m.

'Good afternoon. I'm Detective Chief Inspector Jackie Lawson.' Her expression was grave. 'A manhunt is underway for four-year-old Abbie Turner, who has been missing since Friday morning.'

We were back at the station, watching the press conference live on television.

'Her mother, Kelly Turner, has been identified as the second victim in the arson attack which took place in the Brick Lane shop on Friday afternoon. Ms Turner lived in Romford.'

At the bottom of the screen, an image appeared. A fair-haired woman was standing in a kitchen. She had a nose-stud and pink tufts in her hair and was leaning over a little girl with brown hair in bunches. The girl was crouching in between her mum's feet, trying to pull white plastic sunglasses off her mother's head. The two of them were roaring with laughter.

A gasp curled round the room.

'It's believed that Ms Turner did not have her daughter with her when she visited the shop, and we are investigating a number of hypotheses. Abbie may be with family or friends. She may be with babysitters. She may be on her own somewhere. She is approximately one hundred centimetres tall and weighs forty pounds. She has brown curly hair which she often wears in bunches. She has a small graze on her right cheek which is now likely to be a scab.'

A close-up showed a grinning face with gappy teeth, a brown scab on her cheekbone and a nick on her nose.

'The Metropolitan Police urgently needs your help to find this young girl. If she's been alone for three days, she's likely to be suffering dehydration, and time is critical. She could be very poorly indeed. We urge anyone with information to contact Detective Inspector Maya Rahman at Limehouse Police Station.'

'Poor kid.' I switched the screen off and looked round at the faces of everyone in the team.

'Boss, I've just had a call from Nilufar Ahmed,' Alexej said. 'Several youth centres are going to hand out "Find Abbie" leaflets and put up posters. And our Media Office are putting shareable posters in police and community Facebook groups, and on Instagram and Snapchat.'

I felt my spirits lift. What had Frazer said about social action? We'd give him social bloody action.

'We'll find her.' I heard the resolve in my voice. 'I don't know how, but we will.'

'So, none of her regular babysitters have her, and Kelly's estranged from her family?' Alexej looked from Dan to me. 'Are we certain she wasn't in the fire?'

'I've double-checked Dougie's reports and the ones from the fire service. The teams combed every inch of the building, and the fire dog was given plenty of time. Even if Abbie had been burnt, Dougie is positive the dog would have smelled her, and that they would have found some of her bones and definitely her teeth.'

'Urgh.' Shen turned away.

'With Abbie's mum dead,' I said, 'gathering data about what she was wearing is going to be extremely difficult. The analysts have been studying Kelly's social media. They are trying to contact her

Facebook friends, so we can get whoever her best mate is to meet a uniformed officer at Kelly's flat. She might be able to figure out which of Abbie's clothes are missing.'

Alexej had his face glued to his monitor.

'I've sent two officers back to conduct a search,' Dan said. 'Laptop, clothes, photos, any further address books or diaries.'

If Abbie had died in the fire, it would be tragic. But if she was alive, it was our job to protect her. All of a sudden, the stakes had got a whole lot higher.

Dan, 1.55 p.m.

Dan left the nick in record time. It was a rush to get to St Katherine's Dock for the flash mob, but he made it with a few minutes to spare. From his vantage point on a bench outside the Dickens Inn, he surveyed the area once more and checked his watch.

The back-up officers were on stand-by out of sight and the local Fire Station was on red alert. The WhatsApp message, which had been sent to the police dummy phone, had said to meet at 2 p.m. outside the Dickens Inn.

'Can you hear me? Over.' He spoke softly into the lapel mic.

'All good,' Jackie's voice came back. 'Alexej's got the mobile. No texts or emails and nothing new on the forum.'

'Thanks. Nil going on here.'

'Standing by.'

Dan sat still. Vigilant. Eyes peeled. They were all praying there wasn't going to be another arson attack.

Suddenly, three teenage lads appeared from nowhere, all attitude and swagger, swearing and joking, and carrying a set of mini-speakers which they set down in the square between the pub and the marina.

'This looks like them,' Dan said into his mic.

'Received.'

Five younger kids arrived from the opposite direction, and an older teen lurked behind them, rugby-scrum muscles and a thick neck. The bruiser-guy gave a nod, and one of the youths who'd carried the speakers took out his phone. An up-tempo dance track burst into the April air. Almost in unison, the youths pulled black bandanas over their jaws and mouths, and Dan shot onto red alert.

'Stand-by, stand-by,' he said into his mic. 'Black masks with the LfA logo.'

The kids leaped into action, whooping and shrieking excitedly. They sang along with the lyrics, throwing energetic moves in time with the beat. The air was a writhing mass of arms, wild and gesticulating, and waving at passers-by.

The track changed, and next it was rap. Two girls skipped over, giggling. Pulled up black bandanas and joined in.

'That's Sophie bloody Williams,' Dan hissed into his mic.

She linked arms with one of the lads and shrieked with excitement as he spun her round. For her, it was exactly as she'd said – escapism.

'My kids are crazy about hip-hop,' said the plain-clothed PC who was standing a few feet from Dan.

Dan was silent. Last thing he needed was a talker.

One of the younger kids began handing out sparklers and matches, and encouraging people to light them.

Dan's stomach lurched. 'Sparkler alert,' he said to control.

The music switched to a house track. The dancing continued, and so did the screams and laughter. Then, the music stopped, as suddenly as it had started, and the dancers all clustered in a scrum, congratulating each other and punching the air. Dan scoured the scene for the bruiser-bloke, but he was nowhere to be seen.

The group was still hyper, clapping each other on the back. They cheered while they issued each other with playful punches. Then they picked up the speakers, and rolled out of view in a wave of adrenaline and noise. Seconds later, the square outside the pub, by the marina, looked exactly as it had fifteen minutes earlier.

'That's it. They've gone. It's all over.' Dan looked round at the plain-clothed policeman. 'What the hell just happened?'

'They've what?' Jackie asked through his earpiece.

'They danced to three tracks of music and cleared off. Little sods. They've wrong-footed us again. It was a distraction, I bet you.' Dan knew they'd been duped.

And try as he might, he couldn't shift the feeling that very soon someone else would be dead.

2 p.m.

In the pool of black blood, the weakened body was defeated. The young lungs spluttered their final breath in the darkness, as though they were calling out, desperately hoping to be rescued, yet all too aware that no-one cared.

Where some deaths were grieved, this one wouldn't be. There'd be no mourners at the graveside, for there'd be no funeral. There'd be no mother's tears, for the mother was dead, and this was a dispensable life.

It was the last breath. A fine mist sprayed everywhere.

He dipped the pistol barrel in the fresh blood and began scrawling on the wall in large, angry letters . . .

Maya, 3 p.m.

The atmosphere in the office had changed completely when I arrived back. Alexej was issuing instructions to two uniformed officers, and Shen was pinning new information on the boards. Dan collared me before I reached my desk.

'You must've been in the lift. I just rang you.' His excitement was infectious.

'What's happened?'

'We've got two men dumping a body at the Manor House site. On the CCTV.' He pointed at Alexej, who had several screens in front of him. 'And LfA has taken their site down. Come and see.' We got to his desk and he opened his browser. 'They've removed the whole website.' The page showed the message:

Not Found
The requested URL / faqs / was not found on this server
Apache / 2.4.29 / (Unix) Server at LfA / Port 80

'I'm relieved it's gone but I don't have a good feeling about it,' I said to Dan. 'Why would they take it down now?' My mind was reeling with possibilities. 'It's got to mean something.'

'Don't know. It's good news about the CCTV though.'

'Can I see?'

Alexej shifted to a large monitor. On the screen, a nondescript-looking white transit van pulled up at the entrance barrier to the Stepney site. The driver swiped a card, the metal arm swung up and the van entered. As it turned a corner, another man was visible in the passenger seat.

'Wind it back a bit, can you?' I leant forward to get a better look. The clock on the camera said it was 01:12:22.

We watched the scene again.

'Have you checked the number plate?'

'Nil return. They must've made up false plates.'

'This has got to be them, hasn't it?'

The camera showed the van driving further onto the site and round the perimeter towards the crane where Patrick Ryan's body was found. The vehicle parked up with its rear facing the patch of grass.

'They get out . . . move around . . .' I checked Alexej's face. 'Typical. Black balaclavas.'

'Here they open the back doors of the van.' He traced their movement over the screen with his finger. 'And heave out something long. That's Ryan. See the red crane with the light on it?'

Next, they lugged their cargo onto the grass.

'Shame we can't make out their—'

'Hang on. They're a similar height, both tall and thin. Like Kenny Hayes and his brother.' I stared at him. 'Is it? Yes, I think that's Kenny Hayes and his brother, John. We've got them.'

Alexej's face was jubilant.

'Guys,' I yelled to the rest of the team. 'Possible IDs on the Manor House CCTV. Kenny Hayes and his brother.'

Dan and Shen gathered round, followed by Jackie.

'We can compare relative heights and frames with our existing photos of Kenny and his brother,' Dan said. 'I agree it looks like them.'

Jackie's voice had relief in it too. 'Now we just need to find them. Manor House Developments must know what swipe card they used at the barrier.'

'Where the hell was their security?' Dan asked. 'The foreman kept emphasising how much equipment they have. Surely it can't be that easy for two blokes in a van to get onto the site and dump a body?'

'You wouldn't think so, would you?' I said gruffly.

Having dumped Ryan's body, the two men tied the bandana over his mouth, took out a canister from the back of the van and emptied its contents over him.

'So, that's the petrol. Zoom in on that, can you? See if it's the same can as the one Mr Walker found at the back of the off-licence.'

Alexej froze a shot and enlarged it.

'It is. It's the same sort.' It was another link with the arson. Perhaps we could trace a supplier and whoever bought them.

Then they lobbed the canister back in the van and drove off the site. 'We haven't got the physical evidence but we've got a good view of it.' Questions were circling through my mind. 'So, Kenny and John – we think – killed Ryan and cut out his tongue somewhere else. At least we know that now. But why? And why choose the Manor House site as the place to dump the body?'

Dan's face was blank.

'Where does the van go from Stepney?' I asked. 'If we can find that, it might lead us to the two men.'

'The techs are still checking the footage,' Alexej explained. 'We've got them going east along Ben Jonson Road and south into Aston Street, but then they turn into the unoccupied part of the Ocean Estate and we lose them. The cameras aren't maintained regularly there, and keep being vandalised. Lots of them on that part of the estate are badly positioned and out of focus.'

'Bugger. That's so frustrating. They must've known the CCTV's bad there. Can the technicians enhance the images?'

'They're doing their best but they're really blurry.'

'Thanks, Alexej. Can you start comparing the photos of the men on the CCTV with Kenny and John's photos? Keep checking other CCTV hosts for a clearer picture of their faces and the van.' I turned to Jackie. 'Dan and I will get over to the Manor House site and find out who the swipe card was issued to. If the photo-comparisons match up, can you do a media appeal for information on the whereabouts of Kenny and his brother?'

'Of course,' she said.

'If that's them on the CCTV, chances are, they're linked to the arson too. We're close to getting the full picture, I can feel it.'

Finally, the net was closing in.

Maya, 4 p.m.

When Dan and I arrived at Manor House HQ in Docklands, rain was bouncing off the pavement. Wind came across the Thames in an icy wall and tore through the gaps in the buildings. Headless bodies crouched under flimsy umbrellas, and scuttled to their destinations.

'It's inevitable that Ryan's body would trigger an internal investigation,' Dan shouted over his shoulder as we entered the revolving glass doors. 'So it bloody should.'

We reported to security and signed in. The lift took us up to the sixth floor, where a twenty-something assistant was waiting for us as soon as the doors dinged open.

'Hi. I'm Kirsty,' she said with a very white smile. 'Mr Mertens is waiting for you.'

'Who's he?' I asked her.

'Yves Mertens is our Group Director of Security. He flew over from Brussels yesterday because of the recent breach.'

That sounded promising.

When we arrived at his office, Kirsty showed us in and introduced us. Yves was a slim man in an understated navy suit and expensive black shoes. I recognised him as the person I'd seen talking to the media. 'Detectives, please come in.' He motioned towards a boardroom-type table which sat at the far end of the room, facing a bay of floor-to-ceiling windows.

'This is a dreadful business,' he said. 'I've worked for the company for nine years and nothing like this has ever happened.' He spoke perfect English with an American twang to his Belgian accent. He began pacing the carpet as he spoke. 'We pride ourselves in having stringent security at all our developments. There's no point me fudging the issue or making excuses. It's clear there have been a number of serious breaches at the Manor House site.' Yves signalled to Kirsty to bring them some water. 'I've seen your TV appeal. This is tragic for Mr Ryan and his family, of course, but I'll be frank with you. I am extremely concerned that any involvement with organised crime could harm Manor House's reputation.' He continued to pace. 'We have a number of back-up cameras, some of which take still photographs. I've sent the images from those to your CCTV Control Room.'

'Thank you,' I said. I'd suspected that telling them about Kenny Hayes' background would get things moving. 'We are here to ask about the site's entry system and how these men managed to get your barrier to let them in.'

'Our HR department issues each member of staff with a unique ID card with a barcode. This acts as a swipe-card and lets them on site. Our security system records the details of every card that's presented at the barrier. In 99.5% of cases, this leads to an individual member of staff. We have a few ID cards which are used for visitors. These are kept in the office at the gate. This was one of them. The men must have got their hands on one.'

'How?' I sat forward in my seat and directed my gaze straight at Yves.

He jutted his jaw and looked awkward. 'I don't know but I intend to find out. I've asked my deputy to find out where all our visitor cards are. As soon as I heard what happened, I deactivated the card-reader and put two guards on the gate, on a twenty-four-hour shift pattern.'

He'd acted promptly but it wasn't going to be much consolation to Patrick Ryan's family. 'There aren't too many options, surely? One or both men are Manor House staff. One of them has borrowed someone's ID card. An ID card has been cloned or one has been modified to override your entry-system.' I studied his body language. 'Can you think of anything else?'

'No. And each of those prospects makes me very uneasy.' He paced over to one of the large windows and stared out over the Docks. 'It could be carelessness. Someone goes to the bathroom and leaves a drawer unlocked? Someone's bag is stolen, and it has their ID in it? I'm not making excuses, simply acknowledging that those things are possible.' He faced us again. 'What bothers me far more is whether either of these men have been on the company payroll.' He was clearly shaken.

Dan spoke. 'Have your staff been debriefed and told to report anything suspicious?'

'I was just discussing the best way of doing this with my team.' He placed his hands on the table. 'With the site closed, everyone is at home. We have a company website and portal, and all our personnel have work email accounts which they are required to check. Perhaps the Met can give us some input on what to do?'

'Of course. I'll put you in touch with our Incident Management team.' I appreciated his cooperation. 'Many of your staff will have seen the news on the television, including our appeals for information. The key thing to convey is that each person's input is invaluable, however insignificant it may seem, and each person has a responsibility to say if they've been careless or lost their ID.'

He was nodding.

311

'How you deal with the consequences is none of our business, but someone must know if they lent their card, left a drawer unlocked or had their bag stolen.'

Dan watched Yves Mertens. 'I agree with Detective Rahman. I'd say there's a high probability that one of your employees knows something. Wouldn't you?'

Maya, 6 p.m.

As long as Kenny Hayes was on the streets, people were in danger.

And we still hadn't found Ali.

After my shift finished, I was determined to keep checking places where someone might recognise one or both of them, in the hope that they would know where I could find them.

This was my third Whitechapel hostel. The two previous ones had drawn a blank. Nicola had told us her husband had stayed here on many occasions. From the outside, it looked like an ordinary red brick building. A house, or small block of converted flats. I pressed the buzzer and was let in. Straight ahead was a glass-fronted reception and a melee of voices floated towards me. A male staff member was having a conversation with an irate male client a few metres ahead.

'No, it isn't alright,' the man was saying, his expression intense and agitated. 'I'm not leaving my stuff. Last time it got nicked.'

The staff member saw me, and gestured to the door to the left of reception.

I knocked on it. Leant through the half-open hatch and spoke to the lady who was sitting behind the glass. 'I'm DI Rahman. I'm here to see Michael Reynolds.'

'He won't be a moment,' she said, and pointed at a row of plastic chairs.

When Michael Reynolds arrived, he had a kind face. He was wearing a black T-shirt with a Pink Floyd logo on the front and 1980 tour dates on the back. A thin ponytail of grey hair lay at the nape of his neck. 'Hello,' he said, and shook my hand. 'You wanted to talk about Patrick Ryan? Let's see if the kitchen's free. Bit hard to find anywhere private in this place.'

'Lead the way,' I said, and followed him along the corridor.

The staff kitchen was the size of a toilet and consisted of a stainless-steel sink, a worktop with a cupboard above it and a wall-mounted catering urn.

I showed him the mug-shot of Ryan.

'That's him. Came here a lot. Nice fella. I heard the news report. Awful.'

'We think that this man may have been involved in his death.' This time I showed him Kenny Hayes. 'Have you ever seen him? The scar on his neck is distinctive.'

Michael shook his head. 'Sorry. Doesn't ring a bell.'

'He's got a younger brother. This is him.' I got out John's photograph. 'They work together.'

He looked blank.

'Could you circulate these images amongst all your staff and volunteers, and to any other services they may have used? You never know. They may have been here once when you weren't in.'

'Sure. I should have a bit of time after we've done tea. I can start sending them round some of the other facilities in London.' He was gazing at Patrick's face. 'I can't believe it. He was enjoying his job when I last saw him, and was over the moon to be off the white stuff.'

I nodded. 'I can imagine. Did he . . . ?' I stopped. 'Excuse me. I need to take this call.' My heart leaped up a gear. I stepped back into the corridor, my stomach doing somersaults. This was the news we'd been waiting for. We'd found Abbie Turner at last. 'Alexej?'

But they hadn't found Abbie alive.

They'd found a body.

Maya, 7 p.m.

At Duckett House, the crime scene cordons were already in place.

'Scumbags. I told you. The flash mob at St Katherine's Dock was a distraction.' Dan sent a can flying with his foot.

'Looks like it.' We were round the other side of the estate to where we'd been previously.

'This shithole's a disgrace.'

'Let's get this over with.' My stomach was a ball of dread.

We reported to the scene guard.

'We've had to extend the outer cordon, Ma'am,' the uniformed officer told us. 'A reporter got inside the block from the rear.'

'You're kidding. Who called 999?' I half-knew what the answer was going to be.

'Suzie James, Ma'am.'

'Christ's sake. That means she was in the building, in the dark, before the firearms officers had checked if there was an active shooter in there.'

The guard nodded. 'It was the first responder who called firearms. By then she'd left.'

A few yards away, at the inner cordon, Dougie was waiting for us, shuffling from leg to leg, fury bursting from his craggy features. 'You wait 'til I get my hands on her. Climbed through a sodding window.' He clamped his hands to his face in exasperation. 'What the hell was she thinking of? She'll get herself shot one of these days.'

'It would have to be her.'

'Trampling all over the blood spatter and firearm discharge. She has about as much respect for forensic science as she does for ethical standards in journalism.'

'Did she get near the body?'

'She's refusing to tell us on the grounds that we've stopped her from reporting on a matter which is of public interest. She rang emergency services and said the child was dead, so she must've been in the room with him.'

'Let me speak to her. She's been due a bollocking for a long time.' I pointed at the flat. 'What have we got?'

Dougie looked from me to Dan. 'You do know who it is in there, don't you?'

'I told her,' Dan said.

'Maya, are you sure you—?'

'It's my *job*.' I held out my hand for protective clothing.

'If you're sure . . . ' Dougie handed suits to us both. 'Professional job, by the looks of it. Two shots. One to the head, one to the heart. And some writing on the wall.'

'Ballistics here yet?'

Dan and I pulled the forensic suits on.

'Inside with Dr Clark and the forensic firearms expert. The blood pattern analyst is on her way.'

'Have we got either of the bullets?'

'Dr Clark suspects that one's lodged in his heart muscle. If we can't find the one that went through his head, he's going to remove the other one when he does the PM.'

'Be good if we can identify the firearm.'

'Even better if we can find it but right now there's little chance of either.' Dougie was shaking his head.

317

'What did he say that day we bumped into him in Brick Lane?' I turned to Dan.

'Kyle's going to kill me.'

'And Kyle is Kenny. Kenny bloody Hayes did this, I bet you.' Suddenly, guilt bit at me. 'I sent Social Services to the squat. I thought I was protecting them.'

'You were,' Dougie said, grabbing my arm. 'It was the right thing to do.'

'So much for doing the right bloody thing.' I pulled away from him. 'What it did was send Ali Kousa to his death.'

'Maya, you followed procedures.' Dan was agreeing with Dougie. 'Minors were living in a squat with Class A drugs, ammo and firearms. What else could you do but phone it in? And Ali had left before that.'

'Maybe, but we didn't follow procedures when we entered the squat, did we? We should've called for back-up. He wouldn't have run off then and he'd still be alive.'

'We thought we were going to a family flat where Ali and Riad lived,' said Dan, 'not a junky squat for homeless kids.'

'He took off because we scared him and now he's dead.' In my mind's eye, I could see Ali's face. Vulnerable and scared. I heard the fear in his voice when he talked to me.

'Look, Maya. We sprung them, and he shot through. It's as simple as that. It was the situation that scared him, not us.' Dan flung his arms in the air. 'C'mon. Let's do what we've got to do here and get out of this place. It gives me the creeps.'

'If we'd looked for him more, things might've been different. Abbie Turner went missing and we launched a manhunt. Ali went missing and we did nothing.' I felt like screaming at Dan for not helping me. For insisting that we focussed on Kelly Turner and

Kenny Hayes. 'Why? Because he's Syrian?' I faced Dan and met his eyes. 'Because he was so scared in his own country, he came here illegally?'

'Yes. That is partly why. And I think it sucks too.' He met my gaze, unflinching. 'But it was also because Abbie is the daughter of one of our arson victims. Ali wasn't. And Abbie is much younger. I know you're angry with me, but I still believe it was the right decision.'

'And now he's dead.' I hated hearing us talk in the past tense.

Dougie placed his hand on my shoulder. 'Dan's right, Maya,' he said softly. 'You looked for Ali as much as you could. Everyone's sorry we didn't find him. C'mon.' He steered me towards the common approach path and into the squat.

Inside, the CSIs had rigged up lights. Like the flat we'd been to previously, there was no electricity and no heating. Three plastic garden chairs were scattered about the room. Cardboard boxes were stacked flat against a graffiti-sprayed wall. A sleeping bag lay over the top of the boxes with a bin liner. On the opposite side of the room, a king-size mattress lay – filthy and stained – on a layer of grey breeze-blocks, butting up against the concrete render of the wall. Lying on his back, in the middle of the mattress, in a sticky mass of congealing blood, was ten-year-old Ali Kousa. In the centre of his forehead, a bullet wound was matted with blood and his child's features were contorted into a hideous expression of agony.

I gasped. It was a truly awful way to die.

Dr Clark was taking fingerprints from the body. 'That's one entry wound. Straight through and out the other side.'

Under the bright artificial lights, the pool of blood beneath his head looked black.

'Where's the bullet?'

'We're not sure if it's in the mattress or somewhere else in the room.'

To the left of Ali's chest, another bullet had torn through his sweatshirt and ripped a hole in his heart. 'Whoever fired these bullets knew exactly where to place them. This isn't a murder. It's an assassination.' I looked away, biting back tears. 'Any idea as to the type of firearm?'

'Kevin says it's likely to be a pistol.'

Around the room the CSIs were photographing the blood spatter and marking out the angles, trajectory and pattern with string. Another CSI was spraying luminol. On the wall, the words the killer had scrawled in blood, seemed a cruel irony.

STREET RAT

A dart of fierce anger jabbed at me. 'Poor kid. He escapes from Syria and manages to get himself to the UK, and he ends up getting drawn into God knows what, living in a squat with a load of junkies and having his brains blasted out.' I took in the room. The bucket in the corner. The empty dope bags on the floor. The used syringe on the ground by the mattress. 'What the hell did he do to deserve this?' I was struggling to keep my composure.

'If it's any consolation, at least he'll have died quickly.' Dr Clark's face was pale. 'He'll have been unconscious almost immediately, and bled out in minutes.'

'What Jackie said is right, Maya,' Dan said. 'This is organised crime. These kids are being groomed and exploited because they're desperate.'

Their words washed over me as something caught my attention. On the mattress, one of Ali's feet was bare where his shoe had come off. Had there been a struggle? Had he been overpowered? Then, on the concrete floor, I saw his trainer. It was a dirty white with broken laces.

And was so small.

'Street rats.'

'It's horrible.' Dan said.

'He said they called themselves "street rats". I thought he meant that was their gang name. What he meant was that was how others saw him, and . . .' I stifled a sob, ' . . . how he saw himself.' I fished in my pocket for a tissue. 'And it's all our fault. We barged in there and terrified him, and he ran off.'

'C'mon, Maya.' Dan's voice was gentle. 'We're all buggered. Let's leave the guys to do their job. The best way we can help is to catch whoever did this.'

I nodded. 'This is one of those occasions where it upsets me more to know that he has no family to notify of his death, than it would to be the person to tell them. No-one to cry and grieve his loss. What sort of life is that?'

'Let's go. The search teams might have news on Abbie. And we'll need to grab a couple of hours' kip before we hit the streets again.'

I shook my head. 'Keep me posted on the manhunt.' I took a deep breath. 'I'll meet you back at the nick. There's something I need to do first.'

Maya, 8 p.m.

I rang the bell a second time. Waited. She was in. The lights were on and I could hear her on the phone in the front room.

A face peered round the curtains. Her expression contracted when she saw who it was.

A few moments later Suzie opened the front door a couple of inches and spoke to me over the burglar chain. 'What do you want, Rahman?' It was a snarl.

'Could I come in, please?'

'No chance.' She patted the top knot in her hair and looked over her glasses and down her nose. 'You can say what you want to say from there.'

I took a deep breath. 'Suzie, I need to speak to you. It's late. It's bloody freezing and your neighbours will hear every word I say, standing here.'

'For God's sake.' She stood back, letting me enter the house. 'What's this about?' she asked, trying to sound far more innocent than we both knew she was. She led the way along a narrow hall into the lounge.

'I need to speak to you about two things.' The room was spacious and cosy, with table and chairs in one corner. Clear surfaces except for a laptop and her mobile phone. Beside the sofa, a few toys nestled in a neat crate and there were photographs of a young boy on the mantelpiece.

'I'll give you five minutes.' She pretended to glance at the clock on the wall over the fireplace. 'I've got split ends to trim and a deadline to meet.'

'The first thing is official. The second is . . . ' I paused.

Her face was belligerent.

'. . . personal.'

'Oh?' She stared, eyebrows raised. Intrigue had eclipsed defiance.

'Duckett House.'

She groaned. 'What about it?'

'You entered a crime scene, knowing very well that the best way of helping the victim was by calling 999 immediately and not trampling over evidence.'

The shrug was a reflex action, and quick as a flash. 'What if he was alive?'

'It doesn't matter. You don't put yourself in danger. You check whether the scene is safe before you do anything else.' I'd seen the toys, and strained my ears for the sound of a child, partner or flatmate. 'You could have got yourself shot. Don't you care?' It was odd to be having a similar conversation with Suzie, to the one Jackie had had with me.

She gave a dismissive shrug. 'Does it look like it?' She gestured to the empty room.

'As unarmed police officers, we are told repeatedly that we mustn't enter a crime scene where there's a possibility that someone's armed. We have to wait until firearms officers have declared the site safe to enter.'

'OK, I geddit. Can you switch the lecture off now?'

'You cannot put yourself at risk like that.'

'What do you care?'

'Enough to come round here and say it.' And I didn't see anyone else doing that.

'That's rich. When we both know it's your precious crime scene that you care about.'

'Of course I care about that. It's our best evidence source. But that doesn't mean I don't care if you get your brains blown out chasing a story. Is a scoop really worth getting yourself killed for?'

She snorted. This time the gesture was more conciliatory than hostile.

'I'll take that as a "no".' I paused. 'Look, I know we've had our run-ins, but you've got to keep yourself safe and you've got to stay off crime scenes. If public interests are your priority . . . '

She flashed me a *piss off* look . . .

'Then not doing things which impede police investigations should also be your priority. OK? Let us do our job, and you do yours.'

'I had no idea you had such a caring side, Inspector.' She pulled her cheeks upwards into a sneering grin.

'And I had no idea that you got scared.' I knew she'd seen me clock the chain on the door. I recalibrated. It was now or never. 'I also wanted to speak to you about something else . . . '

'Ah. The *personal* matter.'

'I gather you covered Józef Feldman's funeral for the paper last year? Rosa's husband?'

She was frowning. 'What if I did?'

'Would it be possible to see some of the photographs you took of the day?'

She was staring intently. 'Why? Has this got something to do with the murders?'

'No. Rosa has just told me that my dad was at the funeral. And two friends of his. We've . . . we've lost touch.'

I could see that Suzie was thinking. 'So, you come round here

324

and give me a lecture, and then expect me to do you a favour? Is that how it goes?'

I'd anticipated she'd take this line. 'We were annoyed about the crime scene, but my concern for your safety is genuine.' I thought about what to say next; hoped that, for all Suzie's defensiveness, she could see that I had been trying to help her.

'And now you want me to do you a favour?' Her face oozed irritation.

I needed to show some vulnerability and now we'd shifted off professional ground, that wasn't hard. 'The truth is I haven't seen or heard from my dad since 1990. I looked online, at the article, and didn't see him in any of the pictures. If you have any other photos of the funeral, I'd really appreciate seeing them.'

Her gaze searched mine while she processed what I'd told her and decided how to respond.

'Twenty-nine years is a long time,' I added, swallowing the emotion I hadn't realised would surface. 'If he's alive, I'd really like to know. But I don't want to start hoping he is without some evidence.'

Maya, 8.45 p.m.

Jasmina and I revived the log fire with some kindling and a couple of fire-lighters, and lit the candles on the hearth. The two of us stood in her spacious lounge, motionless, as the yellowy light from the fire flickered over the photographs which lay like jigsaw pieces on the Persian rug in front of us. Many of them had been in the family for years: faded black and whites, old Polaroids which Dad had taken, school photographs and family photos – all snapshots of our lives. Jaz. Sabs. Mum. Dad. Me. And the faces of friends we no longer saw but hadn't forgotten.

Next to them, the images from Józef Feldman's funeral, which Suzie had printed out, changed the story we'd thought we'd known for all those years. They suggested a new reality which was going to take some getting used to.

I stared at each image in turn. 'If Dad's alive . . .'

Jasmina's husband, Rubel, appeared in the doorway with Dougie close behind, carrying a tray with steaming mugs and a box of Jaffa Cakes on it.

'Here you are. We made you some tea.' Rubel padded across the carpet. From his trainers and jogging bottoms, I guessed he'd recently been for a run or was about to go.

'The Jaffa Cakes were my idea so make sure you leave me some,' Dougie teased.

I appreciated his attempts at levity. 'Sorry to turn up uninvited, Rubel.'

'Don't be silly.' He placed the mugs on coasters on a drinks table. 'You're family, and it's not every day you discover that your long-lost father might be alive after all.' He gestured to Dougie. 'And I haven't seen this fella since I got back from Pakistan.' He cast his eye over the rug. 'Just think. If you hadn't helped to carry in Mrs Feldman's shopping, you might never have found out that Kazi was at the funeral.' There was an expression on Rubel's face that I'd never seen before.

It was true. It was almost as if fate had thrown Rosa and I together – except I didn't believe in that sort of thing. 'You know the old iPhone that Mum's got?' I said to my sister. 'The one she uses to listen to Bangladesh Radio. For months now, I've suspected that Dad gave it to her.' I took the Forensic Services print-out out of my bag and handed it to Jasmina. 'I had it tested for prints.' I looked over at Dougie, and his eyes held mine for a moment. You might get good news, bad news or no news, he'd said, when I told him what I was planning to do. Right now, I had no idea which it was. He'd known Jasmina and me for over ten years. He'd watched as the cross-currents of grief and longing swirled in my life. Every day he'd seen me bury each tiny piece of hope that Dad was alive, and seal them over, one by one.

Jasmina traced her finger down the data on the A4 sheet. 'Finger print patterns are inherited. Those obtained from the phone show very close similarities with yours and mine?'

'Yep.' I felt guilty for not telling her sooner.

'Are you sure they aren't mine? Or yours?'

'Please don't hate me. I gave them your prints and mine. Got them from our phones.'

'Jeez.' She walked over to the window and drew the curtains. 'When you rang and said you had news, I wasn't expecting this.' She glanced at the photographs again. 'You might have asked before you took my fingerprints.'

'I know. I'm sorry. I did it in a fit of impetuousness.'

Jasmina was solemn.

'Sabbir wasn't alive when that phone appeared in her room at the residential home, and I made sure I wiped the surfaces clean a few weeks before I took it. So, unless she's got a secret visitor who happens to be a family member, they've got to be Dad's prints.'

'I can't believe he's alive.' Jasmina's voice was soft and she took my hand. 'Look. Have you noticed? There are no family photos after the day Dad left. We stopped being a family that day, and never realised. Dad left and the longer we went without hearing from him, we closed the circle, piece by piece, over his absence.'

'None of us have got over it though.' It was true. Mum's life had stopped the day he left, and we had spent all the years since wondering what happened. I felt Jaz's eyes searching my face. 'Something that's always confused me is why we decided he was dead.' My mind was awash with thoughts along the same lines as Jaz. 'If he'd died, he would've been identified, and we would've been notified. There would've been a funeral. That never happened so the most likely explanation is that he left us – by choice, or because something happened.'

Dougie was standing beside me now, and he gently put his arm round me. My mind was racing, and it was a comfort to feel contained. Held.

'I don't remember any of us talking about it,' Jasmina said. 'What might have happened, yes, but you're right – it is as though we collectively decided to believe he was dead.'

'Was it because that was easier than believing he'd chosen to leave us and was out there,' I waved my arm, 'happily living his life somewhere else?'

Dougie pulled me closer.

'I don't know.' Jasmina's voice was thick with emotion. 'It makes sense, I suppose. If he's been alive all that time, what do we do now? We can't suddenly become a family again.'

I had no idea either. I pointed at the image of Dad in the Feldmans' back garden with Józef, Ody and Cyril. Me on Dad's lap. 'I remember that day. Mum was ill, and she was annoyed that Dad wasn't home, so I said I'd go and fetch him. I remember the blackberries. Must've been late summer, was it?' I pulled myself out of Dougie's arms, kneeled down on the carpet and picked the image up. I peered closer, inspecting every millimetre. 'It's so weird. I can vividly recall this photograph being taken. Me on Dad's lap. The men playing cards. The garden at the back of Rosa's shop. But I have no idea what they were laughing about, or who took the picture.' I swallowed. 'I knew Dad, Józef, Ody and Cyril were friends but . . . ' I studied the image Rosa had given me again. The four men sat in shirt-sleeves, perched on crates in the garden at the back of Rosa's shop, playing cards and drinking beer from bottles.

As I pored over the images, I became aware of a thought scratching at the edges of my mind, a sense that something had been awry that day. Suddenly, sitting here on the carpet, I felt a tide of grief pour through me. I sniffed and swallowed. 'The one thing I remember more than anything was that Dad didn't want to go home.' I tried to lock into the memory, to feel my way back into what had happened.

I'd smelled Dad's tobacco.

Seen the blackberries, the playing cards, the bottles of beer.

'I told Dad that Mum had sent me. He was worried about her

and he wanted to know if she'd eaten, but he kept wanting to delay going home.' Warm tears tumbled down my cheeks. I turned to face my sister who slid to the floor and gently took my hand in hers. 'Like he dreaded it.'

The tobacco.

The beer.

Perfume.

'There was a woman.' I pulled my hand free and clasped it over my mouth. 'That's it. I remember her perfume. He didn't want to go home because there was a *woman* in the back garden at the shop.'

Jasmina put her arms round me. 'Didn't you know?'

I shook my head. 'Wait. Did you?'

'I thought we all knew.' She looked at Rubel and Dougie. 'That day he said he was going for a haircut? And came back without one and with lipstick on his neck? Oh, God, Maya. I'm so sorry. I really thought . . . '

I was trying to take it in. I felt hot all over. How could I have wiped the memory out? Had I simply papered over it?

'It's bound to feel weird.' Jasmina dried my face with a tissue. 'It does for me too and I wasn't there. In a way, I think I knew less about Dad than you did. You always had such a . . . I don't know how to describe it . . . special bond with him. That's why I assumed you knew.'

'Is that why he left us?' I stammered. 'For her?' It was as though a bolt of electricity had shot through me. 'Who was she?'

Jasmina's expression was scared. 'I honestly don't know. I never met her.'

'Do you know what really upsets me?' I faced my sister. Turned and looked at Dougie and the words came out in a whoosh. *'I've never seen him look that happy.'* Thoughts shook loose in my mind.

They swirled, making me feel giddy. 'There's so much about his life that we don't know. It's like . . . there was the dad we knew and loved . . . and this whole other person who's a stranger.'

Jasmina dabbed at my face with a tissue.

'To think he's been alive all this time,' I said, stupefied. 'Where the hell has he been living?'

'And what does Mum know about it all?' Jaz looked as bewildered as me.

There were so many questions and so many unknowns. Within those, I was certain of one thing. I'd missed Dad with a ferocious intensity. If he was still alive, after Józef's funeral a year ago, I wanted to see him.

At the back of my mind, I was aware that I had a case to solve and was due to meet Dan in a couple of hours. Whatever the consequences, I was going to find my father, and that meant doing something I should've done a long time ago. I had just enough time to do it now. 'We've never known what Mum knew,' I said. 'I'm about to go and see her, so perhaps we will finally find out.'

Maya, 10 p.m.

When I arrived at the Woodside residential home, visiting hours were over. I wasn't meeting Dan for a couple of hours and I wanted to show Mum Suzie's photos.

The duty manager was in the office with a couple of the care assistants, enjoying a rare quiet moment. 'Hi, Maya,' he said. 'Go through. She's still up.'

Suddenly I was aware that I hadn't had time to wash the streets from my hair and clothes, and buy some flowers. Today, the dread which usually tugged at me when I approached Mum's room had been eclipsed by a bubbling determination to find out from Mum what she knew about Dad's disappearance. Tucked in my bag were copies of some of Suzie's photos, and the print-out from the forensic services laboratory that I'd been carrying around for the last few days. Would I tell her about all of it? Best to play it by ear, depending on how she was.

I knocked, and pushed the door open. A blast of warm air hit me. 'Hi, Mum,' I said gently.

She was sitting in the armchair beside her bed, watching the news on TV.

'Keeping up with what's going on?' If she was watching the news, it was often a good barometer of how she was feeling.

'It's that shop, Jasmina. I'm sure it's the old bagel shop.' She fixed milky green eyes on me.

'Yes, it is.' I tried not to wince. 'It's me, Mum. Maya.'

Her attention was back on the television.

'The police are investigating the fatal shooting of a ten-year-old boy in a Mile End squat earlier today,' the news reporter said.

'Shall I switch that off, Mum?'

'I'm watching it.'

' . . . appealing for information from anyone who was near the notorious Ocean Estate . . . '

'I saw your sister on the telly yesterday. Have you seen her lately?'

I put my hand on the radiator by the window and closed the curtains. Reminded myself, as I always had to, that it was common for dementia-sufferers to get confused, but it didn't remove the sting of being called by my sister's name. Perhaps, given she seemed to remember the bagel shop, it was a way in to talking about Dad? Or was that wrong? 'I was talking to Rosa Feldman, Mum. The lady who ran the newsagent's opposite the old bagel place. Do you remember her?'

'The Jewish couple?'

'That's right.'

'Dad was friends with her husband. Wasn't he?' I fished in the plastic folder for the photograph I'd printed out. 'She showed me this photo of them.' I placed the faded image on her lap. It was the one of Dad, Józef, and their two friends outside the barber's.

The image drew her attention and seemed to pull her out of her haze. 'Switch that racket off, Maya, will you?' she snapped suddenly. 'I can't think with that noise.' She examined the image pixel by pixel, much in the way that people study paintings for content, texture and tone. 'He's dead, isn't he?'

My stomach lurched. But she was pointing at Józef. How did she know? 'Yes. A year ago.' Should I tell her the news about Dad or was it kinder to keep quiet? How I wished there were rules for what to do and say. 'Józef's funeral was local. They had a traditional parade in the street.'

'Oh?' Mum's residential home was in Stepney so she wouldn't have seen the procession, but she may have read about it in the local paper.

'Rosa Feldman told me Dad was at the reception. Did you know?'

She frowned, and her eyes glazed over. 'You told me that.'

'Yes, just now.' What did she mean? 'I've only just found out.' Was she getting mixed up? 'Did someone tell you before now?'

'I must be getting confused again. I remember Józef.' She looked at the photograph of Dad, Józef, Ody and Cyril. 'And the other two *look* familiar.' She pointed at Ody. 'Who's this one? I recognise him.' Mum began rubbing her wrist.

'That's Odyek Atyeno. I think they called him "Ody". He was at the funeral too.'

'The funeral?'

'Yes, Rosa Feldman told me that Dad and Ody were at Józef's funeral a year ago.'

Loss pulled at Mum's features. She placed her index and middle fingers on the picture of Dad, and it was obvious how much she still missed him. Why hadn't she talked to us about him more? Told us what had gone on?

'Rosa told me that Dad was playing with her granddaughters at the funeral reception, and telling them about the canal.'

'Kazi loved the canal.' Her watery smile faded as her mind slipped sideways. 'Do you remember that time he took you, Maya and Sabbir fishing? It was a scorching summer.' She sniggered. 'You all came back drenched, but no-one would tell me what happened.'

I fell into the memory. The four of us clambering into the old

334

wooden boat. Me, the youngest and shortest, struggling to climb in. 'The boat capsized, and we all ended up swimming.' Why hadn't we told Mum what happened? It was time to change tack before we both got lost. 'I've brought your phone back so you can have the radio on again. It needed a new battery.' I took the old iPhone from my bag and placed it on her bedside table; felt a twinge of guilt because it had needed a new battery, but I hadn't told her I'd taken it for fingerprint testing.

Mum had drifted now, and her expression was glazed.

'Shall I get you some fresh water?' I took the plastic jug and beaker over to the sink, swilled them out, relieved to have the time to collect my thoughts. Mum and I were both wading around in different versions of unknowing: Mum, it seemed, couldn't reliably remember whether Dad was still alive, and I needed reliable evidence. The fingerprints on the iPhone were more recent than Suzie's photos from a year ago. 'Mum, has Dad visited you recently?' She'd first told me this a year earlier and intermittently since then.

'Kazi?'

I had to hold my nerve. 'Yes.'

'You know perfectly well he left us.'

'Uh-huh. But you've said a few times that he's visited you. Here.'

'Have I?'

'And Jasmina said you'd told her that you'd woken up and found Dad here, and then he disappeared.'

'Argh. My memory . . . It's like everything's slipping away . . . ' It was as though she was genuinely trying to reach through the fog and recall what she'd experienced.

'If Dad was at Józef's funeral a year ago . . . ' I had to say it, I had to tell her, ' . . . it means that he's probably still alive now.' I took out the image that Suzie had printed, of Dad, Cyril and Ody, sharing a drink to commemorate Józef's life.

Her eyes were wide now, gaping with the years of not knowing.

I passed her the photo, and quietly said, 'Mum, I'm sure Dad's still alive.' I tapped on his image, and summoned the courage to voice the question I'd wanted to ask for twenty-nine years. 'Did you know?'

And once the question was out, I felt a rush of relief and release . . . followed by a thud of fear.

What was it?

Why had we all been so scared to broach the subject?

Maya, 10.30 p.m.

I sped away from Mum's residential home, still reeling from the day's events. It was hard to shake the feeling I'd had at the squat, when Ali ran off, that we would never see him alive again. In my head, as I drove home, scenes of Ali's dead body, and the room where he'd been shot, were playing on a loop. I'd known the crime scene was not going to be pleasant, but this was as though the images were lasered onto the back of my eyes, and much as I tried to blink them away, they came back. I saw the fear in his eyes. Heard his voice, saying over and over, 'He kill me. He fucking kill me. And all of us.'

Then, there was the stuff with Dad.

When I arrived home in Mile End, I hoped I could leave the day behind. As I opened the flat door, I got a waft of burning logs and chilli con carne. In the lounge, Dougie was half-asleep, iPad on his lap and the telly on.

I stuck my head round the door. 'Hi. I'm going to . . . shower and balcony,' was all I managed, and the only thing I caught that mattered was the kindness in his smile.

*

Twenty minutes later, I was out of the shower, my skin prickling in my pyjamas from the heat of the water. On the kitchen balcony,

I sat on a plastic chair, cradling a bowl of chilli and staring at the inky shimmer of the night sky. The canal felt full of ghosts. Under the gaze of the full moon, Johnson's Lock was bathed in light. The lurking strangers were mere bushes and undergrowth. The shadows, which were usually shrouded in darkness, tonight were tricks of the light.

TUESDAY

Dan, 1 a.m.

It had been a long night. It was well after midnight, and Maya and Dan had made little progress. They'd been on the streets for two hours, searching for people who knew Patrick Ryan and the Hayes brothers. So far, several people remembered Ryan from various locations around London, but none knew Hayes – or would admit to it.

They were leaning against a wall, drinking watery tea that they'd bought from an all-night van.

'I've booked my ticket to Sydney,' Dan said. 'Cleared it with HR. I'm off in a week.'

'That's great news,' Maya said. 'The girls will be so excited to see you. And you'll catch the end of the summer.'

He chuckled. Maya hadn't met the girls yet, or Aroona, but he had a feeling they'd get on well. 'The smell from that van is making me hungry. I'm either going to get a bacon sarnie or suggest we call it quits for the night. What's your shout?' He stood up.

Maya was deep in thought again. After Ali's murder, she'd been alternately quiet and hyper, and was more determined than ever to find Kenny Hayes.

'Maya? Do you want a sarnie or shall we knock off?'

'What? Oh.' She paused, frowning. 'Sorry. I can't for the life of me figure out why Ryan would've had a row with someone at the youth centre. He'd have known it could jeopardise his role there.

Why risk that when he'd worked so hard to get his life back on track? Everyone's told us how much he was enjoying his volunteering.'

'It does seem odd.'

'In her statement, Nicola Grant said Ryan wasn't naturally aggressive. What if it wasn't the way Nilufar's colleagues saw, and the other guy started on Ryan or deliberately provoked him? Maybe they wanted to get him into trouble or out of the way?' Her voice was animated. 'We know Hayes and his brother were using the youth clubs to recruit kids to LfA. What if Ryan knew what they were doing?'

'And confronted them, you mean?' Dan asked.

'It's possible, isn't it?' Maya's expression was determined. 'Nicola told me that Ryan was principled, and spoke up when he saw something that wasn't right. That could be why they killed him and cut his tongue out. He knew what they were up to and threatened to go to the police?'

Dan sensed that Maya was onto something. 'Ryan was dead when they brought him to the Manor House site. They didn't need to douse his body with petrol unless they wanted to suggest a link with the arson.'

'Same with cutting his tongue out and tying an LfA bandana over his mouth.' Her voice was quiet now. 'All three things are symbolic, aren't they? Ryan knew something that whoever killed him wanted kept quiet, I'm sure of it. Not necessarily who the arsonists were, but something that was enough to make someone want to get rid of him.'

Maya, 7.30 a.m.

By sunrise, and after four hours sleep, I was back at the office, spooning sugar into a mug of extra-strong coffee while HOLMES loaded on my PC. The sound of footsteps caught my attention.

Alexej stopped at my desk, drumming a bunch of papers with a pen. 'Still nothing on Abbie,' he said, his voice tight with worry. 'Another search team is about to set off.'

'Oh, God. I hope they find her today. I was about to check for updates.'

'Good news though. Our old boy, Arthur Monro, called in late last night. Originally, he thought the person he saw going into the rear garden at the soup shop on the morning of the arson was female, but he's seen the images of Ali Kousa on the TV and says that's who he saw.'

'Is he sure? Why would Ali have been going into the soup shop garden?'

'Arthur says he's definite. He recognised the white trainers. He's coming in this morning to give a statement.'

'Shit. That means Ali could have torched the soup shop.'

'Yup.' He added Ali's name to the suspect list. 'What do you want us to do?'

'Can you give me a minute?'

'We've circulated Kenny Hayes' photo and description as widely as we can. And his brother's.' He fiddled with a paperclip while he thought. 'You can't miss Kenny because of his tattoo, and six feet three isn't common. John's younger and —' He stopped. 'John's a student at New City College . . . ' He pointed at my computer. 'Is your update log open?'

'Be my guest.' I was still thinking about Ali as our arsonist. 'Did you write down what Arthur Monro said?'

'Yeah. Here.' Alexej tossed me his notebook and put HOLMES on full-screen. 'Look. Shen checked with New City College's registry but I'm not sure she remembered to include his aliases.' Click, click. 'Kenny Hayes used the aliases Kyle Cox and Karl Cox. And . . . ' He traced his finger down the list of students named John.

John Nugent
John Brodi
John Hamilton
John Davison
Jon Kadare
John Arnold
John Cox

'*Bingo,*' Alexej shouted. 'John Cox. We should be able to get an address now. Unless he's using an alias, of course.' He checked the time. 'I'll speak to the Registry as soon as it opens.'

It was a breakthrough at last.

While we were waiting, I resumed reading Alexej's notes on his call with Arthur Monro. The person he described sounded like Ali. 'Did Arthur mention Ali having a bag with him?'

'Don't think so. He's due in at nine. I'll ask him.' He returned to his screen.

'Assuming New City College's records are correct, it means

that Hayes has got his kid brother involved with criminality, as we suspected. What a scumbag. He doesn't give a shit who he drags into his vile world, does he? I wouldn't mind betting those two are holed up somewhere.' I rubbed my dry eyes. I was wracking my brain for where else we could get John's address from so we didn't have to wait for the Registry to open. It was so frustrating to have another delay.

'It's exactly what he did in Manchester and Salford.' Jackie had joined us and was circling Hayes' mugshot on the board. 'He started with drugs and quickly diversified. He regularly changed his habits and locations, and fired and hired to avoid being caught. I wouldn't mind betting Kenny's behind the arson and Ryan's murder. It's exactly his style. If anyone poses the slightest threat to his business, he takes them out.'

I sensed that what Jackie was saying was true, but I had a nagging feeling that it wasn't the whole story. Kenny Hayes might be the common denominator, but I couldn't see any tangible reason for him to want to burn down Rosa's shop, or the soup shop. I was sure there was more to it than— 'That's it. I've got it.'

I stood, facing Alexej and Jackie.

My body ran hot then cold as the realisation took shape in my mind. 'I thought it could have been any of Kenny's recruits, but it's been under our noses all the time. Ali's the person who got the shop wrong.' I got up and went over to the board. Pointed at the SMS and looked at Jackie. '"The shop on right wiv a star above a blue front door." It's such an easy mistake to make. If they weren't sure, most adults would check, but a kid might not. They'd assume the adult gave them the right information. If they were in a panic, living a life of chaos and fear, they'd be even less likely to check.' All eyes were on me. 'Ali's English isn't good either. When I interviewed him on

345

Friday, he got his left and right mixed up. I reckon he got the wrong shop and that's why Kenny killed him – not because he brought the social workers to their door, but because he ballsed up a job.'

Alexej jumped out of his seat and joined me at the boards.

'I knew whoever made the mistake was going to pay.' I said. 'You were right, Jackie. Kenny will not stop at anything.'

Maya, 9 a.m.

Nicola Grant opened the door looking very different from the way Dan had described her. Gone was the make-up and the expensive clothes. She had greasy night cream plastered all over her face and was wearing pyjamas. Her skin was red and blotchy from crying, and her eyes looked sore.

'I rang a few times but kept getting your voicemail,' I said. 'I would like to ask you a few more questions. Could I come in?'

There were no signs or sounds of either daughter in the flat.

She closed her eyes and took a deep breath, as though needing to inhale some patience, some strength perhaps. 'If you have to,' she said unenthusiastically, and she stepped back for me to pass her into the flat.

'Sorry if I woke you.'

'I've had migraine. I got up to get the girls ready for school. Alan's just dropped them off and gone to work. I went back to bed.'

She took me into the lounge. 'Has something happened?' she asked over her shoulder.

'We've received some information which puts the arson in a fresh light. As we believe they're connected, that affects how we are approaching Patrick's murder.'

Nicola's face was pale, so I waited for her to sit down. She sunk onto a chair and attempted to straighten her hair.

'We believe that Patrick may have met the man who killed him during the period when he was sleeping rough. Unfortunately, we have little knowledge of the people he hung out with, if he made any friends, who he got into rucks with. Can you help us?'

Nicola's face changed immediately. 'Do you think so?' Concern and protectiveness replaced her irritation. 'I've been going over and over all the people he met, trying to think who might want to hurt him. All the times I saw him, and followed him, and went to meet him. I kept engineering things so I would bump into him, just to check he was OK. I was convinced he was going to get murdered on those bloody streets.' The words came out with a whoosh of emotion, followed by deep sobs.

I waited a few moments. 'Can I make you a cup of tea or something? I'm aware I've barged in and it's hardly likely to help your migraine.'

She dabbed at her nostrils with a soggy tissue, and blew her nose. 'Thank you.' She checked the clock on the wall. 'I can take a couple more Migraleve actually.'

'While I put the kettle on, could you cast your mind back? Did Patrick ever mention meeting a man called Kenny Hayes? Sometimes he used the name Karl or Kyle.'

Her face registered nothing.

In the kitchen, I flicked the kettle on to boil and took two mugs from the draining board. While I was waiting for the water to heat, I let my gaze wander round the room. A solid wood worktop lay over a breakfast bar, and high stools had been fashioned of the same wood. A cream retro fridge occupied a corner, and matching cream cabinets nestled against the walls under soft lighting. It was a lovely room. Clearly Nicola Grant's new husband earned good money, and they were very comfortably off. On the wall over the radiator, someone had assembled a collage of photographs. At least a third of these had Patrick in. With Nicola and Amanda; with both girls; on his own; in his hard hat, boots and reflective gear at the Manor House site; on their wedding day; with a few of his peers on the trading floor at the bank. One image in particular caught my eye. In it, Patrick Ryan was eating some food from a paper plate. In the background, several guys were also tucking into food, including a very tall one.

'Nicola?' I yelled towards the lounge. I leapt over to the door and shouted down the hall. 'Can you come in here a second?'

It was Kenny. The pinched features. The small skull. The ugly tattoo. The door-frame height.

'What is it?' She was shaking.

'Do you know this man?' I pointed at the photograph.

She screwed up her eyes to get a good look. It wasn't a brilliant picture. Slightly out of focus. 'Hold on. Let me get my glasses.' She turned and scanned the room. Grabbed them up from the worktop by the fruit bowl.

I unpinned the photo and passed it to her. 'This is the guy we think may have killed Patrick.'

Nicola studied the image and I wondered how she felt, staring into the face of the person who'd killed the man she clearly loved deeply. 'I have no idea who he is.'

'Are you sure?'

She peered again. Squinted.

'Does he look familiar?'

She shrugged. 'No.' She put her hand out to steady herself. 'This man killed Patrick?'

'We think so. Who took this photograph? Where was it taken?'

'I must have taken it. Amanda never came to Saturday Soup. I wouldn't let her. It's the charity hot food thing at Waterloo every week for the homeless. Volunteers cook food and bring it down. I help them. It was a way of making sure that Patrick got a hot meal at least once a week and I could keep tabs on him. The volunteers talk to the men and women, trying to help them get fixed up with hostels, GP services, dentists, showers. I still help out because I know how tough the streets are.'

'Did the same people come every week?'

'A lot of them were regulars, yeah.'

'Can you get me the contact number of the Saturday Soup coordinators? I need to call them. One of them may know where this guy lives.'

*

Ten minutes later, I'd got through to Phil Harmond, one of the Project Coordinators at Saturday Soup. I'd taken a copy of Nicola's image on my phone and emailed it to him.

'Yeah. I do recognise him,' Phil told me over the phone. 'Can't miss that ugly scar down his neck, can you? Seen him recently too and gave him short shrift. His hair's shaven now and I don't think he's still staying in hostels. I think he's living in someone's flat. Name's . . . hang on . . . oh shit, what is it now? Kyle. That's it. One of the guys kept calling him "Kylie" to wind him up, and he went apeshit. A whisker away from head-butting the chap. What's he done, by the way?'

I explained. 'Does anyone know where this flat is?'

'No. But one of the women mentioned that he wasn't homeless. She was petrified of him. Said something about drugs and the Ocean Estate. That any help?'

'Definitely. Thank you.' Hopefully Alexej had got an exact address from New City College by now.

'I'll get this picture out to as many services and people as I can then. See if anyone can help you with a proper address.'

I rang off. The team would be relieved. After years evading custody and justice, Kenny Hayes' days were numbered. In the short time since Friday, he'd been behind four deaths. I was sure of it. Not to mention Indra's unborn child, and little Abbie, who we were still desperately trying to find. I couldn't wait to get him into an interview room and court.

And a prison cell.

Maya, 10.30 a.m.

'You're through to the incident room at Limehouse Police Station. DI Rahman speaking.' I gestured to Alexej to record the call. 'How can I help?' The caller had insisted on speaking to me.

'Hello, yes.' It was a man's voice. 'My daughter saw something in a mums' Facebook group about that missing girl? Abbie Turner?'

I waved my arm in the air to attract Dan.

'The thing is, I think I've heard a child crying in the flat next to mine. I didn't say anything at first because I thought it was a cat, but I'm sure it isn't and Julie, that's my daughter, she said that the girl's been without water since Friday and that if I thought it was a girl I had to tell the police . . . ' The words came flooding through the receiver. 'And if it is that little girl, I've heard the noise since Friday and—'

'Slow down a minute.' I had to make sure he didn't hang up before I got the address. 'You did the right thing, calling in. Thank you. Let's start at the beginning. Where are you ringing from?'

'One of them new blocks on the Ocean Estate in Stepney. Coley House.'

It was one of the posh blocks I'd seen with Dan. I checked on the telephone system that the man's phone number had come up.

'Not sure who the flat belongs to but two fellas have been staying there for the last six months. Brothers, I think. Right dodgy and all. One of them's got an ugly tattoo down his neck.'

It had to be Kenny and John. But what was Abbie Turner doing with Kenny Hayes?

The man took a gulp. 'Look, you need to get a wriggle on. If it's her in there, I can't hear her anymore. I haven't heard a peep since yesterday. For all I know, she might already be dead.'

Maya, 11.30 a.m.

The helicopter was hovering over the recently developed part of the Ocean Estate. It was a rare sight these days, making the buildings shudder. The drone of the engine was deafening, and weighed down on the sprawling mass below. We had to move quickly before Kenny did a runner from the flat he'd been living in.

Firearms officers had the battering ram in position. 'Three, two, one, *go*,' the voice ordered. At the exact moment they rammed the door of the flat, the helicopter switched its siren and lights on. The door crashed open.

'*Armed police!*' The team leader was in front. 'The building is surrounded. We are armed and ready to fire.' They swarmed in, a parade of blue and black.

From inside the flat, a startled dog let out a series of rapid-fire barks.

I'd been told to wait for the all clear, so I stood back, with the paramedics, holding my breath, praying Abbie was still alive.

'Get the dog. Someone get the bloody dog,' the ARU team-leader yelled.

I strained my ears for shots inside the flat. *Please may Abbie be safe.* And we needed Kenny Hayes and his brother alive too.

'I repeat. You're surrounded. Stay where you are, both of you. Hands on your head. Against the wall.'

I held my breath.

Shouting.

A girl screamed.

'Get off her. Taking your filthy hands off my daughter.'

His daughter?

The dog's bark was like a machine gun.

'Put your hands on your head, Mr Hayes. It's all over. You are surrounded. Keep your hands where I can see them and send the girl over to me. NOW.'

There was a loud crash.

More screaming.

Then, 'All clear. Over.' The voice came through my earpiece. 'Suspects apprehended. One minor, and we've got the girl. Repeat. The girl is alive, but she needs emergency treatment now. Send the paramedics in. Over.'

Thank goodness. We could finally bring Kenny and his brother to justice. We just had to hope that Abbie Turner wasn't too far gone.

Maya, 12.30 p.m.

Back at the station, the atmosphere in the incident room was jubilant. Abbie Turner was alive – although critically ill in hospital – and we'd finally got Kenny Hayes and his brother in custody. But I couldn't shift the feeling that several pieces of the jigsaw were missing. A succession of ideas paraded through my mind. We were fairly certain that Ali had meant to torch Rosa Feldman's newsagent's but set the soup shop on fire instead. We also believed that Kenny and his brother had killed Patrick Ryan and Ali Kousa. But we didn't have a handle on what any of their motives were to complete the picture and assist with charging. Ali wasn't alive to tell us, and Kenny Hayes was hardly going to cough unless it meant him worming out of culpability or reducing his likely sentence.

Jackie was waiting at my desk, looking elated. 'We've got the van that Ryan was transported in.'

'You're kidding?' I took my coat off and deposited my phone and keys on the desk.

'A couple of planning officers from the council were there to assess the development of the block where the squat is. They'd seen the media coverage of the raid on the flat, so when they stumbled on Kenny's van, they called in. As we suspected, it was dumped where the CCTV isn't working.'

'Bloody typical. They've let the place rot for years and now a kid's been killed there, they decide to develop it.' I swore under my breath. 'Let's hope they find some blood and dog hair in the van.'

'Your wish has just come true. Dougie's team are doing the forensic tests now. He says it's a blood-bath in the back so I think that's a given. The chassis number is registered to Hayes, so there's no doubt it's his.'

As I absorbed the news, my thoughts kept sliding back to motives. 'Something's not right, Jackie. We've missed something, I can feel it. Why would Kenny care about torching Rosa's shop? Sure, they're involved with LfA, but it's hardly a high-profile property – even if the fire grabbed headlines, why start with the shop? What was in it for them?' I began logging into HOLMES. Until— 'Wait a minute. We've been looking at this wrong.' I grabbed up my car keys and phone, and pulled my coat off the back of my chair.

Jackie was staring at me.

'I've had an idea. If I'm right, it fills in the missing pieces.' I checked the office clock. 'I won't be long.'

Curiosity was written all over Jackie's face.

I was out of the incident room before she had time to ask where I was going or mutter about procedures.

*

Twenty-five minutes later, I was in the rear garden of Rosa Feldman's newsagent's. I watched the person I'd known since I was four tug handfuls of bindweed and brambles from the ground. The midday sun slanted on the panes of the shop's first-floor windows.

Tomasz had his back to me and must've heard me approach as he spun round. 'Hi,' he said, and he lobbed the weeds onto a growing pile by the fence. 'She needs a gardener. The constant up-keep is too much for her.'

For a moment, I caught a boyish look on his kind features.

'D'you remember when we were kids, and I'd order stock for the shop when Dad was out? Mum would cover for me and tell Dad that she'd put the order through.'

'The Black Jacks?'

'It drove me nuts that Dad didn't give a shit about the shop. He'd sit around with his mates, playing cards, drinking, smoking, chewing the fat, while Mum worked her butt off behind the counter.' He picked up a damp Rizla packet and a rusty can. 'I wanted to help because the old man wouldn't, but he couldn't stand me "interfering", as he called it.'

Even then Tomasz had identified a problem and taken matters into his own hands.

'I saw the news.' He was pulling at brambles again, wrenching at the tangles of thorny branches, using his foot as leverage to snap their lengths. 'That boy set fire to the soup shop.'

'Yes. It's very sad. He made a dreadful mistake – we don't quite know how yet – and ended up killing Simas and his female friend.' I studied his tells. 'What we don't understand is why a ten-year-old kid would torch a shop.'

'Is that why he was killed? For torching the shop?' Tomasz's voice was casual, as though he was having a chat with a pal in the pub. He suspended his handful of weeds mid-air while he waited for me to answer.

'We believe so.' Was I imagining it or had he flinched?

He knew that his mother's shop was the intended arson target, and that we'd ruled him out as a suspect because, unlike his sister and brother-in-law, he wasn't short of money. I shouldn't have given him the information about Ali's murder, but I'd planned what I needed to say, and my gut instinct told me that the human angle was key. The next bit wasn't going to be easy. 'Do you know someone called "Kenny Hayes" by any chance?'

'I should imagine the whole country does. He's been plastered over the news for the last few days.' He carried on pulling up weeds. 'Has he really been recruiting kids to crime?'

'Yes.' He'd taken the hook. 'We're fairly sure he's responsible for the death of Patrick Ryan and Ali Kousa, the young boy, and we know he was involved in the arson at the soup shop.'

'Really?' Tomasz dropped the weeds on the pile and leaned against the fence.

I nodded. 'Except, a bit like Ali, I can't figure out what his motive could be.'

'No idea, I'm afraid.' He tried to make his voice sound detached. It was the sort of thing you might say if someone asked your opinion.

'I expect it was financial. Money's the only thing that matters to Hayes, and Ali was sadly in the same situation. If Hayes said he'd pay Ali to start the fire, I'm sure it was a pittance and he probably never handed all the cash over.' I paused, not taking my eyes off Tomasz. 'But Kenny Hayes wouldn't come cheap. And it got me thinking about who would have that sort of money.'

'Yes, I see.' He was kicking at the dirt with the tip of his shoe, and moving the soil around in a circular motion with the sole.

'And it reminded me of a few things that you and Agnieszka said about your mum.'

'Oh?' His face drained of colour, and he spoke with a hint of a stammer. 'Like what?'

I kept my voice steady. Calm. 'It's obvious how much you care about her and—'

'Of course. She's my mother. She's seventy-five and she's on her own now.' Business-like was back again. 'She adored Dad but her life with him wasn't easy. She made excuses for him all the time, and rarely complained, and she's struggling even more now because Dad let the shop go.' He took out his phone and checked the time.

'When you said you'd tried everything to help her, and had given up, I wondered whether that was true.'

'What d'you mean?'

'Are there things you ruled out, things you considered?'

His brow crunched into a deep frown. 'Lots of things. I bought her a house, for God's sake. I've given tenants notice to quit, so she had somewhere warm and dry to move to. She wouldn't agree to any of it. Her GP told her she was jeopardising her health, continuing to live at the shop, and she even ignored him.' He was shaking his head. 'It was as if she gave up when Dad died. Like she didn't care if she dropped down dead in that bloody place.' He coughed. 'It's not easy watching someone you love suffer.'

'Like I say, no-one doubts how much you care about her. And you're hardly short of money so you'd have nothing to gain by forcing her out of the shop . . . ' I let my words sink in. 'And I'm sure you wouldn't have intended her to get hurt in the fire . . . '

I felt Tomasz's eyes searching mine for clues as to whether I was being serious.

'Are you suggesting what I think you're suggesting?' he finally asked.

'I'm wondering whether you paid Kenny Hayes to set fire to your mother's shop, to force her into moving out without having to make a decision or feel bad.' If I'd known, all those years ago, that I was going to have this conversation with Tomasz . . .

He used his foot to turn a plastic bottle crate on its head and sank onto it.

'Did you know Kenny was going to recruit Ali for the job?'

He was silent.

'And somehow Ali set fire to the wrong shop, and then Kenny killed him.'

Silence.

'Tomasz, please tell me I'm wrong.'

'Is that what you'd like to hear?' His words were so quiet I barely caught them.

'Of course.'

He was leaning forward, his head in his hands. 'I wish I could say that.' He rubbed the stubble on his chin and seemed to be considering what to say. 'It was a stupid idea. I told him to make sure that Mum was not in the shop. She was never meant to get hurt. I don't know how that kid got the wrong shop. I can only think that Kenny gave him the wrong information and—'

'That *kid* had a name. His name was Ali Kousa, and he probably misunderstood the message because he didn't speak good English.'

'Maya—' He let out the sigh of someone deeply burdened. 'I told Kenny to make sure that he did exactly what I asked. He was to do it himself. No-one was to be in the building or near it. It was to be a small fire, in a contained area, enough to force her to move out, but it wasn't to put anyone in danger or destroy the upstairs where her belongings were.' He was shaking his head, bewildered.

'Surely you knew that Kenny never does anything himself?'

'No. I've realised I don't really know him at all. I was stupid to trust him. Simas, the woman and Ali? They're all dead because of me, and all because I thought this would help Mum.' With that, Tomasz put his head in his hands.

I was looking at a truly broken man.

Maya, 2.30 p.m.

An hour later, I entered the custody suite with Jackie. Samples, prints and swabs had been taken from Kenny Hayes, and he'd been escorted into an interview room with his solicitor, Mike Taylor.

Hayes was sitting across the table from us. He was leaning over, scraping grease out of a join in the wood with his thumbnail and tracing the movements with his gaze. From the top of his head, scalp-flakes drifted onto his hands and the table.

'That's the caution over with.' I took a deep breath and swallowed down the anger which had been welling up for days. It wasn't just Simas, Kelly, Patrick and Ali. It was Indra, Abbie, Amanda and Nicola. And in many ways Ali's murder upset me the most. 'Tell us about this man.' I slid a photograph across the table. 'For the benefit of the tape, I'm showing the suspect exhibit number 3725.'

Hayes sneaked a look at the image. Curled his lip and sniffed. 'No comment.'

'You see, several eyewitnesses have testified that you've been living in a flat belonging to him on the Ocean Estate for around a year. The new, luxury ones, where we arrested you. So, would you like to try that question again? Do you recognise him?'

'No comment.'

'Mr Taylor, could you make sure your client knows that it may harm his defence if he later relies on something which he hasn't mentioned during questioning. I'm sure you understand the middle part of the police caution, but does he?'

The solicitor leant towards Hayes and delivered a few curt sentences to him.

'Yeah, I know him,' Hayes snarled.

'By what name?'

'Tomasz Feldman.'

'Have you been paying to live in his flat?'

Hayes scoffed. 'You from the Housing Benefit Office or something?'

'It's a simple question. You either have or haven't been paying to live there. Which is it?'

Hayes looked at his solicitor for a steer. The man nodded.

'I have.'

'If we checked your bank accounts, would we find a regular amount being paid from you to him?'

'Good luck with that,' he sneered.

'Why's that? Did you pay him in cash?'

'When I paid him.' He scoffed.

'Where did you get that cash?'

'I have a little flutter on the horses, don't I? Get lucky sometimes. Know what I mean?'

'I see.' I deliberately stretched my pause out. 'When our officers searched the flat, where you've been living, they found a Glock 19 with your fingerprints on it. What can you tell us about that?'

'No comment.'

Jackie's body twitched next to me.

'It has no-one else's fingerprints on it,' I said.

'State your question, DI Rahman, please.' The solicitor's voice creaked with anticipation.

'If we tested it, other than fingerprints, what do you think we may have found on it?'

'No idea.'

'Might the gun have had blood, skin cells and tissue on it?'

'No comment.'

'What about cells which belong to Ali Kousa, the Syrian boy you groomed into crime and then shot? Would it have those?'

'I take it you have evidence for these allegations, Inspector?' Taylor asked.

'I do.' I slid another image across the table. 'This boy. We have lots of witnesses who confirm that you know him, so please don't bother trying to deny you do.'

Hayes was staring at the ceiling now, lounging back in his chair with his arms folded. I could see the angry tattoo on his neck, and as he spoke his skin parted round the colours and patterns like ugly sores.

'I'm trying to figure out why, though. Why would you assassinate a ten-year-old boy who's a homeless asylum seeker? Who's here without any family or money?'

'They're filthy street rats,' he hissed. 'That's why.'

I'd guessed he'd fling this at me and I kept my face neutral, deliberately not letting him see how appalling I found his expression. Instead I let his words hang in the air by jotting in my notepad and nodding to myself.

'Useful street rats, though, no?'

'You what?' He practically spat the words.

'Did Ali Kousa do something to you? Or disappoint you in some way?'

Hayes' face flickered with confusion. 'No comment.'

'You see, we did find Ali's blood, skin cells and clothing fibres on the Glock in your flat.' I pushed a forensic services print-out across the table at the solicitor. 'And paint from the wall where you wrote "STREET RATS". If you didn't kill him, can you explain how those came about?'

'No comment.'

'We have your DNA on the discharged syringe on the floor where Ali was shot, and your finger and footprints in that squat room. Would you like to tell us about that?'

'So? I've been there loads of times. Circumstantial, innit?' He glanced at Taylor, puffed up.

'We also have your fingerprints on the petrol canister which was in the Walkers' back garden. Along with Ali Kousa's prints too. No-one else's. Just yours and Ali's.' I fixed my gaze on his. 'If you weren't involved with the arson at the soup shop, how else could those prints have got on the canister?'

'No comment.'

'Perhaps you need to have another word with your client, Mr Taylor, about not mentioning something which he might want to rely on later?'

Taylor gave Hayes a nod.

'I don't know.'

'Who lit the match? You or Ali?'

'DI Rah—'

'Apologies. I forgot to mention that we have an eyewitness who's testified to seeing Ali Kousa going into the back of the soup shop the afternoon of the fire.' I slid Arthur Monro's statement to the duty solicitor. 'The thing is, we believe that Ali got the wrong shop. Is that what happened, Mr Hayes?'

'No comment.'

'Did you tell him to set the newsagent's on fire and somehow he screwed up? Is that why you killed him?'

'No comment.'

'What would you say if I told you that when you switched on the mobile, which you used to text Ali the shop details, cell site data told us it was in your flat?'

He sat up at this. Mumbled to his brief out of the corner of his mouth. 'What's she on about?'

Taylor peered over the top of his glasses at the print-out. 'Let's move on.'

'So, unless you want to carry the can entirely, I suggest you tell us why you did it, and who else was involved?'

'It wasn't me.'

'Who was it then?'

'No comm—'

'Don't even try that, Mr Hayes. At the moment, we've got you for the arson at the soup shop,' I deliberately counted out the offences on my fingers, 'the manslaughter of Simas Gudelis and Kelly Turner, the abduction and murder of Patrick Ryan, and the murder of Ali Kousa. And a string of exploitation, drugs and firearms offences. Not to mention Abbie Turner. How's that sounding?'

'Like he'll never see daylight again.' Jackie could barely contain her glee.

Hayes paled in front of me.

'So, we'll leave you with your solicitor to have a think about how you'd like to proceed. Mr Taylor, perhaps, for now, you can take your client through the sentences for arson, double manslaughter, and double murder? Interview suspended at 1520 hours.'

Maya, 4 p.m.

'Interview resumed at 1550,' I said. 'Present: myself, DI Rahman and DCI Lawson. We'll move onto the next stage of the interview, Mr Hayes.'

He drained the final dregs of water from a plastic cup and lounged back in his seat.

'Abbie Turner. Your daughter.'

'Where is she?' Hayes lunged towards me as he snarled the question, his face bursting with anger.

'Sit down, Mr Hayes. She's recovering in hospital and then she'll be going into foster care.'

'You can't do—' He crushed the cup in his hand.

'Nothing to do with me. It's Social Services. Thanks to the posh CCTV at the flat you've been renting from Tomasz Feldman, we have evidence that Kelly brought Abbie to you on Friday morning. That's correct, yes?'

'S'pose.'

'Did you know your daughter's mother was going to visit Simas Gudelis on Friday?'

'No comment.'

'Because here's where I'm stuck,' I said. 'If you had anything to do with the arson, you would have killed your daughter's mother . . . ' I felt my guts crunch as I uttered the words. 'And effectively deprived your daughter of both her mother and father for the rest of her life. How are you going to explain that when she grows up and asks what happened to Mummy?'

'She wasn't meant to get hurt. Neither of them were.'

'Who wasn't?'

'Kelly and Simas. We were meant to give old Ma Feldman a fright. That's what he asked me to do. But that stupid Paki kid couldn't even get that right. He got the wrong bloody shop.'

I was filling in the blanks. 'Let's rewind a moment. I take it the "Paki kid" is Ali Kousa?' I made sure Taylor had clocked the racist language.

Hayes checked in with his lawyer. 'Yes.'

'Who asked you to do what?'

'I needed somewhere to lie low for a year, didn't I? Feldman let me stay in his flat free in exchange for setting his ma's shop on fire. No-one was meant to get hurt. It was supposed to happen when she was out. The idea was she'd claim on her insurance. Cushty.' He smacked his forehead with his palm. 'I didn't want to risk doing it myself, so I left the petrol for the Paki boy and gave him instructions. I might have known that dipstick would get it wrong. I told him it was the shop on the right with a star above a blue door, and texted it to be sure. Long story short: he set fire to the soup shop and not Mrs Feldman's, and Simas and Kelly were inside.'

'So, you shot Ali?'

He shrugged. 'It wasn't just the cock-up. I knew he'd blabbed to his mate, Riad, and John had seen him cosying up to you. I felt pretty sure he'd open his trap and get us all in trouble.'

'Moving onto the murder of Patrick Ryan. Tell us about the van you used to transport Patrick Ryan onto the Manor House site.'

'No comment.' Leaning forward in the chair, and propped up on his elbows, he had his hands folded behind his head and was studying the table again.

'We have evidence which shows you and your brother dumping Patrick Ryan's body at the Manor House site on Saturday night, and you'll be glad to know we've found your van.'

'Where?'

'Where did you leave it?'

'No comment.'

'On the Ocean Estate.' That shocked him. 'A law-abiding member of the public called in. We've just got the forensics back. What do you think we found in it?'

'No comment.'

Taylor slapped his executive pad down on the table. 'What have you found in it, Inspector?'

'Blood from Patrick Ryan and Ali Kousa. Dog hairs which match those we found on Ryan. Drugs. Firearms. Ammunition.' I handed Taylor a copy of the forensic report and leaned towards Hayes. 'Enough to put you away for a very long time.'

Kenny Hayes cackled, and let his long body flop back in the plastic chair, arms folded, and one leg crossed over the other. His gaze was fixed on the ceiling. Bored and devoid of empathy.

'You left something else in the back of your van, didn't you?'

'What?'

'Patrick Ryan's tongue.'

Water spurted from Taylor's mouth and sprayed over the table. 'Excuse me, I . . . ' The solicitor dabbed at the surface with a cotton handkerchief.

I fixed my eyes on Kenny's face, hoping for a reaction, but there wasn't one. 'Forensics have confirmed that it belonged to Patrick Ryan.' I waited for Taylor to sort himself out. 'I bet you were chuffed to get hold of a Manor House ID card? Big site like that? Quite a coup.'

He gave a tiny shrug, not realising that the gesture made him seem smug.

'You can get anything on the internet these days, can't you?'

'Nah. Wasn't the net. Some chick gave it to me.'

I smiled at Taylor. 'Thinking now about why you murdered Ryan ... we know from various witnesses, including youth club workers, that you and your brother have been grooming kids and teenagers into organised crime and modern slavery. We also know that you've been using Facebook groups and websites like LfA to recruit.' I slid testimonies over the table to Taylor. 'We know that Patrick Ryan had been volunteering at a number of youth centres, and a staff member has testified that Ryan and your brother, John, had a ruck at the one on Coley Way a few weeks ago. Is that correct?'

'Poncey do-gooder. He was happy to get his gear off me for years until he got clean and then, guess what? All of a sudden, he's a born-again anti-drugs campaigner. Forever on his pissing soap-box, preaching away to the kids about the dangers of drugs and pathways and the internet. Like they don't know. These kids make their own minds up.' He flicked at one of the pieces of paper on the table.

'And what happened?'

'He kept schtum for years. But when he got a job at that posh development, he decided that he didn't like what I was doing. He wanted to make out like he was better than me. He called me out. Then did the same with my brother in front of everyone at that poxy centre. I wasn't having that. He wanted to pretend he was all Mr Respectable on his fancy building site. Well, I thought I'd give all his mates there a present. Know what I mean? Every time they think of Ryan, they'll think of his dead body.' Kenny laughed. 'Ryan said we were getting kids into crime and he couldn't ignore it any longer. Dirty hypocrite, if you ask me.'

'But that *is* what you've been doing, Mr Hayes,' I said.

'I was helping them out. If it wasn't for me, they'd have been homeless, starving and skint.'

'By getting them into crime and drugs?'

'I'm going to come in here, if you don't mind. DCI Lawson, for the benefit of the tape.' Jackie was bolt upright. 'We've met before. Haven't we, Mr Hayes?' Jackie's voice cut through the room like a laser. She leaned across the desk at him. 'In Manchester.'

Hayes snorted down his nose and mumbled.

'I'm sure you remember Rob Harris and Jay Drury? Those two boys were . . . twelve years old. You're recruiting them younger now, including your own fifteen-year-old brother?'

'You leave my brother out of it,' Hayes shouted.

'DCI Lawson,' the solicitor emphasised Jackie's rank, 'as you know, my client was not charged with any offences on that investigation. Please move on.'

'Let's discuss the murder of Ali Kousa.' Jackie sat back. Tapped her biro on her fingers. 'In that room at Duckett House, we found your DNA. And we found it on Ali's body.'

'DCI Lawson.' The solicitor put his pad on the table. 'If you have evidence against my client, please state what it is.'

'If the firearm which killed him had been discharged at very close range, there'd be blood, skin and tissue on the barrel. We've established that the Glock 19 that we found in your flat has all of these on it, but we also have gunshot residue from that gun on Ali's skin and clothing, plus skin cells and hair which belong to you.'

Hayes stared at his brief. 'You got this?'

'I need a word with my client,' Taylor said.

Maya, 5 p.m.

Across the table from Dan and I, Tomasz Feldman sat hunched in his chair, looking dazed. His eyes bulged with shame, and he looked as though he'd aged ten years in as many hours. As I hadn't cautioned him in the garden at the shop, we had to go over some of the questions again before we could move on.

'Did you tell Kenny Hayes to make sure no-one got hurt in the fire at the newsagent's?'

'I told him to make sure the building was empty, and to get Mum involved with the flash mob when the fire started, and far enough away that she'd be safe. I knew she loved music and dancing, and wouldn't be able to resist leaving the shop and joining in.'

'How did you learn that the soup shop had been torched rather than your mother's shop?'

'Several friends called me. I was at the bar and got a dozen or so calls from people in Brick Lane.'

'Were those calls the first you heard that he'd got the wrong shop?'

He nodded.

'Did Mr Hayes call you?'

'No. We agreed he wouldn't. I called him that day when you came to the bar.'

'How much did you pay him to perform the arson for you?'

'Five grand. And six months free rent.'

'In cash, presumably?'

'Yes.'

'How do you know Kenny Hayes?'

'I've known him since we were kids. Not well, but we both grew up round here. He left London and went up north a few years ago, and when he came back to Brick Lane, I tried to help him out. I didn't realise that his criminality had got worse not better.'

'Did Mr Hayes ever tell you how he made a living?'

'I knew he used to deal a bit of dope, but he told me he'd stopped and that's why he was skint. He said he was trying to get clean.'

'Except he isn't skint at all. He's got several thousand pounds in his lock-up.'

'I didn't know that either. He told me he couldn't afford to rent a place. He wanted somewhere to lie low and run his business from. I believed him. I feel like a bloody idiot because I can see now that he used me.'

'What do you mean?'

'I paid him to set fire to Mum's shop. Instead of doing the job himself, as we agreed, he got some poor kid to do it, and I've now got tangled up in organised crime and murder.'

'We'll make sure the CPS know the full facts.' It was hard not to feel sorry for Tomasz. It was such a stupid thing to do but I could see how the idea had grown from his exasperation and worry. 'Were you aware that Mr Hayes had a daughter?'

'No.' Shock registered on his face. 'I'm beginning to realise that I didn't know much about him at all.'

WEDNESDAY

Maya, 8 a.m.

When I arrived at the Royal London Hospital, they'd just finished shift handover on the ward. Abbie Kelly was sitting up in bed, not far from the nurses' station, playing with another child. Laughter and squealing reverberated around the vast open space, and I wondered whether the four-year-old had taken in the fact her mum was dead.

The nurse looked up from her monitor. She spoke softly. 'Social Services were here last night. She's going into foster care.' I saw regret in her expression. 'Poor kid. Still, she's young. The best we can hope for is that she gets adopted by someone loving, someone who will help her to put the past behind her.'

'I hope so.' Unless Abbie decided to visit her father in prison, she wouldn't be seeing him for a long time. Kenny Hayes and his brother, John, were due in court in the next few days. It was hard not to wonder if her life would have been different if she'd had a different dad, or if her mum had been able to escape prostitution. 'How is she?'

'A few scratches and bruises but given she's been locked in a room for four days, with hardly any water and no food, she's lucky to be alive. If she weren't healthy, she wouldn't have survived.'

'He didn't—?'

'No. He was drugging her though. If you hadn't rescued her, she would've died soon. But the doctors didn't find any evidence of sexual abuse.'

'Oh, thank goodness.' I sighed with relief. 'Hayes undoubtedly wanted her dead. His lifestyle depends on him being ready to run at any second, and you can't do that with a small child.'

The nurse looked incredulous. 'On the positive side, the psychologist has seen her. She said Abbie's attachment to her mum was secure. Just shows that parenting comes naturally to some people, despite their circumstances.'

'No compensation for losing her mum, of course, but it's good news,' I said.

'The main thing is that it will help her to bond with foster carers and any adoptive family members.' A huge smile spread over the woman's face. 'I'll take you over. She's made a friend already.' She gestured to the boy, who was laying out toys on the little girl's bed.

'Hello, Abbie. I'm Maya. Have you made a new buddy?'

The girl fixed large brown eyes on me. 'Are you a friend of Mummy's?'

'Sort of. How are you feeling?'

'Can I go home soon? Where's Mummy?'

'I think the doctors and nurses want to look after you a bit longer.'

Her face fell but then she was distracted. 'Not there. Here.' She shifted a piece of Lego. 'This is Joshua. He's got a poorly foot.' Abbie clipped the plastic pieces together. 'We're making another hospital so that there will be room for all the sick children.'

The boy continued to lay out pieces on the sheet.

'I need you for a moment, Joshua, please,' the nurse said, and she held out her hand to steer him away so I could talk to Abbie.

I showed her a photograph of Ali. 'Have you met this boy before?' She nodded.

'Was he a friend of your dad's?'

She screwed up her face. 'Don't think so.' She had a worried look.

'That's OK. Do you know his name?'

'Uncle Ali. He's not from here. He's not my real uncle either.'

'What about this man with your dad?' I showed her another image. 'Do you recognise him?'

She continued to hold the Lego and leant towards the image to get a better look. 'That's Uncle John. He's my real uncle.'

'That's excellent. Well done. Shall I come and see you again soon?'

She nodded profusely. 'If you like. Can you bring Mummy?'

Maya, 9 a.m.

Rosa was standing in the doorway of the newsagent's when I arrived. She had a primrose-yellow scarf round her neck, and hope glimmered in her eyes in a way I hadn't seen since I was a child.

'Best thing for it,' she shouted over the top of the rumble and thud from the bulldozer, and gestured to the remains of the soup shop. 'She can start again. We all can. I should have sold up when Józef died.'

Across the street, Indra's thin frame was visible next to her sister's stronger build. She was talking to two men in suits.

'Agnieszka's gone home.' Rosa turned to face her own shop and I followed her inside. The shelves were finally empty, and crates bulged with items for Rosa to sort through. 'The new owners will gut the place and sort the damp out. It's what it needs. I don't know how I didn't see it.' She was gathering up a few remaining pieces of stock and stacking them on the counter for the removal men. 'Basildon Bond notepaper?' She attempted a feeble laugh. 'No-one writes letters anymore, do they?'

'Not so much, no.' It was something Mum would say.

She flipped the CLOSED sign over on the door and turned to me. 'Thank you for what you said. Józef did help his father. They worked together for years. I don't know where I got the idea from that I couldn't let Tomasz help me. Stupid pride, I suppose.' She sighed, and regret crept into her face. 'Józef was so hard on Tomasz.

Refused to accept his ideas or help. I thought I had to be like that too otherwise I was being disloyal to his memory.' She looked over at the racks of trendy mobile phone covers and battery packs. 'Those were Tomasz's suggestion and they were one of our best sellers.' She laughed now, a proper laugh.

'Have you thought about where you'll move to?' I asked.

'I won't stay round here now. So much has changed, and none of it is going to change back just because I'd like it to. I've lost my husband, and now my son. My future is with Agnieszka and the children. Apparently, Tomasz has bought a house for me in East Ham. I'll wait 'til I feel a bit stronger and I'll probably move in there.'

'That's a good idea. You'll have your own independence, and you'll have company close by when you want it.'

'I'm struggling to get my head round Tomasz paying someone to set fire to this place. Did he really believe it would do me a favour?'

'I think so.' As I said it, I wondered again whether I believed it. Was the gap between the Tomasz I'd known as a child and the one he was now so wide? I didn't think it was. 'He said he found it upsetting to see you struggling in the shop and feeling guilty.' I could clearly recall his face when he spoke to me yesterday. 'He thought a small fire would solve things for you.' As I said it, I realised that in a way, it had.

'What's tragic is that his decision has resulted in so many people getting hurt.' Rosa looked like she was on the verge of tears and I found myself sniffing back my own.

'I know.'

'I would like to see him. Hear what he's got to say. Can you arrange it?'

'Of course. He wants to see you too.'

'Will he go to prison?'

'Most probably, but we don't know. We're discussing charges with the CPS.' I pointed through the shop window. 'Did you know that your son had developed a crush on Indra's sister, Marta?' I wouldn't mention the baby. I'd leave that to Tomasz to decide on.

'Oh?'

'He told me.' I recalled how he'd talked about Marta when I told him about Indra's baby. 'Seems he fell in love with her.'

I watched Rosa's expression. She placed the packets of pale blue envelopes, and the box of Pritt Sticks, into a crate and inched towards the glass. 'And did she . . . ? Did she love him too?'

I remembered the giggling I'd heard when the two of them came home together. 'I think so.'

Rosa reached for the door handle.

'Shall I put that lot in a crate for you?' I gestured to the pile of things on the counter by the till, taking the opportunity to give Rosa some space.

The doorbell dinged and she walked towards Marta and Indra. She must've called them, because they spun round, and the two younger women walked towards the older one. Rosa opened her arms and she and Marta fell into a hug for a few moments before Indra joined in.

Maya, 10 a.m.

In the distance, daffodils lay in clumps on the grass and dappled April sunshine fell through the branches of the cemetery's oak tree.

A male social worker stood next to Riad Farzat at Ali Kousa's grave. Another man stood behind them. Rima and I were a short distance away from the men, and we watched the official lay out Ali Kousa's shrouded remains to face Mecca. A few metres from us, Sophie Williams and her mother looked on.

'Forgive him. Pardon him. Cleanse him of his transgressions and take him to Paradise.' The imam's voice was sombre, and it reminded me of Sabbir's funeral.

'Their whole village was wiped out by an air strike.' Rima spoke softly. 'He and Riad may as well be brothers. They travelled all that way together. It took them months.'

As she spoke, it was such a relief to let the tears fall.

She passed me a tattered piece of card. A photograph.

'Is that Ali's family?'

She nodded. 'He brought it with him. Riad saved it from the squat. I promised to give it back to him, but I thought you'd like to see.'

'That's so kind. Thank you.' It was his mum, dad, four boys and two girls and an older couple. 'Is that him?' His eyes were recognisable and the quiff of hair.

'Yes, he was the youngest.'

At the grave, the imam was still talking.

'We've found Riad a foster home with a Syrian family here. That's the father, up there. I visited them yesterday and Riad seems to like it.' She grabbed my hand. 'Fingers crossed they'll keep him on. It's the middle of term, but we've found him a place at a school too.'

The corners of my mouth lifted. 'I'm delighted to hear that.'

The men placed the wooden planks over the grave and sprinkled soil.

'It's so weird. For twenty-nine years, we've all acted as though Dad was dead. It must've been a defence mechanism.' I looked at Rima's kind face. 'But underneath, I've been convinced that Dad was alive. I just wouldn't let myself believe it because I knew it would hurt too much if it wasn't true.' I let the sun warm my face for a moment. Jasmina and I had the morning off and we had arranged to see Dad's friend, Ody, after the funeral. 'Now we're pretty sure he is alive, I don't know what to do with the information.'

'Oh, Maya.' She took hold of my arm.

'It might have been twenty-nine years ago but the evening he disappeared is still vivid in my mind. Before he left, he said, "You children be good for your mother" and part of me knew he was saying goodbye.'

Rima squeezed my arm.

'People don't leave their families for no reason. Do they?'

'It'll come out in due course.'

'Yes.' I glanced over at Jasmina, who was waiting under the oak tree. 'What's bothering me is that, for all those years, the thing I wanted most was for Dad to come back. And now I'm scared – what do you do when the thing you think you've wanted most looks like it's about to happen?'

'You take it a step at a time, and do what you always do,' she said. 'You feel your way through it, with your friends and family around you.'

The ritual was over now. From a distance, the imam gave us a nod and Riad's new foster father gave a polite wave.

'He said to thank you for . . . They couldn't have afforded the—'

'I know.' I smiled at her. 'It's the least I could do. I wanted Ali to know that his life mattered, and that people cared about him.'

A short distance from the gathering, by the cars, Tomasz Feldman stood in between two police officers. He was handcuffed, and as he watched the ceremony, the morning light briefly graced the tears on his cheeks. He saw me looking and lowered his head in shame. At the office, this morning, his and Kenny's charges were being agreed with the CPS, and John, who was a minor, was being processed.

Over by the tree, Jasmina was waiting alone and I waved.

'I'm going to head off,' I said to Rima. Even at a hundred yards, I could see from my sister's expression that she felt as excited and impatient as me. But, like me, she was worried about what we were about to find out.

I glanced over at the grave, with a child's body in it, and freshly sprinkled soil. 'Go well, Ali,' I whispered, and I turned and walked towards the oak tree and the daffodils. And my sister.

Acknowledgements

This novel would not have been possible without the input and guidance of numerous people. Firstly, huge thanks to Clio Cornish, whose fabulous editorial skills helped me to shape and sharpen Rosa and Maya's stories. Secondly, thanks to my agent, Adam Gauntlett, for his unwavering faith in me.

I'm hugely grateful for the help I've had with the police and fire procedural elements of the book, without which many details may have been taken from the telly! These people have asked to remain anonymous, but have been incredibly generous with their time and expertise. The book is fiction and I believe that drama trumps realism, so all inaccuracies and flights of fancy are mine.

Thanks to Dave Sivers, for beta-reading while he was on holiday, and to Liz Barnsley for a second beta-read later on. Huge thanks are also due to the crime fiction community, who are incredibly generous, supportive and encouraging.

I began drafting *Out of the Ashes* straight after finishing my debut novel, and it then lay in skeletal form for a couple of years before I set about re-writing it. As with the first in the series, the plot and characters grew from people I've met, places I've spent time in and things I've become interested in. In 2002, when I was teaching A-level Psychology in East London, I was teaching about conformity and obedience during the Second World War. I was struck by how awful it must have been for Polish Jews and Christian Poles to be forced into collaborating with the Nazis, and by the courage of those who risked their lives to help the Polish Jews.

At this time, I was working close to Brick Lane, and often walked round the area, absorbing information about its history and people. I became interested in what lies beneath the cyclical nature of immigration into the East End. Ethnic groups have always arrived, settled and moved on. This is what inspired the characters of Rosa Feldman and her family, and many others in the book. Something else which Rosa struggles with is change, as does Maya's mother. I'm fascinated by denial and resistance to change because they can be incapacitating.

Thanks so much for reading the book. If you've enjoyed it, do please spread the word. You can follow my news on Twitter @VickyNewham and my website is https://www.vickynewham.com/.

ONE PLACE. MANY STORIES

Bold, innovative and
empowering publishing.

FOLLOW US ON:

@HQStories